GALLOWS

THE BANE OF THE NORTH
BOOK 1

By A. C. Salter

This novel is a work of fiction. Names, characters, and events are products of the author's imagination. Any resemblance to actual persons, living or dead, is entirely coincidental.

Copyright © 2024 by A. C. Salter

All Rights Reserved
No part of this book may be used or reproduced, in any manner whatsoever without written permission except in the case of brief quotations embodied in critical articles and reviews.

This is a British English version and all spellings are edited as such.

Other books

The Daughter of Chaos series

Eversong
Shadojak
Ethea
Winter's End
Seeking Chaos
Darkest Wish (Prequal)

The Dylap series

Dylap
The Night Fae
Blood Thorn

Merry Wish

The Bane Of The North Series

Gallows Born

Dedication

As always, for my wife, children and grandchildren that make up Clan Salter and give me the inspiration to keep writing.

BORN OF THE GALLOWS

1

Gallows Born

The entire village of Crookfell turned out for the hanging. A rare occurrence on the fringe of the Northern frontier known as Fug's Descent, where the days were hard and the people harder.

Dirty faces stared from the squat stone walls surrounding the timber huts and hovels; children watched through open fingers from the fences that held the pigs. Others ventured as close as the mud-churned space by the well that constituted the village square. They huddled together, slack-jawed and stoney-eyed, as they watched the hangman tighten the noose around the girl's neck, adjusting the rope before giving himself a satisfactory nod.

Even the Baron watched on from his carriage on the crest of the hill, not daring to enter Crookfell proper should his people turn on him for ordering the death of one of their own.

"She didn't do it," Gelwin pleaded, pulling on the arm of the hangman, which earned her a cuff around the back of the head.

"Please, our Nel isn't a thief. She wouldn't…"

Gelwin flinched as the executioner made to strike her again, but her husband, Dodd, dragged her away, shaking his head as he muttered apologies to the hooded hangman.

"Leave it, Gelwin, or he'll hang you alongside your sister," he hissed.

She struggled like a cat as he dragged her back amongst the solemn crowd, cursing with the effort to keep her still.

"She didn't do it," she pleaded with each sob that escaped her.

"It doesn't matter. His Lordship said she did, and so she did," Nan Hilga, the village elder said, sucking on her lone tooth as her only eye focused on the gallows. "Girl should have been tried by Crookfell folk, not condemned by those at the castle. She should never have been taken on as a maid, foolish girl."

Gelwin wished that her sister had never stepped foot inside the castle. She'd changed from the first day she was taken on, and now her young life would be snuffed out at the end of a slipknot.

"And if you ask me, it wasn't the silver she pilfered. She was messing with the Baron's son, young Shankil. She'd taken something alright, his lordly seed," Mary chuckled into Hilga's ear.

Gelwin might have thumped the nosey crow in her gossiping mouth if she hadn't been thinking those same thoughts.

Swallowing her next shuddering breath, she focused on her younger sister, facing death on the gallows and seeming every bit her timid eighteen years.

Nel lifted her head, chin trembling as the unforgiving rope bit deep, creaking as the hooded figure stepped up behind her and placed a boot on the stool she was standing on.

Her eyes locked with Gelwin's, a weak smile tightened her lips, teeth clenched as she shook with fear yet seemed to accept her fate.

Through her husband's unforgiving grip, Gelwin tried to smile back yet caught the simple shift of the hangman's foot as the stool slipped away.

"Nel!" she cried, fighting Dodd as her sister dropped with a sickening crack.

Her body snapped taught, head sagging forward, and face hidden beneath dank hair.

Through the silence, the timber frame creaked, the rope swayed, and the people of Crookfell watched.

Gelwin tore herself free from her husband's clutches, took several steps towards her sister and then collapsed, knees driving into the cold earth.

Through her sobs, she thought she heard someone from the crowd mutter.

"Hangman knows his stuff; broke her neck instantly."

"Aye."

Gelwin retched into the mud and then forced herself to stare through her tears.

The executioner looked past the crowd and up at the hill, gave a nod to The Baron and then stepped away; job done.

Gelwin glanced to the top of the hill, and The Baron stared back, face as grim as Death's.

She held enough to kill The Baron thrice over if hatred alone could hurt a man.

He blinked first and with a simple flick of a hand, signalled for the driver to ride on.

"May the Fug take you, Baron Shankil," she whispered, her gaze never leaving the carriage until it passed through the castle gates.

"Don't you go cursing the Baron," Dodd scolded as he took her by the elbow and yanked her to her feet. "You know others in the village would like nothing more than to prattle on you just to win favour with his lordship."

Gelwin pulled herself away from him and cast furtive glances about the folk before regaining her composure.

Dodd was right, though she hated to admit it.

The sawing creak of the rope cut deep into her core with each swing of the limp body, Gelwin's own flesh and blood. Yet she could no longer stand to look at her sister. Not without retching again.

She was alone in the world now. The realisation made her feel even more isolated from the village folk. Nel had been her only living relative.

She took another shuddering breath and touched Dodd's arm for support.

They couldn't take the body down until the sun had begun its descent – the black work of burial must be done only after The All-Mother had finished blessing the land.

"Take me home," she said to her husband, turning her back on the gallows and the small crowd who still gawped at the macabre sight as if making sure they got their coppers worth of the event.

"Wait, what's that?" Gobbin shrieked.

The swine herder had one hand covering his mouth while his other pointed towards the gallows.

Gelwin would have ignored him if it wasn't for Gobbin's wife gasping and giving the sign of the Fug as she prayed to The All-Mother.

Other women were suddenly hiding behind the men, desperate fingers making out the sign of the Fug to ward off evil.

Gelwin turned to see what had their attention when her blood turned to ice.

Nel's body twitched.

Gelwin gripped Dodd's arm, feeling him tremble beneath her fingers, or was that her own body shaking?

Fear clutched her heart as she watched Nel's belly move as if there was a crazed badger lodged inside.

It twisted and writhed, stretching the rough-spun dress out as if swollen with child, yet Nel's head and limbs remained still.

"Tis the demon Black Sviel himself," Gobbin wailed as he made the sign of the Fug and slowly backed away.

The hangman, who had now removed his hood and tidied his things away, ventured back onto the platform, stooping to get a better look.

More familiar with death than the villagers, he placed hands on knees as he peered closer, his pinched face tightening into a frown.

He stretched his finger to the hem of the dress, gripped it as if it might suddenly catch fire, and then slowly lifted it.

Gelwin didn't want to watch but couldn't tear her eyes away.

The dress rose past Nel's shin, the flesh already mottled with dark blue veins, to reveal a head hanging upside down.

It slowly sank lower; a small body coated in a dark red muck followed it, then two tiny plump arms.

A child sitting on the pig fence began to cry and ran to his mother, who gathered him into her arms while sobbing in fright. The rest of the people watched on, astonished horror paling all but one face.

Old Nan Hilga leaned against her staff, sucking on her tooth indifferently.

Gelwin dug her nails into Dodd's arm as the creature flopped out of the corpse and fell to the wooden planks beneath Nel's swaying feet.

Mrs Gobbin feinted. Her body struck the ground with a thud, yet nobody moved to help.

Gelwin was rooted to the spot as the hangman let go of Nel's dress and squatted closer to the demon spawn, hitching his britches past his knees to make the journey easier.

He gave a simple shrug and then stood.

"It's only a bairn," he pronounced. "Dead."

The word was lodged in Gelwin's mind, and she fumbled with it several times before properly understanding. A Bairn? Nel had a baby?

Nan Hilga raised an accusing finger toward the hangman.

"It is a corrupt fiend who hangs a woman with child. You killed two Crookfell people today," she said, hobbling out of the crowd to the gallows, her glower never leaving the executioner.

"True, although I was not told, and so the fault lies elsewhere," the hangman replied, not seeming phased by the scrutiny. Everyone knew that the people from the castle were above the folk of Crookfell.

Gelwin watched, transfixed as Nan Hilga stopped beneath Nel's dangling body and craned her aged head over the baby beneath, still attached by chord to its mother.

"May you be with Nel in the afterlife," Gelwin muttered, blinking away tears.

She moved toward the gallows, wanting to look at the babe, to hold it to memory as proof of its existence, yet Dodd held her firm.

"What's done is done," Hilga said, glancing up from the baby to regard the villagers.

She stamped her gnarly old staff into the earth and made the sign of the Fug.

"Crookfell has lost two of its own today. Whether they deserved the way they passed through the final door or not, may The All-Mother take them into her embrace."

The folk around the damp square mimicked the sign, placing fist to chest and then head, gazes cast down.

Gelwin put her fist to her heart and then pressed it to her head, fighting the sob that threatened to burst from her chest.

With the words said, the folk began to leave, Mrs Gobbin having been dragged up from the floor and flung over the smith's shoulder, the only one strong enough to carry her.

"Come Gelwin, let's get you home," Dodd said, steering her away from the gallows and through the few people who remained.

A silence hung heavy in the village, solemn and brooding. A gust picked up from the north, washing down the mountain before it swept through Crookfell, forcing Gelwin to clasp her shawl tight around her.

It disappeared as abruptly as it came, leaving the silence more potent than before.

The few remaining in the square began to leave, and Gelwin followed.

Her boots squelched through the mud; it spattered her legs, yet she didn't care. You can always wash mud away, unlike today's sorry affair. No amount of scouring will ever clean the impurity of it.

She took another step when a high-pitched scream erupted behind her, piercing her very soul and rooting her to the spot.

The scream was followed by another - the unmistakable wails of a newborn - sorrowful, hungry and scared.

She whirled on the spot and watched as Nan Hilga, still standing by the gallows, leaned down to the body beneath her sister's dangling feet, head shaking from side to side. The hangman returned to the platform to stand beside the elder as he stared down.

Gelwin's heart thumped harder with each painful cry from the bairn, and before she knew what she was doing, she had halved the distance to the gallows.

"Gelwin, no," Dodd demanded, grasping her hand, but she shook him off.

"Gelwin. I forbid you to go any closer," her husband growled.

Without thinking, she pushed between Hilga and the executioner as she reached down to the baby, but before her fingers touched the bare pink flesh, the old woman gripped her wrist.

"Think on, lass. You do this, and there'll be no going back."

Gelwin couldn't think, could barely breathe and felt close to feinting herself.

Another growl from over her shoulder.

"It's cursed. Gallows born. It belongs to Death, Gelwin. As your husband, I forbid you to touch it."

She felt his arm snake around her belly and pull her away, yet she dug her heels into the ground and held firm to Hilga's staff, which was driven into the earth.

"Are you sure, lass?" Nan Hilga whispered.

Gelwin clenched her teeth and nodded, eyes never leaving the squirming bairn on the rough timber.

Hilga gave a single nod, sucked on her tooth and then rounded on Dodd.

She struck him around the head with the knobbly end of her staff.

"Behave with your sharp tongue, Dodd Berkson," she scolded, raising the staff as if to strike him again. "Now get yourself home, prepare hot water and find clean linen."

The beginnings of an argument curled his lips, but the words fell away as he glimpsed the looming staff poised above his head.

He backed off, gave Gelwin a hurt expression and then trudged away, muttering to himself, pushing through the gathering crowd of villagers who had quickly returned.

Gelwin put her back to them as she crouched to the platform and removed her shawl. She delicately picked up the baby and wrapped it around him, seeing that he was a boy.

"Shhh, now little one. I've got you," she cooed, her gentle voice still laced with fear as she brought the small bundle to her chest.

He was small, even for a newborn. Swollen, lumpy, covered in a dark muck, but one of the most beautiful things Gelwin had ever held.

"Don't just stand there, give me your knife," Nan Hilga demanded, rounding on the hangman.

He handed it over without question, and Hilga cut the cord, which bound the baby to his dead mother.

"I suggest you hurry home, lass. Wash the bairn and have that idiot husband of yours take his hounds outside. I'll be over as soon as I can. I'll need to brew a special broth."

Gelwin could only nod as she rose and held the baby tight.

She glanced up at her sister swinging above and pressed her cheek to her cold barefoot.

"I'll care for him, Nel. I swear an oath to the All-Mother that I'll protect him with all that I've got. I'll treat him as if he's my own."

"Go, lass," Hilga hurried her.

The crowd parted for Gelwin as she made her way across the square. Stoney faces regarding her, judging her as if she were mad.

"The thing's cursed…"

"Gallows born…"

"It will bring blight to the village…"

Gelwin put her head down and kept putting one foot in front of the other, not stopping until she arrived at the door to her single-room shack. The rest of the folk followed her there.

She went inside and closed Crookfell behind her.

Dodd was waiting, a cauldron over the fire with water coming to the boil. The linen they were gifted when they were wed was laid out on the straw pallet.

Dodd glared at her as she sat on the chair by the fire, rocking the baby, who had mercifully quieted. The three hounds paced around his feet, ears flat and tails between legs as they sensed the growing tension in the confined room.

"I forbade you, Gelwin," he said, looming over her, fists clenched so tight that they had become white. "And yet you still bring that…that thing into my home. You've cursed us is what you've done. You couldn't leave it, could you?"

"No. I couldn't leave him to die," she said, keeping her words as level as she could so as not to worry the baby. "And I'll not be changing my mind, either. Our nephew will be living with us."

"It's no nephew of mine. And the entire fugging mountain will freeze over before I let you keep it in here with us. I'll not stand for it, and nor shall the village."

"Calm your temper, husband. And don't use language like that in front of him. I'll not have you bringing the Fug down on us to spite the bairn."

Dodd stepped closer and raised his arm to backhand her.

Gelwin raised her chin in defiance. It wouldn't be the first time he'd hit her, and it most likely wouldn't be the last.

Yet the strike never came.

"May the Fug take you both," he said, breathing deeply as he lowered his hand and crossed the room. He grasped his foraging spade before flinging the door open.

"I'll bury Nel, then I'll be up at Kel's," he said, not meeting her gaze. He gave a subtle nod to the hounds, and they eagerly padded out with him.

Gelwin knew they'd be trouble later. Kel, short for The Drum and Kettle Tavern, was where Dodd spent most evenings, getting lost in his cups before stumbling home in the dark hours, stinking of sour ale - drunk, hasty with his hands and heavy with his fists.

The baby began to cry again, so Gelwin sang a lullaby, rocking him within the crook of her arm while she dipped a corner of the linen into the warm water and began to wash the filth from his skin.

By the time she had finished, three loud knocks had come on the door before it swung in, revealing Nan Hilga.

The elder hobbled inside and closed the door behind her, but not before Gelwin caught the rest of the village standing beyond the threshold, trying to stare past the old woman.

She rested her staff against the table, placed a small tin urn on the floor and then sat in the only other chair.

"Alright lass, let's have a look at him."

Reluctantly, Gelwin gave him up and placed him into the open arms of Nan Hilga, a woman who was the leading authority in Crookfell and its only healer and herbalist.

The moment the baby was in her arms, it opened its mouth, peeled its lips back, and wailed.

Gelwin reached back for him but was stilled by a glare from the old woman.

"He's healthy enough," Hilga said as she opened the linen and poked around the small pink body, turning him over and probing the spine and limbs and not seeming at all phased by his cries.

When she had finished, she passed him back to Gelwin, who was only too pleased to have him back in her arms.

"There are no wet nurses in the village, and I doubt any would help if there were, so you're going to have to feed him this broth, nothing else, mind," Hilga warned as she lifted the urn onto the table and raised the lid.

Through the steam, Gelwin could make out an off-white liquid that gave off a sour-sweet odour.

Hilga produced a small bottle from her cloak and ladled the broth into it. She then cut a small square of the linen, placed it over the mouth of the bottle and tied string around the neck to hold it in place.

Gelwin took the bottle and held it close to the baby's mouth, tilted it so the liquid soaked into the linen and then pressed it to his shaking lips.

He soon quieted and began to suck on the cloth.

"You know how to wind a bairn, keep him clean, warm, safe?" Hilga asked, scrutinising Gelwin with her good eye.

Gelwin nodded. She had helped when Nel was a baby while her mother was tilling the fields or bringing in the harvest.

Hilga sucked on her tooth as she nodded, satisfied. She rose, grasped her staff and glanced around the squalid room, tutting.

She hobbled to the door but paused before opening it.

"I won't lie, lass. You've got some hard times coming. Folk around here won't make it easy for you and the bairn. And that husband of yours is a useless lump. You'll need to be thick-skinned and thicker-spined."

"Aye," Gelwin said back. "Thick-skinned is nothing new to me, Nan Hilga. And thank you."

"Don't thank me yet, lass. I'm still unsure it was the right decision, but I'll not go against it."

The door closed, leaving Gelwin alone with the baby, who was greedily sucking on the bottle.

She took up the lullaby again, rocking him back and forth and wondering how strange life was to have started the day by knowing you would be losing your only family and by the end, gaining another.

Where one life ended, another began. Maybe that's how it worked in the world. There were a finite number of souls to go around, and the All-Mother could only release one when one returned.

2

Trial by Fug

Crookfell village is situated beneath the foothills of the Galodis mountains, wedged on the frontier between the Kingdom of Alialis and the rim of the Fug - a halo of fog that circles the mountains from the base of the foothills to the sea cliffs on the other side of the range, some three hundred leagues away.

The Fug rises and falls each day, the silver vapour touching the fringes of Crookfell with its haunting chill, full of howls and threats, before rising once again toward the mountains - never breaking its choke on the frontier as if the very mountains breathed.

Legend has it that the mountains contain the remains of a dead god, its tormented soul trapped within a final breath that remains close to its once immortal body.

None venture within the ring of the Fug, save a few daring heroes seeking glory and a name for the songs. Yet all that passes through the vapour never returns.

Those brave enough to go close to the substance hear the tormented screams of the demons trapped within - the snarls and growls of bodiless animals, the cackling of evil, and the wails of the tortured.

To touch the Fug was to die. Humans and predatory animals, even birds, disappeared if swallowed by the vapour.

On rare occasions, the Fug would thin, the veil of fog becoming translucent enough for the brave and foolish to pass through. Yet these rare occurrences bring other dangers, for those who dwell beyond the halo can also come into Alialis.

Raiders.

The savage people of the frontier that live within the foothills and forests cross into the Kingdom in small raiding parties - stealing, killing and burning.

It is for this reason that the Northern Keep was built. Garik Castle. It sits threateningly on a hill a league from the base of the Fug's lowest reaches. At any one time, the Castle holds a battalion of the King's Own foot soldiers, a company of cavalry, a column of archers and a dozen score royal knights.

Their purpose is to retain control of the Northern frontier, pushing back any invaders and raiders from within the Fug.

Trapped between the castle and the deathly halo of fog is Crookfell - home to peasant land workers and farmers that keep the Castle and its people fed. And although the villagers have protested on many occasions with the Baron to allow them to live within the castle walls safely, he denies them the right, using them as a barrier and first contact with any raiders that come across the Fug. Crookfell is the first means of an alarm should any attack be imminent.

This was one of the reasons why Gelwin believed the people of the village to be as stoney-hard as they were. They had no choice.

****

It had been a long night. The bairn slept in short, fretful bursts, waking with a scream and not relenting until Gelwin had him in her arms and plied him with the broth. After feeding greedily, he would fall asleep, only to wake a little while later demanding more.

She spent the gruelling hours with one eye on the baby, the other on the door for when her husband stumbled through, reeking of ale. Yet that moment never came.

Dawn had come, and Dodd hadn't returned. He had probably found his way into crow-mouthed Mary's bed. It wouldn't be the first time, and the trollop was welcome to him.

Exhausted, she lay the baby on the pallet and tiptoed to the fire to place another log into the dying embers when a fierce knocking came to the door, hammering her full awake again and startling the bairn.

She picked up the baby, wrapped him tightly, and opened the door.

Dodd was standing on the threshold, grizzled-faced and looking as tired as she was. He was wild-eyed and stank of drink. Behind him stood the entire village, glowering at her and pointing at the baby.

"Dodd, what have you done?" Gelwin asked, yet she could guess as she took in the stern faces before her.

"It's one thing to defy me," Dodd said, stepping back to join the villagers. "It's another to defy Crookfell. We had a meeting last night, and nobody wants it here."

His bloodshot eyes drifted to the baby and back up to meet Gelwin.

"It's cursed. Gallows born, and the only place it belongs is in the ground with your Nel."

Gelwin didn't know she was going to slap Dodd until after her hand had connected with his jaw, snapping his head to the side and smarting her palm.

"Don't you speak my sister's name, you pathetic cretting," she said, anger lacing every word.

The baby's cries rose to a full-pitch wail as Gelwin scanned the villagers, seeking any help.

There was none.

Nan Hilga pushed through, her staff parting the folk as if it were coated with thorns.

For a moment, Gelwin thought she had found someone on her side, yet it wasn't to be.

"I'm against it, lass," Hilga said, smacking her lips together as she drew closer, shooing Dodd out of the way with her staff. "But the village has spoken, and as it's elder, I must listen."

"They're going to kill him?" Gelwin said, clutching the baby tighter.

"No lass, they demand trial by Fug."

A sob escaped Gelwin as she backed through the door, wanting to shut the village out.

"That's still a death sentence," she growled, desperation clawing at her, pulling the world out of focus until she collapsed.

The momentary blindness left her, and she found herself on the floor, Hilga standing over with the baby now in the old woman's arms.

"Come lass, walk the baby to the trial stone. You can do that, at least," Nan Hilga said, her voice gentler than Gelwin had ever heard.

Like a lost lamb, Gelwin rose and followed the elder, feeling a numbness settle over her as if she wasn't in her own body and was simply a passenger watching from above.

The crowd paced behind them, Crookfell in its entirety walking as one, making sure they got what they asked for.

A cold drizzle swept through the village, a glistening film clinging to the surfaces and shining in the early morning rays.

It would have been beautiful on another day, yet with the Galodis mountains looming above and the silver veil of the Fug on its descent towards them, it was hideous.

They came to the edge of the village, long grass sprouting from the ruins of an abandoned barn, beyond it a slight stretch of ground that ran the length of Crookfell, no wider than two carriages long. It was the perimeter, a no-man's land between the tip of Alianis and the Fug Frontier.

On the far side was an ancient forest thick with oaks and elms, willows and birch, twisted and joined together.

The first wisps of the Fug began to seep through it as it continued its path, spreading out to its fullest.

Between the two places, in the middle of the no-man's land, was a pony-sized rock that jutted out from the bare ground like a broken tooth.

The trial rock. The final place where the ghastly vapour touched before it began returning to the foothills.

The folk of Crookfell remained by the abandoned barn, none daring to venture further.

"Will you come with me, lass?" Hilga asked as she hobbled on, crossing the empty land to the rock.

Gelwin matched her pace, walking beside her, gaze never leaving the bairn.

They stopped before the great rock, and Hilga placed him gently on the top, tucking the shawl around him.

The elder's only eye stared at the approaching Fug that had now blotted out the forest on the other side of the clearing and was making its way to the rock.

"If you've any parting words, lass, now's the time."

Gelwin drew a deep breath; any words choked down with the tears that were running freely down her face and sinking down her throat.

"I'm sorry," was all she could manage as she leaned down to place a kiss on the baby's head.

She felt a hand in hers and looked down to find that Nan Hilga was grasping it tightly as she began to pull her away.

At first, Gelwin resisted, her heart feeling heavier than a smithy's anvil, but the numbness returned, and she found that she was easily led back. It was something the elder was doing to her.

They reached the safety of the ruined barn, and together, they turned to face the approaching Fug.

It flowed like a billowing fog, spreading out in silver plumes with weaving tendrils probing the ground as it came.

Gelwin had seen it most days. It came, and it went, part of village life on the edge of the Kingdom. It was a constant that she had been used to, yet now, when it affected her personally, she saw it for the evil that it was.

The Fug. God's breath, Halo of the damned – words which she'd heard but never thought much on. Now she understood.

The vapour came on, the ghostly veil stretching far out of distance left and right, the first wisps finding the rock, and the Fug began to engulf it.

Without a thought, she let go of Hilga's hand and ran across the empty land, bare feet slamming into the earth as she propelled herself toward the baby.

"No," she screamed, the word tearing from her starved lungs as she watched the Fug swallow him.

She was almost there, she reached out, fingers pushing through the cold embrace of the fog, yet found only rock.

"No," she repeated, catching dark shadows moving from within the vapour, heard the rumbles of a growl, the roar of a beast and the shadows closed in on her.

Terror raked claws along the flesh within the Fug, tightening its grip as it began to devour her too.

Then, with a feeling of vertigo, she was wrenched free, falling back onto the damp earth, Dodd and Gobbin collapsing beside her.

"Stay down, lass," Hilga warned as she stood over her, facing the retreating fog, her staff striking the rock as if reminding the god's breath where its boundary lay.

Gelwin raised her head to watch the wall of fog recede into the forest, slipping through the twisted trees to begin its ascent up the foothills, taking Nel's baby with it.

"It is done," Hilga announced, shaking her head as she regarded the villagers. "Now go about your business, the lot of you, else it might come back to claim more."

The folk of Crookfell didn't need telling twice. Making the sign of the Fug, fist to heart and then head, they swiftly departed the perimeter to go about their daily work for the castle.

Dodd grasped Gelwin under her arm and hoisted her to her feet.

She flung it off and shoved him away.

"Get your fugging hands off me," she spat, putting her back to him to stare once again at the empty rock.

"Gelwin?"

She felt Dodd step closer, but Hilga intervened.

"Go on with you, you too, Gobbin. Leave the lass be."

"It's not fair. That poor little might," Gelwin sniffed between tears once the men had gone.

The rock was cold and merciless, and there was no sign of the baby being there at all.

"Life isn't fair, lass. Not for the likes of us simple Crookfell folk. Not for anyone. And I dare say that if that poor little might had grown up in the village, his life would have been as tough as yours. Perhaps he is where he should be. And by The All-Mother, he should be with Nel."

"Nel," Gelwin repeated, the name coming out choked.

She still hadn't allowed herself to fully grieve with all that had happened since yesterday.

"I want to be alone now," she whispered once she regained control. "I'll pick some foxgloves for Nel's grave. They were her favourite."

Nan Hilga placed a hand on her shoulder.

"You do that, lass. Take the day to be with her. Tomorrow is a fresh start."

Gelwin waited until the elder had ambled back into the village before her gaze rose once again to the Fug. The wall of fog was already over a league away and rising up the foothills.

It would be back, of course. Twice a day, like the tides on the coast. It will return to the rock in the evening. Maybe she'd come back.

A shiver ran through her as the feeling of terror returned, that single touch which almost was the end of her.

"Fug you," she cursed up at the mountains and then stomped away.

Nel's grave was a small mound of freshly dug earth covered by rocks to create a cairn. It was on the fringes of Crookfell, in sight of both the mountain and the castle, sitting alongside a weeping willow.

"At least Dodd found you a nice spot," she said to the mound as she knelt and began to place the foxgloves around the headstone. "The idiot isn't much use for anything else."

With the last two flowers, she twisted the bottom of the stems together and curved the flowers over to create a heart. She laid it on top of the cairn.

"He was beautiful, Nel. I hope he's with you now and you both find peace. Something which I doubt he would have found with me."

The air stirred around her, the limbs of the willow swaying gently, rocking side to side - as Nel had done on the gallows.

No, Gelwin thought, shaking the thought away before it sunk her into melancholy.

The day was shrinking fast and the sun was beginning to set. She had spent most of the day picking flowers and keeping herself busy. Now, it was time to return. With any luck, Dodd would have already taken himself to the tavern.

She kissed her hand twice, once for her sister and once for the bairn and placed her palm on the headstone.

Then, with a heavy heart, rose and began the walk back to the village.

The path took her past the ruined barn marking the perimeter and skirted along Crookfell, heading toward the pig pens. The few folk still about nodded a greeting, yet none could look her in the eye.

By now, it was almost entirely dark, and the Fug had reached the edge of the forest, making its way across the no man's land to the rock.

Gelwin kept her back to it, unlike the people about her who watched it with weary fear, making the sign of protection before going about their business once again.

Fools, the lot of them, Gelwin thought. She'll never again make the sign of the Fug - wretched cursed thing.

A baby's cry suddenly carried on the wind, a fearful wail of pain and hunger.

Gelwin touched her heart. She was hearing things - a ghost of the bairn she had briefly held.

She was about to continue when the cry came again; this time, others glanced up from their work.

Slowly, she turned to look out beyond the ruined barn, her gaze casting across the narrow stretch of the perimeter to the rock that jutted halfway between Crookfell and the forest.

There, lying in a familiar shawl, was the baby.

"No, it can't be," Mary gasped, shaky hands covering her mouth.

Gelwin stepped close, pushing back any feeling of hope. But the more steps she took and the closer she got, the hope grew.

By the time she had reached the barn, she was running, the Fug receding at the same pace away from her, away from the village and back into the frontier where it belonged.

A cry erupted from behind her, but she paid it no heed. Her whole attention was on the rock and the baby.

"Gelwin, no," came Dodd's booming voice, accompanied by the panicked words from the villagers.

"Go to fugging Hell, the lot of you," Gelwin muttered to herself as she reached down and plucked the baby from the rock.

She brought him to her chest, feeling his little heart thumping against hers, and his cries quieted, sensing the love coming from her. How could he not? She was shaking with it.

"Nothing has ever been returned from the Fug," Nan Hilga said through wheezing breaths, the only person who dared come to the rock with her. The elder must have run to get to here as swiftly as she did.

"Never in all my years and the years before has the Fug returned a soul."

Gelwin hugged the baby tight.

"I'll not give him up," she said, watching the folk gather about the barn, Dodd ahead of them and staring on confused.

"And nor should you, lass," she said, turning to regard Crookfell.

"Listen up," Hilga demanded as she drove her staff to the ground and glowered at the gathering crowd. "You asked for a trial by Fug, and so it has come to pass that the Fug has seen fit to return the bairn. He is one of us. Any of you wish to argue the point may come sit upon the trial rock and seek an audience with the Fug itself."

Her words were met with a silence, yet none dared to argue the point. Even Dodd stood quietly, and as the rest of the village began to leave, he followed, head down.

Gelwin watched until he was gone, wondering if she had lost him forever and if she cared.

"Here now, what's this?" Hilga asked as she pulled a corner of the shawl away to reveal the baby's arm.

Gelwin was shocked to find a black mark around the fleshy part of his forearm. A ring of forest thorns tattooed below the elbow that reached all the way around. The artwork was so intricate that it appeared almost real, as if a single thorn on the tattoo was sharp enough to pierce her skin.

"What does it mean?" Gelwin asked.

"I don't know, child. I've never seen anything like that before. But best to cover it up. You don't want anyone to see."

Gelwin studied the thorns; they seemed to throb in time to the baby's breathing.

"Is it the mark of the Fug?" she asked.

Nan Hilga clenched her jaw as she sucked on her tooth.

"No. This is something else," she said, placing her aged hand over the baby's belly. "And he's been fed."

Gelwin stared at the retreating silver vapour as it flowed through the trees on the other side of the empty ground.

"What man has the power to walk within the Fug?"

Nan Hilga shook her head as she pulled the shawl over the baby's marked arm and gestured towards the village with a flick of her staff.

"No man has that power, lass. Whatever fed and marked the bairn is no man. Let's get this little one under a roof and away from prying eyes."

Gelwin turned her back on the trial rock, the ascending fog and the mountain it was returning to, but not before putting her fist to her heart and then to her head.

"Thank you," she whispered as she began her walk home, matching the elder step by step.

"Can Crookfell demand another trial?" Gelwin asked as they passed the pig pen and the glares from Mr and Mrs Gobbin.

"No. They already did what was in their power. The harshest trial a soul could take, and the bairn proved himself to not only the village but to the mountains and to the Fug itself. But listen here, they won't make it easy for you."

"Maybe the castle?" Gelwin asked, her gaze briefly flickering across the large keep on the hill a league away.

Hilga barked a laugh, sounding part cackle and part strangled cockerel.

"He's the bastard-born son of the young Shankil; of that, I have no doubt. And most probably the reason the Baron had your Nel hanged, waiting until his son was out of the way down South and playing war. If the castle gets wind that Nel's baby breathes, he'll become an easy target. Yet this isn't what concerns me the most, lass."

Nan Hilga paused beside the village well and leaned in, her face coming so close that Gelwin could see the veins of the elder's good eye, her other hidden beneath an old patch.

"Bastard born he may be, but he also has another father."

Gelwin shook her head, "Dodd will help. He needs a few weeks to come around to the idea. He won't..."

"Hush, lass, I'm not talking about that dolt. Do you forget where the bairn was born?" Hilga said, raising her staff to point towards the gallows, which had been dismantled and lay in a pile on the ground. After its use, the castle offered the wood to Crookfell, but none would touch it as the suspicious folk deemed it cursed.

"Gallows born. The bairn's father isn't only the son of the Baron, but also Death himself."

Hilga stared at Gelwin momentarily, allowing the words to sink in before she began hobbling through the village again.

"Think on that, lass. The folk of the village have a reason to fear him."

Gelwin held the baby tight as her shack came into view. She felt the stares from the people around her, heard the hushed tones of gossip and fought the urge to run.

She held her chin high, crossed her threshold and slammed Crookfell behind her.

3

15 Years Later

Bane saw the open hand coming. Smelt the stale ale on Dodd's breath, the spit flying from his rebuke, and the anger seething through narrowed eyes.

Experience told him that the strike would hurt, that it would leave him dazed with white dots fizzing at the corners of his vision. He could easily duck the cuffing, but that would only infuriate Dodd more, fuelling the hate that leached off Bane's sole guardian.

Experience also gave him a narrow path that sat between the two.

Shifting his feet, Bane leaned away in the same direction as Dodd's open hand, twisting his head so the palm struck the corner of his brow. He rolled with the blow, feeling the stroke - strong enough for Dodd to think he had caught a solid cuff yet weak enough for only a glancing touch.

The mark below his leather vambrace suddenly flamed and then died away, leaving an irritating itch.

"And the next time I tell you to catch the hound before he eats the truffle, you damn well do," Dodd growled, nostrils flared as he regained his composure.

An ale-laced belch escaped him as he gathered his foraging pack and pointed further into the forest.

"Now find me some mottled lichen, and make sure you scrape it fresh from the bark itself. None of the rotting stuff in the roots. The old bat Hilga is paying good coin for it. Go on then, go," Dodd ordered, hands on hips.

Bane ambled away, the largest of the hounds pacing behind, nose to ground and sniffing enthusiastically in the earth.

"You can stop that sniffing now," Bane said when they were out of earshot, running his fingers through the hound's fur. "It's not like you can actually find anything. And when you do, you eat it and get me into trouble."

The hound glanced up, tongue lolling from his mouth.

Bane smiled and rubbed behind the dog's ears, earning a soggy lick.

"I hope that truffle was worth it. Now be a good dog and find me some lichen."

The hound put his nose to the ground and began to sniff again, tail wagging as he meandered along the deer track.

They came past an ancient oak tree, and Bane glanced through its twisted branches and found what he was searching for.

"Wait here," he ordered the dog, then leapt up, grasped a low-hanging branch, hooked his leg over, and hauled himself up. The climb was easy enough as limbs and burghs were everywhere, and with the autumn having stripped it of leaves, he made short work of reaching the trunk.

He retrieved a small knife from his belt and began to scrape the lichen from the bark, placing it delicately into his knapsack.

"At least Dodd will be happy," he muttered, staring down at the hound, which had begun to pace impatiently around the oak. "No. Dodd's only happy when he's in the tavern."

He jumped down, landing deftly beside the hound and began to head back to Dodd but paused.

The hairs on the nape of his neck began to tingle, and the mark on his forearm beneath the vambrace began to itch again.

He got the strangest feeling that somebody was watching him.

He slowly turned on the spot, peering into the forest's dark shadows, scanning as far as he could through the foliage and depth of the trees, yet saw nobody.

He absently rubbed at the thorns beneath his leather arm guard and trudged back to Dodd, who was squatting on the edge of the forest, staring out at the village and sipping whisky from a flask.

"About time, boy," he said, rising and stuffing the flask into his jerkin. "You've got a busy day ahead of you, so you better look sharp and make your way back to Crookfell.

Bane gave a single nod as he handed the knapsack of lichen over. Dodd didn't like it when he spoke.

"You've got bellows work at the forge for the rest of the morning. Make sure he pays you two coppers mind. Midday, you'll be wood splitting over at Camwell's place," Dodd explained, counting the tasks off with dirty fingers. "That'll also be two coppers. After that, get yourself round to the Gobbin's place. He'll not pay unless you're there on time. And bloody well make sure he pays you two coppers too. That one will try to swindle you."

Dodd spat on the ground as he frowned at his fingers.

"That's two coppers from the smith, two for Cam and two more from Gobbin which makes," his gaze travelled into the sky as he puzzled towards a number.

"Six coppers," Bane said and earned himself a glare.

"Don't you get smart with me, boy. Yes, six coppers," Dodd said, holding up five fingers. "And don't you come back with a mark less."

Bane nodded and set off towards Crookfell, swiftly passing Dodd and expecting a cuff round the back of the head for good measure. Thankfully, he was too quick and made his way across the damp grass to the track which took him to the village.

Dawn had not long arrived, and a natural mist that clung to the hills began to dissolve with the day's first rays, revealing the castle that stood sentinel on the tallest hill. Bane had never been in the castle; he'd never left Crookfell. But had watched the knights and soldiers coming and going through the portcullis and wishing that one day he would be one of them.

The track took him along the outer edge and followed the empty ground between the village and the mountains - the salt-scoured no man's land which divided the Kingdom from the frontier.

He stopped to watch the descending Fug as it came down the foothills and billowed through the tree line on the other side. The silver fog moving in a way unlike the dissolving mist.

Leaving the wet grass, his feet crunched over the scrubland as he paced towards the Trial Stone that lay at the centre of the dead ground and marked the limit of the Fug's reach.

Alone, as nobody from the village came this way, Bane stopped before the massive slab of rock, close enough to touch if he stretched his hand out.

The Fug now totally engulfed the edge of the forest, hiding the trees within its ghostly form before spreading out towards the rock, moving at the speed of a fleeting deer.

Bane remained rooted to the spot, gaze never dropping from the fog, the god's breath, the halo of death, which had been a constant for his entire life.

Nobody truly knew what it was. Or so Gelwin had told him years ago. Yet she also said to him that she didn't believe it to be evil.

A pang of sadness came over him at the memory of Gelwin.

Ten summers ago, he was standing at this spot, along with Gelwin, Dodd and Nan Hilga.

He feared the latter two, but not as much as he feared the choking cough which had plagued Gelwin. She's had it for weeks, and it was getting worse. To the point that she knew her time was coming to an end.

They had been here so that Dodd could swear a blood oath to the Fug.

Bane remembered how Gelwin's husband had attempted to argue his way out of it, stating that he was no blood kin and that he loathed the child he was forced to keep under his roof.

"I'm not asking you to love the child, Dodd. Just to put a roof over his head and keep him fed until he's big enough to fend for himself," Gelwin said; her insistence and Nan Hilga's threatening presence finally broke him into agreeing.

The three of them had cut their palms and let their blood fall together on the stone as the Fug approached.

They watched silently as the silver vapour flowed over the stone, its advance slowing to a stop and then flowing back, taking any trace of blood with it.

The oath was made and sealed.

They had buried Gelwin two weeks later.

He and Dodd dug the grave beside the mother he had never met. Together, they built the cairn, stacking the stones methodically so that it would last. Both working in stunned silence.

Nobody from Crookfell came to witness the prayer to the All-Mother, which was said by Nan Hilga.

Before the elder left them to their grief, she told Dodd to think on his oath, eyeing Bane with her wild eye.

"A roof and food, nothing more," Dodd had yelled after her before glowering at Bane and then headed off to the tavern where he spent the following days.

Bane watched the Fug retreat across the barren land and into the forest, its circumference shrinking as it crept towards the foothills as if rising to choke the mountains themselves.

A sharp ringing of iron striking iron brought him out of his thoughts and back to the now.

The sound was coming from the village, more specifically, the forge where the smith had begun hammering out on his anvil. Bane should have been there already.

Putting the Fug behind him, Bane ran the rest of the way to the village, putting his head down as he passed the folk heading out to begin tilling the fields.

The large door of the forge lay open, a wall of heat hitting Bane as he entered the gloom, the glowing coals from the forge giving the only light.

Girant towered above the anvil, his thick arm holding the hammer, pausing above a molten strip of iron as he glanced up to meet Bane's eyes. He nodded towards the bellows; Bane returned a single nod, plodded over to the huge contraption of wood and wax cloth, and began to pump.

Within moments, sweat had begun to stick his woollen vest to his back, and he blew his dark curls from his face with each panting breath.

"Keep her steady," Girant said in his booming voice as he placed the length of iron he had been hammering back into the coals.

The trick was to keep the temperature level, working the bellows so that the colour of the coals remained between a bright yellow and white.

Girant didn't say much yet was one of only a few adults who acknowledged Bane and refrained from calling him boy.

By mid-morning, all the muscles in Bane's body ached with fatigue, and he'd sweat so much that he believed he was drying out; the heat in the stifling room only added to the discomfort.

Girant tapped him on the shoulder and handed him a cup of water. Bane mercifully took the offering and downed it in one. Girant refilled it for him.

He wondered if life would have been different if Gelwin had settled down with someone like the smith instead of Dodd. Hard-working, never brought trouble home, worked an honest living.

A while back, he had entertained the idea of approaching Girant to become his apprentice. But the smith and his wife had their first son the same year. He was four now and would soon be working in the forge.

Bane threw the cup of water down his throat and then began pumping the bellows. Keeping busy made the time go quicker, and it wasn't long before Girant once again tapped him on the shoulder and gave him the two coppers he was owed.

As always, Bane nodded and then headed out into the noon-day sun.

The Camwell's cottage was a small wood and thatch home at the edge of the village where the family kept the castle supplied with wood and kindling. He arrived in time to catch Mrs Camwell scolding her son. She had her back to him and didn't see his approach, unlike her son, Dew, who had spotted him and tried to hide the smirk on his face.

"And when that boy gets here, you'll make sure he cuts and splits the entire pile. He'll earn those two coppers."

"Yes, Ma," Dew replied.

"And don't you speak with him mind; he's gallows born that one. Cursed and rotten all the way through."

"Yes, Ma."

"And where's your sister? She's supposed to be coming with me up to the castle. This load won't shift itself."

"I don't know Ma."

Mrs Camwell sniffed as she picked up her skirts and turned to leave, startling herself as she realised Bane was standing behind her.

She gave him an accusing stare before sidling past, making sure not to step too close. Dew earned himself a sidelong glance before she marched back into the village.

Dew waited until she had disappeared before grinning.

"So, just how cursed are you?" he chuckled.

Bane laughed. "No more cursed than you. Now, let's have a look at this pile of wood."

"You don't want to do that," came another voice, younger and higher in pitch.

Belle dropped from the elm she had been hiding up, her dress covered in twigs and leaves.

"It's huge."

"But with the three of us at it, it won't take long to get through," Dew said. "Come, we better get around back before we're seen talking with the gallows born."

Bane followed the siblings to the rear of the cottage, stretching his sore muscles as he went. Although they ached, he was smiling. He looked forward to coming to the Camwells. Dew and Belle were his only friends. They were often left alone with their father away felling trees all day and his mother delivering wood and kindling around the village. It was the only time Bane felt relaxed enough to speak.

"See, huge," Belle said as the three stared at the stack of logs.

Dew was a summer older than Bane, while Belle was a summer younger. With them living just out of Crookfell, they hadn't grown up with the children in the village and so didn't share their prejudices.

Bane wandered to the stack, picked a log and stood it on a tree stump next to the pile.

"Better get started," he said as Dew handed him an axe.

The log split with a satisfying thwack. The two halves falling to either side of the stump.

Bane wrenched the axe free from the stump while Dew picked the halves up, and Belle placed a new log down, ready to be split.

Thwack.

They'd done it this way for years. Each having their own little task making, the entire job three times faster.

"I asked my Ma what Bane meant," Belle said as she placed another log down. "She said it's what people call something that is trouble or a hindrance. Like, the bloody Fug is the bane of my life."

"Belle? You can't say that, and don't curse the Fug." Dew said.

Thwack.

"No, it's fine," Bane said, pausing to brush wood chips from his unruly curls. "Gelwin named me it because of that very point. I am a bane to the village," he laughed. "Never to Gelwin, though. It was more of a joke, I think. But it stuck."

"So why don't you change your name?" Dew asked. "It's not like anyone uses it. They all call you Boy."

"You could be anything. I wish I could choose a new name. Nelly-Belle sounds like it should fit someone dumpy. Like Mrs Gobbin."

Thwack.

Bane burst into laughter, and the axe missed its mark, striking the log on its edge and sending it tumbling from the stump.

Dew chuckled as he watched it go while Belle placed hands over her face and laughed hysterically.

The laughter died down when the log rolled to a stop.

"I like Bane. It fits, and it's what Gelwin gave me."

"Bane it is then," Dew said as he picked up two more halves from the ground.

They talked and laughed as they worked, the pile of logs shrinking faster than Bane would have liked. With his friends, this was where he was happiest, and it would soon be time to leave.

After splitting the last of the logs, Bane struck the stump and left the axe embedded. Another routine they had was when the work was done, they climbed the large oak on the edge of the yard and watched the Fug tide roll down the mountains.

Sitting on a branch wide enough to accommodate the three of them, Belle brought out a cloth parcel wrapped around cheese. She handed it to Bane.

"I couldn't finish lunch earlier," she said, staring ahead into the foothills. "And I know that you've probably not eaten today."

Bane stared at it.

"I usually eat when Dodd feeds the hounds," he said, still not making a move to eat the cheese. It was one thing to accept friendship but another to take food meant for them. Especially when he knew how hard everyone worked to get the meagre food they could afford in the village.

"Belle," he began, but his words were cut short.

"No, I saved it for you. He puts you to work all day and treats you like a dog. That's not right, and it's not fair."

Dew, sitting on Bane's other side, was nodding.

"She's got a point. And we'll be fed later."

Bane's belly chose that time to grumble. He tried to cover it with a cough, but Belle's knowing smile told him she had heard it.

He undid the cloth, and his belly groaned again. It was all he could do to stop himself from ramming the cheese into his mouth in one go.

"You know, if your Ma caught us up a tree with me eating your food, she'd likely bray you so hard the raiders would hear it."

The cheese tasted every bit as good as it smelled.

Belle watched him eat, her face lighting up with each mouthful.

"Most likely," Dew agreed.

"Beautiful," Bane said after finishing the cheese and handing Belle the cloth back.

Her eyes widened as he spoke, cheeks flushing red.

"The view from up here, I mean," Bane added, gesturing out towards the snow-capped mountains, the forest full of a hundred different greens and the silver band of fog that swept up and down, bringing all the colours into contrast.

"No place else like it," Belle said, seeming not too happy all of a sudden.

"Although, none of us have ventured further than the castle boundaries," Dew put in.

"When I'm a soldier, I'll travel," Bane said. "Just like my Da, wherever he is. Whoever he is."

Belle patted his hand, leaving her palm atop it.

"How do you know your father is a soldier? I thought nobody knew but your mother, and she was," began Dew, then shrugged as he nodded toward the village square where the gallows had been erected for a single hanging fifteen summers ago.

Bane shrugged.

"It's what Gelwin told me. I've no reason to doubt her."

He was the bastard son of somebody, so why not a soldier? Better that than being the son of the gallows, or Death, as the folk from Crookfell believe. And he didn't share the same chestnut hair and brown eyes as the locals. He was the only person in the village with dark hair and grey eyes.

"I think someone is coming," Bane said, bracing himself to jump out of the tree.

"As long as it's not my parents, I don't care," Belle said.

"Yeah, let them see us with you. It's about time people started treating you right," Dew agreed.

"I've got a reputation to keep. I can't be seen with the likes of you two," Bane laughed as he jumped down from the oak and grinned at his friends. Belle was shaking her head while Dew let out a laugh. They both joined him on the ground. A moment later, they heard voices.

Kulby Gobbin swaggered into the yard, a head taller than the three friends he had with him. Sixteen summers old and as big as most adults in the village. Mainly because his father, Mr Gobbin, was the pig herder and kept his family well-fed on the swine he bred.

He stood beyond the logs that Dew had stacked, folded his arms, and stared menacingly at Bane.

The three friends he had with him, two other boys of the same age and a girl called Meg, matched his stance, faces pinched as if they smelt something foul in the air.

"Hey, Drip, tell the boy that if he's finished here, he can make his way over to my farm. I've got my thrust and jab to work on," Kulby said, his thuggish friends sniggering.

"My name's Dew, not Drip. And you can tell him yourself, he's right here," Dew snapped, folding his arms. Although the same height as Bane, they both were a head shorter than Kulby.

Kulby stepped closer, the toes of their boots almost touching, and Bane noticed that Belle had balled her hands into fists, they trembled by her side as she took in Meg's measure.

"I don't speak with it, nobody does," Kulby said, poking a finger into Dew's chest to emphasise each word. "Now tell him, Drip, or I'll test how sharp that axe is on your scrawny body."

Dew wasn't going to back down, neither was his sister, and Bane couldn't let them get hurt because of him.

He raised his chin, caught Kulby's attention and gave him a single nod, letting him know he understood.

"I think it knows where it has to be," Kulby said, stretching himself to his full height and shoving Dew before putting his back to them.

He pushed the stack of split logs over before sniggering. "Let's head back; I feel the curse has lingered here too long. Maybe it'll rub off on the Camwells too."

Belle approached him, teeth clenched and fists rising toward the older boy's back until Bane caught her around the shoulder.

"They're not worth it," he said, hoping the thuggish group continued walking and didn't turn around.

Silently, Bane began to pick up the fallen logs and restacked them. Dew and eventually Belle helped once she regained control of her temper.

"When you're getting bashed while Kulby practices his sword skills on you, do you ever get the chance to hit him back?" Dew asked.

Bane placed the last log back on the pile and smiled.

"Once or twice, when his father isn't watching."

"Good. Then make sure you give him a good one today from me," Dew said, picking up the axe and slamming it back into the stump.

"And one from me too," Belle said, handing him two coppers.

Bane was reluctant to take it as the siblings had done as much work as himself but knew they would insist. He placed them in his pocket.

"Will your parents need me tomorrow?" he asked.

"I'm sure they will. There's always plenty of wood that needs chopping. And with Winter fast approaching, the castle is beginning to stock up," Dew said.

"Will you both be here?"

"Of course, unless my ma demands that I go with her on her errands," Belle said. "I'm sure she's trying to find me work in the village or at the castle."

Bane waved them farewell and strode into the village, finding Kulby and his father by the pig pens.

They both sneered as he approached, ensuring he didn't give them too much eye contact.

Kulby was already dressed in a boiled leather jerkin, britches and helmet. He swung his wooden practice sword, making lunges and cutting the air inches above Bane's head.

Bane ignored him as he grabbed a battered shield and strapped it to his arm before grasping another practice sword.

"Now stand there, boy. And none of your funny business or dodging. I'm paying good coin for you and for Master Jarl," Mr Gobbin said, his jowls wobbling with each word, appearing much like a pig from one of his swine herds.

"I'll get a few jabs in before he comes," Kulby told his father before rounding on Bane, who had brought his shield up to catch a blow from Kulby's sword.

His shoulder jarred and caused the tattooed mark on his forearm to suddenly blaze.

"What was that?" came Jarl's voice as strode up beside Kulby. The former knight stepped so quietly that none of them had heard his approach; his soft leather garb, of a much higher quality as befits a retired knight, was dark and soaked in any daylight that came through the shredded clouds above.

His lip curled as he took in their measure, keen eye glancing over Kulby.

"Have you been practising the thrusts I've taught you?"

"Yes, Sir," Kulby answered, stepping away from Bane as he demonstrated, thick arm jabbing, the point striking an imaginary foe.

Jarl shook his head as he ground the teeth in his square jaw.

"Pathetic. Your feet are too close together for a start, your balance is completely off, and you lead with your arm. Where does the thrust begin from?"

"Shoulder?" Kulby answered, face screwed up in concentration.

"No," Jarl said as he stepped into Kulby, hooked a foot around the back of an ankle, dipped his shoulder and knocked him clean off the ground.

Kulby landed on his back, head smacking the dirt and dropping his sword.

"It starts from your feet, like any attack. And if you don't have your feet, you will inevitably fall," Jarl growled as he stalked around Kulby and his father. "Are you sure you have what it takes to become one of the King's Own?"

"He's a fast learner, Sir. I can promise you that," Mr Gobbin said, wringing his fat hands as he backed away.

"We shall see. But since you're paying for my time, it matters not. Now, get up, lad. If we were on the battleground, you'd have been twenty times dead by now."

Bane fought to hide the smile as he watched Kulby squirm, the mud from the pens clinging to him as he struggled up, the boiled leather he was wearing made him more cumbersome.

"Up, lad. Now, over to your foe and adopt a fighting stance. Your leading foot in front of the other, shoulder width apart. No, not like that, like…well, look at your friend. His feet are set perfectly."

Bane had already planted his feet and adopted a defensive stance. The way that Jarl had been trying to teach Kulby to do over the two years.

"He's no friend of mine," Kulby said as he stepped before Bane, rolling huge shoulders while shaking his head. "He's nothing."

Jarl ignored the words as he gripped Kulby's sword arm and yanked it into a better position, nudging his foot a little wider.

"Eyes on your enemy, lad. You'll not see his attack coming if you don't look at him."

Bane watched the older boy before him, a head taller and a good deal wider than himself, dressed in armour and having a thicker shield and heavier sword. He braced himself for the onslaught – this was going to hurt.

"See an opening, attack," Jarl said as he began to pace around them.

Bane held his breath as Kulby lunged, the tip of his wooden sword clattering against Bane's shield, the impact sending a shock up his arm.

"Pathetic," came Jarl's words as he paced around them. "Keep at it."

The lunge came again, Kulby leaning into the thrust, lips pulled back in a rictus grimace. He followed it up with another and a third jab, each stroke hitting the same place on Bane's shield.

"Use your size, lad, hit higher."

Bane brought the shield up, caught the next blow, adjusted his feet and edged back, deflecting the next and the next. He kept his blade in check, although he had ample opportunities to strike out.

Over a couple of years that he had been the practice dummy for Kulby, he had watched and absorbed as much from the lessons as he could.

His job was to be a live target, nothing more - as Mr Gobbin harshly pointed out on the last occasion when Bane allowed his arm to slip and caught Kulby under his chin with the hilt.

"Get under his defence; use your strength. You're twice his size, for pity's sake," Jarl hissed as he came around the back of Kulby, caught his elbow, and raised it. "Feet, you dullard, feet."

Kulby was panting now, red-faced and sweating; his helmet was slipping to one side, yet he kept the thrusts coming, aiming to get inside of Bane's shield.

The splintered wood rattled with each blow, yet Bane caught them all, angling the shield to deflect some of the impact.

"Twenty score thrusts, and you haven't broken his defence. You're going to make a weak soldier, lad. Heavy, hungry but weak as an old sow," Jarl said, raising his face to the sky. "By the All-Mother, why do you inflict me with such a dimwit for a student."

"Because I'm paying you good coin," Mr Gobbin said," scowling at Bane as if it was his fault.

Jarl sighed, shaking his head resignedly.

"Of course, of course. Alright, lad, if that attack isn't working, change tactic. Remember the other moves and forms I've taught you. Jab, slice, cut – use them."

Bane saw each attack come. A slice aimed at his neck, a cut coming low to his exposed thigh, followed by a jab to the ribs.

He caught them all, deflecting and shifting his feet to keep himself from toppling. The days spent working the bellows in the forge and splitting logs up at the wood yard had strengthened his muscles, allowing him to stay upright.

Kulby screamed with frustration, throwing his shield away and coming at him with his sword grasped in both hands.

The wooden blade crashed against Bane's shield from above, again and again, Kulby's weight driving each blow.

Still gripping the smaller sword, Bane struggled to catch each blow with the shield, the old wood feeling heavy and beginning to come apart.

"Die, die, fugging die," Kulby hissed with each strike.

Bane's forearm throbbed with the effort of holding the shield, which had now shed the rim and the upper portion above the straps.

"Enough, lad. Too much aggression," Jarl shouted from behind Kulby, yet it seemed that the huge youth wasn't listening.

The shield took one more hit and fell apart, leaving Bane exposed.

"Enough, I said," Jarl yelled.

Kulby brought his sword down, spit flying from gritted teeth, a demented hatred pouring from wild eyes brimming with excitement.

Bane watched the blade descend, arcing for his head, a crushing blow which would more than likely kill him.

Gelwin suddenly filled his mind, smiling proudly. The only person who had ever shown him love, who had ever cared for him.

"Make it through today; tomorrow will take care of itself," she said. The words she always spoke at the beginning of each day in the village. A mantra that kept them going.

Bane stepped into the attack, caught Kulby's blade with his own, hooked his foot behind an ankle, dipped his shoulder and drove through.

He spun about and adopted a defensive stance as Kulby slammed onto his back in a shower of mud.

A stillness settled around them as if time itself needed a moment to digest what had happened. Kulby's winded breath broke the silence, followed quickly by Jarl's full-hearted laughter.

"I've been paid to teach only one student, but it seems as though two have been learning," Jarl said, smiling at Bane, an intrigued puzzlement settling into his hard features.

Mr Gobbin rushed to his son, slipping in the mud as he struggled to pull him upright. His crimson-faced glower soon turned to Bane, who realised that he had gone too far this time.

"Don't expect me to pay you, boy, not after this. I knew it was a mistake to hire you. Gallows born cursed wretch that you are."

"Easy, Gobbin. The boy was only protecting himself. Your lad was about to stove his skull in," Jarl said, his gaze rolling over Bane as if seeing him in a different light.

Kulby was wheezing hard when he removed his helmet and threw it into the pig pen.

"I'm going to crush him," he said, large hands balling into fists. He shrugged away from his father and picked up his sword.

"That'll cost you extra," came Dodd's voice as he sauntered into the yard, stepped between Bane and Kulby, and stared up at the large youth.

Kulby seemed ready to swing for Dodd, but the large hounds at his feet soon changed his mind.

"That'll be two coppers," Dodd said, holding his hand out to Mr Gobbin. "Same time tomorrow?" Dodd asked, offering the swine herder a cocky grin.

Mr Gobbin eyed Jarl, who shrugged.

"Your lad will learn to be a better fighter with someone like him to practice against," the retired knight said, nodding toward Bane.

"Fine," Mr Gobbin said begrudgingly, tossing the coins to Dodd, who plucked them out of the air.

Bane left the practice sword and what remained of the shield with Mr Gobbin before hurriedly catching Dodd and the hounds up.

As they left the yard, Dodd thrust his knapsack at Bane.

"Old bat Hilga wouldn't accept the lichen from me. She wants you to deliver it yourself."

Bane slipped the knapsack over his shoulder and handed Dodd the coppers for the day's work, knowing that by the time the next Fug tide came, most of it would have been spent.

Bane nodded as he watched Dodd head directly for the tavern in a jauntier swagger now that he had money to spend.

Why would Nan Hilga want him to deliver the lichen personally?

4

The Return of Shankil the Younger

As night came on, Bane crossed the village, avoiding the few folk around as he made his way to Nan Hilga's shack. The small stone home was on the fringe of the forest, and because of its closeness to the dark woodland and only a few spans from the edge of the Fug tide, people only visited if they really needed to.

Smoke spiralled from the crooked chimney stack, and a potent odour of moss and mushroom stew poured out of the open window. The warm glow from an open fire flickered within, revealing the shadows of two people. One was tall and wiry while the other was stout, leaning against a staff.

"It wasn't easy to get. I was almost caught sneaking from the King's library. I'd have been doing the hangman's dance if I had. I hope it was worth it," said the tall one.

"If it were easy, Glance, you wouldn't be paid so richly. And I'll need to study it before knowing its worth. Now, what news of young Shankil. Is he up at the castle already? I'll wager the Baron will be glad his son has returned safely."

There was a pause in the conversation, the taller shadow slinking away.

Bane chose that moment to knock on the door when a blade suddenly appeared at his throat, pressing to the point of breaking his skin.

"Are you lost, friend?" came a hushed voice by Bane's ear.

It was a local accent, deep yet young. With the threat of his life currently pressing against steel, his mind was rushing through his options – which were few at that moment.

He was about to tell the stranger the truth when his belly grumbled, filling the silence.

The shack door opened to reveal Nan Hilga standing on the threshold, glaring out at them.

"Leave the lad be, Glance. He's expected," the elder said, sucking on her tooth as she inspected him with her wide eye.

The blade instantly lifted away, and the stranger stepped into the light pouring from the doorway.

He was tall, about thirty summers and moved with the grace of a shadow cat. His dark cloak swayed as he gave a theatrical bow.

"Forgive me, young squire. One can't be too careful with enemies lurking across the Kingdom."

Bane rubbed his throat where the knife had been, wondering how the man had managed to slip outside the shack and sneak up behind him so swiftly and without making a sound.

Bane gave the man a single nod, taking more details. His clothes were dark green and well used, although of a soft and high quality leather.

The man gave him a wink as he pulled the hood of his cloak over his head.

"If you'll both excuse me, I've matters to attend to up at the castle," he said, then slipped into the forest's shadows, vanishing within moments.

"But the castle is the other way?" Bane said and then realised that he had spoken without being addressed.

Not that Nan Hilga seemed to notice.

"Glance doesn't use the well-travelled ways. He's a lurker of the shadows, that one. Now, come in, lad, let's have a look at you."

Bane followed the elder into her home while pondering her words. Surely, she meant to look at the lichen she had bought, not him. Yet it seemed that the old lady had it right.

"Sit," she ordered, pointing to a stool by the fire, a cauldron of bubbling stew steaming above it. "Are you hungry? Speak, lad; you've no need to remain quiet around me."

"Yes," Bane said, his mouth watering as his belly grumbled again.

Nan Hilga scooped a generous amount of stew into a clay bowl and passed it to him along with a wooden spoon.

"Eat then, lad. You'll not need airs and graces with me."

Bane began to spoon the stew down, the moss mushrooms tasting every bit as delicious as they looked. Before he had finished the bowl, Nan Hilga ladled another portion in.

"How's things at home? I've noticed that Dodd is staying close to breaking his blood oath. That dolt thinks more of his hounds than you."

Bane swallowed the stew in his mouth, feeling uncomfortable with the scrutiny. Although he felt nothing but resentment toward him at home, he still felt loyal to Dodd.

"He does what he can."

Hilga nodded in a way that said she thought otherwise.

Bane placed the empty bowl on a table and brought out the knapsack. He felt uncomfortable with the elder and wanted to be away. He planned to visit Gelwin and his mother's cairn before going home.

"That's not the reason why you're here. Set the lichen down and remove your vambrace."

Bane's gaze dropped to the leather guard around his forearm and back up to meet Hilga's intense stare.

"My vambrace?"

Hilga sucked on her tooth as she opened a wax parcel on the table to reveal an old book.

"That's what I said. Glance has used his skills to retrieve this tome for me for the very purpose," she said, tapping the book and then staring down at his arm.

He didn't want to remove the vambrace. Gelwin had bought it before she died and made him promise that he would never take it off. But Nan Hilga was the village elder. He couldn't refuse her.

Reluctantly, he untied the chord that bound it, the same knots Gelwin had tied before she passed through the final door.

The vambrace clattered onto the table, falling open to reveal long and deep scratches along the inside length. Bane was sure they weren't there before, and nothing could have done that while he wore it.

Then he glanced at the forearm that had been hidden for all these years and gasped.

"Remarkable," Nan Hilga said, leaning closer and grasping his arm with cold fingers. "When last I saw this mark, it was a single ringlet, no thicker than my finger, that banded below your elbow. You were but a day old."

Bane couldn't take his eyes off the mark that now spread from the base of his elbow to his wrist joint. The intricately tattooed thorns were longer now, the vine which bound them thicker and wound in a weaving pattern as if it had grown, the first spikes of new thorns poking along its length. It stood out starkly against the white flesh beneath, not having touched sunlight for half his life.

It looked real as if the tattoo was alive. If he ran his finger along his arm, he was sure he would cut himself.

"Does it hurt?" Hilga asked, rubbing her thumbs along the outer edge and stretching his skin apart. The thorns moved with her, although they didn't stretch in the way his skin did.

"Sometimes," he admitted. "What is it?"

He couldn't help the worry that was now rising within him. Gelwin had explained what she knew about it, which wasn't much. He had been taken by the Fug on his first day in the world and then returned bearing this mark.

Hilga let go of his arm and opened the book. She flicked through the pages, raising her head to glance at the tattoo now and then until she stopped and brought the book closer, putting it alongside his arm.

The image in the book matched the thorns on his tattoo.

At first, Bane felt relief; if someone had copied the image into a book, then the mark had been made before. But then he caught the worried expression wrinkling Nan Hilga's brow.

"What do you know of the raiders that live in the foothills on the other side of the Fug?" she asked.

"They're heathens, made up of many tribes that worship the mountain. They raid the kingdom whenever the Fug wanes thin enough for them to cross the veil,"

Bane said, telling her what he had picked up from the hushed conversations of others over his years in the village.

"Heathens?" Nan Hilga said, raising an eyebrow. "No, lad. There is so much more to them. They're Norsemen. Vikings. They're much cleverer than the folk around here give them credit for. They have to be to survive in the foothills where the Fug tide rolls over them every day. Nobody knows how they do it, nor do we understand how they thrive in the harsh land. Their clan ways are full of honour and tradition, remembering their fallen gods, one of which they believe is buried in the mountain. That's why they don't leave."

Bane tried to decipher the writing that accompanied the picture in the book, but he couldn't read.

"Of the traditions, the most sacred and rare ritual which only the bravest and strongest warriors can attempt is the Tide Hunt, to seek the Wycum. It is where a warrior is permitted to seek out a legendary creature that dwells within the veil of the Fug. And if the warrior survives long enough to find the Wycum and prove their worth, they will be tattooed with the blood from the god in the mountain."

Bane traced a finger along his arm, following the vine as it swirled over his skin.

"So, all these warriors have the same mark, this mark of the Wycum?"

"None. Nobody in living memory has ever found the Wycum and returned. They copy it, the elders of the tribes creating their tattoos, much like the drawing, which was most likely copied from a captured raider. It is like most other legends, simply a story."

Nan Hilga suddenly slammed the tome shut, startling Bane.

A sharp pain erupted in the finger, absently tracing the tattoo. It was bleeding from a thorn that had punctured his skin.

A thorn that should be made from the ink of his tattoo, yet it was solid.

Nan Hilga sucked on her tooth as she gripped the tip of the thorn between finger and thumb, the skin on his forearm puckering until she yanked it free.

His flesh stung where she had plucked the thorn, burning with heat as another thorn rapidly grew from the vine to replace it.

Bane couldn't believe what he was seeing. Blinking as he watched the new thorn darken and settle back into a tattoo.

Carefully, he ran the tip of a finger over the area, feeling that it was flesh once again.

"What does it mean?" he asked.

"It means a great deal. However, I need to study the tome before I know more. And even then, it may not hold the answers."

"So, I am Wycum marked?"

Hilga blinked and dabbed at the corner of her watery eye with a hanky before staring right through him.

"It appears so," she said, handing him the vambrace back. "Whatever happens, you need to keep it hidden. Tell no one."

Bane left Nan Hilga's shack feeling somewhat lost. He couldn't steer his thoughts away from his arm, and the more he worried over it, the more it itched.

Before he knew where he was, his feet had carried him to Gelwin and his mother's cairns, yet before he emerged behind the great willow which stood sentinel over them, he noticed two horses tied close by.

Instinctively, he crouched behind a rowan tree and saw two people he didn't recognise standing above the graves, conversing in hushed tones.

Although hidden mostly within shadow, he could tell from the quality of the boots and garb that they were not from Crookfell. And nobody from the village owned a horse.

"I'm sorry, Bailin, I know you loved her," said the shorter woman, and by the sound of her accent, she was from the castle.

As a breeze caught the willow, its branches shifted enough to allow the moonlight through, revealing a beautiful face.

The other hugged the velvet cloak tighter to his shoulders as he turned to the woman, a haunted look about his stern face.

"She was everything to me, Felina. Everything. That cruel bastard had no right to order her death. And now I know why he sent me South. Why he risked his only son."

Felina stepped closer, putting an arm over Bailin.

"We don't know that. Our father may have,"

Bailin shrugged away from her, jaw clenching with emotion.

"Of course he did. He couldn't risk the two of us having a child. Couldn't allow his precious Shankil blood mix with the likes of a commoner."

"Is that why you stayed away for fifteen years? Father ordered your return a year after she died."

Bailin shook his head, tears glistening from grey eyes.

"Once I received your letter, I sent Glance back here to find the truth of it. When he confirmed it, I did not need to return. Instead, I threw myself into every battle I could. I pleaded with the King to send me to the front line, to go where the fighting was thickest, to put myself front and centre of any vanguard I could," Bailin said, hand screwing into a fist. "I wanted to die. I wanted to be with Nel, and I also wanted to punish Father."

"Bailin?" Felina muttered, reaching out to him, yet her brother shrugged away once more, returning only a callus laugh.

"It seems that even Death doesn't want me. But I'll keep putting that to the test. I'm returning South."

"Bailin, you can't. We need you here. With Father's failing health, you'll be the next baron. Besides, he has brought the autumn festival forward in your honour."

"My body may be at the festival, yet my mind will be sunk so far into a wine bottle that I'll not be present. As soon as my men have rested, we'll be heading back. Hopefully, this time, death will welcome me."

Bane crouched lower as the man kissed his hand and touched his mother's headstone.

"I was to give you this, Nel," he said, retrieving a necklace from around his neck. A small ring hung from its links.

Bailin placed it around the headstone and stepped away. He smiled sadly at Felina before pacing into the night. The sound of him climbing onto a hidden horse and galloping away soon followed.

Felina cried softly for a moment, hands covering her face, when Bane felt an overwhelming sense that he shouldn't be there. That he ought to leave the woman to grieve. Yet this was his mother's grave and Gelwin's resting place.

Then another thought occurred, if Bailin left on a third horse out of sight, and there were two still tied up, whose was it?

"Got you," came a harsh voice as thick arms enveloped him, and he was hoisted into the air.

Bane thrashed his legs, momentarily getting his britches caught in the rowan tree he was hiding behind before being dragged free.

The next thing he knew, he was dropped at the feet of Felina, hands still gripping his shoulder and keeping him in place.

"I found this one watching you, my Lady."

Bane recognised the voice, and when he glanced up, he saw Jarl. The old knight returned the stare, confusion deepening the lines in his face.

The Baron's daughter looked down at him, narrowing her grey eyes.

"Do you know who he is?" she asked, addressing Jarl.

"He's of the village, my Lady. A boy who gets coins for doing odd jobs. Although why he's here, I cannot say."

"Then perhaps he can. Have you a name?" Lady Felina asked.

"Speak, lad," Jarl demanded, gripping tighter to his shoulder.

"Boy, my Lady. They call me Boy," Bane answered.

"What kind of name is Boy? Everyone has a name."

"Gelwin called me Bane, my Lady. And my friends, too."

"Gelwin? Is this her cairn?" Lady Felina asked, gesturing behind her. "Is that why you were here, visiting her?"

Bane nodded.

"Gelwin and my mother, Nel."

Felina gasped, her hand pressing against her chest as she stared into the darkness where her brother had gone.

Bane then caught the glance she shared with Jarl and sensed his life was in danger. The light whisper of a blade drawn from a sheath behind him was confirmation.

Lady Felina composed herself as she inspected him further.

"How is it possible? Nel was hanged before her baby was born."

Bane looked at the moss-mottled stones that covered his mother.

"She was, my Lady. I came a few moments later. They say I was gallows born."

"I've heard such rumours," Jarl said. "That there was a child born in Crookfell to the gallows. Yet I believed them to be only rumours."

A tear rolled down Lady Felina's cheek.

"Gallows born? How truly awful," she said, stepping closer and reaching out to touch his jaw. Her hand slipped down his chin, and she gently moved his face to catch the moonlight.

"You're exactly like him when he was your age and those eyes…How much did you hear?" she asked.

"And don't lie, lad," Jarl added.

Bane contemplated telling them that he heard nothing and had only arrived a moment before he was caught, yet the thought of lying in front of the cairns made him feel dirty.

"I heard enough to understand that my mother had found love before she died. And in the end, that's what killed her."

Lady Felina let go of his chin, her hand now trembling as it covered her mouth.

Bane got the impression that his life was about to end, that Jarl would stab him in the back to hide the secret.

It would be morning before Dodd would realise that he was missing. And that would only be because he was needed to earn coppers for the tavern. Dew and Belle would miss him, he was sure. Nan Hilga might. Yet would also see his passing as a problem solved.

"My Lady, may I speak freely?" Jarl asked.

Felina nodded; clearly, she didn't fully control her emotions to speak.

"From what I've known of the lad, he's a wily character. Perhaps a lot brighter than he appears. I think he grasps the nature of the situation and the importance of not saying a word. After all, his life would be the first taken if the people in the castle suspected."

Lady Felina nodded, her tight lips softening into the sad smile which matched her brother's.

"Do I have your word, Bane? Do you swear not to tell anyone of this night? Of what you have learned?"

Bane dipped his head the way he saw the folk of Crookfell do whenever a knight or high-born passed through the village.

"I swear it, my Lady. I won't tell anyone," Bane said, raising his head and meeting Lady Felina's gaze so that she could see he was telling the truth.

Bane felt Jarl's hand rise from his shoulder, the weight of death rising with it.

Felina reached Nel's headstone and retrieved the necklace Bailin had placed there.

"I don't doubt this would have been stolen by daybreak," she said, delicately lowering it over his head. "As a token of trust between us, I give you this offering, Bane."

Now the necklace was around his neck, he could see that it was pure silver, and the ring that dangled above his chest was gold with a ruby set at its centre.

"You'll never be recognised as more than the bastard offspring of my brother and, as such, hold no claim to any title. Do you understand?"

Bane nodded, then flinched as Lady Felina leaned closer, grasping him. He thought she might clutch tighter, a threat for him to keep quiet, but instead she kissed his head.

She said nothing more.

Bane watched her untie the reins of her horse, stroking its neck as she offered him a smile.

"I'll be watching you, lad," Jarl said before joining Lady Felina. He held her horse while she mounted and climbed onto the other. He gave Bane a nod, then steered his mount about and followed Lady Felina through the trees as they set out towards the castle.

When they were gone, Bane sat between Gelwin's and his mother's cairn, grasping the ring to get a better look.

It must be worth enough to buy his own house. Perhaps a farm and several horses, maybe more. It was undoubtedly worth enough to start a new life. But he was sure of one thing: if Dodd caught him with it, he would take it. He would be accused of stealing if someone else found it on him.

Then his gaze fell to his arm and what lay beneath his vambrace. The mark of the Wycum.

The more he thought about it, the more the markings itched.

He wished Gelwin was with him. She always knew what to do. Not that today's events would have been made any easier with her being here, only that he had someone to share them with.

With a heavy sigh, he removed the necklace from his neck, pulled a fist-sized stone from his mother's cairn and shoved the token of trust deep within the dark crevices of the grave.

If he ever needed it, he knew where to go; if he didn't, then his mother had more right to it than he did.

5

Shadow Leopard

The cuffing came early, and as half-hearted as Dodd made it, Bane still caught it on the side of his head, twisting in the direction to take the sting out of it.

He didn't know what he had done to deserve this one.

"By the All-Mother, my head is throbbing," Dodd complained, absently rubbing his hand.

With the cuffing out of the way, Bane stepped away from the man, his fetid breath spoiling the morning air with stale ale.

Dodd fumbled in a knapsack and retrieved a slack handful of dried meats. Most likely chicken.

He tossed a couple of chunks to the hounds and then handed Bane what was left.

"Forgot to feed you yesterday, so have double," he chuckled, which turned into a fit of coughing.

Bane put the meat inside his pocket. He was still full of Nan Hilga's stew the previous night, so he would keep the chicken until later.

Dodd belched, hiccupped and then sat heavily on a tree stump, crossing his legs and resting one boot above the other upon the roots.

"Take Chewer and find me some truffles. And don't be long. You've got plenty of work today."

Bane nodded, whistled for Chewer to follow and then set out into the forest, the huge hound bounding after him.

"And no eating what you find," Bane said, stroking the hound.

They came across the same deer track they found yesterday, its winding path leading them further into the thicker part of the forest, heading up towards the limit of the Fug.

They passed the oak where he found the lichen, and Bane paused. The strange feeling of being watched came over him again, and his mark beneath the vambrace began to itch.

He stared into the brush, peeking into the shadows and trying to see through the foliage, but saw nothing.

Then Chewer found a scent.

"What is it? Truffles?"

Chewer put his nose to the ground, large ears flopping side to side as he nuzzled the earth, and then, tail wagging enthusiastically, he began to work along the deer track.

It wasn't long before he paused, raised his head and sniffed the air, tail wagging faster.

"What is it?" Bane asked, the hound acting differently than usual when he found a truffle.

Bane stared into the underbrush where Chewer was now whimpering with excitement. He took a step closer and peeled back the bracken that was in the way to reveal a small hollow beneath a fallen tree.

An odd-shaped shadow lay trapped beneath the trunk. Bane was wondering what shape it was when the shadow stared back with bright green eyes. The pupils were vertical strips that widened when they focused on him.

It was a shadow leopard.

It was a small one, or maybe a youngling. Bane had heard Dodd once talking with one of the villages, saying he once saw one as large as a pony. Man-eaters, apparently, and trained by the raiders to fight alongside them in battle.

Staring at the small creature trapped beneath the fallen tree, it was hard to see why.

"It's alright, little one, I won't harm you," Bane said as he edged closer, offering the animal his open hand to sniff.

The leopard screeched, and a paw whipped out, catching Bane on the palm and raking its claws through his skin.

"Ouch!"

Bane glanced down at his hand and found four long cuts across the fleshy part of his palm, blood beading along the edges.

Chewer tried to barge past him, barking at the cat, yet soon whimpered again as it curled its lips back in a snarl, revealing long fangs and sharp teeth.

"Easy now," Bane said, hauling Chewer back and ordering him to wait.

It was clear that the leopard was frightened. One of its legs was caught under the thicker part of the fallen tree; claw marks scraped deep into the rotten wood where it had struggled to free itself.

"Hungry?" he asked the cat, crouching down close yet keeping out of harm's way should it try to attack him again.

He guessed it to be the size of the smallest hound. Its black coat shimmered as it moved, revealing a pattern of dark grey rings and dots that covered its body.

"Easy," he whispered, seeing the teeth clash together. It wasn't hard to imagine how a leopard the size of a pony could easily tear a man apart.

Bane reached into his pocket and pulled out the chicken he had been saving. He held it closer, allowing the cat to catch the smell.

It hissed at him, yet its gaze fell to the meat, nostrils working as Bane brought it closer.

A paw whipped out and snagged the meat from Bane's hand, and within a moment, the leopard had devoured it, its tongue licking the grease from its lips.

"Good, now let's see if I can free you."

Bane slowly crouched lower to where the fallen tree met the ground and found that the leopard's leg was wedged, pressing against the roots beneath.

No wonder it wasn't able to dig its way out.

The leopard snarled again as Bane edged closer, but it seemed the animal wasn't as quick to swipe him with its claws again.

Keeping his movements slow, Bane pushed his hands as far under the trunk as possible and tried to lift and roll it away.

But it was no use; the tree was too heavy.

"I'm going to need a branch," he told the leopard, who began to scrape at the rotten wood again.

Bane kicked through the bracken and foliage until he found a suitable branch.

Returning, he wedged one end as far under as he could, prising it against the roots and putting all his weight on it.

He strained, arms shaking with the effort, and just as he was about to give up, the tree slowly rose high enough for the leopard to drag itself away.

When it was clear, Bane let go of the branch, sank to the ground and leaned against the trunk.

The leopard looked ready to run, but Bane noticed it limped as it took a few cautious steps.

It sniffed the air, turned to regard Bane and then came back to him, sinking heavily to the floor, most likely too exhausted to go.

Bane reached out and gently stroked its back, feeling how soft and thick the fur was. He was ready to pull away should the cat decide to bite, yet it seemed to enjoy it, leaning into his body.

He caught Dodd's impatient shouts further away in the forest, and Chewer began to pace impatiently.

"I'll be back later," he said. "I'll try and bring you more food. If we can build your strength up, you'll be able to find your way home."

The leopard began to purr, a deep rumble from inside its chest and then began to sniff Bane's injured hand, its rough tongue licking the blood from his palm as if cleaning the wound.

When it was done, it lay its head on his lap and stared up at him with large green eyes regarding him intently.

"You're not so vicious," Bane said, smiling at the cat and noticing a long silver stripe running down its flank - maybe an old scar.

He wondered where it had come from. They were supposed to stick to the foothills and mountains on the other side of the Fug. Maybe it had found a way through.

"Boy?" came Dodd's voice again, this time closer and causing the leopard to raise its hackles.

"I better go," Bane said, slowly moving away from the animal. "Stay hidden until tomorrow."

Bane stroked behind Chewer's ears as they both returned to Dodd at the edge of the forest.

"Well?" he demanded, seeing that Bane had returned empty-handed.

Bane shook his head and then prepared himself ready for the cuffing.

For the second time that day, he rolled with the contact of the open hand, so used to it that he barely felt it anymore.

"Fugging useless. Now, get yourself back to the village. Working the bellows, splitting wood and then back over to the Gobbin's place for sword practice," Dodd said, counting the tasks off. "Two coppers from each, mind. So that will be five coppers in all," he said, holding four fingers up. "Now, get on with you. I'll have to find the truffle myself. You'll be lucky if I feed you later, boy."

Bane set off at a run, putting distance between himself and Dodd. The man was unpredictable with a morning ale head.

As he passed the Trial stone, he gave the sign of the Fug, glancing momentarily at the silver fog which was making its way through the forest to the space of land.

How had the shadow leopard managed to get across it?

A fierce wind had picked up by the afternoon, gusts catching his woollen shirt and lifting it from his body as he split the last log. His muscles ached from working the bellows all morning and chopping his way through the pile of logs, but it was now mercifully over.

Dew picked up the halves and stacked them before joining him at the now-empty stump.

"Did you hear about the autumn festival? The Baron is bringing it forward in honour of his son's return," Dew said excitedly.

"Mother's up at the castle today," Belle added as she leaned against the oak. "Most likely trying to get a peek at his Lordship. According to her, he was quite attractive back in the day. Still is, according to those that have seen him."

"Belle," Dew scolded.

"It's true. Well, he hasn't been here in fifteen years, so he might have changed, I suppose."

"And he's old enough to be your father," Dew said, shaking his head.

Bane only knew how true that statement was.

After the events of yesterday, he was glad of the hard work and the company to keep his mind from mulling over everything.

"You're not saying much," Belle said, giving him a worried look. "Has Dodd been heavy-handed again?"

Bane shook his head.

"No more than usual," he said, wishing he could tell his friends about what had happened at his mother's cairn and what was under his vambrace. Yet he was sworn to secrecy on both occasions.

Belle seemed to take his silence as confirmation.

"What is it, Bane? You can tell us," she said, approaching and taking his arm.

Bane sighed, touched by the affection from his friends.

"I found a shadow leopard this morning. In the forest, while foraging," he admitted, wanting to share at least something.

"Fugwash," laughed Dew.

"I swear by the All-Mother," Bane said, raising his face to the sky. "I found a shadow leopard."

He then explained what had happened and how he had helped free the trapped leg.

"And it fed out of your hand?" Belle asked, scrutinising his face should he be lying.

"I want to see it," Dew said, his sister agreeing with him.

Bane shrugged.

"I don't see why not. But we'll have to go this evening after I've finished at the Gobbin's place. And after Dodd's gone to the tavern."

Dew and Belle glanced at each other, broad smiles lightening their faces.

"And if you have any spare food, bring it. The poor thing was starving. And probably a lantern if you can. It gets dark quickly in the forest."

"Of course," Dew said, then changing the subject. "Did you really put Kulby on his back yesterday?"

Bane grinned.

"It felt good. If I get the chance, I'll do it again today. If I leave now, I might be able to finish a little early. I'll meet you at the Trial Stone as soon as possible."

Bane made his way to the pig pens, where he found Mr Gobbin and Kulby. The pair were grinning as he arrived, the younger already wearing his boiled leather armour and helmet.

"I dare say you're going to hurt some today, boy," Mr Gobbin said, his many chins wobbling as he spoke, his sausage-like finger prodding Bane's chest with every other word. "You'll not be pulling any stunts on Kulby like you did yesterday. Understand?"

Bane wanted nothing more than to say that Kulby had brought it on himself, yet knew that would only land him in trouble with Dodd, and he enjoyed the lessons he was receiving from Jarl. He didn't want to ruin it, and so he nodded.

"And I've sharpened my sword for you, boy," Kulby added, running his thumb up the edge of his wooden blade, his grin widening.

"Nobody puts me in the mud, you got that?" he asked, then struck Bane's thigh with the sword.

Pain shot up his muscle, the sharpened edge almost biting through his britches, yet Bane fought not to show it.

Clenching his teeth, he nodded and wandered over to his practice sword, which he found to be a few inches shorter, with fresh saw marks along the squared point.

He felt the presence of Kulby looming behind him and braced himself for another blow, but mercifully, Jarl chose that moment to show up.

"Over here, you two," he growled as he dismounted his horse. He threw the reins at Mr Gobbin, who fumbled to catch them.

"Have you shed yesterday's animosities, lad," he asked, directing the question at Kulby. "You'll be on your back more often than not when you begin your proper training, and if you don't learn to have thick skin, you'll soon find yourself in a world of hurt."

Kulby's narrowed eyes briefly found Bane before he turned to the old knight.

"It's forgotten."

The knight slapped him on the shoulder.

"Good, now show me the forms I've taught you."

Kulby stared at his feet as he placed them apart, setting one foot in front of the other, changing his mind and swapping them around. He put his shield before him and raised his sword to the side.

"What form is that? Because it's not one that you've learned from me," Jarl said, folding his arms.

"It's Stalking Crane," Kulby said, face going red.

"Like Fug it is, lad. Now show me properly, Stalking Crane."

He shook his head as Kulby swapped feet, his sword clattering over the rim of his shield as he swapped it from a wide position to a narrow one.

"Surprised you're still here," Jarl said in a hushed tone so only Bane could hear. "I thought you'd be halfway to Hamlinshire by now. That would have been the wise thing to do."

"I don't know anywhere else but here. I've never left Crookfell," Bane whispered, not used to an adult talking with him without a trace of disdain in their voice. "And I want to be a soldier. Like my father," he said, meeting the man's gaze.

Jarl stared at him, face unreadable as greying hair blew across his weary brow. His eyes never left Bane as he brushed the strands away.

"I've fought alongside Lord Bailin. Before I retired and became bodyguard to Lady Felina, that is. There isn't a man more dangerous on the battlefield than Bailin. His skill and prowess with the blade is something right out of the songs."

Jarl's attention returned to Kulby, who had given up and stood there, shield resting in the mud and his sword cocked over a shoulder.

"What's the point in forms, anyway," the large youth groaned, his cheeks squashed up in the chin strap of his helmet. "It's always the strongest that crushes the enemy in the end."

Jarl unfolded his arms as he approached Kulby, unsheathing his sword and letting the daylight play along its steel, the lethal edge glinting.

"Wait, now, what's this?" Mr Gobbin demanded, stepping between the knight and his son, fat wobbling as he began to control his rising panic. "I've paid good coin for you to teach, not to threaten, Sir."

Jarl stopped before them reversed the grip on his sword and held it toward Kulby.

"And teaching is exactly what I'm doing," Jarl said as he not too gently shoved Mr Gobbin aside. "Now take my blade, lad."

Kulby stared at the sword and then up to his father.

"Don't look at your father, lad. You want to know what the forms are for; take my sword."

Reluctantly, Kulby dropped his shield and took Jarl's sword from him, a nervous tension settling over the group.

Bane watched on, wondering where this was going. Knowing Jarl, there was a lesson about to be taught.

"Grip it properly. Give the weapon the respect it deserves. Now, kill me."

"What?" Both Kulby and his father said together.

"You heard you mutton-brained oaf of a child. Use the sword I've given you and kill me."

Bane couldn't believe what he was hearing. He stepped closer, unsure what was happening, a sinking feeling filling his gut.

"Bloody, kill me!"

Kulby flinched as the knight shouted and then slashed at him, gripping the sword in two hands and blindly swinging it.

Jarl leaned away from the first swing, setting feet wide apart as he ducked beneath the next.

"Swaying Foxglove," he said, arms held aloft as he turned and dodged a thrust, the steel coming within an inch of skewering him.

Jarl pivoted on a heel and rolled behind another slash, elbow dipping to collide with Kulby's ribs.

"Stalking Crane," he said, his body flowing from one form into another, and Bane recognised the position of the limbs and angle of the body before the knight ducked another cut and twisted away from a savage slash.

Stalking Crane flowed into the Minstrel Star, which became Spinning Rock, each stance having a particular shape.

Jarl called each of them out, catching Kulby with a slap to the cheek, a kick behind the knee, and ending with a gentle shove to the chest.

Kulby toppled backwards, but not before Jarl easily plucked his sword from a flailing arm.

"Death's Last Kiss," he said, standing over the fallen boy and placing the tip of his blade to Kulby's heart.

"What's the point in forms?"

Jarl leaned closer, a wicked grin curling his lips.

"Forms keep you alive. Unless your enemy learned them better. Now get up."

Bane hid the smile threatening his face as he watched Kulby clamber to his feet, panting like a hound after a chase.

Jarl stared past him and met Bane's gaze.

"Stalking Crane," he snapped.

Without thinking, Bane set his feet apart, cocked his elbow out and raised the sword over his head, tip pointing down.

Jarl stepped closer and paced around him, nudging the toe of his boot to the back of Bane's heel to move it in a fraction.

"It's almost halfway decent," Jarl said with a satisfactory nod. Then, turning his attention back to Kulby.

"See, he gets it, and I haven't even been teaching him. Now stand beside this lad and bloody learn," Jarl snapped and waited until Kulby stood beside Bane, red-faced and wheezing.

"Good," Jarl continued, adopting the same stance. "Now, Falling Grace," he said, shifting weight onto his other leg, swiping the sword down as he went and manoeuvring into another position. "Silent Star."

"Wait now, Sir. I'll not be paying you to teach the boy. He's only here for Kulby to hit," Mr Gobbin said, thick jowls positively throbbing.

"Well, it wouldn't harm the swine-filled lad to be occasionally hit back. And he's already wearing armour on top of the rolls of fat that are protecting his body."

"Now listen here, you might be a knight, but I'll not be paying for that urchin to learn. He can sod off back to Dodd if he's not needed here."

Bane didn't want to go back. He wanted to learn from Jarl and become a soldier, like his father - now he knew who he was.

Jarl breathed deeply as he stared from Mr Gobbin to Bane.

"Fine," he said, shaking his head.

Bane felt his world sink beneath him. He was so desperate to be taught the way of the blade that nothing else mattered.

He watched Kulby smirk and needed to unclench the fist which he wanted to drive into his face, but Jarl hadn't finished speaking.

"I'll pay for the lad myself. Here, take half your coin back," the knight said and tossed the swine herder a mark. "If you don't like it, you can find another tutor."

My Gobbin frowned as he bent to retrieve the coin, yet said nothing. Jarl was easily the best instructor of the blade from the castle; if he lost him, he wouldn't be replaced.

Bane felt indebted to the knight so much that he didn't know what to say.

Jarl turned his attention back to them, narrowing his gaze both on Bane and Kulby.

"Now, the pair of you, keep your eyes keen, listen hard and learn.

"Stalking Crane," he shouted.

****

Clouds set in in the evening sky, bringing on night more swiftly than usual.

Bane rolled the stiffness from his shoulders and back as he walked through the village. Jarl had put them through many forms, shouting until they got it right - or as right as Jarl let them get away with. Bane promised himself that when he had time alone, he would practice them, doing them over and over again until he mastered every single one.

Dew and Belle were already at the Trial Stone when he arrived. Warm light glowing from a lantern and illuminating their faces.

"Thought you were never coming," Dew said as they set off for the forest. "You were lucky that the Fug tide had already been and gone; otherwise, we wouldn't be here."

"I don't mind it," Bane replied, glancing up into the foothills and seeing the halo of fog shrinking away towards the mountains.

"Well, you're simply odd. How come you're late?" Belle asked.

"Jarl put us through it today," Bane said. "And he has given half his earnings back to Kulby's father so he can teach me too."

"Really? That's wonderful. But why?" Belle asked.

Bane shrugged; he couldn't explain without breaking his oath and didn't want to lie to his friends.

"Did you bring any food?" he asked, changing the subject.

"A bit of mutton I kept by after dinner," Belle said, retrieving a small hanky from her pocket and handing it over. "Haven't you eaten?"

"Not yet, but this isn't for me. It's for the leopard."

Dew chuckled.

"I'm still not convinced you've seen one," he said as they entered the forest.

Bane took the lantern and led them through the trees to where he left the leopard that morning.

He pulled the bracken aside to reveal the small hollow where the fallen tree lay. Yet the leopard wasn't there.

"It was here," he said, then watched as the shadow beneath the trunk slinked out and sat before him, large green eyes narrowing over his shoulder to where Belle gasped.

"It's real," Dew said as he came closer, hunkering down to stroke it.

The leopard swiped at his hand, bared teeth catching in the lamplight, yet it was only a warning. The paw came short of striking.

"It's alright, they're friends," Bane soothed as he placed the lamp on the log and squatted down.

The cat inspected Dew and Belle suspiciously, walking around their feet before returning to Bane, where it rubbed its head against him, long ears tickling his arm.

"It's beautiful. Will it bite me?" Belle asked.

"Try giving it the mutton. It'll know you mean it no harm," Bane said.

"She, it's a she," Dew said, folding his arms and leaning against an oak.

Bane glanced up at him.

"How can you tell?"

Dew laughed.

"How do you think?" he said, nodding to the leopard. "She's lacking something."

Bane felt like an idiot. Why hadn't he checked?

Belle slowly approached; the mutton held before her as if it were a charm to ward off evil.

The leopard raised her head, sniffed at the meat and then turned her gaze on Bane as if she were asking permission.

"Go on, we brought it for you," he said and smiled as she swiped the mutton from Belle's hand in a blur of motion, startling the girl, who fell back and landed on her rump.

Dew laughed, which earned him a thump in the leg from his sister.

"Ouch! You didn't have to hit me," Dew complained.

"Well, you didn't have to laugh. Now help me up," Belle said and was hoisted from the floor by her brother.

"We best keep our voices low in the forest," Bane warned, staring out into the shadow yet couldn't see much further than the lamplight. "Trappers and maybe raiders still lurk amidst the trees."

The leopard suddenly dropped the meat and hissed as somebody stepped into the lamplight.

"Trappers and raiders, aye?" said a man dressed in dark clothes.

Dew squeaked as he dragged his sister behind him, fumbling for a belt knife, which he dropped.

"Glance?" Bane said as he rose, stroking the leopard to calm her from pouncing on the newcomer.

Glance gave a theatrical bow before lowering his hood.

"How did you sneak up on us so silently?" Belle asked, her hand covering her chest as she gathered herself.

Glance grinned.

"It wasn't hard. I'm sure if there were any raiders in the woods, they could have sneaked an entire clan up on you. You should listen to Master Bane; voices should always be low in the woods."

Master Bane? What did the rogue know? Or was he mocking him? He wasn't familiar with people speaking with him, especially adults, and he didn't know how to react.

"And why are you out in the forest alone?" Glance asked, looking at Dew and Belle. "You're the Camwell children."

Dew folded his arms.

"How did you know that? And also, what business is it of yours?"

He tried to stick his chest out, but Bane could see that he was easily a head shorter than Glance, and his shoulders were nowhere near as wide.

Glance chuckled as he leaned against a tree, an easy smile coming to his lips.

"I know all kinds of things, all kinds of business, and it is mine to hold or to sell for the right price. How did you come by a shadow leopard, Master Bane?"

"I found her this morning. She was trapped, and I freed her."

Bane didn't mind talking with the rogue. If Nan Hilga trusted him, then he had no reason not to.

"I better take her back up into the foothills where she belongs," Glance said as he hunkered down to stroke the cat.

"But she's Bane's," Belle said, coming to stand by him. "If he wants to keep her, then it is up to him."

Glance laughed.

"My dear girl, have you seen a full-sized shadow leopard?"

Belle's lip went firm as she shook her head.

"And do you know what they can do to a fully grown man, even one in armour?"

Again, Belle shook her head.

Glance then narrowed his eyes on Bane.

"Do you want to keep her?"

Bane stroked the cat, who nuzzled into his hand. He did, yet knew on some level that it would be impossible.

"I doubt the village would take kindly to a shadow leopard. They'd no doubt try to kill her," he said.

Glance slowly nodded.

"You've found the truth of it, Master Bane. Fortunately, I found you before she bonded with one of you."

"Bonded?" Dew asked.

"It's what the raiders breed them for. Even wild shadow leopards will bond with a human. Only one, but when they do, they become bonded for life. They become the other's shadow, as it were," Glance explained.

"I only found her this morning," Bane said, wishing there was some way to keep her.

"It doesn't work like. The leopards are full of honour, much like the clans of raiders on the other side of the Fug. They must feel that the human they bond with has saved its life. That they owe a debt. There's a ceremony where the cats are given the gift of food and then offered the taste of the human's blood, whom they wish to bond with. Once that happens, they are bonded."

Bane looked at the cuts in his palm where the leopard had struck him with her claws earlier.

"Bane, what's the matter?" Belle asked, concern wrinkling her brow.

"This morning, after I freed her from beneath the tree, I gave her a piece of chicken," he said and then met Glance's gaze. "At first, she didn't trust me and had swiped at my hand."

He held the injury up for them to see.

"Then afterwards, when she was free and had eaten the food, she licked my wound clean."

Glance stood and gripped Bane by the shoulders hard enough to hurt, and the leopard arched her back, teeth bared as she hissed at the rogue.

"She has bonded with you, lad," Glance said as he eased himself off. "Now there's no uncertainty. She must come with me. And tonight. Any delay and the bond will become stronger."

Bane unconsciously reached for the leopard and ran his fingers through her thick black fur.

She nudged into him, head pressing against his chest and began to purr.

He believed he could feel the bond now. It didn't only go one way; he felt a kinship with this shadow leopard, more so than any of the hounds at home, some of whom he had raised since pups.

Belle came closer, her hand hovering over the cat before she leaned away.

"Bane, she has to go, for your sake as well as hers."

"Where will you take her?" Bane asked, fighting the urge to pick the leopard up and to leave.

"North. Back into the foothills where she belongs. She's still young, and with any luck, she'll bond with another. Or will return to the mountains to live out her life as shadow leopards should. You're doing the right thing, Master Bane."

Without another word, Glance bent down and scooped up the cat, tucking her beneath his cloak so her legs and, more importantly, her claws were held firm. She struggled until Bane lay a palm to her head.

"It's alright, Glance won't hurt you," he soothed, which seemed to settle her.

"But North will take you beyond the Fug. That's impossible. Nobody can get through the wall of fog," Dew said.

Glance grinned as he pulled the hood of his cloak over his head so only his jaw was visible.

"There are ways, and there are ways," he said, and then, with a theatrical bow, set off through the trees, soon disappearing into the gloom.

"He's vanished just as quick as he came. I can't even hear him," Dew said as they stared after the rogue.

"Is he really going through the Fug?" Belle asked.

"It's what he said," Bane answered as he picked up the lamp, which was beginning to dim. "Let's get you two out of here before the oil burns up."

Belle stumbled as they began, gripping his hand to steady herself.

She didn't release it.

6

Alruna

Alruna heard the Tide bell and knew that she was running out of time. The Fug would sweep over her within moments, and she would be caught out in the open like a lame raven.

She worked her fingers as fast as she could, threading the last strands of her hair into place and cinching it off with string.

Done.

She let her warrior braid fall to her shoulders as she sought shelter.

A dull sky hugged the mountain and foothills, casting great shadows over the outcropping of rocks she was hiding amongst while the women of her clan left the goats they were herding to seek refuge in the communal burrow.

She put her back to them and stared down into the Southlands and the grey castle sitting on a hillock, the squat village of Crookfell in between.

Alruna briefly wondered what it must be like living outside of the Fug tide. It must be easier not to have to shelter twice a day, but as her father said, that luxury brought a softness to the Southerners.

Another tide bell rang. This one was from the edge of her village, which meant she had the time of a single breath before it would claim her.

It was a stupid decision. She should have been with the goat herders or in her home burrow with her father instead of hiding out in the open only to defy him and put her hair how she wanted it. She was a clan warrior after all - or would be as soon as she reached her sixteenth winter - a single moon away.

Crows took flight from a twisted birch close by, and the silver fumes of the Fug cascaded down towards her; the impenetrable wall engulfed all as it came, swallowing everything, including her, if she didn't hurry.

Putting her back to the fog, she dashed down the hill and slid to a halt beside the closest burrow door, which lay buried a hand's width below the ground. She yanked on the handle, yet it was shut firm.

"Fug sanctuary," she bellowed as she knocked on the wood. The runes carved into it began to frost over as the god's breath approached.

Nothing.

More birds took flight from the trees around her, indicating that the Fug was bearing down.

"Odin's stones," she growled as she left the burrow door and darted further down the hill, boots sliding in the damp earth as she came to the next burrow.

She kicked it with the heel of her foot.

"Open up, Fug sanctuary," she shouted, kneeling to bang harder.

She put her ear to the rough wood slats and heard no movement from within.

Spending time out in the open to braid her hair now seemed an immensely foolish thing to have done.

Further on, she caught movement and saw a burrow door open, a face peering above the ground.

Their eyes locked before the head disappeared, and the door slammed shut.

"No, you fugging, don't," Alruna shouted as she sprinted towards the last burrow at the edge of the clan village. There were no further places beyond to hide.

"Fug sanctuary!" she screamed as she dived onto her belly and began to bray her fist into the door. "Fug sanctuary."

The silver fog had now covered her tracks, swallowing the village whole and was rushing towards her, snarls and hissing catching her ears through her pounding of the wood and above the thumping of her heart.

"I know you saw me, Ganlin. Now open up. Fug fugging sanct…"

The door was flung open, and she fell into the burrow beneath.

She landed hard, face smacking into the packed mud floor, driving the wind from her chest.

Howls and screams from the passing Fug above battered the door, shaking it violently in its timber frame. The beasts within the halo that would have ravaged her.

It soon ebbed away.

When her vision cleared and she regained control of her breathing, she sat up and faced the others in the burrow.

An old hag and a boy a winter older than herself.

A single candle lit their grim faces, narrowing eyes focusing on her and revealing the confined burrow with a single chair and a shelf cut into the earth walls on which the candle was sitting.

"Thank you," Alruna mumbled reluctantly.

"Foolish girl," the hag said, shaking her head. "Does Boran know you were out during Fug tide?"

"Probably thinks you're milking the goats, where you should be," the boy said, smirking as she rose.

"I'm no milkmaid, Ganlin," she snapped, stepping up to him and raising her chin. "And you should have given me sanctuary when I asked for it. You saw me."

Gamlin shrugged.

"Maybe I thought you were one of the howlers or another demon trying to break free of the fog. But it doesn't matter. I saved your life, and you owe me a life debt, Alruna Lothrun. Isn't that right, Nan?"

The hag nodded, her glower never leaving Alruna.

"And the life debt owed by the Chief's daughter is a mighty thing," Ganlin continued, cocking his head as the tide bell rang further down the hill, letting them know it was safe to come out.

"And now you can go back and tell him. You owe me."

He punctuated the final word by stabbing her in the chest with a thick finger.

Alruna clenched her teeth, an anger rising within her, yet she couldn't argue the point. She had foolishly risked her life and now owed a debt to this oaf, all for the sake of braiding her hair.

She pulled her gaze from him, gave a nod of thanks to the hag and climbed up the steps to push open the door.

The brightness of the day blinded her as she climbed out of the burrow, took several steps, and then stopped.

Gamlin had followed her.

"You're mine now."

Her fists were balled so tight her fingers began to throb.

Slowly, she turned to face him. He was tall; even at seventeen winters, it was clear he would make a large man with broad shoulders to match. He had muscular arms, a chiselled chin, and already the makings of a blonde beard, his matching warrior braid trailing down his back.

He leaned cockily on a quarterstaff, hungry eyes taking in every inch of her.

Alruna breathed deeply and settled the fire raging within her as she stepped closer to Ganlin.

"Fight me," she said, willing her limbs to stop shaking, "and give me the chance to win my debt back."

Ganlin raised an eyebrow.

"I don't need to fight you. I already own you. And you can start by taking that braid out of your hair. No wench of mine will be a warrior."

Although fear began to seep into her anger, she fought to show only a cool calmness.

"Do you really think my father would believe you and your nan? It would be my word against yours."

Gamlin frowned and was about to argue when Alruna raised her hand to stop his argument before it came.

"But beat me in a fight, and I'll come willingly. I'll tell my father that I owe you a life debt."

Gamlin sucked on his lip, his frown slowly dissolving.

"Just a single fight, you and me, whoever cries Freya first, loses," she said, raising her arms. "I'm unarmed, and you can use your stick."

"Quarterstaff," he corrected, nodding as he watched her step closer. "And you may as well cry Freya now; I've also been training with sword and axe, but my Da reckons I'll be more at home with a hammer,"

"Yes, it must be those big, thick arms of yours," she said, lowering her voice seductively.

Ganlin's grin widened as he flexed an arm, his muscle stretching the rough-spun wool.

He momentarily dropped his gaze to his bicep, and Alruna made her move.

Ganlin wasn't the only one learning weapon skills. Her father had been teaching her ever since she could grasp a stick, a handle, a hilt. It had been brutal, but she loved it.

In a single fluid motion, she kicked the quarterstaff from under Gamlin, caught it as it spun and drove the butt end into the soft flesh beneath his ribcage.

Gamlin doubled over, face burning red as he fought to breathe.

Veins throbbed in his temples as he lunged for her, yet she easily sidestepped him and drove her foot up into his stones.

A mouse-like whimper escaped him, bulging eyes turned accusingly to her as he slowly toppled over and curled up into a ball, hands held between his legs.

"I'll be ten times the warrior you'll be, you dung heap," Alruna growled, raising the quarterstaff and bringing it down on Gamlin's side.

He yelped as it made contact.

"Freya," he whimpered, raising a hand for protection.

The air made a whooping sound as she brought the quarterstaff down again.

"Freya, Freya," he squealed and watched as she brought the weapon back for another crack; her fire was burning hotter than the forges of Asgard.

A huge shadow leopard crept up beside her, a mass of grey fur, teeth barred as it padded between her and the fallen Gamlin. Then, the quarterstaff was suddenly wrenched from her hands, and her father was standing there, glowering with all the wrath of Odin.

He said nothing. He didn't need to. Alruna could feel the thunderhead of rage beneath Boran's stare.

"Life debt," Gamlin spluttered as he rose into a sitting position, a trembling finger pointing at Alruna. "I claim a life debt for giving her Fug sanctuary."

Her father's grey beard caught in the wind as he stared down at the man on the ground, ice-blue eyes unreadable.

"I am grateful for your charity, lad. No doubt you did save her life. But see here, she was about to kill you," he said and tossed the quarterstaff on the ground beside him. "So, I also saved your life. You now owe me a life debt, no? The way I see it, the one cancels out the other."

He briefly held the boy's gaze before glancing at Alruna and nodding back up the hill. He marched away, his shadow leopard stalking after.

Alruna breathed deeply as she stared after her father. She was in a lot of trouble.

Ganlin's whimpering brought her attention back to him.

"My life debt is cleared," she said, then set off after her father.

"How long had you been there?" she asked after her father remained quiet.

"Long enough. I swear by the All-Father, you're going to be the death of me. When you didn't return home before the tide bell, I came out looking for you. And when you didn't arrive at the communal burrow, I felt sick to the pit of my stomach. And for what?" he demanded, lifting her warrior braid and tossing it into the air. "For this? I've told you to wait until you're old enough. There are rules, and being the chief's daughter doesn't mean you can break them. Even more so than anyone else. Do you understand?"

Alruna nodded, pressing her lips tight to stop the coming retort. She hated hurting her father. He had a challenging task to do, solely bringing her and her brother up alone while still being in charge of the clan.

"I'm sorry," she said and began to untangle the braid, her long blonde strands at the mercy of the gusts as they whipped about her face.

"When it was done, she smiled up at him. He never stayed angry for long.

"So, you watched all of it?"

"All of it," he admitted, the severity lifting. "Long enough to see you put that idiot on his back. It was a good move, and the kick to the stones was an added bonus."

He came to a stop, a worried look creasing his brow.

"You let your anger rule you again, Alruna. He'd already pleaded Freya's mercy, but you still attacked."

Alruna knew that her temper had ruled the moment. If her father hadn't intervened, she would have done some severe damage.

"You and Raif are all I have. And when I'm gone, and Raif takes my place as Clan Chief, he will need you. And if you're determined to become a warrior, you'll have to start using this," he said, tapping her softly on her head.

Alruna hated it when her father talked about his passing, about his age and frailties.

"Is Raif still putting himself up for the Tide Hunt later?" she asked, changing the subject.

Her father nodded.

"Your brother has earned the right. He's planning on heading into the Fug this evening. That's why I've come to find you. So, you can wish him luck."

Alruna caught the tinge of worry in her father's words.

"Wish him luck and maybe say goodbye," she said. "Can't you talk him out of it? You know how dangerous it is."

They began walking through the village again, Geri, the grey shadow leopard, prowling beside her, head nudging her hand until she stroked her behind the ears.

"It is his right, Alruna. And the rest of the clan will be looking at him to lead them soon. If anyone should attempt the Tide Hunt, it should be him."

"But what if he can't find the Wycum? What if he doesn't come back?"

She loved her older brother, who had become almost a second parent when their mother died several winters back. The thought of losing him to the Fug, to anything, worried her. Perhaps that was why she had lost it with Ganlin.

"He will come back. Raif is ready. If anyone deserves the mark of the Wycum, it is he."

Alruna glanced at her father's Wycum mark, a thin ring of ivy circling his forearm below the elbow. It was faded now, the single weave with a smattering of leaves which marked him as clan leader. It was hard to believe that the blood of a god was used in the tattoo.

Other villagers had already emerged from their burrows, fire pits lit with roasting meats being turned on spits above flames.

They nodded and smiled at Boran Lothrun, their Clan Chief, as they strolled along, some of the men placing fists to chests, a greeting from one warrior to another.

"Where's Geri's young welp that I gave you? I've not seen her around in days."

Alruna sighed, her heart sinking again.

"I don't know. The last time I saw her was when she chased a rabbit down into the gullies. She went beyond the boundary and still hasn't returned."

Alruna wanted nothing more than to track the leopard cub, but she was forbidden to track beyond the boundaries. She'd waited the rest of the day and only returned because of the Fug tide. Her only hope was that cubs would return to their mothers every few days until they were strong enough to hunt for themselves. Either that or she had found a way up into the mountains to live a life as a wild leopard.

"It might be for the best," Boran said, offering her a smile which cracked his grey beard. "Keeping shadow leopards isn't easy. And most see them as burdens. That's why I'm the only one in the clan to have one. They're hard to train and almost impossible to discipline. Isn't that right, girl?" he chuckled, stroking Geri's huge head. The leopard leaned into him and almost knocked him over.

Alruna shrugged. She'd only had the cub a few days before she went missing. But she wanted to be like her father. If she ever returned, she would make sure to bond with it. Maybe that's what it needed.

They came to their home at the top of the village, a simple log hut with a single chimney. The burrow lay beside it, door open and ready for when the next tide bell came to signal the return of the Fug as it made its way up the hills to the mountain.

Raif was sitting on a bench outside the hut, sword on his lap as he ran a sharpening stone along the blade.

"What happened to your hair?" he asked, an easy smile reflecting from the steel. "No, let me guess, you had it in a warrior braid."

The stone made another scrape before he placed it in his pocket and stood, slipping his sword into its sheath.

"Only one moon left before you can do it," he laughed, tussling her hair.

Alruna wriggled away from him but couldn't stop the laughter bubbling out of her.

"That's if she makes it to the next moon before offering herself to another idiot in a life debt," her father said. He was about to say something more when another warrior, Hadlo, came striding up the hill, wolfskin covering broad shoulders and the large hammer he wore on his back.

"Chief, a word," he said, leading their father away. "I've got news from across the boundary," he said, his voice a low grumble yet still audible as they plodded down the hill. "Young Shankil has returned, and the Baron will bring the Autumn fair forward."

Alruna watched them until they disappeared into the thicket, along with the conversation.

"Are you really doing the Tide Hunt?" she asked, slumping onto the bench Raif had been sitting on. "I don't want you to."

Raif cocked his head back to catch a brief glimpse of the sun as it found a gap in the clouds. His dimples deepened as he grinned, casting his gaze back up the mountain.

"I'm as ready as I'll ever be, and if I'm to take Da's place, I'll need to be Wycum marked. Besides," he laughed, placing a hand on the hilt of his sword as he leaned closer. "If I don't get one soon, you'll beat me to it."

He playfully ruffled her hair again before leaping away as she lashed out with the toe of her boot.

She missed, of course. She always did.

"Oaf," she laughed as she jumped from the bench and grasped the practice blade hanging from a hook by the door.

The heavy lump of iron was given to her by Raif last year. His old sword, which their father used to teach him with.

Raif ducked her attack, easily sidestepping while drawing his blade.

Steel clashed against iron as they circled each other, a rapid succession of thrusts and jabs easily parried by both siblings as they worked to break each other's defences.

"What did Da mean about this life debt? Have you been promising yourself to some boy or planning on leaving to join another clan?"

Alruna caught an arcing blow; it jarred her shoulders, yet she angled her blade down, the metals screeching in complaint as they slid until the cross-pieces came together.

"Ganlin," she gasped as she shoved Raif away, sweeping her feet behind his heel, yet he saw it coming and skipped over it.

"Not the boy who I'd have thought could steal your heart," Raif said, effortlessly deflecting her cut and then digging his elbow into her ribs.

Alruna grunted, tried not to show it had hurt, and then pressed back with a low lunge.

"He gave me Fug sanctuary and then demanded a life debt."

Blades clanged, and she lost her footing, stumbling further up the hill, yet she kept to her feet.

The view of the village below, the forest, the silver halo of fog and the vast countryside beyond was beautiful. She loved her home, the village and the foothills she grew up in. But her brother's Wycum Hunt later in the day tainted it.

"What? You're his now?" Raif asked, dropping the point of his sword to the ground.

Alruna didn't waste the opportunity; she dropped to one knee, reversed the grip of her sword and thrust the hilt into Raif's thigh.

He groaned as he slipped away and then came back, the point of his blade flicking dirt into her face.

As she leaned away from it and sliced her sword back, she realised that it had been a ruse.

Too late, she caught the crosspiece of Raif's blade with her shoulder and was knocked onto her back.

Her brother's shadow passed overheard as he placed a knee against her chest and a sword to her neck.

"Not bad, little sister," he said, grinning down.

He left his ankle exposed, in easy reach of her weapon, yet it would have been a cheap shot, and she couldn't guarantee that she wouldn't slice through his tendons and do permanent damage.

She let her sword fall to the ground.

"Please tell me you've not given yourself to that idiot Ganlin."

Alruna rolled from under him, picked her sword from the floor and slipped it into its scabbard.

"Of course, she didn't," her father said as he stepped around the hut and took the sword from her. He was grinning as he placed it over his shoulder.

"She challenged him for it and then put him on his arse. Kicked ten shades of Asgard out of him before I intervened."

Alruna shrugged.

"He had it coming."

Raif was rubbing his thigh where she had caught him with the hilt.

"No doubt. So, what did Hadlo want," Raif asked, staring down at the village where the giant warrior was skinning a rabbit, large hands making light work of degloving.

Boran stared from his son to his daughter and then back, creases making deep furrows of his brow.

"We've got to bring the raid forward by a few weeks. The Baron is throwing the Autumn fair early in honour of his son's return."

"But I'm still going on the Wycum hunt," Raif said, mimicking a scowl of his own to match his father's.

"And I shan't stop you. I wish you would wait until after we've struck out against the castle."

Alruna could tell he wouldn't be dissuaded by her brother's clenched fist and gritted teeth.

"Fine," Boran said. "I shan't fight you on this; Odin knows you're going to need a clear head. Rest up for now. And you won't be alone. Hadlo's lad is joining you."

Raif's posture changed at the mention of his friend.

"I knew Jhora was thinking about the Hunt. I'm guessing he thought I stepped down now that the raid had been brought forward."

Boran sat on a log and placed Alruna's sword on his lap.

"No. He knew you wouldn't do that. But I'm going to tell you what I told him. You'll be going into the Fug together. Not competing or aiming to beat each other to reach the Wycum first. If you do that, you'll both end up lost to the fog. You'll be working as a team. You'll have each other's backs, and by the All-Father, you'll both return, Wycum marked or otherwise. Do you understand, Raif?"

"Yes, father."

Boran narrowed his gaze on his son and studied him for a while before nodding.

"Good. Then rest up. Both of you. Evening tide will be here soon, and I want you to be ready."

They spent the rest of the afternoon in the hut, eating mutton and sharpening swords. Hadlo and his son Jhora came to join them. Alruna was uneasy about her brother committing himself to the Wycum Hunt. She felt a little better knowing that Jhora was going with him, but it still caused an ache in her chest. Most warriors didn't return, and those that did were changed. It was rare that a warrior was marked. Out of the entire clan, only her father had one.

During the day, her father and Hadlo had pulled Raif and Jhora aside, speaking quietly so only they could hear. Alruna tried to sneak closer to listen, but when she was noticed, her father sent her out to collect firewood.

When she returned, the mood in the hut had changed. Raif and Jhora were silent, casting glances at their fathers. Alruna asked her breather what was wrong, but he told her nothing.

When they heard the first tide bells ring through the chilling air, they began to make their way to the burrow at the back of the property. Jhora bolted the heavy trap door above, closing them in.

Her father lit a candle as they all waited for the Fug to pass.

The two young warriors stared at each other as each bell tolled, coming closer as the halo swept through the village.

"Please be careful," she whispered to Raif as she hugged him.

He put on a brave face, but Alruna saw through the ruse. He was more nervous than she had ever seen him. As was his friend, Jhora.

The next bell rang, indicating that the Fug was almost upon them. Then, the growls and howls appeared above, claws scratching along the wood of the trapdoor, teeth gnashing, and the fierce snarls of hidden beasts rattled it in its frame.

Raif was now pacing back and forth, the energy within him leaching out as the wild noises eased.

He turned to his father and they held each other's forearms in a warrior grip.

"May Odin shine bright along your blade," Boran said, the phrase repeated by Hadlo to his son.

And as the next tide bell rang, they climbed the ladder, shoved open the trapdoor and were out.

Alruna set off after them, an exciting tension firing through her body as she gripped the ladder's rungs, but her father held her back.

"Steady, Alruna, let them go."

Alruna fought the urge to kick him off, yet he released her.

Night air rushed through her as she leapt out of the burrow and chased after her brother, pumping her legs for all they were worth. Yet they seemed feeble as Raif's long powerful strides carried him away and towards the retreating Fug.

There is a reason why only the strongest and swiftest warriors got to attempt the Wycum Hunt: they are the only ones fast enough to catch it up.

Would she have joined him if she could? Had a female warrior ever even attempted the Hunt? She doubted it.

Her chest was heaving as she watched her brother draw his sword and charge into the fog, Jhora on his heel.

"You better return, Raif Lothrun," she bellowed with what was left in her lungs.

She came to the end of the village and rested against a bell post, sucking air in as she fought the tears which stung her eyes.

Warriors didn't cry.

By the time her father and Hadlo joined her, she had regained her composure, staring up the hill as the silver vapour made its way up the mountain, taking her brother with it.

"They'll return with the next tide," her father said, nodding as he spoke as if having to confirm it to himself.

"Aye," agreed Hadlo, a wetness to his eyes he brushed away as his gaze never left the halo.

It would be bad - it would be profoundly bad if anything were to happen to Raif, yet Boran still had her. Jhora was Hadlo's only offspring, and with his wife long ago in the ground, he would have nobody.

Swallowing the creeping trepidation within her, she slipped an arm through her father's and another through Hadlo's.

"Come on, you old goats, let's find you some mead," she said and pulled them away from the view of the mountain. Otherwise, they'd be staring at it all night - as would she if given the chance.

"Aye, lass," Hadlo said. "Mead would be good."

Both towering above her, the pair of them felt like children in her arms, both seeming lost.

"What's Geri got?" Boran asked as they watched the shadow leopard sitting down and licking a small black shape. "Loki's trickery, it's the cub."

Alruna ran the rest of the way to the hut, sliding to a halt before the giant cat as she focused on the cub.

It was her.

"Freki," she said, her knees sinking into the earth as she picked up the cub and hugged her.

She felt thinner as if she hadn't eaten in the days she was gone.

The tears prickled her vision again, from her brother's Hunt, from the pent-up anger of the fight with Ganlin, and now as the loss she felt for the leopard melted away.

"Where have you been?" Alruna asked, running her finger down the thick black coat, along the silver scar on her leg, which she noticed had a scrape. The moment her finger touched it, Freki hissed.

"It's alright, girl. You're safe now," she said, speaking softly as she set her down in front of Geri again, the smaller cat snuggling into her mother.

"I'll not let you out of my sight," Alruna promised her, yet caught the cat's eyes staring back down the foothills to the forest as if she would like to be elsewhere.

7

Final Glimpse

Bane worked the bellows, prickly heat stinging his back as the sweat rolled down his spine.

He kept the airflow steady as it streamed across the coals, glowing white and illuminating Girant's smile as he turned the length of iron, dipping it further into the forge, the impurities fizzling bright until he withdrew and placed it against the anvil, the ring of the hammer filling the blazing chamber.

"Good lad, well done," the smithy said.

Bane turned to face him, his hands almost sliding from the handle of the bellows at the remark.

Nobody had ever complimented him before. He wasn't even sure what he had done.

The smile forming on his lips died as he realised that Girant wasn't talking to him, but his son who had stumbled into the room, struggling with a jug of water almost as tall as himself.

"Place it down there, Tomm, that's it," the smithy said, glowing with pride as the toddler did as his father asked, face beaming with delight.

"Now run along to your mother."

Bane couldn't help but feel the smile creeping back as he watched the giant of a man grinning after his child.

What must it be like to feel a father's love? Tomm was a fortunate boy. He couldn't have chosen anyone better in a father.

The thought of his own father, or the man that sired him, was at the forefront of his mind for the rest of the time at the forge. Who would he be now if Bailin Shankil had married his mother? Or even if his mother had lived. Would he be living in the castle? Would he have servants of his own?

He was daydreaming about riding a horse alongside Bailin Shankil when Girant tapped him on the shoulder and dropped two coppers into his palm.

The autumn air cooled his muscles as he walked through the village to the wood yard. His shoulders and arms ached from the work, but it was a pleasant sensation.

Dew and Belle watched him approach, smiling as they led him around the back to the log pile.

"It's the biggest yet," Belle said. "For the festival next week. The castle wants double the normal amount."

"For all the meats and puddings they'll be cooking not to mention the fire pits that'll be covering the hill for the celebrations. I can't wait," Dew said as he handed Bane the axe. "It's going to be the best one this decade."

Belle placed the first log on the stump, and Bane struck it true, the halves falling either side for her to pick up.

"Are you looking forward to it?" she asked him, smiling beneath her long hair.

Bane returned the smile.

"Not really. I've never been before, and I'll no doubt be left here. Somebody must watch Crookfell."

Belle's smile dropped.

"Why?"

Dew placed the next log down, and Bane split it.

"Because Dodd gets three coppers from Gobbins, the forge and your parents, and then a further copper for each home I watch."

"You'll be here alone?" Dew asked.

Thwack.

"I'll have Chewer with me. It's been that way since we buried Gelwin."

"Then I'll stay with you," Belle said, picking up the split logs and tossing them to Dew, who clumsily caught them."

"And miss out on the festival?" Dew said, shaking his head in disbelief. "And Ma and Da won't allow it. Not now that you've got a job at the castle."

Bane looked down at his friend, her grimace towards her brother slowly evaporating.

"A job?"

Belle nodded, her cheeks taking on a tinge of red.

"A maid. Beginning in the kitchens until I've learned the correct etiquette to conduct myself around the castle."

"*If* you learn. You should see her in the evenings, practising how to curtsy and walk properly," Dew said until half a log struck his chest.

"Maid? But you can't," Bane said, the words spilling out before he could call them back.

Belle turned to him, the red in her cheeks becoming crimson as she scowled, hands on hips.

"Why not?"

Bane wanted to tell her that his mother was killed because she was a maid up at the castle, wanted to explain that the Baron ordered her hanged because she carried the child of his son, yet didn't know how to shape it into the right words without giving away who his father was.

"Well?"

Bane shrugged, catching Dew's eye for help, but he only watched on, an eager grin curling his lips.

"Because I don't want you to," he said, unable to think of another excuse.

Belle's scowl softened as she stepped closer and gently placed a hand on his, a strange expression reaching her eyes as she stared at him. Her chest rose and fell a little quicker.

"Tell me why, Bane. I can always change my mind and seek work in the village. For the right reason."

She was leaning closer still, making Bane lean away, a warm, awkward heat rising in his stomach.

"Because," his palms began to sweat on the shaft of the axe.

"Yes," Belle pressed, lashes fluttering.

"Because who else will pick up the halves after I've split them?" he blurted out in a single breath.

Belle clenched her teeth, brows coming together as she stepped back, slamming her boots into the mud.

"If that's all you see me as, Bane, just a simple girl that's only good enough to pick up wood from the floor, then I'll begin at the castle as soon as I'm able," she snapped, putting her back to them as she marched off towards the house. She paused on the doorstep, glowered over her shoulder and then pushed inside, slamming the door behind her.

"What did I say?" Bane asked, wanting to apologise to Belle, although he didn't know what he was apologising for.

Dew snorted as he stared after her, shaking his head.

"Girls," he said, as if it was a puzzle there was no solving. "We better get stuck into this lot. With only the two of us, it will be hard going."

Bane drew his gaze from the cottage, and the small silhouette, staring out at them, hoisted the axe onto his shoulder and split the next log.

New sweat ran in beads down his back where old sweat had dried, leaving him with the sensation of prickling heat. The last log was now split, and Bane waited for Dew to stack the halves with the rest before giving him the axe.

He stared into the distance as he flexed life back into his fingers and saw a large dust cloud above the valley that hid the King's Road.

"What's that?" he asked as Dew joined him.

"That'll be young Shankil, heading back to the wars. When Ma was at the castle yesterday, she overheard an argument between the Baron and his son. The entire castle heard it. Anyway, the son told his father that he wasn't staying for the festival and was making preparations to leave."

"He's going? Now?"

Bane felt an overwhelming sense of loss and couldn't understand why, and before he knew what he was doing he had already crossed the yard and was making a direct line across the valley.

"Bane, where are you going?"

Dew's question went unanswered as Bane picked up the pace, his long strides breaking into a run as he made his way through an orchard, the leaves having already fallen and the fruit harvested the previous moon, fine branches whipping him as he struggled through until he was out in the open.

The ground rumbled beneath him as he sprinted up the valley wall, his thighs and calves now burning and joining in with the rest of the muscles he had used that day.

As he crested the hill, he looked down onto a large contingent of armoured men marching in ranks along the King's Road - the leading pair carrying flags which snapped in the wind. One was the King's Own standard and bore the head of a roaring lion on a green background, while the other was of House Shankil, a black mountain leopard surrounded by a silver halo on a red background.

Bane gathered his breath as he watched them march past, armour clanging and steel glinting, faces set in grim determination. It seemed the two ranks went on forever, passing from view as they reached the bend in the bottom of the valley.

Behind them rode the cavalry. Perhaps fifty riding in pairs, the horses snorting plumes of vapour and dust as their iron clod hooves clipped along the road. The riders wore a similar armour to the foot soldiers, although they were of better quality and on their helms, they wore red and green plumes, their steed's reins emblazoned with the same coloured cloth.

Higher ranking soldiers rode behind them, sleeker mounts and comfier saddles. The small group of men wore velvets and long capes, although they were still in either the King's or the Shankil colours. They talked with each other as they rode, not keeping to any particular formation. They were most likely knights and in charge of the small army.

None of them gave Bane the slightest bit of interest. Then came the final horseman. This one rode at the rear of the group of officers. Dressed in black leather to match the colour of the large charger, he rode. The shield strapped to the side of his mount was heavily battered and marked with countless scratches and cuts, but Bane still recognised it as belonging to house Shankil. He also recognised the rider.

Bailin Shankil, his father.

Bane felt a lump forming in his throat, a tightness in his guts. Bailin rode his charger as if ready to charge, a tense energy coming from him as if eager to be at war.

He wore no helm, his dark hair clinging to his grim face with the drizzle passing through the valley.

As he drew level with Bane, Bailin's grey eyes caught him and held him fast. His lips parted in shock as their gazes locked.

Bane's heart thumped wildly, sorrow struggling with anger fighting to hold him back, to prevent him from screaming 'Father'.

Sorrow won.

The lines of soldiers marched on, the cavalry, the knights, taking Bailing with them. The Baron's son watched from his black charger for as long as he could, turning in the saddle to hold the gaze, until the bend in the valley wall stole that away and, with it, their link.

"Father?" Bane said aloud, stepping towards the road as if he would join them. He watched the procession of wagons and men following the cooks, the stable hands, the staff that set the camps, which dug the latrines and did all the menial tasks that an army required.

He could easily slip within them, blending amongst the wagons and the dirt. Someone would surely need an extra labourer.

He took another step when a shadow of a horse came up behind and devoured him.

"Father? Such a simple word, but one that could easily slit your throat," came a deep voice.

Bane gritted his teeth as he slowly turned to stare at the man on the horse.

Dressed in dark green and wearing a jaunty grin, the man bowed his head.

"Glance?" Bane said, feeling suddenly exhausted.

"Aye, Master Bane, luckily for you. Anyone else might have taken you to the castle for the Baron to finish you off. Lady Felina meant it when she said you must keep your lineage secret."

"How did you know about that?" Bane asked.

Glance's grin grew wider.

"It's my job to know everything. Besides, she told me. She holds no secrets from me."

"Why?" Bane asked, still unsure whether he trusted the man or not. Then he remembered he needed to be at the Gobbin's place.

"Are you in a hurry, Master Bane? Shouldn't you be with Jarl for sword practice?" Glance said as if reading his mind.

"How…"

Glance tapped the side of his nose with a finger.

"My job, remember. Let me ride you there."

He offered him a hand. Bane stared at it, looked back to the clambering wagons and men following the army, and then back up to Glance.

He took the hand and was easily hoisted up onto the saddle behind the secretive man.

"You weren't thinking of joining them, were you?"

Bane was beginning to feel irritated at how the man seemed able to read his mind.

"Maybe."

The horse began trotting back down the valley, its gait bouncing Bane in the saddle and forcing him to tightly grip Glance's waist.

"First time on a horse?"

"Aye," Bane said, unsure of the unfamiliar movement. If only Dew and Belle could see him now. They would never believe he had ridden on a horse.

"Why does Lady Felina tell you all her secrets? Do you work for her?" Bane asked as the horse reached the valley floor and began to pace more leisurely through the long grass.

"Kind of. She's my sister. The Baron's my father, and Bailin, you're Da that can never be, is my brother."

Bane let the words sink in. How hadn't seen it before? The rich voice and perfect speech, the expensive clothes and sleek mount.

"You're a Shankil?"

Glance snorted.

"By the All-Mother, no. If I was, things might have been different. I'm the bastard-born son of the Baron. My mother was his mistress."

"But he didn't want to have you killed?"

Glance shook his head as he guided the mare between large oaks, the wind picking up and ruffling his cloak.

"There was no need. Both Bailin and Felina are older, and since I was born out of wedlock to his whore mistress, as the Baroness liked to call her, I was of no threat to the title. Instead, he made me swear allegiance to him. I serve the Shankils and the throne."

"Your father ordered the execution of my mother," Bane said, the anger from earlier returning. He didn't want to direct it at Glance, but knowing that he was the

Baron's son made him feel as though riding on his horse was somehow betraying his mother.

"He did. Holding the seat in the north is hard; it takes a hard man to do it. And has done some tough tasks to hold power, killing threats being one of them."

"My mother was no threat," Bane snapped, releasing his grip on Glance's waist, yet quickly held tight again when the mare shifted to skirt around a ditch.

"Not her, but you were. Still are - if he knew the truth of it. But I've no doubt he regrets his actions now that he has lost his favourite son. Bailin has no plans of returning."

They came to the edge of the village, and Glance steered the horse into the shadows of a cops of trees.

"I'll go no further. Best you're not seen with me, Bane."

Bane slid off the saddle and paced around the front of the mare. He didn't know what to say. What could he say? Notwithstanding the fact that he almost joined the band of stragglers following the army and leaving Crookfell for good, there was a lot to digest. He was still playing with the idea of running back. It wouldn't be hard to catch them up.

"Now, don't go running off to join my brother on his suicide campaign," Glance said, proving once again that he could read minds. "And mind you keep your secrets."

Bane took in the man again. Still youthful, although his eyes held a worldly experience he'd noticed in Nan Hilga.

"Why are you helping me?" he asked as Glance turned his horse about, ready to leave.

"Isn't it obvious, Bane? I'm your uncle; you're my kin. Besides, you've got more than a few secrets, and I believe you have a great story ahead of you," Glance said, his gaze dropping to Bane's arm.

He unconsciously gripped the leather vambrace as if he could hide it from the scrutiny.

"Now keep your head low; become the unseen while seeing everything."

Bane nodded.

"That's something I'm well practised in. Did you manage to take the shadow leopard across the Fug?" he asked, wondering what had become of the mountain cat.

"Yes, I left her at the foot of a clan village. She'll be found and taken care of. Now off with you."

Glance steered his horse in the opposite direction and then trotted away, heading back toward the forest.

Bane watched until he vanished within the thick canopy before realising that he should have been at the Gobbin's place by now.

Mr Gobbin was shaking his head, jowls wobbling as Bane ran between the pig pens. Kulby was absently swinging his sword, slack jaws hardening as he watched him approach.

Jarl was leaning against the wall, arms folded and face tilted towards the afternoon sun. His head slowly turned to Bane, a subtle nod, an easy smile.

It quickly fell away.

"What in Fug's name has you late to a battle, lad?" the retired knight growled. "No, never mind. Stand next to that soggy pudding and show me your forms."

"Yes sir," Bane said, grateful that he didn't press him with further questions.

He picked up the remnants of his battered shield, the wood loose and the brace looser. It only remained fixed on his arm because he wedged the vambrace tight into the crook. His sword was in a worse state.

The hilt was missing, and the blade was several inches shorter. It wasn't much larger than a knife.

He picked it up, held it out and glanced at Jarl.

The trainer shrugged.

"Use whatever tools are to hand," he said. "Now, show me your forms."

Bane took a breath, set his feet shoulder-width apart, and began the forms. Working through the sequence he had been taught and had practised earlier when Dodd had sent him scavenging in the woods.

He slipped smoothly from Stalking Crane to Silent Star, the sword becoming part of him, his legs and arms flowing naturally as if in a dance. The blade swept about, elbows tucked in as he reversed the grip – Falling Grace - pivoting on the balls of his feet, planting a solid heel, dipping the knee, raising the shield – Rising Tide – dropping the shoulder, levelling the sword, thrusting forwards – Widow's Kiss.

"Shameful," Jarl snapped, spit flying as he rounded on Kulby. "Feet further apart. You're as clumsy as one of your sows. Keep the wrist supple. No, you sack of fat."

Bane heard the noise yet was lost to the forms, the flowing sequences, the dance of steel.

Floating Nettle – Spinning Thistle – Noon's Embrace. He was dropping into Slicing Locus when pain erupted in his shoulder, and his world spun around before his face hit the dirt.

"Focus, lad," Jarl snapped at him, heavy boots griding into the mud beside his face as he loomed above. Bane felt hands grip his tunic, hauling him to his feet. "You've been practising your forms, but what's the point if you don't see what's happening outside your space? An archer ten feet from you would have an easy shot. Stay aware."

Bane's cheeks flushed with the rebuke, yet he remained quiet, only nodding that he understood.

"Now, the pair of you face each other. It's time to spar."

Bane rolled the stiffness from his joints as Kulby stalked closer; the swine herder's son had a grin beaming beneath his helmet.

"Let's see how well you defend yourself with that stick," he whispered, giving a swing and making the air whistle.

Bane glanced over to Jarl, holding his shortened sword – lacking a crosspiece – for him to see, hoping he would stop the bout before it began or at least find a more suitable weapon. But if he saw, Jarl had no intention of stopping anything.

"What are you waiting for, attack," he demanded.

Bane barely had time to right his grip before Kulby's first blow came, the larger, heavier sword cracking against his and almost knocking it from his grasp.

Being caught off balance, Bane tried to right his feet, stumbling from another blow caught on his rattling shield, the impact passing through the rotting wood.

He struggled into a defensive stance. Oaks Limb, he thought, yet as he brought up his shield, Kulby dipped his shoulder and rammed into him, using his bulk and height to take him off his feet.

The stone wall was unforgiving as he slammed into it, jarring every bone in his back.

He caught an advancing shadow and rolled out of the way as Kulby's blade struck the stonework where his neck had been.

Clambering to his feet, Bane once again looked to Jarl, yet the old knight did nothing but fold his arms, nodding over his shoulder.

Born more from instinct than practice, Bane ducked, felt the air pass over his scalp, and then buckled over as a boot slammed into the back of his knee.

Once again in the mud, Kulby pressed the attack, bringing his sword down onto Bane's chest, his blade whipping out and deflecting it a heartbeat before ribs were broken.

"Stay in the dirt where you belong, scum," Kulby said, hawking up phlegm from his throat.

"Poke him good," whooped Mr Gobbin from the side, eagerly bouncing on his feet while slamming a fist into his palm.

Heat built in Bane's stomach, a dark, brooding anger that had been smouldering in the background all day, drawing from the raw emotions of watching his father leave, from the revelations of who he was, the unfairness of life and how it had shaped the few years he had been in the world.

The anger grew, building from the pain in his shoulder, in his muscles, from within his chest – pulsing with each beat of his thumping heart, in rhythm with the fire that flamed along his arm beneath his vambrace.

The phlegm hit the dirt beside his head, strings of it left behind on Kulby's wobbling chin as he laughed.

"I said fugging fight," Jarl demanded, and as if the words were a catalyst, a spark to oiled kindling, Bane sprang to action.

He leapt from the ground, rising shield first, the rim, or where the rim would have been if the lump of wood had been whole, struck Kulby in the gut.

The swine herder's son had enough time to draw a ragged breath before Bane stepped through and drove the fist gripping his sword under Kulby's armpit, slamming into the ribs beneath.

It had been a good hit. Bane felt the impact through his body, yet the boiled leather he struck bore the brunt of the force.

A stunned Kulby looked from Jarl to his father and then settled on Bane, astonished pain evaporating to leave only rage.

"I'm going to gut you for that," he screamed as he came on, blade already swinging, sweat shining beneath his helmet.

"You can try," Bane growled under his breath as he met the attack, pivoting on his heel, dipping a shoulder and turning the sword with his own, driving it down – Falling Grace – a subtle shift of the hips – Rising Tide.

Kulby yelped as Bane's blade found the gap beneath his armour, digging deep into the flesh of his belly.

"Fugging gallows born runt," Kulby screeched as he spun, sword and shield coming as one.

Bane easily leaned out of reach and arced his shield arm one way while cutting his sword the other – Spinning Thistle – Stalking Crane.

His blade slashed along an exposed neck and then drove the point under a flailing arm. Two moves which would have killed if the sword had been real.

"What are you doing, boy? Get back at him," Mr Gobbin demanded, catching Kulby and turning him about before pushing him on.

Bane was prepared, knees bent, weight on his back foot, ready to spring forward.

The attacks came in a tangled flurry of mistimed and misjudged brutal blows.

Bane effortlessly danced between them all, parrying, blocking, dodging – flowing from one form to another, his rage now gone, leaving the embers of a fire within, ready to burst into an inferno when called for.

"Fugging die."

The words spattered out in three rushed breaths, Kulby heaving with exhaustion, yet the blows still came. They were now so slow and laboured that Bane could anticipate where he needed to be, adopting the form to get there.

"Spawn of Death, son of a thieving whore," Kulby spat, his shield arm now dangling by his side, his sword waving pathetically before him as if he was water dowsing.

A single ember within him burned bright, and Bane caught the next cut with his sword, knocked it away as he stepped inside Kulby's guard and drove his elbow into the sternum.

The effort hadn't been hard, no overly excessive energy, simply accurate and well timed, but the effect knocked the larger, bulkier boy clean off his feet.

Bane felt the need to breathe, holding himself back and not following his instinct to drive a boot into Kulby's head.

"You can't do that," Mr Gobbin bellowed as he rounded on him, gripping him roughly around the collar and shoving him away.

Bane allowed himself to be manhandled, not fighting back and not meeting the swine herders' eyes.

"You're just here as a target, understand, boy," he growled, fetid breath as foul as Kulby's.

"Leave the lad be," Jarl said as he stepped away from the wall he had been leaning against. "You're paying me to train your son. Part of that is taking a hit. It'll teach him better for the next time."

"There won't be a next time if he does anything like that again," Mr Gobbin snapped, fat finger shaking in Jarl's face.

Kulby struggled to his feet, bent over, and his dinner splattered against the floor.

"He's only winded," Jarl chuckled, holding up his hands. "He'll get worse than that once he begins training at the castle.

"If he goes," My Gobbin said, narrowing his eyes on his son. Then turned to Bane. "And as for you, boy, I'll be docking a mark from your pay."

Bane swallowed the argument that was rising to his lips. If he went back to Dodd without the full two marks, he would no doubt get a cuffing, but if he tried to talk back with the swine herder, he would likely end up with nothing.

Kulby straightened up, his chest wheezing with each breath. His already red face went the colour of beetroot as he turned to Bane, the knuckles around the hilt of his sword turning white.

But Bane had already set his feet apart, knees bent and was ready for the attack.

It didn't come.

"That'll do for today," Jarl said, slamming a hand down on Kulby's shoulder and guiding the boy towards his father. "Now you've taken a hit in the sternum; you know exactly where to strike a man to bring him down."

"Aye," Kulby croaked as he shrugged away from Jarl, narrowing his eyes on Bane for a moment before he followed his father towards the pig pens. Mr Gobbin paused, turned and tossed a single mark into the mud. The grimace that followed told of no argument.

"I profoundly doubt he'll forget that in a hurry," Jarl laughed when they were alone. "I'd watch him tomorrow if I was you."

Bane slid the battered shield from his arm and left it on the wall with the shortened sword as he stooped to pick up the coin. He brushed the dirt from it as Jarl dropped another mark onto his palm.

Bane closed his fist over the coins and smiled up at the knight.

"That was a good hit. The trouble with bullies like Kulby is they make the worse victims. To keep the lessons going, might I suggest you play a little gentler next time? Another battering like that and the pig-coddled lump of fat will refuse to pick up a sword again."

Bane nodded, pulling his tunic tight about himself as the wind picked up. Now that he wasn't moving, he felt the cold seeping into him.

"So why were you late?" Jarl asked. "Were you at the King's Road?"

Again, Bane nodded, feeling like Jarl was trying to read his mind.

"I hope you weren't getting a fool notion that you might join young Shankil on his mission south."

Bane breathed deep, his voice catching in his throat.

"He saw me," he said, a gust catching the wetness in his eyes. "He recognised me, I think."

"Then you're a fool, Bane. Seeing you would only lead to sowing doubt into his already clouded mind. You shouldn't have gone. Dammit, boy, I even warned you to forget who you think you are."

Bane blinked the wetness away, the spark of anger returning.

"I wanted to see him before he left. If what I heard at my mother's grave was true, then he has no intention of coming back."

He almost spat the final word, chin raised, and hands balled into fists.

"I wanted one final look at my father."

Jarl glared around them; nostrils flared, temples pulsing until he calmed himself.

"Bane, if word got back to the Baron of who you are, how long do you think you will live? I've seen men killed for less. And if Bailen does fall in battle and Lady Felina's son becomes the heir, you will become a threat to him."

"But I don't want it. I don't want anything."

Jarl slowly shook his head.

"It's not what you want, but others may try to use you. Lady Felina is taking a risk already by letting you live. And if things should change, who do you think she shall send to eliminate the threat? That's right," Jarl said, poking himself in the chest with a thumb. "My blade is sworn to protect her."

Bane found himself slowly nodding. He already knew this and knew the consequences.

"Then why agree to teach me sword lessons?"

Jarl sighed as he offered him a weary smile.

"To keep you close, of course. Best place to watch over you. And you remind me of Bailin when he was younger. You're the spit of him, and the way you move, the way you carry yourself – it's as if you're the same being, only twenty years apart."

Bane studied the knight. Long grey hair catching the wind, resting easy against the wall, although he could spring into action in a heartbeat. He was likely the most dangerous person he knew.

"Would you kill me?"

Jarl pressed his lips together, brows drawing close and nodded.

"If it's any comfort, I would take no pleasure from it," he said, patting his shoulder. "I'll see you here again tomorrow. And remember, use what tools are to hand."

Bane watched Jarl mount his horse and trot away before he, too, left for home.

A small part of him wondered if he would have joined the army on the King's Road. And if he did, what might his life become?

8

Raif's Return

Alruna knelt in the damp grass, idly stroking the shadow leopard as she watched her father and Hadlo return.

They'd been gone all morning, wandering the perimeter of the foothills, searching for any sign of her brother and Jhora.

She could tell from her hiding place behind a squat ash tree that they had found nothing.

They ambled past, her father's shoulders drooping lower than usual, his head downcast. Hadlo, the giant Viking, was pacing in the same manner. Geri padded between, grey fur catching a rare beam of light as it came through the perpetual clouds.

From her hiding place, Alruna waited until they had passed before revealing herself.

"Still no sign?" she asked, thinking that she might have at least startled them, but they knew she was there.

"Nope. But it's still relatively early. They'll be here on the next tide or the one after."

"And it's not a good idea to hide upwind of us. Especially when you've been bathing," Hadlo added in his booming voice. "You smell too clean to be in the woods."

Alruna raised her arms and sniffed her pits.

"No, I do not. Take that back, you overgrown toad-bunger, or I'll make you plead for Freya's mercy."

She stalked closer, Freki limping along beside her.

"Toad-bunger?" Hadlo laughed, her father joining in. "And Valhalla will freeze over before you make me plead for Freya's mercy."

Alruna leapt against the trunk of an oak and boosted herself off, landing on Hadlo's back.

The warrior didn't miss a step or even act as if she was now sitting on his broad shoulders, straddling the hammer he had strapped across his back.

"You're too clean. You smell like a Southerner," Hadlo chuckled. "Have you been in the castle baths, scouring the hard work from your skin with oils and salts?"

"They do that?" she asked, scrunching her face up, although the thought of soaking in hot water did sound appealing. There was a spring on the other side of the mountain, which steamed every so often. The water stank of rotten eggs but was supposed to have healing properties. Some of the other clans used them frequently.

Hadlo suddenly sidestepped, and she was caught in the face with the naked branches of a rowan, knocking her from her perch.

She rolled off the warrior's shoulders and landed deftly on the ground, Freki stalking beside her and hissing up at the huge Viking, who was laughing again.

Geri turned her large head, ears flattening as she growled at her cub. Freki soon quieted.

"Have you cooked us up any breakfast?" Boran asked, forcing a smile as if trying to occupy his mind and not fret over his son, which Alruna knew he was doing.

"Da, you know I can't cook. Nor sew, clean or do any of the wench stuff you've been attempting to force on me. You want breakfast; you can cook it yourself."

Boran raised his brows, and he grinned.

"Well, can you at least hunt? Bring back a couple of rabbits," he said, taking his bow from his back and handing it to her with a quiver of arrows.

"Or squirrels, if you can manage. The boys will no doubt be hungry when they return."

Alruna slung the bow over her shoulder and hung the quiver on her belt.

The scowl she had adopted dissolved as she stared at the ageing warriors.

"I'll bring back meat just so long as you two old fools can dig up some carrots without draining the rest of that barrel of mead."

She clicked her fingers at Freki, and the leopard cub followed her into the tree line.

"And make sure you're back well before the next tide," her father called after her.

She spun to face him, walking up the slope backwards and giving him a mocking bow.

Her smile fell away when she was out of sight of them. It had been a front to hide her fear for Raif. She would have thought he would have been back with the first Fug tide yesterday. And when he hadn't shown up the previous night, her gut told her something was wrong. Now, after the third tide had passed and there was still no sign of him, she knew.

She took a ragged breath, unslung the bow and tossed it to the ground before slumping against an ancient birch, the silver bark flaking from the trunk as she slid to the roots and curled her knees up to her chest.

The tears ran freely down her face, gathered at her chin and falling to the earth. An ache settled into her stomach, clutching tight as an image of her brother lying dead in the grass came to her. He was cut open, his insides steaming as they slopped out of a gaping hole.

She shook it from her mind before it anchored itself.

An impulsive flash of the worst horror her brain conjured. It wasn't true. It couldn't be. Raif was alive, she knew it, and he would be back with the next tide.

"You better not be dead, Raif Lothrun," she said, choking on the last word.

Freki padded through the brush, sat at her side, and began to rub her body up against her, head nudging against the damp cheek.

Alruna let out one last shuddering breath as she hugged the leopard close to her chest. Then she rose, gathering the bow and slinging it back over her shoulder.

Her father didn't expect her to come back with anything. She wasn't the best shot with a bow, but she guessed the task was given to fill her day.

"Come, Freki," she said, sighing the last of her grief. "Let's at least go back with something."

They trod lightly as they stalked into the woods, Alruna placing her feet between fallen leaves and twigs, stepping on the balls of her feet as Raif had shown her.

She kept to the shadows, crouching low as she scanned the trees around her, picking out the scampering as squirrels darted between the burghs above.

If she waited long enough, the squirrels would come down to begin foraging on the floor. That was the time to shoot.

She removed her bow slowly, slid an arrow from the quiver and nocked it, only partially drawing the string back. She wasn't strong enough to hold the full tension for any length of time.

Freki prowled beneath the bracken and foliage on the other side of the tree, which the squirrels were up. The cat was all but invisible in the dark greens; only her narrowed eyes could be seen.

A breeze picked up, ruffled the branches, and several leaves slowly spiralled down; then she saw it.

Through the canopy of the low branches, she glimpsed a deer. Its head was up, ears back, and nostrils flared, yet it couldn't see them.

Slowing her breathing, Alruna gently pulled the string back until her fingers brushed her ear, aiming along the shaft, the sharpened iron point settling over the deer's chest.

The next breath she held, made a silent wish for Odin's luck and let the arrow fly.

Alruna let out the held breath as she watched the arrow fly harmlessly past the deer, grazing a tree before skittering into the underbrush.

The deer leapt away deeper into the woods, Freki giving chase until Alruna called her back.

It would do no good if the shadow leopard ran off again, and besides, she wasn't fast enough or large enough to bring so large a prey down. Maybe in a few months.

The cat stalked back and circled Alruna before sitting on her haunches, staring at the gap the deer had disappeared through.

In truth, she hadn't wanted to kill today. Perhaps she had subconsciously aimed wide and intentionally missed. Things might have been different if her brother was back home and safe, yet the trepidation that had been haunting her since he left didn't need adding to with a death at her hands.

"Come on, Freki, let's head back."

She slung the bow and headed home. By the time she arrived, the first tide bell began to sound from below the village. The trap door to the Fug shelter was already open, and her father was poking his head out.

"Nothing?" he asked.

Alruna propped the bow against the shack wall and motioned for Freki to enter the shelter.

"No. I'll go back out with Raif when he's home," she said as she swung her legs over the hole and dropped through.

Hadlo was already perched on one of the two benches, taking up the entire length, a large carrot wedged in his mouth.

"Those are for cooking," she said, sitting on the bench opposite.

"No point in cooking them when there's no meat to go with it," he laughed.

The tide bell at the edge of the village rang, and Boran climbed down the steps and closed the hatch behind him.

"How did you know I wouldn't bring anything back?"

"Because you're not a hunter," her father said, passing her a carrot.

She shoved it in her mouth and snapped off the end; not really hungry but knew that her body needed something.

Another bell rang, but it was almost drowned out by the crunching of carrots inside the shelter.

"Reckon they'll be on the edge of the village, Raif and Jhora," Alruna said, lowering the carrot to hear the rush of the Fug passing above the hatch, the wild hammering, scratching and growling momentarily rattled the frame until it was gone.

Then, wedging the carrot between teeth, Alruna rushed up the ladder, pushed open the door and was up and running after the retreating silver fog.

"Raif?" she called as she slogged up the hill to the edge of the village. "Raif?"

Nothing.

Freki was at her side, staring uneasily at the Fug as it made its way up the mountain.

"Stop fretting, Alruna," her father said as he caught her up, placing hands on his hips as he heaved in the air.

"He'll be back with the morning tide; they both will," he added as Hadlo joined them, teeth clenched as he stared up the mountain.

Alruna couldn't sleep that night. She lay awake on her cot, Freki snoring soundly at her side. Every sound that came through the window be it born from the wind, animal, or the footfalls of the sentries that patrolled the village, she thought might have been her brother coming home.

It wasn't until dawn arrived that she realised she'd been awake the entire time, and judging by the way her father groaned as he went outside to relieve himself, he hadn't either.

By the time she dressed, had splashed cold water on her face and made her way outside, Hadlo had arrived.

"Today," the giant warrior said, grinning up at the mountain and the returning Fug. "They'll be home today."

"By Odin's stones, I hope so," Boran said, placing an arm over Alruna. "This one didn't sleep a wink."

"Neither did you," she said, shrugging from under his arm.

"Truth be told," Hadlo said, stretching his neck and clicking the tendons in his thick muscles. "Nor did I."

A bell sounded from up the mountain, indicating that they didn't have long before the Fug came down.

Living in the foothills since birth, Alruna was so accustomed to the rising and falling halo of fog, the Breath, that she didn't think she needed the bells at all. But then, she was young. The bells were more for the elderly who forgot what part of the day it was. Yet, most of the elderly spent their time living inside the shelters.

"Come on then, let's get in," her father said, pulling up the hatch and allowing them to climb inside. The cats leapt down last before Boran closed it and slid the bolt into place.

"Now, no running off like you did yesterday," he warned. "I'll not have you breaking an ankle or injuring yourself."

Alruna rolled her eyes, sure she couldn't be seen too clearly under the candlelight.

"I won't," she said, feeling the tension in the shelter rising with each bell that tolled.

They remained quiet until the Fug passed over, and then unable to contain herself, she shoved past her father and clambered up the ladder, throwing the door open before scrambling out.

"Alruna Lothrun, get back here," her father growled after her, but it was too late; she was free and running up the hill.

"Raif?" she bellowed, Freki bounding beside her as they ascended the steep slope into the woods. "Raif?"

She slowed as she caught a shape in the grass further up. It was dark and unmoving.

The vision that had flashed through her mind yesterday returned.

Steam rose from the shape, a foul smell of blood reaching her as she took a step closer and then another.

The shape was a man, hunched over and facing away, dried blood clinging to the shreds of clothes, bare arm resting over his head, slack fingers a sickening black. A sword lay in the grass, fallen from an open hand - a sword which she recognised.

"Raif," Alruna choked as she dropped beside her brother, reaching out and grasping his hand.

It was colder than glacial ice, the fingers themselves frozen together.

"No," she gasped as she gripped his frost-coated tunic and pulled him over. His head lolled to the side, nose tinged black and open eyes staring up into nothing.

"Is it him?" her father said, his words coming from behind as he approached.

Alruna nodded as she took in the rest of her brother: a long gash across his fur trousers, blood congealing in the open wound, a foul smell of decay leaching from the many other cuts that covered his body.

"Blade or beast?" Her father said, straining to control the emotion in his voice as he sank to his knees beside her.

"Both," she mumbled, a numbness settling over her.

Hadlo paced the area around them, hands to mouth, as he bellowed his son's name over and over again, but his only answer came from the unforgiving wind and the tide bells descending towards the bottom of the foothills.

"May you be dining in the halls of Valhalla," Boran said as he reached for the fallen sword. He was about to place it on his son's chest when it suddenly rose.

"Not…just…yet," Raif croaked, his words sounding like they were strained through mill stones.

Alruna swallowed tears as she watched her brother blink and slowly ease himself onto his elbows.

"Raif," Alruna blurted out as she leaned over her brother, grasping his face in her hands and planting a kiss against his forehead. Her lips stung with the cold of his flesh.

"Jhora?" Hadlo demanded as he noticed Raif was alive.

Raif slowly turned his face up to the great warrior and shook his head.

Alruna couldn't look up at her father's second; she didn't think she could bear the grief he would be showing, yet couldn't unhear the muffled cry as Hadlo paced away from them, leaving her with guilt.

"Did you find the Wycum? Are you forest-marked?"

Raif dropped his gaze to the ground, struggling to breathe as he replied.

"No," he said, then lay back down as if the energy needed to speak had drained him. "The mark has already been given."

"We'll speak more about it later. Come, let us get you home. It would be best if you had rest and a healer from the looks of you," Boran said, grasping his son's arm in a warrior grip. "Alruna, fetch Old Ma Bunt. And tell her she'll need cat gut and a paring knife. The frostbite will need cutting away."

Alruna didn't want to leave her brother but knew the extent of his wounds meant that he wasn't in the clear yet. She was soon off running back to the village, Freki easily keeping pace with her.

By the time she had returned home with Old Ma Bunt, Raif was on his pallet, a woollen blanket covering him and nursing a bowl of steaming stew.

The old healer glanced at him and shook her head, smacking her lips together.

"Bloody fool," she scolded as she pulled the blanket back to inspect him further. "Wycum Hunt indeed."

She grasped the blackened hand, turning it over and not caring how much Raif was wincing.

"You're going to lose some of these," she said, tapping the black fingers, "and if you somehow don't end up with infected wounds and you survive the week, you'll no doubt have plenty of scars. But I dare say you'll enjoy them, as men do. Bloody fools the lot of you."

She raised her eyebrows at Alruna to gain support from the only other female in the room, yet Alruna couldn't give it. She was looking forward to earning some scars for herself.

Raif kept quiet as the healer worked on him, falling in and out of fitful sleep, murmuring incomprehensible words.

Alruna hoped he remained in that state as she watched the healer cut off the blackened fingers and sew the healthy flesh over the stumps. Mercifully, he didn't lose any from his sword hand. Even so, she guessed that he would feel a sense of loss at having parts of him missing when he awoke.

When she was done, Old m Bunt left, leaving instructions that Raif must rest and sleep.

"I knew he should have waited until after the raid," Boran said as he rose from his stool. "I'll go see how

Hadlo is fairing. He's most likely several tankards of mead down and spoiling for a fight."

Her father paused on the threshold and glanced at his son.

"I'll be back before the next tide to help you take him down to the shelter. If he wakes, make sure he eats.

"Draugr," Raif suddenly said as he opened his eyes and glanced about him. When his gaze fell on his father, his posture softened. "I need to talk with you. About what I saw in the Fug and what the Wycum told me."

"You need to rest, Raif. Old Ma Bunt will have my hide otherwise."

"No, Da, this is important. Draugr, there were Draugr in the Fug. An entire army of them."

Alruna had heard of the Draugr before. A Mythical army of the dead. Fallen Viking warriors that are sworn to fight in Odin's name. But they were only myths; they were not real.

Boran glanced about to make sure nobody could hear before stepping inside and closing the door.

"Draugr. Are you sure?"

A film of sweat broke out on Raif's face as he nodded.

"When Jhora and I stepped inside the Fug, it was them that attacked us. They came at us one at a time, testing us, testing themselves. They were strong, and we could only kill them by removing their heads. Jhora..." Raif fell into a coughing fit, leaning over as he heaved.

Alruna went to help him, but her brother pushed her away.

"Jhora was killed by an ancient Draugr, a sword driven through his chest. I fought on, killing many more until a chief bested me," Raif spluttered, waving a bandaged hand, missing a couple of fingers, over the various wounds that the healer had sewn shut. "But instead of killing me, he said I had honoured the Draugr. That I may pass through to seek out the Wycum."

"If the Draugr are amassing, then war is coming. How many were there?"

Raif locked eyes with his father.

"A number so great there is not a name for it. Countless. Perhaps every Viking warrior that had ever fallen in battle, right back to when the ice giants ruled the North. And now, Jhora is part of them."

"When I was released from the Draugr and the Fug, I found myself on the mountain near the summit. I spent a night huddled in the craggy rocks before I climbed to the top. There, I found the Wycum."

Raif reached for a jug of water, clumsy hands shaking as he attempted to lift it. Alruna took it from him and guided the spout to his parched lips.

He drank deeply, water dripping down his chin until he wiped it away with the sleeve of his arm.

"It was then that she told me the mark had already been given. Another holds claim to the clans."

Boran glanced at the fading tattoo on his arm, his hand covering the ring of ivy.

"Did she tell you who?" he asked.

Raif shook his head.

"The only reason the Wycum let me go was so that I could deliver a warning. She said an old god is waking in the far South. It's coming to finish what it started a thousand years ago. It's coming to claim the fallen body of the god in the mountain."

"Our mountain?" Alruna asked.

"Yes," Raif said, staring into the fire. "That's why the Draugr are gathering."

"But the gods are no concern of ours," Alruna's father said, although the deep frown lining his brow told otherwise.

"If this southern god succeeds and takes the mountain, then a darkness will consume the world," Raif said, then broke into another fit of coughing.

Alruna patted his back, a feeble gesture, but there was nothing else she could do for her brother.

"Draugr, southern gods, a new mystery leader of the clans – if there's any truth to this, then we must tell everyone. I'll be back before the next tide," Boran said, then closed the door behind him.

Raif's coughing fit subsided, and he eased his head back to his pillow.

"It sounds terrible. A nightmare. Do you believe it?" Alruna asked, taking a damp cloth and wiping the clammy sweat from her brother's brow.

Raif grasped her hand tightly with his own, the one which still had all the fingers.

"I wish it were but a dream. But I saw it, Alruna, with my own eyes, and I believe what I saw."

She could see the fear he was holding back; feel the trembling muscles through his body. For the first time in her life, she realised that Raif was scared. That he was vulnerable, much like herself.

She would have tried to find words of comfort, but Raif finally succumbed to sleep, his panting breaths easing.

Her father returned several hours later, along with two other warriors from the village. They carried Raif down into the shelter, along with his pallet. There was no point bringing him out after the Fug had passed, only to take him back the next morning.

"I'll stay with him," Alruna told her father as she made herself comfortable on the bench. She couldn't stand the thought of Raif sleeping down here alone.

"What of Hadlo?"

Boran glanced at the other men who had remained with them in the shelter, sighing as he shook his head.

"As expected. Like a drunken bull searching for someone to vent his rage on. Trouble is, nobody will go near him."

Alruna filled the brazier with logs, sparks floating out of the open hatch, rising into the darkness. She sat back on the bench, trying to stay awake; Freki curled up on her legs, her weight a comfort. Yet sleep claimed her, pulling her into a dreaming world of Draugr, gods and darkness.

The next thing she knew was she was shaken awake, her father having climbed into the shelter and closed the door behind him.

"You were out all night," he said, the tide bell tolling in the distance.

"And you were snoring," her brother added as he sat up, flexing broad shoulders as he offered her a wink. "Like a banshee in a hurricane."

"I did not," she protested, mimicking Raif's grin, although she didn't see the usual twinkle in his eyes.

They waited until the Fug had passed before clambering out into the open, broke their fast with bread and cheese sloshed down with Yuht, a hot drink of goat's milk and honey.

"You're looking a lot better," Hadlo said as he lumbered up the hill towards them, red eyes swollen and shoulders stooped. He crashed down on the ground beside Boran, smelling of stale ale and wearing thick scabs along his knuckles. He caught Alruna staring at them.

"Only three of them; I was drunk," he shrugged, stating how many he had bested in a fight before he was either beaten or was too drunk to stand. Alruna guessed the latter.

Alruna wanted to hug the grieving Viking. He'd lost his son and now had no family. Yet it wasn't the Viking way. Jhora had a good death and fell with steel in hand - how all warriors wished to go. Honouring Odin, the All-Father.

"Aye, I feel much better," Raif said, not meeting the huge warrior's gaze. "Fit and ready to go on this castle raid."

"Are you sure," her father asked, absently stroking Geri, who was curled at his feet, chewing on a bone, teeth cracking through to the marrow beneath.

Raif nodded, all humour now gone as he nodded grimly.

"I failed and didn't get marked by the Wycum. I must still prove to myself that I am worthy to lead. Perhaps the Wycum will mark me then."

"But Old Ma Bunt said you must rest," Alruna said, knowing her brother was far from ready to fight. Yet she saw the determination in him; he wouldn't be persuaded.

"Yes. Front and centre. If the Draugr couldn't kill me, then the Baron and his tin soldiers won't be able to."

"There will be no front and centre," Boran said as he leaned closer. "I've already spoken to the other warriors; we're going in with stealth. We need to take a hostage. One to bargain with for supplies, cattle, steel, gold."

"They won't bargain for just anyone," Hadlo said. "It'll have to be someone important."

Boran nodded, a knowing grin proceeding his words.

"And I know which one. And it'll be an easy snatch with young Shankil already on the King's Road and days away."

Alruna listened to them plan the mission, other warriors from the village had arrived throughout the morning to take orders, add suggestions and begin preparations. Even Ganlin was there, although he avoided eye contact with her.

She was given menial errands, fetching mead and lighting fires, and one other warrior asked her to make herself useful and sharpen his blades.

She told him where he could shove them.

"So, do we all know what we're about?" Boran asked later in the afternoon after the talking had been done.

It was met by nods and grunts of approval until Alruna spat into the fire and rounded on her father.

"You haven't said where I'll be," she said, scowling at the other men about the fire. "I'm as good a fighter as any of these old farts and better than some."

Her gaze fell briefly on Ganlin, who had the good sense to look away.

"A raid is no place for a wench," said a warrior squatting beside Hadlo. Ferric was a scrawny man who was more sinewy string than muscle, but he had a reputation for being fiery and bloodthirsty in a battle - a berserker with a hungry axe on a battlefield.

"It's no place for a feral rat, but you seem to find your place in them," she said, knowing that it was a risk to push Ferric the wrong way, but if she was to be taken seriously, then she needed to prove herself. She couldn't allow Ferric to mock her because of her gender.

"What have you been feeding her, Chief, fire beetles?" Ferric laughed, others about him joining in.

They stopped when Alruna slipped her dagger from the hidden sheath on her wrist and threw it at Ferric.

The blade bit into the toe of his boot, sticking erect. It had been a good throw, although she had been aiming for the mud beside his foot.

Too late now, she needed to follow it up, there was no backing down.

Ferric's face contorted into rage, cheeks blazing red as he looked from his boot to her, hands balling into fists, chest filling as he stuck it out.

All was quiet as Alruna squared off to him, swallowing the rising fear, meeting his glower with one of her own.

Freki stood at her feet, hackles raising and lips drawn back to reveal long teeth.

She knew she had pushed too far; Ferric was a proven man and couldn't be seen to be cowed by anyone, especially a wench shy of her sixteenth winter.

"What's up? Are you cycling through your moon's blood?" Ferric spat, fingers getting twitchy on the hilt of his sword.

Alruna didn't know what would happen if he drew it. Could she best him or would she be humiliated in front of the clan's best warriors, including her father and Raif.

Grim faces stared back, apart from Ganlin's, who watched on with an amused smile.

"The only blood cycling will be your own," Alruna found herself saying, her temper getting the best of her mouth, her own hand slipping down to the hilt of her sword. The much heavier, clumsy slab of iron that she used for practice. Unlike the sharpened lighter steel on the hip of Ferric. Steel that could easily find its way between her ribs.

An icy cold rushed through the hill, born from a rising gust, yet it seemed she was the only one feeling it and willed herself not to shiver as it clutched her core.

Ferric stepped closer, her dagger wobbling but still defiantly standing erect from his boot, sinewy muscles flexing beneath his tunic as he ground his teeth.

Then a grin split his beard as he tipped his head back and laughed. A loud, throaty cackle echoed around the hillside.

Others joined in, and Alruna felt the coiled tension within her lift, making her feel light enough to float.

"Here," Ferric said, pulling the dagger from his boot and handing it to her. "You've got bigger stones than some of these lads."

The berserker turned to face her father.

"I'll take her in my party, Chief. I could do with someone to show some of the others what being brave means."

Alruna noticed he glanced at Ganlin as he spoke, yet her attention was on her father, intent on what he had to say.

Either her actions had proven that she was ready or that she was far too foolish to risk on a raid.

"Fine, she goes with you," he said, nodding to himself, although Aruna recognised doubt in his countenance.

There would be words later. She also noticed that Raif was quiet, his head tilted to one side as he regarded her.

Had she crossed a line, or were they simply worried?

"It's settled then," her father said, returning her to the now. "In three days, we will attack on the night of the Autumn festival. Now go and prepare."

A wave of excitement ran through Alruna as she watched the warriors leave amidst back-slapping and laughter. She was going on a raid.

Then the trepidation crept in – she was going on a raid.

9

Night of The Festival

Bane left the wood yard earlier than usual. There was no wood to chop and only a few stacks of logs to split into kindling. Dew and Belle were already gone, having joined most of the villagers at the castle grounds, no doubt enjoying the festival. He didn't pass anyone or see any other souls until he reached the pig pens where he found the Gobbins, Kulby grinning eagerly at him as he made his way across the yard to the wall where the battered shield and shrinking sword were. Beside Kulby were his three friends. The two boys sniggered while Meg laughed as she elbowed Kulby.

"This is going to be worth missing a couple of hours of the festival," she said.

Five days had passed since he had put Kulby on his back, and each day, his sword had shrunk, another couple of inches cut from the blade.

He picked up what was left now, which wasn't much. The wooden practice sword was little more than a handle missing a cross-piece and only two inches of splintered blade. It was now shorter than a small knife.

He picked up the broken shield; the brace had now been removed, so there was no way to fix it to his arm.

How was he supposed to fight with these? Not that he had been doing much more than defend himself the best he could over the last few days.

Jarl looked on from across the yard and nodded subtly before gesturing for Bane and Kulby to step into the middle.

"Work through your forms," the old knight ordered.

Bane planted his feet and began to flow into the first, the shield slipping with each movement and the useless lump of wood in his other hand making him feel foolish.

Surely, Jarl could see that the Gobbins had now cut so much of his practice sword down that he wouldn't be able to defend himself. Yet if he did notice, he wasn't doing anything about it.

"Think I'm going to enjoy today's bout, boy," Kulby said as he twisted through his forms beside him, his movements clumsy and ill-timed. "Think I want to break something. Maybe one of your arms, maybe both," he sniggered. "And my friends are here to watch."

The bruises and welts from the previous bouts still smarted and ached over his torso and limbs, and the nasty lump on the crown of his head had been throbbing ever since he took a battering yesterday.

"Fugging useless, the pair of you," Jarl growled as he circled them, grasping Bane's wrist and raising it. "You can't perform Downward Scorpion if its stinger is hanging loose by its side," he said before turning on Kulby. "And you have about as much poise as a fat sow."

"Today, this sow's got teeth," Kulby replied, dropping his sword arm as he stared at his friends. "And I'm getting hungry."

Bane thought the remark was as stupid as the person saying it. Unaware that Jarl had mocked him.

Jarl curled the arch of his foot around the heel of Kulby's boot and shoved him over.

"The only place pigs have on the battlefield is in the bellies of those fighting. Understand?"

Bane felt a little satisfaction as he watched the bulky boy struggle back up, face crimson as he looked to his friends and then to his father, yet Mr Gobbin didn't say anything.

"By the Blessed Mother, I'm sick of the pair of you. Go on, face off. Let's get this over with."

"But," Bane began, staring from the cumbersome broken shield to the stick in his other hand. Yet, as Jarl glared at him, he knew any argument would be wasted air.

"Begin," the knight barked.

Meg and the boys laughed as Kulby stepped closer and, using his iron clod shield, butted Bane's damaged shield, and it instantly broke apart. He followed it through with a swipe of his sword.

Bane tried to catch it with the splintered wood in his hand but misjudged the block and instead had the full force of Kulby's blade strike the top of his knuckles.

Pain pulsed in waves through his hand, a white-hot heat erupting as his fingers went numb. He wouldn't be surprised to find that something was broken.

How would he be able to pump the bellows in the forge tomorrow with a broken hand? Yet as Kulby advanced on him, an eagerness radiating from the armoured boy, he knew he couldn't dwell on it.

His hair brushed Kulby's blade as he instinctively ducked beneath a surprise attack, the heavy youth following it up with an elbow to Bane's jaw.

Tears stung his eyes as he stepped away, tasting blood in his mouth as he caught Jarl shaking his head in disappointment.

Shadows shifted as Kulby came on again, giving Bane no warning, just a mass of armoured fat, thick arms clumsily swinging a length of sharpened wood and a heavy shield.

Bane tossed the useless strap, which was once attached to the equally useless shield, and gripped the handle of the once whole practice sword with both hands.

He took a blow from the rim of Kulby's shield to his shoulder before he planted his feet and pivoted away from a downward slash.

The larger boy put too much weight behind the blow and carried himself over, becoming unbalanced.

Bane continued flowing into Dancing Thistle, swinging both hands under Kulby's arm and striking his ribs.

It was a solid impact, the splintered remnants of his blade poking true until it snapped off on the armour.

"Unlucky," he heard Jarl chuckle as Kulby rounded on him, smiling maniacally at seeing him unarmed and coming on with more vigour: Meg and the boys whooping with anticipation.

Bane tossed the useless lump of wood away, expecting the knight would undoubtedly end the bout now, yet as he watched the wooden blade cut the space before him, he knew that it wasn't the case.

Rising Sun rapidly became Prowling Heron as he leaned away from the sword chop aimed at his neck and stepped back from the shield's rim.

With nothing to fight back with, or to parry or deflect, Bane found himself weaving and ducking, spinning and turning, then a flash of white heat erupted as he took the blade under his chin.

Dots fizzled on the edge of his vision. He shook his head to clear them in time to see the flat of the shield hit his chest with the full weight of Kulby behind it.

He felt weightless for an instant before his back struck the mud, his head bouncing once before coming to a rest.

"I thought I taught you better than that," Jarl said, his voice far away. "Wasting my time, my coin…get up and fight back."

Bane was about to shout, fight with what? Yet before the words formed in his bleeding mouth, the knight answered him.

"Fight with the tools to hand."

Kulby's boot came slamming down from above, and Bane rolled from beneath it, feeling the heel scrape down his side.

He kept rolling as Kulby followed the stamp with a kick, the toe of his boot catching his thigh.

Bane's tattoo beneath his vambrace flamed with heat, hotter than a bathing stone, yet he brought it up to meet the descending sword.

The thick arm guard took the brunt of the force, yet the impact jarred his body. But he was already moving.

Floating Maple Seed - his free arm spun horizontally, hand catching the shield's rim, gripped tightly, wound it back.

Downward Scorpion - his other hand, which would have held a sword, curled into a fist and drove it into Kulby's nose, and he felt the cartilage give beneath his knuckles.

Whatever tools are to hand.

Kulby screeched in rage, bunched up cheeks burning crimson, a deeper red than the blood splattered across them giving him a demon like quality.

"Fugging whore spawn retch," Kulby spat, coming at him with such venom that Bane barely dodged the thrusts and jabs, each aimed for his face.

Then the shield's rim collided with his head, and he reeled back, fell into a Jarl and was shoved off again.

Without thinking, his hand curled around the hilt of a sword; he gripped it tighter and yanked it free.

A flash of silver as the blade in his grasp ascended, caught Kulby's descending sword.

Steel met wood, and he severed it in half.

He dipped his shoulder, stepped through and rammed the larger boy off his feet.

Kulby landed in the mud, arms flailing wide, a stunned slackness to his pig face.

Bane continued the form – Stalking Heron, Falling Dawn…

He was lost to the steel dance, the sword in his grasp – Jarl's sword, which he somehow found and slipped free – arcing gracefully down, slipping through the weak defences.

"Enough!" Jarl shouted, the sharp order breaking through Bane's state lost to the forms, bringing him to an abrupt halt.

He stared down his arm, the wrist, the silver crosspiece, and along the length of sharpened steel to the tip, which was hovering above Kulby's throat, his breath fogging up his reflection along the razor's edge.

"Easy now," the knight continued as he reached around Bane and gripped his sword, pulling it away from Kulby's neck, the boy blinking through tears.

"Kulby?" came Mr Gobbin's shrill voice, laced with panic. "What did you do?"

Bane felt the large man's meaty hands as they shoved him away from his fallen son.

Behind him, he heard the sharp intake of breath from Meg, and the boys fell silent.

He could only watch as the swine herder knelt, gripped Kulby under the arms and yanked him up.

"You tried to kill him, boy," he piped over his shoulder. "You Death spawned son of the gallows. Evil. Pure evil is what you are."

"Mr Gobbin," Jarl began, hands raised as if he could reason with the swine herder who brushed past him, leading Kulby away, lips pulled tight as he wailed.

"I paid good coin for you to teach my son," he said, red jowls wobbling. Yet you used Kulby to teach that wretch."

"I taught both boys the same, but only one learned while the other bullied," Jarl replied.

Mr Gobbin snorted.

"That will be the final time you teach my son, and you," Mr Gobbin spat, taking his beady eyes from Jarl to Bane, "will not receive a single grot from me for today, not tomorrow or ever again. And I've a mind to take my own sword and give you what you deserve."

Jarl let out a laugh.

"If I allowed it, then I'm sure you would end up in the dirt, like your bully of a son."

Bane watched them leave, unable to think of what to say. What words could undo what had happened?

The boys followed Kulby. Meg paused momentarily, brows drawing together as she looked at him in a way she had never looked at him before, as if confused, cheeks flushing red. No longer was there venom in her eyes. She glanced at the door the Gobbins disappeared through, shrugged and then set off towards the castle.

Bane turned to Jarl, who was shaking his head.

"When I said use what tools are available," Jarl said, nodding towards the wall where Bane noticed a rake and shovel propped up in easy reach. "I didn't mean you to take my own sword."

Bane was about to apologise when the knight began to laugh.

"I mean, it did the trick - better than the gardening tools, and you accomplished what you set out to do."

Bane shook his head.

"No, I didn't. I never meant to hurt him, and now look, the lessons have ended," he said, listening to himself as the words sunk in. "I held back over the last few days, even though Kulby tried his best to hurt me, even though they had cut my practice sword down to nothing."

Jarl snorted as he slipped his blade back into its sheath.

"About that," he said, smile widening into a grin. "It was me. I cut a couple of inches from your sword every day. And loosened the nails in your shield."

Bane stared at him, not comprehending why the knight had done what he had done.

"You're a lot better than you give yourself credit for. I could see it, recognised the ability in you. It's rare, and you need to realise it for yourself."

"I almost killed Kulby."

Jarl stared into the dirt and the imprint of where Kulby had landed.

"I didn't expect you to use my sword. I probably should have seen it, really. You move like your father. Unpredictable and deadly."

Bane stared at the knight, feeling both elated at the recognition of who his father was and sad that he might never meet him.

"Is there no way for you to carry on instructing me? I'll give you what I have. The necklace and ring that Lady Felina gave me."

Bane was hopeful that this might be enough, yet as he watched Jarl scratch the back of his neck, not meeting his gaze, he knew that it wasn't.

"Sorry, lad. If this week's lessons hadn't ended how they did, I'd have been stopping them anyway. Now Lady Felina's son is reaching the age to begin training; my priorities have changed."

"So, these last few days were hard intentionally?"

Jarl nodded as he took Bane's hand and dropped two marks onto his palm.

"I wanted you to learn as much as I could teach you in those few days. You've got the basics, lad – could probably hold your own against most in the village with a blade. Keep practising your forms, do them over and over until you're doing it in your sleep."

The knight placed a heavy hand on his shoulder, gripping him momentarily before releasing.

"Look after yourself, Bane. Perhaps our paths will cross in the future. Hopefully, on good terms."

Bane watched him leave, gripping the coins in his hand so tightly that he lost all feeling in his fist.

With a heavy heart, he trudged away from the swine pens, the grey clouds finally giving up holding back the tears and releasing them. Thick drops splattered his face and his shoulders and soaked into his clothes.

The weather matched his mood, yet as foul as it was, he was glad he was alone. Truly alone.

The unforgiving gusts buffeted him as he collected Chewer from home; Dodd had already left for the festival, like the rest of the village.

"Come on, boy," he grunted to the hound as he began the slow plod around the dwellings before heading out to the wood yard.

****

Alruna hunkered low as she darted across the barren strip of land that separated the foothills from Crookfell, one hand grasping a bearded axe while her other rested on the hilt of the sword swinging from her hip, preventing it from tripping her over.

Freki padded easily at her side, a silent shadow as they joined the rest of the small party, huddled into the corner of a small ruin, possibly a barn.

Ferric was peering around the corner; eyes narrowed against the hammering rain.

"The village is empty. Seems like they all went up to the castle for the festival. Trusting lot, aye."

Alruna felt a pang of relief; their job would be a lot easier if there were no one to fight. Then again, if there was no one to fight, how could she earn respect from this raid? How could she prove herself?

It had been a hard few days as they prepared for tonight. Raif and her father going over the plan, instructing her where she had to be, how she had to behave, to make sure she listened to Ferric and not to try anything foolish.

She had laughed them off, a fierce bravado that had weakened the closer this evening came, the excitement at going out on a raid being replaced with trepidation. Yet she would be nowhere else.

Tonight, she would prove herself.

"Listen up," Ferric said, drawing the small group together as he wiped dank hair from a wet face.

"The rain will cover us, but I still don't want you making any noise. As planned, Alruna and I will head over to the forge and see what steel we can take," he said, jabbing a stubby finger at Ganlin and Krip, "You will head straight to the pig pens. String them together and head back here."

"Aye," the pair said in unison, both trying to sound keener than the other, yet Alruna could smell their fear. They were both equally green to the raid as she was.

"Well, get gone then," Ferric growled, thumbing toward the pig pen. He then turned his attention to Alruna.

"You ready, lass?"

Alruna gritted her teeth and nodded. Then followed Ferric as he darted into the gloom, his dark clothes soon becoming lost against the darker night.

Swallowing the lump in her throat, Alruna set off after, wondering why she had painted blue lines across her eyes if nobody was there to see. But at least she got to tie her hair in a warrior's tail.

Mud splattered up her boots as they ran. Her grip on the ground was a slippery one, and she became extremely mindful of the sharpened steel in her hand and the other swinging from her hip.

From what she could see of Crookfell, it wasn't much bigger than her village. The shacks and hovels were similar, as were the low clouds clinging to them.

She was about to dart across a gap to the large building, which was the forge, when Ferric paused and motioned for her to keep still.

As she crept closer, Alruna could see a lone figure standing beneath the eaves of the forge, using the overhang of the thatch to shelter from the rain.

"It's a boy," Ferric whispered, slipping a dagger from his belt. "He'll need taking care of."

Alruna studied the boy. He was of an age with herself. Taller and with a solidness to his shoulders. Any other features were hidden within shadow.

"No. I'll do it," Alruna offered, the words passing her lips before she could take them back. What was she thinking? But as she watched Ferric slide his dagger away, a wicked grin splitting his face, she knew she was committed. At least this way, she would prove herself.

"Freki, with me," she hissed as she stalked around the back of the shack they were squatting against and made her way to the next before approaching the boy from his blind side.

She wondered about using her sword, possibly sliding it across his neck or even running him through but thought better of it. The axe would make a swifter end with less risk of the boy screaming out.

Placing one boot in front of the other, she gently sneaked as close as she could; the boy's head was turned away, hands shoved inside his armpits as he huddled himself to keep warm.

He was all hard lines, subtly muscled without an inch of fat - a solid jaw appearing beneath unkempt hair. There was a sadness in him. A melancholy mood to match the foul weather.

He would be even sadder if he knew what was about to happen.

Holding her breath, she took another step, closed the distance and raised the axe.

It was easy to split a skull, Raif had once told her. Like splitting a turnip – a simple thunk through the outer shell and the juicy stuff spills out.

Alruna remembered laughing at the time. She wasn't laughing now.

The boy caught her movement and spun, eyes making large circles as his mouth fell open.

"What, who…" he muttered, then gazed at her raised axe and backed away.

She caught Ferric dashing towards him, blade in hand from over his shoulder.

The boy heard the slapping of feet, turned, and somehow managed to dance out of harm's way, moving fluidly.

He eased back, putting a little distance between them, yet didn't run.

"Try to flee, and I'll set my cat on you," Alruna said, stepping around to the front of the forge, axe still held above her.

To his credit, the boy stood his ground, gaze meeting hers with the greyest eyes she had ever seen. A large hound lumbered from the edge of the building to join him, its muzzle sniffing the ground as if searching for truffles.

"Are you going to kill me?" he asked, and there was no hint of fear in his voice, no tremor.

"Aye," Ferric said, stepping towards him until Alruna grasped his arm.

"I said he was mine," she insisted, wishing she had gone to steal the swine instead. But warriors didn't prove themselves by robbing a couple of pigs.

Ferric shrugged from her grasp, lips curling into a grimace.

"Get him in the mud and be quick about it. Your Da will be here soon. I'll see what I can pilfer."

She waited until Ferric had opened the forge and disappeared inside before gripping the haft of her axe tighter.

"You don't need to kill me," the boy said in a way which sounded as though he was trying to help more than plead for his life. "I'm the only one here. Everyone else is up at the castle. Even if I ran, I couldn't bring anyone back until long after you've gone."

"Shut up," Alruna hissed, knowing the boy was right.

"And I don't believe you want to."

Alruna flexed her shoulder and heaved the axe up high.

"I said shut up."

The boy watched her, not raising his arms in surrender or whispering silent prayers to his false gods – acting as if he accepted what was coming.

"I've never met a child of the Fug before. That's what you are. Children of the Fug, raiders. My name's Bane."

He even offered her a smile. It was pleasant and fit the rest of his features well.

"What? I don't care," she said, yet the venom had now dropped from her words, and she slowly lowered the axe.

Freki sniffed the boy's dangling fingers, her tongue darting out to taste him, and then, like a traitor, rubbed her head against his leg and began to purr.

"Hello again. I see you're not limping anymore," the boy called Bane said, kneeling to stroke the leopard.

When he caught her glowering at him, Bane used that disarming smile.

"I found her last week, trapped under a fallen tree. It's a wonder she's alive."

"Freki, come here," she said, calling the cat back.

Freki lifted her head and glanced at her but didn't move.

"Freki," Alruna snapped, slapping her thigh. Anger flamed through her as Bane gave a final stroke down Freki's back before gesturing her to go.

Reluctantly, the leopard prowled away and paced around Alruna's legs before sitting down, her gaze falling back to the boy.

Now, even if she wanted to kill him, she may have to fight her cat, and she couldn't do that.

"What now?" Bane asked.

She wished he would shut up. Maybe a glancing blow to the back of the head might quiet him, but the thudding of fast-approaching feet stole her attention.

A trumpet piped through the wet night, short blasts from the castle, letting her know they were running out of time.

The feet belonged to her father, brother and Hadlo; something slung over his broad shoulders.

They stopped before them, Hadlo dropping the bundle on the floor. It was a boy in finely dressed clothes, tear tracks down his cheeks, soft lips trembling as he tried to crawl away from Hadlo, frightened eyes never leaving Geri as the huge leopard padded closer.

"We've got what we came for. Lady Felina's son. Cuthbur, is he called? A Damn fine hostage," her father said, staring back the way they had come. "But the guards and many knights are heading our way. They'll be on us in no time, so grab what you can. We need to go." Then he noticed Bane standing there and instantly reached for his sword.

In the same instance, Ferric emerged from the forge, three lengths of iron under his arms and a hammer and tongs tucked into his belt.

"I told you to end him," he hissed, standing in the doorway and shaking his head. "I knew I should have been the one to gut him. Full of bravado up at home, wench, but once in the thick of it, you lose your mettle."

Heat pulsed through Alruna as she spat on the ground, thinking that she wouldn't find it as hard to sink her axe into Ferric's head. But her anger was also steered towards Bane. She wouldn't have been in this dilemma if he hadn't been there in the first place. And the way he had looked at her - still looked at her, had caught her off guard.

"If he's here alone, just crack him round the head and shove him in the barn. We need to go. Now," her father said, glancing up the hill to the castle and the men on horses that were rapidly advancing, spanning out in a line that covered the hillside.

"Leave him," Raif said, "It's not as if he can stop us, and the alarm has already been raised."

"Fair point," her father agreed, although she still felt as though she had been cheated out of something. Would Raif have killed him in her place? Most likely. And now Ferric would spread the word of her failure at killing a soft Southerner.

She would deal with him later. Nothing could be done about it now. Maybe a glancing blow to the back of the head for good measure.

Alruna turned to face Bane, yet all she saw was a fist taking up her entire vision, and the world abruptly turned black.

10

Death Giver

Bane's heart struck harder than a hammer on an anvil. His bowels turned to water as he watched the group of raiders arrive; the largest, a giant of a man, dropped something that he'd been carrying into the mud. At first, it appeared to be a sack or bundle until he watched it wriggle.

It was a boy, maybe a summer or two younger than himself, dressed in fine velvets that were being spoiled by the wet earth. He cowered away from the largest shadow leopard Bane had ever seen as it prowled closer to him, sniffing the air.

Chewer whimpered beside him, then darted inside the forge, tail hidden between his legs.

Bane fought to steady his breathing as the group focused on him, hard stares, flexing muscles and a lot of sharpened steel. But at least the girl's axe was hanging by her side as she talked with the older man, possibly her father.

"We've got what we came for. Lady Felina's son. Cuthbur, is he called? A Damn fine hostage," he growled.

Cuthbur?

Bane studied the boy. Even through the tear-tracked cheeks, the swollen eyes and trembling chin, he saw Lady Felina in him.

"They're coming; we have to go," the younger man said, glancing back the way they had come, the trumpet blasts piping out from the castle, the thunder of fast-approaching hooves.

The knights from the castle would be here soon. But they will be too late to rescue Lady Felina's son, and more than likely himself.

The thought came an instant before he acted. It was so small a space in time that he didn't know what he was doing until he was committed.

A single step, light and swift, the momentum driving his fist towards the girl's jaw.

Bane thought she could have been pretty beneath the blue paint and the anger twisting her features. A hostile beauty that had been on the brink of killing him with her axe, the shaft of which he gripped as he simultaneously punched her in the face.

The girl, Alruna, as her father called her, turned at the last heartbeat and his fist struck her cheekbone, rocking her head back.

If he could, he would have apologised. He had never hit anyone, not counting Kulby, and never thought he would ever hit a girl. Not that she wouldn't be able to fend for herself. She seemed more than capable a moment ago when she was threatening him with an axe.

Guilt came swiftly as he thrust himself backwards, grasping Cuthbur under an elbow and shoving him inside the forge.

The boy stumbled and then collapsed on the threshold, fear rooting him to the spot.

Bane didn't have time to soothe him, not that there was much point to it if he could. He couldn't fight five hardened raiders and two shadow leopards.

"Fugging southern rat weasel," the girl spat, rubbing her cheek where he had struck her, the older man pulling her close for a look, yet she yanked away, drawing her sword.

"Should have killed you already. That'll teach me."

She spat on the ground again, the rain sweeping down in sheets drowning the gesture, yet from the rage in her glare, Bane got the point.

He set his feet and adopted Swooping Eagle, albeit with a different weapon. The principle should be the same, and at least he had a steel blade, even though it was in the shape of a bearded axe.

Alruna advanced, teeth clenched until the younger of the men gripped her arm.

"No. I'll do this. It needs to end swiftly," he said, freeing his sword.

"Raif, no," Alruna argued but had already been dragged back by the older man, nervous glances cast back to the advancing knights and soldiers from the castle.

"Drop the axe, boy, and you can walk away," Raif said as he advanced, sword scraping from its scabbard. Death was at the end of it, his death. He was about to die before the forge where he had slaved over the bellows for so many sweaty hours.

Fear shook him like a violent wave that he once heard Dodd talk about, that crashed against the cliffs on the far side of the forest. He often wondered what it might look like – he guessed he would never find out.

The raider named Raif was now before him. His features were much like Alruna's – a brother perhaps. However, the tip of his nose was blackened as if he recently suffered frostbite.

"Drop the axe," he said again. Not angrily, not an order, just a simple request.

Bane heard Cuthbur sniffle behind him, a whimpering that set Chewer whining. The pair of them sounded like a chorus of despair.

"I can't," Bane replied, feeling his palms slick on the axe shaft, rain mixing with sweat, making his grip slippery.

He'd been a wretch his entire short life. A Bastard, Gallows born, spawn of Death. The village hated him, and the All-Mother knew he didn't owe them a jot.

But he wouldn't run. At least he would die proving them all wrong. Yet there would be nobody around to witness it.

He caught Alruna's eager grin behind her brother, a bead of blood running down her chin.

Raif shrugged as if he didn't mind either way. Then his shoulder dipped as he came on, a two-handed grip bringing his sword slicing across.

Bane wasn't ready.

Dancing Thistle hurriedly became part Crouching Cat, part Swooping Gul, as he clumsily brought the axe about and somehow caught and deflected Raif's blade.

Bane caught a flicker of surprise in his opponent's eyes, felt satisfaction and then staggered as the warrior came on with three more cuts, the final biting below the head of the axe and severing the head.

The blade landed with a wet thunk a few feet away.

"Raif, hurry," the older man urged as the thundering of hooves came closer. The huge shadow leopard at his side snarled - large teeth bared as it began to pace.

Sighing and tightening his lips in a gesture that said, 'I did warn you', Raif thrust his sword at Bane's exposed chest.

Born from reflexes alone, Bane turned with it, bringing his arm down and parrying the blade with his vambrace.

He felt the leather give and then fall away, exposing his flesh, the blade sliding along it, scraping over the thorns which somehow deflected the steel.

Fire erupted along his wrist and ran the length of his forearm, yet he continued the turn – Floating Ash Seed – the stump of the shaft in his hand became his focus as he put the remaining strength into a downward thrust, aiming for Raif's exposed thigh but met only empty air.

His weight carried him over and the dance became a wild windmilling of arms as he fought to remain upright.

"Wycum marked," Raif said, his words coming through the loud snarls from the cats, the hammering of rain in the mud, the thundering of hooves and the louder crash of Bane's beating heart – yet he heard him.

Wycum marked.

His heel found a slick patch in the earth, sent his foot from under him, and his world pivoted on its axis.

Amidst the ensuing chaos, his absently flung arm, the one on fire, caught against a soft branch; he felt a tug as it snagged into the bark, and then as it ripped away, hot water spattered his face.

Somewhere in the maelstrom of his mind, he knew there was no tree there, but it soon became lost with the rest of his panicking thoughts.

He crashed onto his back, the wind driven from his lungs. He struggled out of Raif's reach, half crawling, half rolling until he was back onto the threshold of the forge.

Leaping to his feet, he turned to face Raif's next attack, the final blow, the cold steel of the raider which would end his life.

It didn't come.

More hot water arced out of the wet night, falling against his heaving chest. No, not water.

Raif's sword clattered into the mud, both hands pressing to the wound in his neck, dark liquid pouring through trembling fingers.

He spat blood from his mouth as he tried to speak, and then, as his eyes rolled back, he collapsed.

"Raif!" Alruna screamed as she rushed to her brother, slipping in the sludge as she caught him. "Raif," the name became a sob.

Bane watched life drain from the man who had tried to kill him. So much blood.

"Chief, we need to leave," the giant warrior said, huge hammer now in meaty hands as he stared up the hill. "Chief."

The old man slowly brought his gaze away from the dying man, blue eyes boring into Bane's for a moment; disbelief, hate, anger – all passed in an instant as he clenched his jaw and nodded.

The giant slipped his hammer into a holster on his back, knelt before Raif, and gently picked him up as a mother would a sleeping child.

Slack arms dangling, head lolling as the giant began to run away from the approaching army.

"Go. Back across the border," the old man said, tears now in his eyes as he grasped his daughter under her arm and propelled her away from the forge. She took several staggering steps before she stopped.

Through her blue paint, through the rain-soaked shadows and through her tears, Bane witnessed a rage, the likes of which he had never seen before.

"I'm going to kill you. Do you hear me, boy? I swear on my brother's life, I will end yours," she screamed, the final word trailing off as her father hoisted her onto the back of the large shadow leopard. The smaller cat, Freki, paused at the edge of the yard, head turned his way before she too vanished out of sight.

Bane stared after them. He was vaguely aware that he had taken several steps out into the rain before he found himself back inside the forge; somehow, the fallen sword, the last owner's blood slick along the blade, was held in his hands, point resting on the floor.

"Have they gone?" came a soft voice from behind him.

Bane opened his mouth to reply, yet no words passed his lips. Instead, he simply nodded, the effort seeming to waken something in him, and his entire body began to shake.

No, not his body, the ground.

Horses charged through the yard, hooves churning up mud as they galloped after the raiders, knights leaning over saddle horns, swords raised as they spurned their mounts on.

Some stopped outside the forge, several knights circling about, horses stamping impatiently, nostrils flaring, steam rising from their flanks.

When one of the knights noticed him standing there with a sword in his hand, he levelled his own blade, and Bane realised that his life was about to end for the third time that night.

More horses galloped past, cutting through the village, mud splattering up the walls and fences and on the other knights.

The man glowering suddenly lowered his sword as he stared beyond him.

"Master Cuthbur?"

Bane felt the boy brush past him as the son of Lady Felina came to stand at the edge of the threshold. He might have said something, even looked the boy's way, yet his gaze fell to the dark pool of blood at his feet.

Another commotion as a fresh rider stopped in the yard and jumped down from his mare.

"Jarl," Cuthbur yelled and ran to the newcomer, quickly swallowed by the older man's embrace. A moment later, the knight had thrown the boy up onto his horse and climbed on behind him.

"I'm taking him back to his mother. See to it that you root out any more raiders from the village," Jarl said before glancing at Bane. "And take our little hero back to his people."

He put heel to flank and turned the mare about, locking eyes with Bane long enough to give a nod and then set off at a gallop back towards the castle.

The other soldier dismounted and paced through the mud to Bane.

"You hurt, lad? You're covered in blood," he asked, removing his helmet to study him closer.

Bane lifted his head from the ground and found that his left arm was coated in blood, gone cold and beginning to congeal. It covered his tattoo, the thorns of which had somehow sliced through Raif's neck, severing an artery.

"None of it is mine," he heard himself say, the words carrying off as if coming from somewhere else.

The soldier nodded, sucking on his bottom lip as he surveyed the ground, the prints and the dark red splats.

"Hero indeed. One brave little man against five hardened raiders and a shadow leopard."

"There were two leopards, Captain," said another soldier coming to join the first. "I was some distance away, but I could make out that there were definitely two, Sir."

The captain turned to his subordinate. "Two? You held them all back with only a sword?"

Bane let out a shuddering breath, the blade in his hand feeling suddenly heavy, his legs so weak that they might buckle.

"The sword was his," he mumbled, glancing once more at the red stain, which seemed to darken the more he watched it.

The captain slapped him heavily on the shoulder, startling him, and he almost fell to the ground with the freight.

"Well played, lad. And by rights of combat, that sword is now yours. And a fine-looking one it is, too," the Captain said, then turned to the other soldier. "Take our young hero back to the tavern where the rest of the villagers are. Make sure he gets food."

Bane heard the captain say more, the words swimming to him as if wriggling through treacle. He couldn't understand them as he was led to a horse and pulled up behind the rider. Chewer was locked in the forge, probably the best place for him.

The next thing he knew was that they had arrived at the castle, the horse trotting through the gates.

On another day he would have been fascinated. He'd always planned on coming to the castle, if not to join the guard, then to at least experience the huge stone structure.

The rider stopped inside the bailey and tossed the reins to a waiting stableboy.

Bane clambered from the horse and followed the soldier down a narrow passageway and through a door. The noise inside was a commotion of loud voices, each louder than the last, as if fighting to be heard above all others.

"In you go, lad, let's find you somewhere to sit," the soldier said, putting an arm over his shoulder and guiding him through the crowds of people.

A pungent odour of sour ale, tobacco smoke and bodies filled his nose as he was ushered to the back of the tavern, the crowd pulling away from him as if he was riddled with the plague, the noise dying down until it became so quiet he could hear his boots scuffing the straw floor.

"Clear the way," the soldier demanded as he, not too gently, shoved a man from a small table and directed Bane onto the bench.

"Stay here; I'll make sure food and an ale come your way," he said before pushing back through the crowded room, leaving Bane alone.

A quietness settled over the tavern. Bane felt the stares, sensed the tension, and he tried his best to make himself small, shrinking into the corner of the cramped room as best he could.

He was still gripping the sword's hilt when a plate of meats and a tankard of ale was dropped heavily onto the table, froth sloshing over the rim to splash onto the rough wood. It made the same pattern as the blood spats on the back of his hands.

The whispers about the room soon became hushed voices, and then conversations began to take back up; some of the words were about him, a mention of gallows born or been cursed, blended with raiders, urgent, angry, most likely directed at him.

"I'm telling you - it was in league with the Children of the Fug. Expect my swine have gone. Fugging boy tried to kill Kulby earlier. Fetch Dodd. He can get it removed."

He didn't raise his head; he didn't need to. He knew who was speaking.

Bane flinched as someone slunk onto the bench beside him. A body pressed up against his and grasped his hand.

"What happened, Bane," Belle asked.

Bane opened his mouth to speak, gazed down to his arm, the outline of thorns showing through a crusty brown layer. He remembered it snagging, a tug, and then a gush of hot blood.

It already seemed like a distant memory, happening somewhere else, to someone else, almost as if it was a nightmare, but he knew it wasn't.

Dew pushed through the crowd to sit opposite, leaning across the table with as much concern in his features as his sister.

"I," Bane began, but Alruna's face filled his vision, dark with hatred, slick with rain and tears, blue eyes smouldering.

"I killed someone," he mumbled, letting his hand slacken inside Belle's, waiting for her to pull free - she didn't.

"What was that?" Belle asked, leaning closer still.

"I'm sorry for upsetting you the other day," he said instead, not trusting himself to repeat the last sentence.

"Don't be silly. It's forgotten. Now, are you going to tell us what's happened?"

"Da says there are raiders in the village; that's why they won't let us go back, not until they've searched Crookfell," Dew explained as he reached for a chicken leg on the plate before them. It was in his mouth before Belle slapped his arm.

"Is that right? Is that why you're here?" Belle pressed. "Are you hurt?"

Before Bane could answer, there was a shuffling of bodies in the tavern as someone pushed through.

"There it is. Now, what are you going to do, Dodd? It belongs to you," came Mr Gobbin's shrill voice, quickly followed by Dodd's shadow casting over the table.

"Well, boy? How come you're here and not watching the village? And who did you steal that sword from? Give it here," Dodd ordered, looming over them as the rest of the village crowded around, eager to see what was happening.

"Guard said he'd killed a raider," the barkeep said from across the bar, absently wiping dirty hands on his apron before pouring ale into a tankard. "Said he'd fought five of them and two shadow leopards at the forge. And rescued lady Felina's son."

"Horse shite," Dodd replied, sneering at the barkeep.

The barkeep shrugged.

"Tis what the guard said. Even paid for the lad's meal and ale. And well, just look at him. He's covered in someone's blood."

Dodd raised an eyebrow, then took Bane's tankard of ale, placed it to his lips and drained it.

Bane knew that it wasn't Dodd's first that night. It probably wasn't his fifth or sixth, either.

Belle gripped tighter to his hand and he felt her intense stare, felt all the tavern was watching him.

"Speak, boy, else I'll take that sword you pilfered and shove it…"

Dodd's words were cut short as Jarl shoved him aside, a fist curled into the collar of his jerkin as he lifted him onto the tips of his toes.

Bane was sure the knight would strike him. A wildness to his manner, an eagerness that was searching for an excuse to hit him. But Jarl took a breath, eased Dodd back to the floor and simply pushed him out of the way.

"Bane, Lady Felina requests an audience with you," he said, loud enough for all to hear. "Come with me."

Belle gasped as she let go of him.

"Is it true, Bane? Did you fight raiders and rescue Master Cuthbur?" she asked.

"Kind of," he whispered to her as he passed.

Through the silence, Bane offered Dew and Belle a nervous smile and then followed the knight out of the tavern. The moment he was outside, an explosion of voices erupted from the other side of the door.

"Whatever they say in there, lad, you did me proud," Jarl earnestly said, pushing fingers through his tangled hair as he stared back at the tavern entrance. "You've more courage and honour than the lot of them put together."

The knight studied him briefly, nodding slowly as he took him in.

"You killed a man. And it's not an easy thing to deal with. It'll be a stain on your mind for the rest of your life.

But remember this, Bane. If you hadn't killed him, he would have killed you. Now come, let's not keep her Ladyship waiting. And it's probably best that I hang onto this for now."

He took the sword from Bane and held it up to a burning torch on the wall. Flames reflected along the blade, making it seem as though it was on fire.

"A good sword. Well balanced and properly cared for. Its previous owner knew how to look after it."

Bane only nodded, seeing Raif's wide eyes stare at him accusingly as his life gushed through his fingers.

They walked through a network of stone corridors, up steps, archways, and down long hallways. Servants and maids paused as they neared, bowed or curtsied to them both. And then they were through to another part of the castle, the stone walls covered with oak panelling, wooden stairs, and tapestries and paintings hung from the white-washed walls.

He may have taken more interest if he wasn't so tired, but it was too much effort to put one foot in front of the other.

They climbed a spiral staircase that rounded onto another corridor. A large door was before them with a guard standing on either side, polished armour gleaming under the candlelight, and even their halberds shone. They wore the Shankil emblem of the shadow leopard on their breastplates, a dark cat on a green field.

They nodded at Jarl as he pushed the door open and ushered Bane inside.

The chamber was large, with a red rug on the floor and paintings hanging from the walls. Lady Felina came out of a door at the other end of the chamber, dressed in a white gown that Bane thought could be a slip or bedwear, yet never seen either before, could only guess. She gently closed the door behind her.

"Bane," she uttered as she turned to him, lower lip trembling as she rushed across the room, throwing her arms around his shoulders and drawing him into a fierce hug.

Bane couldn't move. He stood there, arms by his side, feeling Lady Felina's chest rise and fall as she clung tighter. He realised it was the first time he had embraced anyone since before his aunt died, over half his life ago.

"My dear, boy. I owe you everything," she whispered, then drew away, producing a delicate cloth from her sleeve to dab at her eyes.

Bane was ashamed to find that her white gown had several dark marks ground into the rich material, yet she didn't seem to care.

"Cuthbur told me everything. Those beasts broke into his chamber while he slept and stole him away. He would surely be dead if it wasn't for your valiant and selfless act."

Another door opened from behind a tapestry hidden from view, and Glance stepped through, swiftly closing it behind him.

"So, the rumours are true," he said, sharing a glance with Jarl, who confirmed it with a nod. "You killed several raiders, single-handedly and unarmed. All while fending off a pack of shadow leopards."

"It wasn't like that. There were five raiders and only two cats," Bane explained, not liking the attention he was getting.

"Only five, he says. And you killed one of them," Glance said, running a finger across his throat. "The rumours are already spreading about the castle. By tomorrow, I've no doubt that the story will have you fighting a horde of raiders."

"Cuthbur tells me it was one of the two who had taken him from his bed," Lady Felina added, dabbing at her eyes again.

"Raif," Bane said, saying the raider's name for the first time since he had killed him. The echo of Alruna screaming it, the anguish, her hatred. Was she out there now, burying her brother?

I'm going to kill you. Do you hear me, boy? I swear on my brother's life, I will end yours.

"Raif, you say," Glance said as he began to pace. "Raif Lothrun, son of Boran, the chief of their clan. A mighty kill indeed."

Guilt caught Bane in the throat and clung to his chest as he tried and failed to push the visions of the night away.

Raif! No. I'm going to kill you.

He wanted to tell them it was an accident. That he had not intended to kill, but the words never reached his mouth.

"Whoever it was, I owe you a life debt," Lady Felina said. "Ask from me anything. If it is in my power, it is yours."

"My Lady, I wish for nothing," Bane said, attempting to bow and feeling as awkward as it must appear.

"Hush now, Master Bane, if my sister is offering you a treasure, you must take it. Don't be coy, name it. Gold? A passage to another place, a fresh start?"

Bane shook his head and then looked to the knight, who was remaining quiet.

"I wish for Jarl to continue teaching me sword skills," he said.

"You know I can't do that, lad," Jarl said, smiling sadly. "I'll be training the new recruits here at the castle, and the rest of my time will be taken up with teaching Cuthbur, now he's coming of age."

"Can I be a new recruit?"

Lady Felina looked to Glance, who held up his hands.

"It is possible, but I'm afraid you must do something which I don't think would sit well with you. All recruits must swear an oath of allegiance to my father, the Baron."

"I can't swear an oath to the man who killed my mother," Bane admitted.

"It's a shame you couldn't hold on a couple of years. My father spends his days now in his bed, mind addled with delirium."

"Glance, that's no way to speak about Father," Lady Felina said, and Bane saw how close the two were, both in looks and how they carried themselves.

"I'm sorry, Bane, I cannot even grant you a place at the castle unless you swear an oath to a Shankil. And I cannot receive it, as a Lady can only have one sworn protector," she said, smiling at Jarl.

The door slowly opened, and a small face peered through, soft features matching his mother's.

"Cuthbur? Did we wake you?" Lady Felina asked.

Cuthbur shook his head as he entered the chamber, dressed in white bedwear.

"I was listening the entire time," he admitted. He stared at Bane, taking in his state and most likely reliving the darker time in the night. Now in the light, Bane realised that he wasn't as young as he first thought. Cuthbur was probably only a year younger than himself.

"Thank you," Cuthbur said. "Without your intervention, I'm sure I would be across the border and cooking in some cauldron by now."

"Hush, Cuthbur," his mother warned.

"And they don't actually eat people. More than likely, you'd have been a hostage, a bargaining chip for them to gain supplies and weapons," Glance put in, earning himself a glare from his sister.

"You must be tired, Cuthbur, go back to bed," Lady Felina said, and Bane couldn't help wondering what it must be like to have a caring mother.

"But I came though because I heard the predicament Bane is in, wanting to be taught skill at arms but unable to give at oath to a Shankil. Well, why can't he swear an oath to me?"

Lady Felina looked to Glance, who was grinning.

"Well played, Cuthbur," he said, ruffling the boy's hair.

Lady Felina stared at Bane, properly taking him in.

"Will you swear an oath of allegiance to my son?"

Bane felt a pang of hope as he looked from the boy to his mother.

"I will," he said and dropped to one knee, head bowed low.

"Do you, Bane…what is your last name?" Lady Felina asked.

"I don't have one," Bane answered.

"Then Bane, do you swear allegiance to my son, Cuthbur Shankil? Will you protect him, fight and honour him on point of death?"

"I do."

"Give me your hand."

Bane felt a light pressure and then a sting as Glance produced a small blade from beneath his sleeve and made a tiny cut on his palm. He did the same with Cuthbur, who winced as a bead of blood stood out starkly on his pale flesh.

Jarl put the sword Bane had won tip first on the ground and presented the hilt to Cuthbur, who grasped it, leaving a bloody handprint. He then tipped it towards Bane.

"Grip the hilt, lad," Jarl whispered over his shoulder.

Bane gripped the hilt tightly, letting his blood mingle with that of Cuthbur's.

"Then it is done," Lady Felina said.

Glance stepped forward and placed a hand on Bane's shoulder.

"Not quite. Bane will still need a patron and a title here at the castle."

Lady Felina sighed.

"What do you suggest, brother? Although I'm sure with your cunning, you already have something in mind."

Glance gave his usual cocky grin.

"You know me so well, Felina. I have been on the lookout for an apprentice. It seems Master Bane here will fit most of my expectations. You'll need educating, of course."

"Yes," Bane said a little too enthusiastically. "But what exactly am I going to be an apprentice of?"

Glance laughed and tapped a finger to his nose.

"A master of the dark. To serve the Shankils as only a bastard born of the same blood can."

By the time Jarl had walked Bane back out into the castle grounds, dawn had arrived. Grey light crept over the horizon and the Fug was descending towards the border that separated Crookfell from the foothills.

From this distance, it seemed as though nothing had happened the previous night, as if the coming of the next day had erased the violence of the dark hours.

He'd been shown to the bathhouse and had scrubbed himself clean, leaving the water a rusty brown colour. Jarl had given him his old rough spun tunic and leather britches to wear. They were too big around the shoulders but were the nicest clothes he had ever worn. He'd also found him an old vambrace that was too large for his forearm but hid the thorn tattoo well.

Jarl escorted him to the castle gate.

"Collect your things, say your goodbyes and put your past in order," Jarl said, staring down the rise to the village. "I dare say it shouldn't take you too long."

Bane smiled.

"I've nothing to collect and Dodd will be thankful to see the back of me."

Jarl nodded.

"Then I'll see you in the practice yard in the morning. Glance will have found you accommodation by the time you return."

Jarl smiled and held out his arm for Bane to take in a warrior's grasp.

"I meant what I said last night. You did me proud. Now go. I'm sure when you begin training in the morning, you'll soon regret your request for me to teach you."

Bane took a few unsteady steps from the castle and glanced at his hands – the hands that had killed the previous night. There was still dried blood caught between the nails. He wondered if it was harder to wash out if you experienced guilt from getting it there. The more guilt you felt, the more it clung to you.

He pulled he gaze away as he made his way to the village, watching the Fug advance its way back into the foothills and caught a tendril of smoke spiralling in the distance. A small fire that seemed at the other side of the world.

11

A Brother's Pyre

Alruna bit her lip to stop herself from crying, yet the harder she bit, the more water spilt from her swollen eyes. She stared away from the curling smoke and dug the tip of her knife into the edges of her fingernails, trying to scrape her brother's dried blood from them. But it seemed the more guilt you felt, the harder it was to remove.

"I promise I'll avenge you, brother," she said, her voice hoarse from the shouting, from the arguing and from the late-night building of the pyre.

Her father edged closer and put an arm over her shoulder, the heat from the smouldering wood, the burning flesh, somehow making her feel colder. She shrugged the arm off and stepped away.

It had been a hard night. A chaotic blur of running through the mud, of floundering across open ground, arrows skittering along the wet earth, the screams of the soldiers chasing, the thundering of hooves, the scrape of drawn steel.

She'd set her sights on her brother, bouncing in Hadlo's arms as they crossed the border and passed through the thicket of trees marking the foothills of the frontier. They'd rested to gather their breaths further in, hiding like cowards behind thick oaks and dense bracken, not that the Southerners would follow them in – even though they would have been easy to follow, leaving a trail of Raif's blood.

Her brother was dead.

She remembered leaning over him, thumping his chest, willing him to draw in breath – hands pressed to the mess at his neck, the shredded flesh where the thorns of the Wycum-marked tattoo had raked across it.

So much blood.

One of the swine had come too close, sniffed the dark stains down her brother, and stuck its tongue out to taste him.

She'd found her knife driven into its head, fingers still wrapped around the hilt, before she realised what she had done.

"It'll need carrying now," Ganlin had moaned.

"Well, fugging carry it," she'd growled back, her blade scraping against bone as she pulled it free.

Alruna had argued then, pleaded to go back, to kill the strange boy who had robbed her of her brother.

Now, all that was left of him was ash and bone, and it wouldn't be long before it was simply ash. The only blood she'd shed that night was from a split lip and the blisters on her hands from splitting the logs for building the pyre.

Now it was dawn and all she could see in the grey sky was the boy. Bane.

"Alruna," her father began.

"I don't want to hear it," she sniffed. "You could have avenged him. Could have killed that demon who took Raif from us."

Other men about the pyre turned to watch the exchange, Ferric going as far as shaking his head. He blamed her. Yet not as much as she blamed herself.

"He was only a boy and was defending himself. If anything, he gave the final blow by accident," her father said.

Hadlo was standing behind him, nodding slowly, face grim as ever.

"Only a boy?" Ferric cut it. "Did you see the marks on his arm? That was a proper tattoo, inked from the blood of a strong god. It ran from elbow to wrist. Full and thick with thorns, real thorns."

The warrior's eyes dropped to the feeble ring around Boran's arm, letting it linger before he carried on.

"Raif said that the Wycum had already marked another. It must be him. And if it so, then the rest of it must also be true. The Draugr in the Fug, the god in the south, raising an army to claim our mountain."

Alruna knew that Ferric had the right of it, yet she didn't want to believe it.

"It was a good death," Hadlo said, deep voice penetrating through Alruna's weakening rage.

She had none left. Sorrow of plenty, an ocean of anger and hurt, a pit full of revenge, but the rage had dropped away, along with her strength.

"There is no good death," she said, then wished she could take it back. Hadlo had to believe there was; he lost his only son only days ago when her brother had stumbled out of the Fug. She hadn't minded thinking that Jhora had a good death then. The added guilt caught a spark of the anger and reignited it.

"And for what? Three swine and a couple of pieces of iron? Is that what my brother was worth?"

"Calm it wench. You should have ended the boy when I said," Ferric hissed. Trying to put all the blame on her while still remaining respectful to her father.

He didn't need to try. Alruna knew she was to blame. Her weakness the previous night at not killing the boy – or not allowing Ferric to end him, had cost her dearly.

Before she knew it, her knife was driving towards Ferric.

It was a pathetic blow, Ferric easily leaning out of her reach and then back-handing her across the mouth.

The pain seared along the jaw where the bruise was already blackening from Bane's punch.

She would have swung for Ferric again, but Hadlo had stepped up behind and wrapped his trunk-like arms around her, pinning her own pathetic arms to her side.

"Easy, Alruna," he whispered in her ear as he pulled her away.

She wriggled in his grip, but he was too strong and caught herself before she stamped her heel down on his foot. He was doing this more for her sake than anyone's.

When she stopped struggling, he let her go.

"Fug the lot of you," she said, taking a final glance at the pile of ash that had once been her brother before setting her gaze to the woods above and stepping that way.

"Alruna," her father called after. "You have lost Raif, you've lost a brother, but I've also lost a son."

"You're not acting as so. Why aren't you raising the clan to spill Crookfell blood?" she shouted over her shoulder, again wishing that she could take her words back and again igniting her rage from the guilt. Maybe that was all that was left of her. A shell of a girl fuelled by anger, guilt and fury.

Her father shouted more, but she pressed through the trees and his words became lost.

The smell of smoke went with her as she climbed out onto the outcropping of rocks. It clung to her clothes - black dust, ash, parts of Raif.

She sat on a ledge and curled herself into a ball, tucking her legs inside her arms, chin resting on her knees as she stared down the hill, catching the castle's outline in the distance, a ghostly silhouette partially hidden within the fog.

Bane was down there.

Freki emerged behind a bush and gently nudged her head against hers, tall ears brushing her face.

"And you can stop trying to snuggle, you traitor. You were all over that boy."

Her words held no anger and so her shadow leopard didn't take them for anything other than loving.

"Stupid cat," she said, leaning closer, putting an arm over her back and hugging her close.

The morning had vanished and evening was fast approaching when Alruna raised her head from the crook of her arm where she had rested it and finally succumbed to sleep. She had no more tears. The rage had subsided, her strength gone, yet her determination to avenge her brother was fuel enough to make her stand.

A distant tide bell rang further up the hill marking the Fug's descent from the mountain. No doubt her father would begin fretting that she hadn't returned.

Freki purred as she padded around her, eager to return to where she knew there was food.

Alruna stopped at a spring on the way back and washed, the cold water revitalising as she splashed it on her face. It was shockingly sharp as she dunked her head into the pool at her feet. She held her breath until her lungs burned before lifting it out, gasping as she shook the water from her hair.

A second bell tolled and she began to pick up the pace, breaking into a steady run, the blood beginning to pump feeling back through her body.

By the time the third bell tolled, she had stopped at the mound of ash that had been her brother.

It was nothing now but different shades of grey powder soon to be lost to the wind.

She bent down and scooped up a handful, slackening her grip to allow it to run through her fingers.

"I'll kill him, Raif, this wretch of Crookfell – this Bane. I swear on your honour I'll slit his throat as he did yours. I'll carve the Fug mark from his flesh, and I'll hunt the Wycum for myself."

Her knife was back in her hand, a habit that was becoming worse of late. She let the rest of the ash fall from her palm before running her blade across it, allowing her blood to mingle with the dusty remains of her brother.

"I swear it on my blood. I will see this oath through."

The fourth tide bell rang and she gave a final nod to her brother and then ran towards home, stumbling on the still dewy grass.

Crows flew around her, disturbed by the descending fog and what lay within it.

"Should have set off sooner," Alruna berated herself as she leapt a boulder and slid beneath a low-hanging branch. Freki bounded beside her, sleek and powerful and easily capable of running ahead, yet the cat chose to keep pace with her master – if she was still her master.

A deer suddenly darted in front of her, leaping from the brush and she lost her footing.

The world turned shades of greens and browns as she tumbled, only coming to a stop as her shoulder slammed into the trunk of an oak.

She rose before the pain hit, her boots already smacking the forest floor as her shoulder began to scream.

It was probably the same deer she had missed with an arrow days ago. Should have killed it. Should have killed Bane.

Her boots slapped harder, arms pumping as she pushed through the tree line and into her village, teeth grinding as she swore never to let something go that needed to be killed.

She was truly a dry well of empty mercy.

Her home came into view, smoke rising from the chimney, a stew slowly simmering in a cauldron within. Further down the slope, the trap door open and her father leaning out, beckoning her on.

"Move it, lass," he bellowed, eyes going wide as he focused on what was behind her.

She caught snatches of snarls and wild growls closing in on her as she motioned for Freki to go on.

The cat jumped down the trap door, tail slipping through the opening as Alruna dived.

Darkness swallowed her, the trapdoor slamming down the same instance as she hit the packed earth, crumpling into a tangle.

The shoulder that she had already struck the trunk of an oak now pounded with each beat of her heart.

When her senses caught up with her, she found that she was across one of the benches, a leg in the air and head craned over so that she was seeing the shelter upside down.

Her father climbed down the ladder, face grim as he folded his arms.

"Cutting it fine, aren't we?"

Alruna swung her leg around and pulled herself into a sitting position, the tendons in her neck clicking as she worked her jaw and rolled her shoulder.

"Got here, didn't I?"

Freki padded over to her mother, Geri, who was sitting on her haunches, watching the humans limber up for an argument. It was as if the cats could sense the tension and decided to sit it out, not wanting any part of the harsh words that were coming.

"Where've you been?"

Her father's questions were short and angry, and she was in no mood for them.

"Clearing my head. I'm not a girl anymore, and I don't need to tell you where I am and what I'm doing," she snapped, flicking her warrior's braid out.

Her father snorted.

"Seems you've got a bloody wish to join your brother. You came this close to being taken by the Fug," her father said, holding a hand, finger and thumb almost touching. "You're bloody foolish and fugging selfish."

Alruna was warming up to fly back at him, clicking the fingers in her knuckles as she stood, yet her father wasn't finished.

"The clan has lost a great warrior, a man that would replace me as leader. And I lost my son," he said, the final word getting caught in his throat, lips pressing tight together, yet the emotion won the battle and it came out as a sob.

Alruna wanted to tell him that he could avenge him. That he should have done it the previous night, that he was becoming as soft and weak as the mark left on his arm. But it seemed the emotion was catching.

She sniffed back the tears, stepped closer and held him.

They both let it all out, giving the pent-up tension release – and like a damned well, once it was broken the water carried on spilling.

When the heaving faded to sobs and that too calmed to quiet, they found themselves sitting beside each other, the Fug long gone and the cats prowling back and forth wanting to be let out.

"Hadlo tells me that Ferric has designs on becoming clan chief," her father admitted, staring up at the crack of light coming through the trapdoor. "He's been spreading rumours about the village that I'm past it. Too old to lead and too weak to fight what's coming."

"I'll kill him," Alruna said. It wasn't said in anger, wasn't cheap words to placate her father. She meant every word of it.

"I'm sure you could. But no. Not yet anyway. A leader doesn't kill those that oppose him. Not unless that's the only option left. And with Raif gone, I need you to step up and take his place. You've a lot to learn, Alruna."

"What? You're going to train me to be leader, to be the next clan chief?"

"Aye. And the first lesson will be that you can't disappear across the border to take revenge," he said, taking her hand and unfolding it to reveal the fresh cut along her palm. "And oath or not, your first priority will always be your people."

Alruna didn't know how he did it, but her father always knew what she was thinking.

"And if this threat from the south is as real as Raif believed it to be, you will be the one to bring the clans together, to join our people with those at the castle."

"But you'll still be Chief when that happens. Even if it's twenty years from now."

Her father shook his head, leaned back so he could meet her gaze.

"No Alruna. Ferric was right about one thing. I am too old. I have been for a while. It was only out of respect from the warriors and the promise that Raif would be my replacement that I remained chief for so long. And if I thought any of them were good enough to lead then I would gladly step aside."

"What about Hadlo?"

Her father smiled.

"He's the best second I've ever had, and I'd trust him with my life. But a great leader needs more than muscle, more than a name and reputation. No, Hadlo is too honest, and people like Ferric will use him. What a chief needs to be above all else is cunning."

Daylight spilled through as her father climbed the ladder and flung the trapdoor open, leaving her behind with her thoughts.

Whatever filled her head before she entered the shelter was now pushed to the back of her mind. It was still there brooding, a smouldering heat that she knew would never leave her until Bane was dead. But now this new idea had taken root. Could she lead the clan, could she be chief?

She emerged into the afternoon, her father already on his chair, a bowl of stew on his lap.

"Go on," he said, nodding back into the shack. "A chief thinks better with a full belly. And that goes double if you're to learn."

It was surely a ploy to take her mind from Raif, yet Alruna was beginning to think it wasn't such a bad idea after all.

12

A New Life

Events from the previous night spun through his mind, glimpses of what had happened, the chaos, and the confusion both in the village and at the castle. Twice now, Bane stopped himself from wondering if it had happened the way he remembered – what parts were facts and what were nightmares that his tired brain had constructed.

His feet took him to the forge; whether he had intended to go there or not, he couldn't say, yet that is where his body had brought him.

The door was wide open, flames from the forge giving a red glow from inside, yet his gaze fell to the patch of mud on the threshold, the scratches and scuffs and the dark stain in the damp soil.

He didn't realise the hammering had stopped until he caught the smithy staring at him from the doorway, arms folded and an old hammer being throttled in a meaty fist.

"I'm sorry," Bane croaked, the words drier than the flames within the building.

He stepped closer and held out the two marks that Jarl had given him the previous morning, which seemed a lifetime ago now.

"It won't cover what was stolen, but it is all I have," he said.

Girant stared at the coins and then slowly shook his head.

"I know what happened," he said, eyes cast down to the darker patch of mud. "You likely prevented a lot more from being taken. And the forge still stands. Those Children of the Fug like to burn things. I'm sure I would no longer have my livelihood if you were not here."

It was the most words the smith had ever said to him in one go.

"Crookfell has wronged you, Bane. I've never liked how you've been treated, but as big as I am, I was too cowardly to act any differently. Listen, I'd happily keep you on if you still want to work here."

The words shocked Bane. Yesterday, they would have made his heart sing, but yesterday belonged to another him, a Bane that didn't exist anymore – a life that ended when his thorns ended another's.

"I'm here to say goodbye. I'm leaving for the castle."

It was the first time he had said it out loud and it felt good.

"The castle? From what I heard you did last night it is a just reward. I wish you well, Bane."

He left the forge with more haste than intended, whether to make sure he didn't take Girant up on his offer or to put swift distance between himself and the remainder of the night's black work imprinted in the ground, he couldn't say. Probably a mixture of both.

Two field workers, idly chatting against the empty pig pens, paused their conversation as he passed. The usual scowls were gone, and one even tipped his hat.

"You did Crookfell proud, lad," the other said, smiling.

Bane didn't know how to respond; he only nodded back before he caught Mr Gobbin coming out of his home, Kulby close at his heels.

They stared at him but soon averted their gazes, Kulby hurrying back inside.

What a change a single night could make.

He tried to put them behind him as he wandered to the edge of the village and into the lumber yard. There was nobody about, no pile of logs to be split. He thought about knocking on the door, even reaching his fist out to do so, yet swiftly let it drop.

What would he say if Mr or Mrs Camwell answered the door? 'Hello, can I come in? I wanted to say goodbye to Dew and Belle, my only friends – who you forbade to even speak with me.'

As he walked away he heard the door open, and as he turned Dew rushed out and took his arm in a warrior's grip. He fumbled it, trying to slap his forearm against his. In the end, he simply let it drop.

"Are the rumours true? Did you fight raiders? Did you kill one? The entire village is talking about it."

Bane was about to put Dew straight, but his friend didn't give him the chance.

"Belle overheard Meg bragging that she knew you – that she was friends with the Crookfell Slayer. Belle soon put her straight. There was very nearly a fight between them. And Ma said that if you came around today to split logs, she'd save you something to eat."

"Really? Crookfell Slayer?" Bane asked, wondering why the girls would fight over him. And why Meg had said what she had.

"I fought only one raider. And killed him by accident," he admitted, saying the words out loud to his friend bringing a fresh wave of emotion.

"Where's Belle?" Bane asked, changing the subject, looking up at the windows.

"She begins her new job today. A maid. You've just missed her. Ma is taking her up to the castle. So, are you staying? Da won't be long with the logs."

"No. I came to say goodbye. I've been apprenticed up at the castle."

Dew's grin dropped - his shoulders too.

"That's great," Dew said, sounding flat. "Apprenticed to what?"

"I'm in training to become a bodyguard to Master Cuthbur," he said, not adding that he was also being apprenticed to Glance for darker tasks, which he was unsure of.

"So, it is truly goodbye. You'll not come back?"

Bane thought that putting his back to Crookfell would be the easy part of his transition to the castle. He didn't count on the goodbyes being the hardest. And one of them wasn't even here.

"I'll come if I can. Or you could come up to the castle."

He knew that his words were lies. Once he begins castle life, he would become one of them, and Crookfell folk don't mix with castle folk. Dew knew it too but kept the pretence for both their sakes.

"Then I'll see you whenever. Good luck with it all," Dew said as he skulked to the doorway, giving a final glance before shoving it closed.

"Say goodbye to Belle for me," Bane called after, but Dew was already gone. He wondered about knocking on the door and speaking with him again. He didn't want to leave things like this. Had he lost his only friend?

He skirted the edge of the village as he made his way to the place he had called home, avoiding people as he cut between the hovels until he stumbled inside the shack he shared with Dodd and the hounds for the final time.

The fire wasn't lit, the cauldron was empty, not that Dodd did much cooking, and the large chamber was dimly lit.

The hounds raising their heads as he entered was the only reason he knew he wasn't alone.

"So, you finally came back, boy," Dodd said from his pallet.

He sat up and propped himself on his elbows, staring through bloodshot eyes and stinking of stale ale.

"Think you're too good for the likes of us now, do you? Wearing your new clothes, strutting around like a hero in a maiden's story."

Bane shook his head, about to gaze to the ground like he always had, then checked himself and met Dodd's stare.

"Missed the morning's gathering, missed the forge. That's five marks you owe me, boy," Dodd said as he swung his legs out of the pallet, belched, and stood.

"Well?"

"I no longer do those things," Bane said, not looking away. "And I only get two marks from Girant, and you never pay me."

Dodd's jaw clenched as he stumbled closer, a thick vein pulsing at his temple as it always did when he was angry, which was most days after a night's drinking.

"Fugging answering me back, boy? Who do you think you are?"

The cuffing came as expected, and Bane caught the glance with the corner of his head and rolled with it. Yet, unlike the countless other times he'd taken a cuffing, he felt the shame.

"And what do you mean – no longer doing those things? You've already lost me three marks with Mr Gobbin and his lard of a son. You'll be heading up to the lumber yard to begin splitting logs. Do you hear me?"

Dodd loomed closer, yellow teeth displayed in a snarl.

"I've just come from there. To say goodbye. I'm leaving today, now. I only stopped by to tell you that your oath is fulfilled. I no longer need a roof over my head. You are free of me."

Bane thought that his words would make Dodd happy, that the man who had made his hateful emotions clear all these years would be relieved to be finally free of him. But Dodd's grimace only deepened, spit frothing at the corners of his snarl.

"No, I am not. You're going nowhere, boy. You're mine, and you will do as I say."

The cuffing came again. A drawn-back fist laced with an anger Bane had never understood. But he had naturally set his feet shoulder width apart – one in front of the other, knees slightly bent.

He leaned away from the fist, caught Dodd's wrist and twisted it down.

The larger man's momentum carried him forward, and as Bane yanked up on the wrist, Dodd's upper body was forced low, his head striking the corner of the cauldron with a sickening thud.

Bane let go of him and stepped away, once more adopting a defensive stance. Dodd pressed fingers to his split scalp. They came away bloody.

"I'll gut you for that," he spat, the hounds cowering away into the corners of the shack, whimpering with the violence in the air.

A strange howl escaped Dodd as he rushed at Bane, sounding much like an injured fox. Fists flew in all directions, head down as he attacked.

Pathetic, thought Bane, and suddenly, the fear that he'd felt all those years melted away. The brutal way the man had treated him, the disdain, the blame for the loss of his wife, the harsh punishment and forced labour – the endless nights going without food, without warmth.

He allowed the first punch to connect, the balled fist landing on the bony part of his elbow, deflected the next with his vambrace and then butted Dodd on the bridge of his nose.

The fox howl became a screech as the elder man dropped like a split log, landing hard on his rump, the back of his head striking the cauldron again.

"Stay down, Dodd. The oath is fulfilled. I owe you nothing. I am nothing to you anymore. You can drink yourself into oblivion now that you have no responsibilities."

Bane felt a pang of guilt as Dodd looked up at him, tears spilling down his cheeks and into his unkempt beard. At that point, he appeared more childlike than man.

"You're all I have of her. My Gelwin," he mumbled, trembling fingers reaching toward him. "Now I have nothing."

"How have I never seen this before? And to think I once feared you," Bane said, stepping away and opening the door, letting fresh air into the feisty room.

"You're nothing but a bully. A sad old spent bully."

Bane stepped out into the day and paused.

"I'm leaving for the castle, but if I hear that you bully again, even if you're harsh with the hounds, I'll come back to remind you how pitiful you are."

Bane slammed the door behind him. A weight that he'd been carrying since before he could remember lifted. It was as if he was born again; in a way, he believed he was.

Others in the village greeted him as he made his way to the castle. Folk who would rather spit at his feet before now slapped him on the shoulder, shaking his hand. He nodded back but kept walking. Let them think he was rude; he didn't owe them a thing. He was free. He had nothing but what he was wearing and that he had borrowed from Jarl, yet his steps were lighter, a smile even creeping onto his lips. Then he glimpsed the forge, and last night came crashing back.

I'm going to kill you. Do you hear me, boy? I swear on my brother's life, I will end yours.

The guards at the castle gates stopped him. He thought they would refuse him entry, that his apprenticeship had been only a dream or a trick to amuse the castle dwellers, but the guards seemed to have a message.

"You must be the young hero. Bane, isn't it? The Crookfell Slayer," one of them chuckled light-heartedly.

"Crookfell Slayer?"

Bane felt his cheeks flush.

"Aye, lad. It's been the talk of the castle. A child villager taking on the might of the raiders and killing the Chief's son. You've got some stones. Anyway, Sir Garik says to meet him at the servant's entrance."

"Sir Garik?" Bane asked.

"Aye, lad. Garik. Lady Felina's half-brother. You know, always wears dark clothes."

"Oh, Glance. Thank you," Bane said and then hurried through the gates and into the castle grounds, wanting to distance himself from the guards before they started to ask questions. He followed the outer path around the bailey, leading up steps to another cobbled path and through a stone arch to the rear of the castle.

He didn't appreciate the size of the building the last time he walked this way. He stretched his neck back to see the top, the spires above seeming so high that they must brush the clouds. Guards patrolled the ramparts below, so small that if he raised his thumb in front of him, it would cover a man.

As he rounded the corner and was about to enter the servant's entrance, he was stopped by a heavy-set man wearing a light green suit with a dark green sash.

"Stop there, child. Who are you, and what business do you have in the castle?" the man demanded, brows rising as he waited for an answer. "Well? Answer me, boy, or I'll have the guards remove you at once."

"He's with me, Randel," came a voice from behind a low wall.

Glance's head appeared above the stonework, an easy smile putting the other man at ease.

"Sir Garik, forgive me. I wouldn't have questioned him if I'd known he was with you."

"No need to apologize. These are dangerous times. Here, let me introduce you. Randel, this is our latest addition to the castle, Master Bane. He's to become the close guardian of my nephew Cuthbur. Obviously, that's some years away yet, and a lot of training between."

Randel bowed gracefully.

"An honour, young sir. And what is your last name, might I ask? So that I may add it to the castle's inhabitants."

Bane was about to say he didn't have a last name when Glance spoke for him.

"Garik, like myself," Glance said, treating Bane to a wink.

"Garik. Very good. And will you be having a chamber in the castle itself?"

"He will indeed, Randel. But I will see to his accommodation. Now, if you'll excuse us, we've a busy schedule for the rest of the day."

Again, Randel bowed.

"Very good, Sirs. Then I will leave you to it."

Bane waited until the portly man had disappeared around the corner before addressing Glance.

"Who was that?"

"Mr Fittle Randel, head of housekeeping here at the castle. He'll be on his rounds making sure that everyone is doing their tasks and where they should be. He's a little stiff, but the castle wouldn't run as well as it does without him."

"Now come, I wasn't lying when I said we had a busy schedule. There's so much that I need to show and explain to you."

"Why did you tell him my last name was Garik, like yours?"

Glance shrugged as he looked down at Bane, placing a hand on both shoulders.

"Because my little nephew, we're both bastards. We cannot take the Shankil name, yet we have noble blood in our veins. In which case, we are named after the castle which we serve. You are a Garik."

"Bane Garik," Bane said, unsure of how he felt about that. What would Gelwin have thought?

They walked through the servant's entrance, the grey stone floor worn smooth, the walls unadorned with only simple oil lamps set into the walls.

"Do you know how many entrances there are into the castle?" Glance asked as they turned down a corridor, the daylight cutting through a narrow slit in the wall to slice through the gloom.

Bane shook his head.

"Six?" he guessed.

"Good," Glance said, nodding. "But you're wrong. There are eight formal entrances to the main building. Three unofficial doors which only a very few know about."

Bane's uncle slowed and checked behind them before leaning closer.

"And four more which only I know about."

He straightened and led Bane up a flight of stone steps, passing a maid who paused long enough to curtsy before hurrying on.

"Garik castle is relatively modern compared to other castles in the Kingdom. It's around three hundred years old. But it was built on top of the ruins of an older castle. It was built after the great war, which caused the Fug. Some of the walls and lower chambers, especially the dungeons and oubliette, are from that earlier castle, yet the foundations are from an even older building. There are places within these grounds that are close to two thousand years old when gods and dragons battled over the land."

Bane didn't know how many two thousand was. He guessed it was a lot.

They continued walking through many other corridors and traversing staircases. Bane could only keep a rough idea of where they were in the castle by which windows the sun shone through.

"Between the old stone, the older rocks, and the latest timber, there are many secret passageways and tunnel networks. Chambers that have been hidden for centuries, deep caverns that nobody has stepped in for millennia and even a long-ago hall, abandoned and locked in time, light never breaking beyond the sphere of a single glowing lamp."

Bane tried to imagine all those rooms, tunnels, passageways, and a hall hidden within the castle and struggled to see where it all must be.

"Is most of it underground?"

Glance nodded.

"Very clever. Most of it. Yet there are large chambers and vaults around the stone works above and even one on the other side of this wall," he said, placing a hand against the cold stone. "And only one person knows where it all is. Well, almost all of it. There are still places deep below which have yet to be investigated."

"You?"

Glance bowed.

"I am a Garik. If anyone should know the castle's secrets, it should be me. And now also you. Now come, let me show you to the kitchens. When was the last time you ate?"

A flicker of an image from the previous night came to him. A table in the inn, cold pie and an ale. He pushed the memory away before it brought back others, yet he knew that he hadn't eaten anything since the day before yesterday. Most likely, it was two days ago when Dew had saved him a wedge of cheese.

"A while," Bane answered with a shrug, his belly choosing that moment to grumble so loud that it filled the staircase they had paused on.

"This way, then. The kitchen is always busy, and Brendle has a larder fit for a king."

Glance led him along more corridors and through a huge banquet hall, although at that moment, it was empty save for a guard standing at either end. The men nodded as they passed, eyes lingering on Bane.

"I take it these are the garments that Jarl found for you last night. Do you not have anything you brought with you?"

Bane shook his head.

"I only had the one jerkin and one pair of britches. Dodd said that the hounds only needed one coat, and so did I."

Bane remembered the tears in his guardian's eyes, the drunken mess he was and the tangle he left him in. He had no more guilt to feel after what he had done last night, yet even if he did, he doubted he would feel any for Dodd.

He raised his arms.

"I'm wearing everything I own. And this was even borrowed."

"Well, we can't have that. Right, here we are."

Glance pushed through a large double door to reveal a huge kitchen.

Steam filled the air, mingling with smoke from several ovens. A wall of heat pushed back at him as he stepped through the thick atmosphere, the bubbling of water, the crackling spit of fat, the chopping of a knife against wood - all mingling with the shouts from a red-faced woman in an apron large enough to shelter beneath in a storm.

"No, cut the carrots thicker, or they'll turn to mush," she shrieked at a man who was chopping veg. He startled at the rebuke and almost lost his fingers.

"Brendle, my angel," Glance said as he glided across the chaos and took the woman's plump hand, placing it to his lips.

Brendle's red face went the colour of beetroot.

"Sir Garik," she said, the anger disappearing from her face as she smiled, appearing decades younger. "You know how to flatter a girl. You've come for food, no doubt."

"I have, but not for me."

Then Brendle's gaze fell on Bane, and her hand went to her mouth, eyes going wide.

"You poor little mite, you're as thin as a broom handle," she said, then clicking her finger at the man chopping the veg, "Drop those carrots and fetch me the cold meats from breakfast."

Her scowl softened as she once again inspected Bane.

"You'll be from Crookfell, I'll wager," she said, placing her hands on her hips. "There's only a single family from there with any meat on them, and that's the Gobbins. Come, sit down over here," she said, clearing the chopping board from a table and slapping the polished timber top.

Bane settled himself on a stool, feeling uncomfortable under the cook's scrutiny.

"Have you a name child?"

"Bane. Garik," he added afterwards, the unfamiliar word rolling around his tongue, and he was still unsure of how he felt about it.

The cook frowned as she stared up at Glance, who had raised his hands in defence.

"No, not mine. Bailin's," he said with a sheepish grin.

"Bailin's?"

Brendle put her hand to her mouth again. "Then he's Nel's?"

Glance nodded.

"Oh, my dear boy," she said, her hands finding Bane's and wringing the blood from them. "That business was awful,"

She was about to say more but stopped herself and remained tight-lipped.

"One of my favourites was young Nel. And you are the spit of Bailin when he was your age. Although, I would never have let his cheeks sink in as far as yours. You need fattening up."

Before she could say more, plates of meat arrived. Cooked chicken, thick slices of ham, mutton legs. Bane's mouth instantly filled with water as he stared at them, the smell lifting his nose as he leaned closer, belly grumbling louder than the spitting fat and bubbling steam.

"Go on, Bane, have your fill," Brendle said before turning to the man again. "Fetch a wheel of cheese and the bread; it's just come out of the oven and will still be warm."

Bane had never eaten so much in a single meal. He couldn't remember ever eating so much in an entire week.

"Now listen, young man," Brendle said when he had finished chewing the last of the chicken legs. "If you're ever hungry, you come straight to me. I'm always here, and there's always food. I won't have an empty stomach in the castle. Not so long as I'm head cook."

"Thank you," Bane said and struggled from the stool, his stomach now so full that any sudden movements might cause a rupture in his gut.

"She knew my mother?" Bane said as they left the kitchen, Brendle waving farewell to them as the doors swung closed.

"I believe so. I was away a lot in those days, yet it seems that Nel left a lasting impression on all she met in the castle, no more so than your father."

Bane recalled the day he'd seen Bailin Shankil at his mother's and Gelwin's cairn. How he'd cried and the way he had left the graves a broken man.

He shook the memory away, another that he tried not to dwell too much on. It seemed that he was doing a lot of shutting down memories lately.

He stifled a yawn as he followed Glance, but his uncle stopped.

"Did you get any sleep last night?"

"No."

Glance grinned.

"Then a full belly is the last thing you need. Come, I'll show you to your quarters."

They passed through a stone archway and into a more richly adorned part of the castle. Bane thought he had been here the previous night when Jarl led him up to Lady Felina's chambers.

"In time, when you officially take on the role of bodyguard to young Cuthbur, you will have quarters on the same floor as his. But until then, you will have my old rooms."

"Yours?"

Glance stopped outside an oak door, gripped the handle and pushed it open.

"It's been a while since I was last in here," he said, gesturing for Bane to step through ahead of him.

The room was impressively large, big enough to cover the entire floor of the hovel he had grown up in twice over.

He ventured further inside, taking in the large four-poster bed with fresh-smelling linen, a deep red cloth hanging between the posts, matching the thick drapes that were on either side of the leaded window, the mountain looming in the distance with Crookfell between. A writing table stood against the far wall, beneath a lamp, shelves of books beside it.

On the chimney breast was a portrait of a battle scene, the soldiers locked in a ferocious fight; some wore the Shankil coat of arms while many others bared emblems of a strange, scaled claw that Bane didn't recognise.

"It's the final battle of Ghrone Deep," Glance said as he closed the door behind him. "It happened in the early part of the last century. Dalen Shankil led the last charge that broke the Ghasten armies. Outnumbered and after fighting for weeks on the southern borders, they pushed the Ghastens back down to the coast."

"Dalen Shankil," Bane repeated, taking in the central warrior, sword bloodied, several dead lying at his feet, and a silver sword held high.

"Our great-great, I forget how many, great-grandfather. The picture was my favourite, so I moved it to my chamber as a boy. And now the chamber is yours.

"Mine?"

Bane turned on the spot, taking in more detail, a heavy wardrobe, a set of drawers."

"Truly?"

Glance nodded, matching the grin Bane was feeling, pulling his cheeks tight.

"One of two. You see, this is where the castle will expect you to be. Where they expect you to sleep and where Randel will come for you when summoned. However, that is only one of two Banes: the bodyguard in training, the soldier, the Slayer of Crookfell. The other is apprenticed to me. The Bane that dwells in the shadows, which is silent and invisible, and only three other people know of his existence. That Bane has another chamber, away from prying eyes."

"I have another room?"

Glance crossed the chamber and opened the wardrobe. He pushed the clothes aside and leaned in. There was a metallic click, and then Glance ducked into the wardrobe.

"This way," he called out.

Bane peered inside the wardrobe, past the many garments hanging on the rail. Another room was on the other side, where the back of the wardrobe should be.

"Be careful to pull the front doors of the wardrobe closed."

Bane shuffled backwards, closing the doors as he went. And then righted the clothes so they hung like they did before.

When he turned, he found himself standing at the foot of a spiral staircase.

"This is where you'll be spending most of your time," Glance said as he ascended the staircase.

In the gloom, Bane could make out the shape of his uncle as he reached for a lamp on a wall hook and struck a flint and steel box to light a flame. An amber glow soon filled the old stonework, revealing the layers of dust and cobwebs that filled the gaps and corners.

"As you can see, nobody ever comes this way. And it's been some years since I ventured this route."

The spiral staircase led them up to a circular room that was bigger than the bed chamber they'd left. The ceiling was high with thick rafters festooned with the dust and webs which covered the rest of the walls and floor. Glance trailed a hand along the stonework as if searching for something, then gripped a long shard of masonry and pulled it free.

Daylight sliced through the air, revealing more of the round chamber.

Another spiral staircase at the far end led up, disappearing into darkness. There was an archway to the side of it and another looming darkness beyond.

"Look down," Glance said, lowering the lamp. "See how there's only one set of footprints. Mine. I've stepped in the same places every time I come through here. I suggest you do the same."

"Because the floor's rotten and might give way?" Bane asked, aware that he had stepped outside Glance's footprints.

"No, the castle is solid, and it'll be so, long after we're gone. Think."

"Then is it so that we know if we're being followed or that someone else has come this way."

Glance clicked his fingers.

"Exactly. As you can see, the layers of ancient dust have left the perfect trap to catch anyone who trespasses in our passageways.

Bane nodded and then stifled another yawn.

"Perhaps we've reached your limit today. It would be easy to get lost in the secret tunnels, and we don't want you falling to your death or getting your head stoved in with falling masonry on your first day as my apprentice. Let's return to your chamber and begin afresh tomorrow."

Bane was about to say that he was fine to continue, but another yawn took him by surprise, and this one set Glance off.

"And now you've got me doing it," he said, gesturing for Bane to return to the staircase.

Careful to step on the same footprints as they came up in, Bane returned to the secret wardrobe door and pulled it open before climbing through.

"Might I suggest that you don't try to go back through without me," Glance said as he closed the wardrobe doors behind him. "Now, it's early evening, and it's prudent that you have a full night's sleep."

His uncle smiled as he crossed the room, resting a hand on the door as he paused.

"You'll find my old clothes and boots in the chest and wardrobe. Some of which I wore when I was your age, so some will likely fit. You're welcome to take what you want. I no longer have use for them. And we will see about getting you fitted with new attire.

"Truly? I can keep them?"

Bane suddenly felt fully awake again. The clothes that he was now wearing that Jarl had given him were the richest garments he had ever put on, and they were shabby compared to what he had seen in the wardrobe.

"Truly. Now get some sleep. You'll be with Jarl in the morning, and as I remember, he's pretty hard on new recruits."

Glance opened the door and was about to step out, leaving Bane alone.

"Uncle,"

Glance stopped on the threshold.

"What exactly am I an apprentice of?"

He took a deep breath before stepping back into the room. Coming close enough to Bane so that he might whisper.

"The darkness. The shadows. You may feel tired now, yet most of our work is done at night. We serve the castle, we serve the Shankils, and the tasks that come with it are many. We'll speak more of it tomorrow with a fresh mind. Now get some rest."

13

Reputations

The white sheets gathered as Bane shifted, the soft cotton sliding over his body, and no matter which position he twisted in, he had never felt more comfortable in his life.

He'd laid back on the four-poster bed the previous evening when Glance left him. Only to see if it was as soft as it appeared. The next thing he knew, he had awoken in the dead of night, shivering with the draft that blew through the open window.

He had then stripped from his clothes and climbed between the sheets, the contented smile never leaving his lips until sleep claimed him once again.

Now he lay there, eyes closed and wishing Gelwin knew where he was, how he was doing. Maybe she did.

He stretched, turned and buried his face into the pillow again, feeling himself float away.

"Master Garik, Sir?"

Bane became aware of knocking at the door to his chamber.

"Master Garik?"

He then realised that Master Garik was himself. He sat up as the door opened, and a young errand boy slipped into his room, nervous hands fiddling with his cap as he stared at Bane.

"Forgive my intrusion, Sir. But you're wanted in the practice yard."

"Practice yard? Fug it!" Bane snapped, finding the morning light spilling through the gap in the drapes.

He'd slept in.

"How late am I?" Bane asked the boy as he clambered from the bed and quickly scrambled into the clothes from the previous day. There was no time to sort through the chest or wardrobe to find anything else.

"I don't know, Sir, but the new fledglings have been swinging practice swords since before I had breakfast."

"No," Bane swallowed, feeling a rising panic, yet it was no good getting flustered.

"What's your name?"

The boy placed the cap back on his head, shifting awkwardly from foot to foot.

"Kip, Sir."

Bane offered him a reassuring smile. It was clear that he was unsure, nervous even. He had to be no older than eight winters old.

"Kip, can you show me the quickest way to the practice yard, and you can drop the 'Sir'."

Kip grinned as he nodded enthusiastically.

"This way, S, what do I call you?"

Bane followed him out into the corridor, closing the door behind him.

"Bane. Did Jarl send for me? Did he seem angry?" he asked, staring about the corridors and trying to get a sense of where he was and looking for things to recognise for when he returned. That was if Jarl didn't send him back to Crookfell.

He couldn't believe he was late for his first day as a fledgling.

"The Master of Arms is always angry when he's in the practice yard," Kip replied, offering Bane a sympathetic smile.

They passed the kitchens and Bane's belly grumbled again. If he'd gotten up earlier he would have been able to eat before he left.

Eventually, they passed through the servant's entrance to the castle and out into the bailey. They followed a cobbled path that hugged the perimeter wall and down steps to the practice yard.

The clacking of wooden swords filled the grassed area, bouncing from the stone walls, accompanied by the harsh tones of Jarl as he rebuked and cursed the young men before him.

"Thank you, Kip. I doubt I would have found my way here as quickly."

Kip nodded and then flinched as Jarl spotted them.

"Fledgling Garik. Get your arse over here and pick up a bloody sword," the knight shouted.

"Good luck, Master Bane," Kip said before he turned on his heels and ran off leaving Bane staring after him.

"Are you deaf as well as late?"

Bane hurried across the open patch of grassland, the wind picking up and cooling his burning cheeks. Everyone was staring. Jarl, the other fledglings, including Cuthbur, who seemed ready to smile but glanced away as his neighbour began to laugh and point at Bane. There was another instructor alongside Jarl, a man with wide shoulders and an ugly grimace. His glare was worse of all, dark eyes smouldering above a beard as black as pitch.

"There are no privileges in the practice yard, Garik," the instructor said as he pointed at a barrel of practice swords leaning against the wall. "Take one and line up."

Bane stepped up to the barrel, picked out the first sword he grasped and pulled it free. It was battered but seemed solid enough.

"Line up, I said," the instructor yelled, spit flying from white teeth.

The fledglings hurried to form a line in front of the two men, some with eager faces wishing to please, others with disdain as if they preferred to be elsewhere; Cuthbur was one of these, and another, a tall, rangy youth of maybe seventeen winters, strolled casually as if the instructors were lucky to have him there.

"I've seen your forms – pitiful," Jarl snapped as he paced slowly along the line, eyeing each fledging, the burly instructor at his side. "Whether you're of noble blood, a son of a high-ranking knight," his glare lingered on the rangy youth, "Or a budding soldier wanting to join the ranks and fight for the Baron, the King, the country – you're all the same, you are fledglings."

He reached Bane, blue stare boring into him and bringing cold sweat to his brow before turning and pacing back along the line.

"It is only day one. You think you may know how to swing that lump of wood in your hands, but you are wrong. You know nothing."

"But rest assured, you snivelling weak-wristed worms, Sargent Bullif and I will sculpt you into warriors."

He paused at the centre of the line and looked up and down.

"Do any of you have any questions?"

"Sir?" asked the rangy one, a cocky grin on his face. "Is it true that a Crookfell commoner bested a band of raiders? A simple turnip plucker by the name of Bones?

My father believes it's nonsense. The villagers don't know how to hold a spade properly, let alone a sword."

He laughed and others along the line laughed with him.

Bane noticed that Cuthbur wasn't one of them.

"The Crookfell Slayer? I've heard the rumour," Jarl said as he approached the boy. "And regardless of what Sir Hemmel says, a man from any walk of life can stick a sharp bit of steel in you."

"But is it true?"

Another boy, one of the eager ones, licked his lips as he stepped out of the line excitedly.

"I heard that he now lives in the castle," he said, pointing back at the huge stone building behind them as if none of them knew where the castle was. "He's taller than an oak and just as wide."

"Get back in line," Bullif snarled, and the boy leapt back, almost toppling in his haste.

Bane clenched a fist around the hilt of the practice sword, feeling a coldness sweep through him, and not from the biting wind.

"My Da said the Slayer strangled a shadow leopard," said a smaller boy, dressed in plainer clothes than the rest.

"Shut up, stable boy. You're Da doesn't know anything outside of rutting horses," said the rangy youth, sneering at the smaller fledgling.

"Have you not listened to a word I've said, Hemmel? All are equal in the yard. Whether you're the son of a knight or the son of a stable master. Do you understand me?" Jarl snapped.

Hemmel sniffed, looked Jarl up and down and then nodded, although that cocky sneer returned.

"The Slayers name is Bane," Jarl continued in a calmer voice. "If you want the facts. And he faced off five raiders and two shadow leopards, unarmed and alone. He stood up for what is right and killed to protect another. And yes, he is now resident in the castle."

Heat rose within Bane, not shame but something of that ilk. He wished the knight would stop talking about him. At least nobody there but Cuthbur knew the truth and he hoped it would stay that way.

"Now pair up. You've gone through the forms, or at least tried to. Now let's see how you fair against each other."

Bane watched as the boys faced off each other, Hemmel surveying the group as if deciding who might be good enough to take him on, chest pushed out as he pointed his sword at the stable boy.

There were nineteen of them, and so with everyone now paired, he was standing alone on the edge, which was fine with him.

He watched as the wooden swords began to clatter against each other, the youths pulling faces, some grimacing with the effort while others flinched, the stable boy even closing his eyes as Hammel viciously attacked with harsh strikes from above, beating his opponent down.

Cuthbur was exchanging blows with another dressed in similar rich garb. Most likely from noble stock, both trying to hit the other's sword and not aiming for the body itself.

Jarl and Bullif wandered between the fighting boys, expressions grim as they shook their heads.

"I've seen more fight in a frog pond," Bullif growled as he stared at Cuthbur. "Aim for the body; you know the forms, and you," he looked to the other, "Stop dancing around like a roosting chicken without a nest."

A scream cut through the fledglings as the stable boy dropped to the ground, a red welt opening up on his brow, but it was his arm that he was holding.

Hemmel stood over him and placed the tip of his sword against his neck. He stared around to ensure everyone was watching before he withdrew his sword and pointed at another boy.

"You, fight me."

The fledgling looked startled and was about to shake his head until Jarl gestured for him to move up to Hemmel.

"You'll get bruises. You'll get welts and grazes, may even break the skin," Bullif said as he continued pacing. "And the more you carry, the faster you'll learn."

Jarl stalked the other way, weaving between the boys.

"And be sure of this, my little fledglings. It's better to learn the thick of your lessons while you hold a wooden sword because when you come to grip steel, the bruises become cuts, the welts and grazes become open wounds and possibly loss of limbs."

Bullif paused beside the stable boy and easily heaved him from the grass as if he weighed no more than a straw doll.

"And if you haven't learned all we can teach before you join the ranks of the army, then your enemies will become your teachers," he said.

It seemed to Bane like it was a well-practised speech, most likely said by the pair each time new recruits came to the castle. But what they said resonated with him.

Bullif pushed the stable boy towards Bane, only managing to stop himself as Bane caught him by the shoulder to prevent him from falling once again.

"Thanks," he mumbled. "Fugging harsh, aren't they?"

He took up position before him, sword held out and ready to attack.

Bane nodded.

"I think they have to be. You've got blood running into your eye," he pointed out.

"Thanks," the boy repeated, wiping a sleeve across his brow. "I'm Bon."

"Garik," Bane replied, feeling that now Jarl had revealed that the Slayer was called Bane, he couldn't use it.

Another yell from a fledgling as Hemmel shoved the boy he was fighting to the ground. He made a show of spinning his blade around his hand and reversing his grip before driving it down into his opponent's chest.

"You ought to be thanking me," he said, raising the sword to bring it down again. "After all, the more bruises, the better you'll learn. Shame there's no one here to give me a bruise or two."

He grinned wickedly as he pointed at Cuthbur.

Bane was sure that Jarl wouldn't allow it, but the knight nodded, although he noticed that the knight's jaw was clenched.

We are all equals in the practice yard.

To his credit, Cuthbur stepped up to Hemmel, nodding to himself as if he was gathering the determination to at least try.

"Ready?" Bon asked, pulling Bane's gaze away from the boy he had sworn to protect.

Bane nodded and set his feet.

Bon came at him, both hands throttling the grip of his sword as he slashed out.

Bane caught the sword with his own, twisting his wrist and deflecting the blade down.

He pivoted into Falling-Star and jabbed with the hilt, hitting Bon in the shoulder. Not so hard that it would hurt but solid enough to feel.

As he finished his turn, he once again adopted a defensive stance, noticing that Bullif was watching, grimace fixed beneath the thick black beard but a subtle dip of the head in recognition of the move.

"Next." Hemmel bellowed.

Cuthbur was on his back, sword in the dirt as he nursed his forearm.

Above him, Hemmel waved his sword around as he chose his next victim.

Bane was so caught up in what was happening with Cuthbur that he didn't have time to react as Bon dipped in low and struck him solidly in the stomach, driving the wind from him.

"Ouch, sorry, Garik," Bon said, stepping away. "It's just that you were so quick the last time that I thought you'd deflect it."

Bane managed to draw in a ragged breath as he straightened up.

"No, my fault. Besides, the more bruises, the better the lesson, right?"

Bon's concern melted away as he nodded, yet Bane caught Bullif shaking his head as he moved on to watch another pair clack swords together.

"Four down, and not a single touch," Hemmel boasted as he stepped over another unlucky fledgling sprawled on the ground.

"I wish someone would give him a good lesson," Bon said, catching Bane's gaze as they stared at Hemmel as he tried to fight two boys at once. "He's been taught sword skills by his father. If you ask me, having a Da that's a serving knight is an unfair advantage."

Hemmel kicked one of the two and backhanded the other, both boys stumbling away, red-faced with shame.

"He's a bully. I've had to deal with one of those before," Bane admitted.

Hemmel caught them watching, disdain curling his lips into a sneer.

"What are you looking at, Garik, is it? Named after the castle. So, you're a bastard, no doubt. And judging by the oversized clothes and gaunt look, not begotten from anyone of note."

Everyone stopped fighting with each other to watch; even Cuthbur lifted his head from his injured arm, head sweeping from Hemmel to Bane and back.

"Don't worry yourself, fledgling. I don't expect you to fight me. You're not worth my time," he said, then turned to face others. "Maybe if I fought three of you…"

"Enough," Jarl bellowed, gesturing for them all to form a line. Glaring at Hemmel as the boy sauntered into position like a prized peacock and shoved Bon out of the way.

"Hopefully, you've all tasted a bruise or two and gotten a feel for a sword in hand. Like I said, you'll all get them and the more you get, the more you'll learn. Work hard for me and Bullif, and we'll make warriors out of every single one of you."

Hemmel chuckled as he raised a hand.

"How am I supposed to learn amongst this shower of wet rats? I'll not get any bruises from this lot of turnip pluckers."

"None of us are from Crookfell," Cuthbur argued, the determination returning to him. "And your height and prior training have you at an advantage."

"Advantage? You're grandson to the Baron. I don't know why you're even here. You'll never need to fight in battles. You'll have us knights doing that for you," Hemmel said, nodding towards Jarl as if grouping himself with the experienced warrior.

Cuthbur gripped tightly to his sword as if he might attack Hemmel, yet Jarl broke the tension.

"Perhaps we have time for another lesson today. Hemmel, step out here. You too, Garik."

The tattoo beneath the vambrace flamed with heat at the mention of his name, yet Bane didn't let it show.

Hemmel cockily sauntered out in front of the line of fledglings, sneering at Bane as he stepped out before him.

"Face each other," Jarl ordered, catching Bane's eye and nodding confidently. "Use the forms you've been taught," he said to the pair of them.

Bane gritted his teeth as he positioned his feet, hearing Hemmel sigh, yet the youth took up an attacking stance with blade arm high.

The fledglings watched on, Bon nodding with encouragement while the others showed sympathy, especially those that had already experienced Hemmel's blade. Only Cuthbur watched on with anticipation, a grin creeping onto his lips.

Bane only hoped that he wouldn't let his future charge down.

"Fight," Jarl ordered.

The word was still ringing in the air as Hemmel crashed forward, sword whipping underarm and catching Bane beneath his sternum, the exact place where Bon had struck him only moments before.

Bane bent over, struggled to catch a breath, caught the flickering of shadow and was struck with a cracking blow to the elbow.

His sword dropped as his entire lower arm went numb.

The shadows moved again, and on impulse, he rolled his shoulder and leaned out of the way as Hemmel's sword came down, splitting the air where his head had been.

"Is that it?" Hemmel laughed as he came on with another thrust.

Bane twisted his hips and allowed the blade to carry past as he spun out of the way.

Before Hemmel whirled on him, he dug the toe of his boot beneath his fallen sword and flicked it up into his waiting hand.

He caught and parried the next thrust, observing how Hemmel moved, seeing his heel pivot as he stepped into the next form, but Bane was already moving the other way, Rising Star – deflecting a slice, the two woods slamming together and sliding along each other's length.

Spinning Thistle – a dip of the shoulder, left arm out for balance, ducking beneath a weak cut, Stalking Crane – dancing away from a high slice, catching a fist with his vambrace.

Hemmel was more skilled than Kulby, yet Bane recognised the next form and saw that his opponent was attacking harshly, overreaching with an aggressive blow.

Bane stepped through, reversing the grip on his sword; twisted so Hemmel's blade missed, the momentum carrying him on, head coming down as Bane's hilt came up.

Gasps escaped the fledglings as Hemmel's head jerked up, his body following it as he fell, landing hard on his back.

Bane kicked the fallen blade away and placed his own, tip first, to the youth's throat.

Hemmel stared up, confusion widening his eyes, a line of blood running from his nose.

"Another valuable lesson," Jarl laughed, slamming a hand down on Bane's shoulder and making him jump. "Never assume the enemy is weak, aye Bane?"

"Bane?" Hemmel said as he sat up, the confusion now replaced by recognition. "Bane, the Crookfell Slayer?"

Murmuring escaped the fledglings once again and even Bullif watched on, still with that grimace of his yet he gave an approving nod.

"Yes," Jarl continued as he grinned down at the youth on the grass. "A simple turnip plucker from Crookfell, a bastard Garik, and the boy who just put you on your arse. There is never a second chance when two men are trying to kill each other. Never assume your enemy is weaker than yourself."

Bane offered his hand to Hemmel, thinking that the boy would most likely slap it away, yet was surprised to find that the fallen youth was smiling as he grasped it and was pulled to his feet.

"If I were to be bested by anyone, at least I can say it was the Slayer," he said, putting fingers to his nose and wincing.

They both stood back in line, yet Bane felt that all of the fledglings were now staring at him. He tried to ignore it, wondering why Jarl had chosen to reveal who he was.

"That'll do for today. I expect you all here tomorrow, on time," Jarl said, gaze wondering over Bane, "and leaving all prejudices behind."

As the fledglings began to place their practice swords away, Cuthbur caught Bane's attention and laughed.

"That was well done, Bane. I didn't get the chance to watch you fight the raiders the other night, but judging by what I saw, I'm sure it was impressive. And Hemmel had it coming."

They both watched him leave, sauntering away from the practice yard as if he hadn't just been knocked down.

"Egos like his never accommodate doubt, but at least you taught him a lesson."

"And I can't believe I had a bout with you – the Crookfell Slayer," Bon said, grinning from ear to ear. "And I even caught you with a blow."

"That you did," Bane laughed, rubbing his stomach where he'd been struck twice that morning.

"Bane?" Jarl called, summoning him away from the others.

Bane left the fledglings at the barrel while he caught up with Jarl, who was now walking back towards the castle.

"I'm sorry I was late," Bane said as he began pacing beside him, knowing that he was about to be rebuked, although he saw Jarl grinning.

They stopped beside the wall, a tall bundle leaning against the stonework.

"In a way, I'm glad you did. They're green, and apart from Hemmel, they couldn't adopt a single form.

Fledglings seem to be getting greener every time we take on new recruits," he said as he picked up the bundle and unwrapped the bindings.

Bane recognised the hilt.

"I managed to find an old scabbard that fits your sword," he said, handing Bane the weapon he'd earned by killing a man.

"It wasn't easy. The blade is an unusual length. It is longer than most swords, and the hilt is larger to accommodate both hands. Although someway shorter than a traditional long sword."

Bullif joined them, dark eyes soaking up Bane and making him feel like he was constantly being judged. "It can be used combined with either shield or axe or more usually alone.

"And you should know, Sargent, it's the style you choose to adopt," Jarl said.

"The scabbard belonged to you?" Bane asked.

Bullif nodded as he grasped the hilt and drew the blade. He held it up to the sun, admiring the steel. He performed several lethal thrusts before slipping it back where it came from.

"Its former owner knew how to look after it, kept the blade keen, the steel oiled. I trust you'll do the same."

"I will. Thank you," Bane said as he placed the belt around his waist and tried to buckle it, yet it was far too big."

"No, lad. The sword is too long to wear like other swords. This one straps to your back," Jarl said as he helped Bane slip the harness over his shoulders.

It was a solid weight that ran down his spine yet wasn't uncomfortable.

"Once you've been wearing it for a while, you'll get used to it," Bullif said.

"And Bullif will be giving you extra lessons with it if you wish to learn. Of course, I'll still be teaching you skills with sword and shield. Now you better run along. I'm sure Glance will have work for you to do."

Bane thanked them and was about to leave when he stopped.

"Why did you tell the others who I was?" he asked, feeling as though he'd been made a fool of.

"Reputation," Jarl answered with a shrug. "The rumours are already flying around the castle. You're the talk in the guardroom, the barracks, the stable – even the nobles are asking questions. And a reputation goes a long way and will offer you favours, gain you friends, and as you're new to the castle, and as Hemmel put it, 'a turnip plucker,' you'll need every advantage you can get. Better you own the name Slayer than the servants begin suspecting someone else and before you know it, a random man from the village will be given the credit. Do you think the likes of Kulby would deny being the Slayer if he was asked?"

Bane knew that Kulby would relish having a reputation like that.

"I don't want it."

"Understandable, Bane. But see it this way: your father, the Northern Death, as some call him, will already have his enemies fearing him because of that name."

"Not to mention that his skill with the blade is unmatched," Bullif added.

"A name is hard to earn. Some great warriors who have fought in every battle south for the past decade still haven't gained a name or a reputation. So, I say this, own it. It doesn't mean you have to be boastful. Let others do that for you."

"Is Bailin…my father, really as good as the stories?"

Jarl looked to Bullif, and they both grinned.

"There's not been the like since Dalen Shankil. Who happens to be a forefather of yours."

"I know. I have a painting of him in my chamber."

"I wouldn't mind seeing that sometime," Jarl replied. "I'll see you in the morning, and don't be late."

Bane nodded and waved farewell, then set off to find his uncle. No doubt he wanted to begin the lessons of this other Bane, which he was supposed to be.

He entered the servant's entrance and, by keeping to the side of the castle that faced the mountain, managed to find his chamber, only having to turn back on three occasions when he got lost.

Someone had been in his room since he had gone. The bed had been made with fresh linen. He guessed it must have been one of the maids. On the table was a lamp, which hadn't been there before, and beside it was a piece of parchment. He picked it up to study yet couldn't read a word of the scrawly writing. The only person from Crookfell who could read was Nan Hilga. There were diagrams to go along with the writing, but there was no point in deciphering its meaning. He'll ask Glance when he shows up.

His gaze drifted to the bed, remembering how comfortable it felt; he took several steps, wondering if he could fit a light nap in, then noticed new garments laid on the chest.

There was a cloak, tunic and britches, all in greens so dark that they were almost black.

They were the same which his uncle wore. On the floor was a pair of tall boots. He picked one up and felt the softness of the leather.

They were most likely the richest pair of boots he'd ever held.

He looked down at his own shabby hand-me-down boots, which were worn thin by Dodd before he passed them on.

If they were left by his chest, along with the dark garments, then they were meant for him.

He perched on the edge of the chair by the table, wondering if his thoughts were true. Should he put them on? Maybe he ought to wait for Glance. There was so much to learn in the castle, so many ways that were alien to him, and he didn't want to get anything wrong.

He unslung the sword, about to place it on the bed, but felt an impulse to pull it free.

The steel rang as it slid from the scabbard, the polished metal catching the rays that came through the window and reflecting them onto the ceiling with all the colours of a rainbow.

He rubbed a thumb along the edge, testing the sharpness. It was the gentlest of touches, but he felt the steel bite and a bead of blood ran over the pad of his thumb.

It was his. He's earned it by killing a man.

"Raif," he said, the name sounding loud in the quiet chamber.

He didn't know why, but he guessed that he ought to remember it. The name of the man who had owned the sword before. Maybe Raif had done the same at some point in the past. Maybe the sword had been passed from killer to killer. Perhaps Bane was only the next in line, a short transition as it went onto the next, the man that would end his life.

The Crookfell Slayer.

Bane slid the sword away and dropped it onto the bed. He then picked up the garments.

Own your reputation.

Bane undressed and changed into the dark green garb, feeling the material's quality and smoothness as it flowed over his skin. And the boots felt as though they moulded to his feet. He put the shoulder harness and sword back on before the cloak, the hilt poking through the top of the neck in easy reach.

He stalked around the chamber, the soles of the new boots so soft that he didn't make a sound.

He twisted this way and that, stretched his arms and spun around. The garments offered him free movement, unlike his old stiff leather tunic, which was restricting.

He went back to the desk and picked up the parchment once again.

He stared at the diagrams and recognised a crude drawing of the wardrobe, lines drawn horizontally and then a large circle and an archway with an arrow pointing through it.

He looked at the lamp and found a small flint and steel box beside it.

It was then that he realised what the images were. The wardrobe, the lines, which represented the staircase, and the circle were supposed to be the circular room above.

The parchment was instructions for him to follow.

Bane checked the chamber door was shut properly and then opened the wardrobe, grabbed the lamp and disappeared inside.

14

In The Shadows

The lamp took on the second strike, and he stowed the strike box in one of the many pockets he found in his jerkin and closed the hidden door in the back of the wardrobe.

A draft picked up and tussled his hair as he ascended the spiral staircase, ensuring that his boots fell into the prints left from the previous day.

He thought about calling out to Glance yet remembered that his uncle had warned him to remain silent in the passageways.

After a single turn, the steps came out into the circular room. The glow from the lamp was barely bright enough to chase the darkness into the corners, yet it was enough to see that Glance wasn't here. The staircase at the other end appeared like a rectangle of blackness, while the archway was fixed in a permanent yawn, the darkness looming beyond.

He took out the parchment and held it to the light, affirming that the arrow pointed through the picture of the archway.

Stepping in the old footsteps, Bane made his way across the circular room to the archway. He held the lamp high, the light catching a mouse that scurried into a crack that split the floor from the stone wall.

Spiders clung to webs in the ancient eaves; several that had been hanging hastily climbed up the silver threads they'd been dangling from, tiny black orbs staring back at him.

He hated spiders.

An eery tingle crept down the nape of his neck, playing with his nerves, and he began to pick out shapes in the gloom.

He felt as though someone else was there.

Swallowing a rising fear, Bane slipped his sword from its scabbard, the steel whispering as it was drawn.

The solid weight of the weapon lent him reassurance as he paced further into the room.

It was littered with broken furniture. Old stools, dining tables, split barrels rotting on the floor and casting strange shadows that seemed to dance as he moved.

The thorns beneath the vambrace began to itch as the tattoo sensed something sinister. The lamp lit him up, a victim, easy to see, easy to attack from the myriad of dark places.

He took another step and heard a scrape behind him.

He whirled, blade raised, but saw nothing but his own imprints in the dust.

His imagination was getting the best of him.

Maybe he ought to return to his chamber and wait for Glance to come to him.

No.

The parchment had been left for him to find. This was a test; he was sure of it.

After a few more steps, he found another archway ahead - or at the least, half the archway. The roof had partially collapsed, a slab of stone leaning at an odd angle on the ground, revealing a small triangular hole barely large enough for him to squeeze through.

He knelt and placed the lamp on the floor, attempting to see further into the hole, but saw that it was covered with rocks and rubble and was impassable.

As he rose, he heard another scrape. This one was much closer and was followed by the intake of a breath.

"Who's there?" he asked, hearing the panic in his own voice.

Was it Raif came back from the dead, wishing to take his sword and avenge his death?

Only his echo answered him.

The scurrying of tiny feet and something ran over the toe of his boot. A third scrape to his right and the sound of brittle wood snapping.

Bane twisted towards the noise, his heel catching a crack in the floor, and he toppled.

He flung out his arms to keep balance, and the lamp gutted out.

"Fug it," he hissed as he placed the lamp beside his feet and searched his pocket for the strike box.

Then spun in the direction of another drawn breath, followed by a sharp laugh – a glimmer of a blade coming towards him.

Bane readied himself for Raif's attack, hastily planting his feet and gripping the sword with both hands.

"Like a scared mouse," came a voice out of the gloom.

Bane turned to the threat and watched a spark arc from a hand and the sound of a strike box being struck. A thundering heartbeat later, and a lamp lit up Glance's grin.

"And you were louder than a Bongalo band on midwinter feast night."

Bane put a hand to his chest and felt the hammering slowly calm beneath.

"I told you to be as quiet as you could in the instructions," Glance said as he placed a glass cylinder over his lamp and the entire room lit up.

Bane produced the parchment from his pocket and held it out to his uncle.

"I can't read," he said, sliding his sword away, or at least tried to. It took a few attempts to find the hole with the blade's tip before he finally slid it away.

"That, my little apprentice, is something that must be remedied. I'll have a word with Mr Pensulby. He's already teaching others. He'll find room to teach you. He owes me a few favours - it won't be a problem. Now, come with me."

Bane hastily picked up his lamp and followed Glance as he began to walk between the broken furniture, walking in a strange loping fashion as he placed his feet down in odd locations.

Without questioning him, Bane did the same, placing his boots into Glance's prints.

"My old master told me that the man he was apprenticed to laid this mess of scrap wood here to hide the other door. Anyone who had the misfortune to stumble upon this chamber would find the collapsed arch and think it a dead end."

"That's what I thought," Bane admitted as he watched his uncle begin to descend a narrow staircase hidden behind a broken table that was on its side.

It went down several steps before ending in an even narrower passage.

"Stay close. There's a long drop further along. One that disappears into the bowels of the foundations."

Walking side on and head bent low, they made their way through the twisting tunnel until Glance stopped.

"Here it is. Now the stone on the edges is a little soft, so step well clear of it."

Glance gripped a rock that was jutting out from the wall and stretched his leg across a hole that ran from wall to wall and was as wide as a man's shoulders.

Not as scary as he first imagined, yet as Bane stared down into the impenetrable gloom beneath, he realised that if he fell through, his body would most likely never be seen again.

"Now, there's a knack to this," his uncle said as the passageway ended. The wall before them was mainly earth and dust, crusting rough stone beneath. There was no way through.

He watched as his uncle turned to face the wall on the left, which looked much the same. But as Bane watched him push his hand through a cleverly hidden hole, he heard a metallic click, and that section of the wall swung inwards.

"This was an opening a long time ago, most likely centuries. At some point, somebody created this hidden door. Simple and effective. Come."

Bane had expected another passageway, possibly even steps to a grimy chamber layered with dust, yet was surprised to find that he stepped through into a cosy circular room with sunlight pouring through tall leaded windows. The floor was cleanly swept, and long, comfortable chairs and a large oak table sat at its centre. Shelves of books covered the walls, reaching twice as high as a man, and a ladder was propped against a thick stone column at one end where a spiral staircase led down as well as up.

"Welcome to our study room," Glance said as he blew his lamp out and closed the concealed door behind them.

The door was cleverly disguised as bookshelves on this side of the wall.

"This is where you'll spend most of your time as my apprentice. Over the next few years, I expect you to have read most of these books."

Bane slowly turned in a circle, staring up and wondering how many pages there were surrounded by. What was that number that Glance had used yesterday?

Thousands?

"There's a wealth of knowledge here, a lot more than you'll find in other libraries, and that's including the King's library down in the Capital. The royal librarian would commit murder to have a chance to enter. Actually, a lot of the books here, my predecessor and I had pilfered from the King's palace. We've got maps and atlases from all around the world, shipping charts, laws, and a list of Kings, lords, Dukes and Barons – where they live and what armies they command. Shelves dedicated to plant lore, animals, the weather…if it's been studied and noted, we will have a copy."

Bane wondered how a human head could contain it all without bulging and springing open like an overstuffed apple barrel after harvest.

"Who else knows about this place?" Bane asked as he felt the plush velvet cushions on the seats and wondered how something could be so soft.

He crossed to the window and peered outside. The mountain was in the distance, the silver halo of fog choking it as it was on its rise.

The view was the same as the one from his own chambers, only higher up, which meant this room was on the same side of the castle as his own.

"Only two people. Me and you. It's the most exclusive library to get into. Now come, let me show you around. On top of the books, you'll be learning a little alchemy," his uncle continued as he motioned for Bane to follow. They entered the staircase and began to ascend.

"If you follow the stairs down, you'll come to my quarters. Like your chamber, the only access to here is through a hidden door."

"But wouldn't somebody count the windows and work out there were hidden rooms up here?"

"No, and I'll show you why, come."

The stairs twisted around twice, light coming in through slits in the walls on both sides which meant they were climbing a tower. The stairs continued, but they paused beside another door, an acrid smell coming from beneath the ancient wood.

"Do you know what alchemy is? The fundamental elements, different metals, medicines – poisons?"

Bane shook his head, noticing a red glow flickering beneath the door as if there was a smouldering fire on the other side.

"Then until you do, this room is out of bounds."

They continued up the steps, which wound eight more times before emerging out into the open.

Harsh gusts swept over crumbling ramparts and whistled through the circular roof, picking up dust and swirling it around.

The grey sky was heavy with moisture, clinging to the greyer surfaces and devouring everything that wasn't stone.

Bane stared through the slits of his lids as he gathered the cloak about him and stepped out onto the roof.

He was the highest he'd ever been.

Moss moulded around his fingers as he pressed a hand against the top of the ramparts, seeing the rest of the castle spread out below him in a network of slanting roofs, hard edges and sharp corners. Chimneys poked up here and there, smoke curling from the blackened spouts, birds' nests wedged into the corners of eaves. The peaks of the other four towers were also below, and the perimeter wall was lower still.

"You see how the ramparts of the other towers only face out, and the walkway on the perimeter has a low wall on the outer edge and a tall wall on the inner?"

Bane slowly nodded.

"Good. Tell me how many men do you see from up here? In the castle and its grounds."

The gusts picked up, dust and dry moss stinging his face as Bane stared down.

"I don't see any."

Glance offered him a knowing smile.

"That's because there's no walkway, upper window or balcony facing inwards. The tower we're standing on is at the centre of the castle. The tallest in Garik, yet it's invisible to everyone – lost amidst the many rooftops and spires. And I've ridden every which way around the lands outside and the only places you can see it from are so far away that it can barely be made out.

"Apart from the hidden chambers and secret tunnels below, it's the loneliest place in the castle."

Another gust cut across the open space, taking Bane's cloak and dragging him off his feet until his uncle caught him.

"And the windiest. You need to bulk up a little. Did you have breakfast?"

Bane shook his head.

"Then your first lesson begins here. I want you to make your way to the kitchens by way of your chamber, fill your belly and then meet me at the stables. And Bane, try to tread more quietly. The secret tunnels will only remain a secret if nobody knows you are there."

Bane retraced his steps, going back down the tower to the study room and through the secret door behind the bookshelf. He was thankful for the lamp as he doubted he would have found his way back without it.

Once in his room, he brushed the dust from his dark cloak and tunic and then went to the kitchen.

"Look at you, Master Bane. In your fine clothes, just like Master Glance." Brendle said, arms wobbling as she placed them on her hips. "Now, I expect you're hungry. Sit right there and I'll bring you some meats."

Brendle didn't let him leave until she was satisfied he couldn't eat another mouthful.

With a full belly, he went through the castle to the stables, where he found Glance waiting with two saddled horses.

He handed one set of reins to Bane.

"I don't know how to ride," Bane said as he took the reins and stared up at the chestnut mare, which suddenly seemed a lot bigger.

"You'll learn as we ride. Now put a foot in the stirrup and climb up."

Bane watched his uncle as he gripped the saddle horn, placed a foot into the stirrup and swung a leg over with ease. He then gestured for him to do the same.

Bane fumbled the reins in one hand while reaching up and gripping the saddle horn, which was the same level as his head. He fished for the stirrup with the toe of his boot, missed several times before locating it, and then managed to swing his leg over after the third jump.

The mare flicked her tail in complaint, ears flattening to her head as she bared her teeth at him.

"The trick is to act confidently. Even if you don't feel it, horses can sense fear and it'll make them skittish. Now come, night will soon be upon us."

Glance clucked his tongue and pressed his heel to his mount's flank.

When Bane tried to imitate him, his mare whinnied and stamped her hoof.

"No fear," he whispered to himself and then tried again, this time putting more weight behind his boot.

"Fugit," he yelped as the horse leapt forwards and dashed past his uncle, bouncing him in the saddle with such ferocity that his teeth gnashed together, and he almost severed his tongue.

"That's it," his uncle called from behind as Bane gripped as tightly as he could, hugging the mare's neck as she launched through the castle gate and out onto the open ground.

The sword rattled against his back, thumping into his spine with each bound, the cloak billowing out behind and flapping like a flag snapping in the wind.

"Confidence, Bane," Glance said as he caught them up, sitting atop his steed with the ease of an experienced rider.

Bane tried not to focus on the ground rushing below him as he willed his fingers to let go of the mane, and with tremendous effort, he pushed himself into a sitting position and forced a grin upon his face.

He couldn't be sure, but he thought he felt the horse slow, her strides becoming less panicked.

"Good. It'll become easier the more you ride," Glance said as they slowed to a trot.

"Who does she belong to?" Bane asked, suddenly feeling as though he ought to be more careful.

"She belongs to the stable master himself. A safe enough horse for you to practice on. You'll get your own in time, of course, but for now, she'll do."

They followed a track that took them to the forest that sat at the valley's edge, overlooking Crookfell. Dusk was approaching and a dark smudge in the red sky told of coming rain.

"Now the most important element of our work is the ability to be silent," Glance explained as they dismounted and tied the horses to the branches of an oak inside the treeline. "The other is to be invisible."

They paced further into the forest until the growing shadows almost swallowed them. The air was cool with a hint of frost to come.

"Invisible? I thought magic wasn't real," Bane said, wondering if his uncle was a wizard or warlock from a fairytale.

"Magic? I've seen it first hand, but whether it's real or not, I couldn't say. When I say invisible, I mean hidden from sight, unable to be seen by others. Now, wait here."

Bane pulled the cloak tight about him as he watched his uncle pace further into the forest, the shadows soon devouring him. He caught a brief impression of the heel of a boot and then he was gone.

The horses whinnied from the tree line, one of them stamping impatiently. Bane strained to hear more, to locate Glance, but couldn't. A woodpecker knocking, a faraway owl hooting, and the scurrying of squirrels as they collected nuts for the coming winter, but there were no human sounds.

He took a careful step towards where his uncle disappeared, wanting to venture after him, but he was told to remain.

"Invisible."

The whisper came directly into his ear, so close he could feel the breath of the person whispering.

He was startled as he spun around, hand going for his sword as he set his feet, yet it was Glance.

"Not magic, only years of practice and wearing the right clothes."

His uncle held out the fabric of his cloak, running the soft material through his finger and thumb.

"It's so dark that I can blend into the shadows, and as long as I touch nothing, it doesn't make a sound."

Bane looked down at his own britches and shirt.

"But why dark green? Wouldn't black be darker still?"

Glance grinned as he moved back beneath the trees, gesturing for Bane to follow.

"You'd have thought so, but no. Things are rarely truly black, including the night," he explained, wandering slowly into the shadows again and pulling the hood of his cloak over his head. "But dark green blends in with most shades that nature throws at us. Yet, remaining hidden has many facets and many skills to gain before mastering it. One of which is how to tread without making a sound."

Bane's very next step snapped a fallen twig, proving how clumsy he must seem. He also noted that Glance hadn't yet made a noise.

"It's not only where you step, but how you step and which part of your foot to set down first."

He signalled for Bane to stop as he walked across a small patch of crisp leaves without disturbing a single one.

"Did you see how I changed which part of my foot to place down each time?"

Bane shook his head as he watched him do it again, this time coming back.

His uncle first placed the toe of one boot down, rolled to his heel as he placed the edge of his other boot down and rolled the other way.

"I'm exaggerating the movements to demonstrate, but do you see how I slip the edges of my boots and the toe beneath the leaves and distribute my weight so I don't crush them?"

Bane nodded, although he still didn't understand.

"Now you try."

Glance chuckled as Bane took three steps and crushed the leaves with each one.

"You're going to have to concentrate. Go slowly until you grasp what it is you need to do."

Bane tried again, working the edge of his boot beneath a leaf as he set his other boot down. One foot was silent while the heel of the other crushed several leaves as he lost his balance.

Glance winced as he shook his head.

"Distribute your weight so the lighter part of you is always leading."

With his next step, Bane leaned away from the leading boot, set it down, and slowly rolled his shoulders so that the bulk of him was hovering over his back foot. He then took another step, leaning on the foot that was already down, placing his boot toe first beneath the leaves and leaning away from it.

He didn't make a sound.

With a nod from Glance, he attempted to take another step, yet his heel caught a twig which snapped so loudly it startled a nearby wood pigeon from a branch.

"Practice. That's all you need. I want you stepping silently everywhere. The castle, the forest, and even the practice yard with Jarl. It will become the way you move from now on.

"What if I can't do it?"

His uncle slapped a hand down on his shoulder.

"You will. Now, keep at it. Your eyes will adjust to the gloom. And the trick to seeing in the dark is not looking directly at anything. If you wish to see something in particular, look to the side of it; you'll make out the outline of it much better."

They stayed there for a while as Bane attempted to step quietly through leaves, over fallen branches and stalk through the darkness, squinting as the shapes of the trees came to him an instant before they touched.

He didn't think he'd ever get the hang of it.

Afterwards, he attempted to sneak up on the horses, yet as soon as he neared, they both raised their heads, snorting with disdain.

Once out of the darkness of the forest, the dull night seemed bright enough not to need torches, even though there was no moon or stars.

"Your eyes have become acquainted with the dark, which gives you an advantage over those that haven't. In time, you'll come to realise that skill will be one of the ones you'll rely on more than most, which brings me to another skill I want you to master. When you wake from sleep, only open one eye."

"Only the one?"

Glance nodded as he untied the reins of his horse and mounted.

Bane untied the reins of his own horse, noticing how his mare's ears flattened, and her teeth were on display.

He swallowed as he placed a foot into the stirrup, gripped the saddle horn and heaved himself up.

"Why only the one?"

Glance clucked to his horse, and they began to trot back towards the castle.

"Because from sleep, your eyes will already be adjusted, and you'd be ready if someone came to slit your throat in the night."

Bane's hand went unconsciously to his neck, and then he regripped the reins as he almost bounced out of the saddle.

"That skill saved my life," Glance revealed, yet said no more, his gaze seeming to have gone far away.

As they drew close to the castle, they slowed and then dismounted at the gate, where they were met with two guards who ordered the heavy portcullis to be opened.

Once inside, they led the horses to the stable, where they handed the mounts over to the stable boys, one of whom was Bon, a fellow fledgling.

When he noticed it was him, Bon grinned as he took the reins.

"How are the bruises?" he asked, nodding down at Bane's chest where he had been struck by both Bon and Hammel that morning.

"Not so bad," he said, realising he had forgotten them. The day had been too full of learning to feel anything but bewildered.

"How about yours?"

Bon shrugged as he began to unbuckle the bridle and remove the saddle.

"I've had worse bruises from being kicked and bitten by this lot," he said, thumbing the horses in the stalls. "Guess we'll get some more tomorrow. Anyway, have you been out hunting raiders again?" he asked, eyes focusing on the sword strapped to Bane's back.

"Bon, less of your yacking. Get back to grooming," came a booming voice from the other side of the stables.

"Yes, Da," Bon said, then rolled his eyes before nodding a farewell. "I'll see you in the practice yard."

"Aye, I'll be there."

Glance was waiting for him outside.

"Tired?" he asked.

Bane rolled his shoulders and felt a soreness down his inner thighs from the horse riding, but he wasn't about to show it as he shook his head.

"Good. The night is still young. I want you to cross the bailey using the shadows for cover. There is a route to the servant's entrance that remains hidden within darkness. Avoid all torches and lamps. And I don't want you to reveal yourself to anyone, not even the guards, unless they challenge you."

Bane stared at the open stretch of ground between the stables and the main building and plotted a route that would keep him hidden. It looked simple enough.

"Tomorrow, after you've finished in the practice yard, you will meet me in the secret study. And this time, try to be silent."

Bane nodded as he picked a route across the bailey, ensuring the shadows overlapped. When he turned to say goodbye to his uncle, he found that he had gone. Vanished.

How had he done that?

Hoping that he would one day be as good at disappearing as Glance, Bane slowly crept through the dark edges of the open area, walking how he had been taught.

His boots still made a light rustling over the grass, and if anyone saw him, they would think him simple or drunk, the way he was walking.

Once on the other side of the bailey, he walked in a crouch along the castle wall, keeping low to avoid light from the burning torches on sconces, placed regularly along the perimeter but not so close together that the flickering halos met.

At the corner, he grasped the rough stone bricks and shimmed up and over onto a narrow path hidden within the fold of the castle itself. It was so dimly lit that Bane had no trouble traversing the path to the practice yard, where he picked a course around the outer edge, crawling at several points where the guards patrolled the walls above.

He paused at the large rock beside the servant's entrance, suddenly becoming aware that he was not alone.

In the darkness of the rock, he saw the shape of a person facing away from him, shoulders hunched over and quietly weeping.

They didn't know he was there, so he must have been quiet enough to not have been detected.

He thought that was an achievement until he recognised the person weeping.

"Belle?"

The figure stiffened, a final sniff before she turned to face him, a brief flash of damp cheek as she caught the light from the lamp by the entrance.

"Who's there?" she snapped, fists balling by her sides.

"It's me, Bane."

He stepped out from the darkness, offering her a reassuring smile. He had expected her to at least return the smile, but instead, a fresh wave of weeping came back in heaves before she closed the distance and flung her arms around him.

"What is it, Belle? Has somebody hurt you?" Bane asked, unsure of what to do.

Belle gripped tighter and then regained control of herself as she eased away.

"It's so good to see a friendly face," she said, about to wipe her tears with her sleeve before she paused and retrieved a handkerchief from the pocket of her apron and dabbed at her swollen eyes.

"No. Well, not physically. It's only that many of the other servants and maids are so mean. They treat me differently because I'm a villager. And that man teaching me letters, Mr Pensulby, uses every opportunity to remind me as such. His expertise is wasted on a Crookfell retch. I wouldn't mind skipping the learning, but Mr Randel, the head of housekeeping, insists that every staff member must be able to read."

She sniffed and then began to smile again, shaking her head as if trying to take her words back.

"Here's me babbling about myself. Tell me about you. I haven't seen you for days."

Bane stepped further into the light, swallowing his anger towards the bullies who were cruel to Belle. If he got the opportunity, he would get even with them.

Belle's eyes grew wider as her gaze travelled from his boots, up his clothes and settled on the sword on his back.

"It is true then. You're the Crookfell Slayer," she said, her lips widening into a full grin which was more like her old self. "And such nice clothes. Maybe I ought to be calling you Sir or something."

"I don't know about being the Slayer, but I can't stop the rumours now they are flying around. And as for a title, you can call me Master," he laughed. "Everyone else seems to."

Belle's laughter suddenly died.

"Really? Then I shouldn't be speaking with you. I've already been in trouble for being over-familiar with anyone above my station."

Bane wished he hadn't told her, yet he only said it in jest.

"Belle, I'm still me. Bane. And I feel more out of place here than anywhere else."

Belle bit her lip as the concern on her brow began to melt.

"Perhaps when nobody else is present," she said, taking a step closer and taking his hand. "Are you living here now? Please say you are. I'm missing home terribly. Even Dew."

"Yeah. Glance has given me my own chamber. You should see it, Belle – it's bigger than the hovel I used to live in, and the bed is so comfortable."

Bane felt Bell's hand grip tighter, that playful grin that made his belly go warm coming onto her face.

"Maybe I should," she whispered, raising a brow.

Bane suddenly felt hot, and he became aware that his palm had become sweaty. He hoped Belle hadn't noticed.

"So why are you out of the castle at night?" he asked, trying to change the subject.

"Finding time to myself. More to the point, why were you out creeping about in the dark as if trying to sneak into the castle unseen."

Bane tipped his head back and barked out a laugh.

"Because I've been creeping around in the dark, attempting to get into the castle unseen."

She playfully slapped him on his chest.

"You're not very good at it," she said, her hand lingering where it was before drawing it back.

A bell suddenly rang from inside the entrance, snapping her attention away and breaking the mood.

"Fug it," she hissed. "Can I see you again?"

Harsh tones carried out from the castle, and Bane thought he caught the words, 'Where is that idiot girl?'

"Of course. We're still friends. I'll see you whenever I can."

He mimicked Belle's smile as it lit up her face, then froze as she leaned closer and pressed her lips to his.

She held it there, eyes fluttering closed, and Bane felt that he ought to shut his too. Yet the moment the thought occurred she pulled away.

"Friends."

Then, with a final embrace, she sped off into the castle, pausing only to glance back at him before disappearing inside.

Bane remained still for a time. The taste of Belle's lips still on his, the heat from her touch, or was that a heat that was coming from simply thinking about her?

15

Bailin Shakil

Bailin pressed the tankard of ale to his lips, felt the cold metal, and smelled the hops from the frothy liquid, yet he didn't have the stomach for it. The confined space in the hastily rigged tent, which was his sleeping quarters and the headquarters as he marched his division south, didn't help.

He placed the tankard down on the map table and earned a frown from his second, Sir Godlin.

"Your mind's been elsewhere these past few days, Bailin. What's up with you?"

Bailin shrugged, put a leg up on the table and placed one boot over the other, feigning indifference, yet Godlin was right; something was on his mind.

"You may as well tell me now. No good when we're formed up on the borders and about to ride into battle."

Bailin wanted to tell him that there was nothing, yet his second knew him too well. They'd fought in most battles on the southern borders together. Had saved each other's lives countless times.

"I think I've seen a ghost," he admitted, unsure of how to put what had been bothering him into words.

Godlin's mouth was full of ale, and he needed to puff his cheeks out to stop himself from laughing. He forced a swallow, choked and fell into spluttered laughter.

"A ghost? Come, my Lord. I've seen you take beasts down fiercer than a mere ghost."

The tent flaps fluttered and snapped in a carrying gust, one cloth wall billowing inwards and almost gutting the only candle.

Godlin's grin faltered when he realised Bailin was being serious.

"Was it Nel?"

Bailin shook his head as he reached for the tankard again, not caring for a drink but wanting something solid to grasp in his hands.

"No. I see her all the time, yet only in my memories. This was days ago, as we left the castle, I saw a ghost. A boy."

Godlin nodded as he listened, absently playing with the end of his greying beard.

"He was standing alone on the side of the King's Road, up on the valley top. Probably no older than fifteen winters. Dressed in the rough spun wool of the villagers."

"A Crookfell ghost, aye? How'd you know he wasn't just a boy who came to watch the soldiers marching past? Some of those young Crookfell folk are thin enough to be wraith-like."

Bailin finally pressed the tankard to his lips and swallowed a large gulp of the ale. It was bitter.

"Because I recognised him. I stared as deeply into him as he stared into me. There was recognition there – too much for us not to be known to each other."

Another drink. Godlin leaned closer; the tent billowed in again.

"Who was it?"

Bailin stared his second in the eye, wondering why he was blathering this to a comrade and not keeping it down with the rest of the pain he'd been feeling. The loss of Nel, the hatred for his father, the eagerness to throw himself into every fight, every battle and willing the enemy to drive steel through him to relieve him of his burdens.

"I saw the same face I see every time I look in the mirror. The ghost was me. A younger me."

Godlin cocked his head to the side.

"You? Dressed in rough spun?" the cocky grin briefly reappeared.

"I saw what I saw. It was a ghost of me."

The tent flap flew open and Shull ducked inside, devouring the rest of the space as he crashed down into the chair beside Godlin.

"Thought we left the foul weather in the north," he said, blowing a drip of rain from the end of his nose. It fell onto his wet uniform and ran over a polished greave.

"That's not all we should have left behind," Godlin said as he poured Shull the last of the ale into a cup and slid it across the table. "It transpires that we've also brought with us a ghost."

"Ghost?"

Shull's brows disappeared into his damp hair as he met Bailin's gaze.

Bailin shrugged. Shull had been with him almost as long as Godlin and had earned his knighthood the hard way. There were no secrets between them.

"Bailin saw a ghost of himself when he was but a boy, and get this, he was wearing rough spun," Godlin said, his tone jaunty as he attempted to keep the conversation light, yet he failed.

They'd been here before, back when Bailin had received a letter from his sister informing him of Nel's passing.

They were dark times. Godlin and Shull had been his rocks then, keeping him from sinking into oblivion. He couldn't blame them for wanting to avoid sinking low again, especially on the brink of another campaign.

"No, wait. Was this back at Garik? The day we left?" Shull asked, swilling the dregs of his ale around his cup. "I thought I saw a boy up on the valley. He was the spit of you when you were younger."

Bailin pulled his boots from the table as he leaned across and grasped Shull's arm with such ferocity that his friend yelped.

"You saw him too?" he asked. "You saw my ghost?"

Bailin hadn't thought that someone else might also have seen the spirit. Perhaps he wasn't losing his mind.

"Bailin, it wasn't a ghost. Only a Crookfell boy. Although I must admit, the likeness to you was uncanny."

"Why didn't you mention this earlier?" Bailin asked, letting go of Shull as he slouched back again, wondering who else might have seen this strange boy.

Shull exchanged a look with Godlin and shook his head.

"Why would I? He was a local boy. I remember thinking that there was something of a Shankil to him. I don't know, maybe your brother or father begat a bastard from a local…"

Bailin knew that Shull was about to say wench or whore but caught himself before the word was out.

"Girl," Godlin put in. "It's not like it doesn't happen."

They could be right, of course, although he knew his loathsome father had learned his lesson when he had begat Glance, and Glance, his younger brother, wouldn't have been old enough to have a child of fifteen winters.

Bailin's blood ran cold.

A clatter followed by a slosh came from the floor, and he realised he'd dropped his tankard.

He didn't care. He was up and pacing around the tent, or at least the few feet where his boots could find clear ground.

The years worked out right. The location, the recognition. Could it be?

The final cog turned and slotted into place. The riddle that had plagued him since Nel's death had finally been solved.

"That was why the old bastard had her killed," he growled, his fist suddenly flying into the central tent post before he could pull it back.

The wood split as a crack rendered up the spine of it, but the tent held.

Godlin and Shull were on their feet, casting a confusing glance at each other.

"Nel was with child. My child," Bailin said, rubbing at the blood on his knuckles and not caring. "He had her killed to avoid any challenges to his seat should I fall. That fugging…"

This time his fist was caught by Godlin, his other arm grasped by Shull as they struggled to keep him from smashing something else.

He tried to pull them off, writhing from side to side, but they had him pinned.

"Easy, Bailin, easy now," Godlin soothed.

Bailin took a breath, calmed the raging fire that was perpetually burning within him and then eased himself back into the chair.

"The child is yours?" Shull asked, hands still held before him, prepared in case of another violent outburst.

"It fits. His age, appearance. Is there anyone in the division who is local to Crookfell? Any of the new recruits, a stable hand, anyone?"

"I believe one of the farriers has taken on an apprentice from Crookfell," Shull said, and Bailin knew that if Shull said it was so, then it was true. The man only dealt with solid facts.

"Send for him," Bailin demanded, hands gripping the sides of his chair as if to rise, then he forced himself to let go. He could do with a drink, but the last of the ale was soaking into the ground.

Shull poked his head out of the tent and ordered a guard to fetch the boy.

"Are you sure you want to know? I mean, what good will it do?" Godlin asked, easing himself back down now that he could see that Bailin was calm.

"We can't turn the division around and march back to Garik. Not when the King is expecting us on the borders by Midwinter," Shull added.

Bailin had asked himself the same question countless times before. After Nel's death when he first suspected something was amiss. More so when he discovered that his father had ordered her hung due to stealing. He'd not believed it at the time. He knew Nel inside and out, and no one was more honest and caring. He'd always strived for the truth, and the harder he pushed, the more distant his father became. But he believed his suspicions enough for it to drive an unshakable wedge between them.

"I need to know."

His friends exchanged another worrying glance between themselves but didn't argue.

The tent remained silent for a time; the only sounds coming from outside were the sharpening of steel, the whinnying of horses, and the laughter of the men as they took time to rest before the continued march at dawn.

The flap opened and the guard stepped inside accompanied by a timid boy of maybe twelve winters. Large eyes took them in as he stepped nervously closer, head switching back to the flap as the guard left.

"You're not in trouble, lad," Bailin said, wanting to put the boy at ease. "What you're name?"

"Nibbin, your Lordship, Sir," Nibbin said, his fingers fidgeting with the hem of his jerkin.

"Nibbin, are you a Crookfell lad?"

Nibbin nodded.

"My Da tills the land with my Ma and brothers," he offered.

"So, you've grown up in the village and know most of the folk?"

"Yes, Sir, Lordship, Sir. Crookfell folk all know each other."

Bailin tried to keep the smile on his face. He wasn't used to dealing with children, and this boy was barely old enough to be anything else.

"And do you know of a boy from your village, a few winters older than yourself, hair darker than most, tall, grey eyes?"

Nibbin shook his head, and he pressed his lips together.

"No, Sir. Nobody like that in the village. We've all got brown hair, apart from Mary. She's got golden hair. Like the raiders. Da reckons that her mother had been sleeping with a raider and…"

Bailin ignored Godlin, who was quietly laughing behind the boy.

"Nobody else? Taller, slim...could look like a younger me?"

"No Sir, nobody like that in Crookfell."

Bailin felt a pang of loss, unsure why when he had nothing to lose in the first place. Or was it because a moment ago he had been a potential father?

No. It wasn't that. It was the link to Nel. The strange, grounding thoughts brought it back to the only person he had ever loved - like it always did.

"Unless you mean, Boy," Nibbin continued, nose scrunching in concentration.

"Boy?" Bailin asked. The way Nibbin had said it as if it was a name, and a condescending one at that.

"The gallows born. I think Dew and his sister called him Bane. He belongs to Dodd, the forager."

"Gallows born? Who was his mother?" Bailin asked, almost demanding. He willed himself to breathe, to calm down before he scared the lad.

"His mother was hanged. My Da watched it all; the entire village did, but it was before I was born. Gelwin's sister, Mel, or was it Nel, was the mother. My Da said she died on the noose, her neck broken," Nibbin explained, mimicking a rope with his hands as he tipped his head to the side and stuck out his tongue, proving that he had never actually seen a true hanging before.

"Boy came moments after. Nan Hilga helped bring him into the world. That's why he's gallows born. My Da said that the village didn't want him and that they tried to give him to the Fug. Laid him right out on the trial stone."

By now, Nibbin had gained all the confidence of a tavern bard that held his audience captive.

"But the Fug gave him back. He's been in the village ever since. Nobody will have anything to do with him, though."

"Do you know who his father is?" Bailin asked, stealing the eagerness from his voice.

"Yes," Nibbin replied. "Death is his father."

The tent billowed in with enough force for the cloth to catch the candle and gut it out, throwing them into darkness.

"Damned bloody field tent," Godlin said as he paced about trying to locate a strike box, but Bailin barely registered him, his world shrinking until it was only himself and of course, the ghost of Nel, which was always with him.

I have a son.

We have a son. Nel corrected. Or his mind did, putting her voice to his own thoughts. He knew she wasn't really with him. But being close to death always seemed to bring her near. That was why he was always in a battle. To be closer to her.

When the candle was relighted her ghost vanished, replaced by both Godlin and Shull with shocked expressions, while Nibbin remained where he was.

Bailin produced a silver coin from his pouch, placed it on the table and slid it across to the boy.

"That is all, lad. Thank you."

Nibbin took the coin, his face lighting up brighter than the shiny metal it was made from.

Shull escorted him out and then closed the flap, leaving the three of them in silence once again. Nobody spoke, but Bailin knew his friends were watching him closely should his rage return, but it was spent.

"I knew you hadn't seen a ghost," Godlin said after a time. "Do you trust what the boy said? I mean, gallows born."

"I have heard that said before. There were rumours around the guards of something like that happening," Shull said, picking up his cup, realising it was empty and setting it back down. "And I saw him with my own eyes. If I were to guess, I'd say the words were true."

Bailin rubbed the stubble on his face, fingers rising over and through his hair. He didn't know what to say. What could he say?

"Are you thinking about returning to Garik?" Shull asked.

"Surely not. I mean, I'd follow you anywhere, you know I would, but it would be unwise to go back on your orders," Godlin put in.

Bailin had briefly considered heading back. If only to get the truth from his father and to lay his eyes on his son again. But his friends were right. Once this next battle had been fought and won, there'd be plenty of time for that.

He was about to say as much when the tent flap came open again and a guard poked his head through.

"A King's messenger, my Lord. He demands to see you right away."

"This can't be good," Shull said under his breath as Bailin nodded for the guard to let the messenger enter.

The man stumbled in, covered in road muck and dripping with rainwater and sweat.

He removed his hat and gave a short nod before handing over a sealed envelope.

Bailin gestured for the man to sit before he fell. He appeared ready to collapse.

He inspected the seal and saw that it was intact before pulling the candle closer.

Using his boot knife, he split the wax seal and pulled out the parchment within.

Bailin read the message and then read it again to ensure he wasn't mistaken.

"What is it?" Godlin asked, sensing something bad.

Bailin glanced up - his friend wouldn't be wrong.

"Fallia has fallen. It's now under the control of the Empire," he said, scanning the message for a third time. "It's in the King's own hand."

He gave the parchment to Godlin to read for himself.

"Fallia. But that city is huge. It holds the largest battalion of ground troops outside of the capital. How can that be true?" Shull asked.

"The Southerners overran it," the messenger said, wild stare catching Bailin as he worked moisture around a parched mouth.

Godlin handed him a waterskin, and the messenger drank deeply, spilling half down his chin.

"They came out of the ground. Sand demons. Writhing up out of the dirt, out of the sewers and cutting the battalion down from within Fallia's own walls. More came from the sea. Striking land with hundreds of galleons, an entire fleet full of soldiers."

The messenger tipped the water skin back again, drinking deeply and then upending the rest over his head.

"Demons," he repeated, wiping his mouth with a sleeve.

"You were there?" Bailin asked.

"No. I was some leagues north, but I saw the survivors, what was left of them. And I heard the stories. I was with the King hunting for forest grouse when the attack happened. By the time word reached us, the city had fallen. We were only a small party of twelve, so the King headed directly to Palsin, which was the closest garrison. He hastily wrote that message on route and dispatched me to find you."

"And we're to head directly to Palsin?" Godlin asked, reading from the message before Shull plucked it from his grasp.

"If a city the size of Fallia can be taken so easily, Palsin wouldn't last long at all. It's a third the size," Bailin said, trying to remember his last time there. It must have been over five years ago when they stopped to regroup before heading to the fringes of the border to chase the Southerners back into their lands.

"How long did it take you to reach us?" Shull asked the messenger.

"The best part of two weeks. Riding hard, swapping mounts at every post and catching sleep in the saddle," the messenger said, forcing his heavy lids back open.

"That is an achievement in itself," Bailin said. "My bedroll is back there. Lie yourself down and grab what sleep you can. We'll be heading out at first light."

"Thank you, your Lordship."

Bailin waited until the messenger had located his bedroll and was on his back within moments, snoring the way of the weary traveller a few heartbeats later.

"Two weeks riding hard," Shull said as he leaned over the maps, a long finger pressing down over the location of Palsin. With a forced march, minimal stops and a clear run down the King's Road, we'd be lucky to reach Palsin within a month, most likely closer to a month and a half."

"And that's if the men are willing. You know how they get when we pass through towns with a decent tavern," Godlin put in.

Bailin crossed the room, picked up his sword and scabbard and began to buckle it on.

"I know. That's why I'm heading out immediately with you and a handful of the younger knights with something to prove. We could do the distance within half the time."

"And you want me to bring the rest of the division down after you?" Shull asked, folding his arms and raising his chin. "And miss all the fun."

"I wouldn't trust anybody else," Bailin said, slapping his friend on the shoulder. "Now rouse the younger knights. I want a score of twenty. And I want them ready to leave within the hour.

16

Challenger

Alruna pulled her cloak tight about her body for the damp night but also for other reasons. Her father was beside her, troubled face lit up by the flames from the fire pit and the stares from the clansmen that formed a circle around them. The deepest scorn cast by Ferric.

Her father might have felt better having Geri at his feet, but shadow leopards were not permitted at the fire pit during a clan challenge. Alruna also felt the loss of Freki, who was back at the bunker with her mother. The two cats would no doubt be pacing around until their return.

If they were to return.

"So, a challenge, is it?" her father said after he let the silence drag out and the hostile stares from the gathered men, which was all the men and some of the older boys from the village.

"Aye, it's a challenge, Boran. And well passed time too," Ferric said, stepping out from the circle of men, chin raised and teeth gritted. "More than a few have said so."

"Is that right?" Boran growled, folding his arms and glowering right back.

Alruna sensed his fear. They both knew this day was coming and had prepared for how they would handle it. But now that the time had come, Alruna was unsure if they made the right decisions.

Hadlo had heard the quiet chattering amongst the clan and had seen how Ferric had bribed, argued and steered others to his way of thinking, which was for himself to take over as chief.

"Aye, that's right," Ferric said, flames reflecting in his eyes as if he were a demon. "Do you think I'd have organised this circle about the fire pit for wenches chatter?"

"I've heard you've been chattering around the men like a wench and have been for weeks. You couldn't come out and challenge me like a real leader might. You've always been a sneaking fugging rat, Ferric."

Alruna hadn't been to any challengers before; there had been none in the village since before her time. And she'd only heard of them from conversations with folk from other clans when trading.

"Sneaky fugging rat I might be, old man, but I've got the stones to lead this clan the way it should. I might have held off knowing that Raif was to take your place. But he isn't around anymore."

Alruna felt Ferric's gaze pass over her at the mention of her brother.

It stung. The heat of anger flashed across her skin, prickling her nerves into action. Weeks had passed since Raif became ash, yet each day was as raw as the last. Her grief was as strong as it ever was.

She bit down on her tongue, swallowed her breath and remained quiet. Ferric was only goading them.

"Is that right?" her father said, teeth flashing as he took a step closer, the tendons in his arms standing out.

"Aye, that's fugging right," Ferric snarled as he paced around the circle, receiving nods and grunts of approval from some of the men eager to please the new potential Chief, while getting an unsure shrug from others, those that were hedging their bets.

Alruna noticed that a few kept silent, yet none wanted to speak against Ferric. Her father wasn't going to get help from the very people he had been protecting for most of his life.

Un-loyal, backstabbing or damn right cowards, the lot of them.

Ferric must have been working in the background longer than she or her father realised.

They knew that the clan was divided on how her father did things. Alruna hadn't realised how much by. This was a lot worse than she had thought.

"And we're all sick of the way you're handling the Baron and his men. It's been years since we raided, and when you finally decided to do it, you only wished to get a hostage. A hostage with which you could use to gain parley to seek a union between us and them."

As he stalked around the onlookers, Ferric removed his tunic and made a show of dropping it on the ground. Muscles bunching as he flexed and tensed. Some of the men shouted encouragement, knowing what was to come.

"We must stand together," Boran growled above the noise. "The threat is approaching. We must stand with the castle, or we all fall."

"Are we to believe the words from your dead son? There is no proof of Draugr in the Fug. He was more than likely hallucinating," Ferric said, grinning like a madman. "Now let's get this challenge done, old man. My men are thirsty, and there's a keg of ale for us to celebrate with. Although," Ferric held a finger to his pursed lips as he winked at Boran. "I believe that is in your hut. Sorry, I mean my hut."

Alruna held her breath and kept her gaze on her boots. She wouldn't react. It was a game to Ferric. A tactic. He was winding them up, forcing a move.

"What do you say, Chief? Do you accept my challenge?"

With the final word, Ferric punched the air several times in rapid succession, faster than Alruna could keep up with.

There was one thing Ferric was known for, and that was fighting. Especially unarmed brawls. Alruna had heard the stories from her brother. Ferric would fight bare-chested - even in battle and would go wild with blood lust.

All eyes were on her father, almost twenty years older than Ferric, thinner, weaker and with bones that were quick to ache and knuckles that clicked and groaned when curled into fists.

If swords were permitted by the men in the circle, then things might have been different. But Ferric was the stronger, the younger, the fiercer fighter, and he had been preparing for this for weeks.

"I accept," Boran said as he spat on the ground.

Alruna knew he had no choice but to accept. To not do so would be to lose face in front of the men.

Hadlo grunted by the side of her father, nostrils flared and itching to fight in his place, but again, if her father allowed it, the men would think him a coward. Nobody could fight for a Chief but himself or his family. And Alruna was his only kin.

Things would have been different if Raif had been here. He could have bested Ferric with a blade or open hand.

"Let's get this done then," Ferric said as he began to pace again, thumping his chest to get his blood up, slapping his face, eyes alive with violence.

He cast them at her, his maniacal grin spreading his ratty cheeks wide.

Her heart thumped, hammering against her ribcage; her palms sweated, and her bowels felt like water.

How could her father appear so brave?

Ferric was now bouncing on the spot, muscles flexing, red where he had been striking himself.

"Come on," he bellowed, gesturing with a hand.

Boran took a breath and then stepped back, leaving Alruna out in the open.

"I choose Alruna to fight in my place," Boran said, earning gasps from the circle of men.

Another gasp escaped Alruna as the cold, damp air bit at her. She drew her cloak tighter as she stared at her father.

His gaze locked with hers, jaw clenched and hard.

He had chosen.

"What?" Ferric laughed, hands now on hips as he stared from her to her father.

"You send your loud-mouthed daughter to fight in your place? What kind of chief are you?"

Boran remained tight-lipped as he glared on, yet said nothing as he waited for the outcome. He may have been carved from stone.

A shiver racked through Alruna as she steadied her breathing, feeling more fear now facing one of her own than she did the night they raided Crookfell.

She stepped closer to Ferric, her boot slipping on the soft earth, earning a laugh from the circle and bringing heat to her face.

"Do you really want to fight me, wench? You can still walk away. It's not your fault your father is a coward," Ferric said, steam rising from his wiry muscles.

Alruna glanced over her shoulder at her father. He hadn't moved - stoney expression revealing nothing. Hadlo seemed more nervous than he did, the giant of a man shifting his weight from foot to foot, a gentle shake of his head.

It had been a hard few weeks. Probably harder still for her father. He was in no fit state to fight. And losing meant banishment, or worse.

Alruna's shoulder trembled as she turned to face her opponent, not much taller than herself, but wider, stronger and with years of fighting experience.

She wondered how to best him unarmed. He was a berserker, so he would be vicious, fast and unforgiving. There would be no art to the fight, only savagery.

Ferric sensed her fear as he slowly stepped closer until they were an arm span apart, making a show for the men.

This would be humiliating, and Ferric would make sure that her father watched everything.

"You've got more stones than your father, wench. But don't think I'll not still knock six shades of snot out of you."

More laughter from the men and Alruna caught Gamlin grinning along with them.

"I tell you what, I'll let you have first strike," he goaded, turning a cheek towards her, yellow teeth showing through his grin.

"Go on, wench, slap me. It'll be the only touch you'll get. Until afterwards, maybe. Then you'll be mine to touch how I please."

Alruna knew there was no backing out. She needed to fight and needed to win.

Ferric opened his arms out to the men as he slowly turned.

"Didn't I always say we were led by a coward with more desire for harvesting than spilling blood?"

When he turned a full circle and came back to staring at her again, fingers twitching with anticipation, he was like a cat toying with a mouse.

"And to give you a little fire in your belly, girl, when I'm done with you, I'll have the bunker your leopards are in sealed shut. Will that make you fight a little fiercer and give me at least some sport?"

She couldn't think about Freki and Geri right now. There was no room for distraction.

"Come on then, girl," he goaded as he shifted his feet, ready to lunge, faked a punch and then drew back at the final moment, laughing.

"I don't know, maybe you ought to fight topless like me."

The toothy grin caught the firelight, and Alruna caught an animalistic desire in his gaze.

"Fight me, wench," he laughed and then cocked his head to the side. "If there was any fight in you, that boy from Crookfell would be dead and Raif would be alive. None of this needed to happen. But that's what sending girls out into raids does for you."

Alruna took another step, only small, should the wet mud cause her to lose her footing again.

"You have the first strike. Slap me as hard as you can, go on," Ferric offered, placing hands back onto his hips. "I'll even shut my eyes."

Alruna knew that she would only have one chance at this. And as cocky as he was, she knew he was right. She wouldn't be able to beat him in a fight. But there was no choice. No backing out.

She took a step closer to Ferric. To the man who had caused this and would see her and her father banished.

If she could strike him with hate alone, she could win, but it would take more than a strong emotion to bring him down.

The men around the circle quieted, all eager to see the first strike, all baying for blood. Her blood.

Alruna slipped her arm from beneath her cloak, raised it and slapped Ferric across the side of the head.

It wasn't the hardest slap. It didn't need to be when her hand was gripping the shaft of an axe.

The flat of the blade met flesh and bone, softness giving way to a wet crunch.

Ferric dropped to his knees, catching himself before he toppled over.

The circle erupted in surprised shouts, one of the men cursing angrily.

Blood ran from Ferric's mouth as he stared up at her, working something around his gums before spitting out a tooth.

"No man is permitted to bring a fugging weapon into the circle," he growled, rising on shaking legs.

He took an unsteady step towards her; bloody lip puckered into an ugly grimace.

"And no *man* has," Alruna replied and struck him again. This time harder.

Mud squelched as his knees hit the ground once more, head tipped back with a large angry welt appearing over a sweaty crown.

Alruna easily sidestepped around a lumbering punch and hit him square in the face with the back of the axe.

She felt the cartilage in the nose break as his head snapped back, yet he stubbornly remained kneeling.

A hand rested on her shoulder as her father came to join her.

"Not as clever as you think you are, aye," Boran said as he crouched so he was at eye level with the challenger.

One of Ferric's eyes was swollen shut, the other bloodshot.

"Fugging coward," he said, red liquid bubbling down his chin.

"Matters none in the end. You're the one in the mud. I'll give you until next tide to leave the village. Only death will welcome you if you return."

Ferric's head swivelled to Alruna, defiance in his ruined face twisting into hatred.

"I'll return. And it will be in the dead of night. You won't see me coming. And I'll slit both your throats."

Alruna imagined him sneaking through the window of her home, killing her father, killing Freki and Geri, and there would be nothing she could do about it because she knew he would kill her first.

There came a thudding crack, and something hot splattered across Alruna's cheek. Yet her gaze was locked on Ferric's head, which was split from the crown, her axe wedged into his skull, and her hand still gripping the shaft.

It took her a moment to realise what she had done. Steel meeting flesh, the two materials at odds with each other.

It wasn't as hard as she once thought it was. As her brother said, an axe blow to the head was as easy as splitting a turnip.

Ferric teetered, eyes rolling before he toppled.

As he fell, Alruna kept her grip on the axe and felt the metal scrape against bone as it came free.

Silence hung in the air. The only sound was the rain drumming into the damp earth and hissing on the fringes of the fire.

She couldn't draw her gaze away from the mess in the mud, the dark blood oozing from the gaping wound in Ferric's head and running into a black puddle.

Ferric had thought she didn't have it in her to kill. Wherever he is now, she guessed that he would probably know he was wrong.

A gust picked up, blowing the hood of her cloak back and she caught her father staring at her, his mouth partly open, brows raised in question.

Alruna was still holding the axe level in her hand, the blade slick red.

Own it, a voice said in her head, sounding a lot like her brother.

Grinding her teeth, she rounded on the circle, the axe drawn back and ready to swing.

"Is there anyone else that wishes to challenge my father?" she yelled, glaring at everyone as she slowly turned, her threaded nerves on the brink of shivering, a shuddering breath escaping her, which she masked with a snarl, pointing the blood-smeared axe at each of the men around the circle.

"No?"

As her glower crossed Gablin he dipped his head and stared at the ground, and she felt a pang of satisfaction.

The rest of the men remained quiet, some looking away, others only staring at the body collecting rain while leaking in the mud.

She paused to stare at the two who had given Ferric the most support, her heart hammering once again as she stepped towards them, yet they too glanced away.

She must look a sight.

When her eyes picked out her father, she saw that he seemed to gather himself, jaw clenching as he addressed the circle.

"I run the clan how I see fit. If you think I'm doing wrong, you come to me and fugging talk. If you sneak around my back," he inclined his head to the body of Ferric, "Then you'll be left for the Fug to collect with the next tide. If you don't like it, then you're welcome to find another clan."

Alruna gathered herself as he spoke, using the lapse of attention on her to regain control of her senses.

She barely grasped what her father was saying, her mind running over what she had done.

She had killed a man.

The circle seemed to sway, and she realised that she had been holding her breath, white dots fizzing at the edge of her vision. It was as if she was experiencing the circle from beyond her body.

"Steady, Alruna," a deep voice whispered behind her, and she felt Hadlo's hand on her shoulder. "Keep breathing."

The taste of vomit came into her mouth and she felt hot and cold at the same time.

"Easy," the hand gripped tighter and she swallowed the bile back down and took a breath.

The world swam back into focus as the men began to leave, some casting glances back to Ferric, others eyeing her suspiciously, but most departing swiftly. She couldn't blame them.

When they were gone, her father turned to her, gaze falling to the axe she was still gripping.

"I think you've done enough damage with that. Put it down."

Alruna slid the shaft into the loop on her belt and prized her fingers from the wood.

"Back in the bunker when we talked this over, and you begged to be the one that should fight for me, I didn't think you had this in mind," her father continued, pointing a trembling finger at Ferric.

Ferric stared up into the night, mouth open and catching water, lank hair fallen across the hole she had rendered.

"What was I supposed to do? He was going to come back and slit our throats. Better I ended him now," she argued, unable to draw her gaze from the corpse.

"She has a point," Hadlo said, sauntering over to Ferric and nudging a leg with his boot. "He would have come back. And the others will now think twice before standing against you."

"Aye? Well, we'll never know now."

Hadlo shrugged as he knelt, grasped Ferric's arm and in a single motion, heaved the body onto his shoulder.

"I'll leave him out for the Fug to claim," he said, adjusting the burden into a more comfortable position. He was about to stride away when Alruna's father spoke again.

"No. We make a pyre. He was still one of us. And the clan won't take kindly to us giving him over. It doesn't seem right."

Hadlo shrugged as if he didn't care either way.

"And Alruna will help you."

Alruna stared at her father, not wanting anything more to do with Ferric, yet from the anger written plainly in his frown, she knew there would be no arguing otherwise.

There were no words said between herself and Hadlo as they collected the wood and built the pyre. Not even when they threw his body unceremoniously on top, apart from the curses Hadlo made as he struggled to light the damp logs in the rain.

"Don't be hard on your Da," Hadlo said after the flames took and the pyre began to burn. "He feels for every clan member lost. Even those that don't deserve it."

He nodded towards Ferric, the corpse's flesh beginning to blacken.

"And he sent you out to have something to keep your mind from maudlin over what you'd done. It isn't easy, killing. The guilt will be with you for a long time."

Steam began to rise from Alruna's cloak, the heat from the pyre beginning to dry her clothes. She caught glimpses of the body through the curling smoke and realised that she didn't feel guilt at all.

17

Night Prowler

A spider scurried over Bane's hand as he worked it along the ancient masonry, groping for the corner of the tunnel in the dark. He fought hard not to flinch, even though the tapping legs left a tingling sensation on his skin.

He paused for a moment to gather himself, trying to see through the corner of his vision how Glance had taught him. But the network of tunnels was so dark that he was unsure if his lids were open or not.

Several weeks had passed since he first came to the castle. Intense weeks of learning sword skills, riding, and reading, all the while practising how to walk silently, how to operate in the darkness and how to move around without being seen.

It had been hard, but he'd loved every moment of it, especially those rare occasions where he had the chance to spend a little time with Belle - as fleeting as they were.

Most nights they would hide beneath the rock near the servant's entrance where they had met on that first night. That time she had kissed him.

It hadn't happened again.

A stone shifted beneath Bane's foot and he lost his footing, striking the side of the wall with a knee.

He allowed himself to get distracted.

It was late in the evening, most of the castle was asleep, and he had traversed from one side of Garik to the other, using a tunnel that his uncle said would lead him up to the third level. His mission was to find the secret door that would come out onto the upper battlements and steal a candle from the Watch Tower without being seen.

There had been plenty of tasks that he needed to achieve for Glance. Stealing a certain spoon from the kitchen, counting the stars embroidered into the tapestry in Felina's antechamber, daub paint on a chimney stack above the guard house – all while being unseen.

He'd completed each task without failure, even though he'd managed to drop a large dollop of paint on a guard's helmet while hanging beneath one of the beams above. It was only by chance that a scuffle between the stable hands had spilt out into the bailey, and the guards needed to rush out to break it up that he managed to get away with it.

He eventually found the edge of the tunnel and worked his hands along the stonework until he touched rough wood.

This would be the secret door.

The wood felt dry as he pressed a cheek to it, listening out for footsteps or conversation from the other side.

Nothing.

He located a bolt and slowly slipped it back.

Glance kept all the bolts and traps around the tunnels well-oiled so as not to attract noise when he used them.

Noise was a friend of the enemy so is best avoided; he had explained to him.

Once the bolt was back, Bane gently pushed against the wood until a sliver of light came through, slicing the darkness and catching the dust moats which perpetually floated in the stale air.

He glimpsed a stone floor, well used but swept clean. A warm glow flickered out of sight, casting a shadow of a lone guard, but something didn't feel right.

The wood creaked as he pushed it open a little more, pausing as the sound filled the tunnel.

Glance would be livid if the secret ways were ever discovered.

The shadow of the guard didn't move.

Holding his breath, he pushed harder and stuck his head through the gap.

The shadow of the guard revealed itself to be a tall table with a lamp standing atop the polished surface.

He wasn't in the Watch Tower at all but in a chamber within the upper levels of the castle. But where?

He must have gotten himself turned around in the tunnels.

The room had a thick rug on the floor and matching drapes covering the windows. A large bed occupied the room, larger than his own.

Whoever owned it must be a high-ranking official, a knight, or somebody close to the Baron.

Bane stepped further into the room and slowly closed the door behind him, seeing that from this side, it was a large portrait of an elderly man on a horse.

There was a single door coming from the corridor and another that led out onto a balcony.

He felt like a thief as he crept to the balcony door to get a better idea of where he was. His hand was on the handle and about to push it when he heard an intake of breath.

Instinctively, he went rigid and then slowly slinked into the corner of the room where there was a partial shadow, hoping that he wasn't seen.

Another intake of breath and he turned around but saw nobody.

The covers stirred on the bed and he realised that somebody was in it.

"Bailin?"

The voice was old, the name slurred as if half asleep.

"Bailin, come closer. Let me see you."

A hand with swollen knuckles gripped the bedpost, and like a corpse rising from a grave, an old man pulled himself up into a sitting position.

"Did you not hear me, boy?"

The man stared Bane in the eye, recognising him as someone else, while Bane recognised the man in the bed.

It was his grandfather; it was the Baron. The man responsible for the death of his mother.

Locked under the intense scrutiny, Bane stepped closer, glad that his hood was up, concealing most of his face.

"Fetch me a cup of water, Bailin. This desert sand is turning my throat to leather."

The Baron was old, his eyes sunken, flesh wasted, and skin papery thin. Nothing like he appeared in the portraits Bane had seen dotted around the castle, although there were some discernible features, the narrow bridge of the nose, the thick brow and grey eyes.

Bane crossed the room to a jug on the nightstand and poured water into a cup.

He felt the gaze of the Baron on him as he did so and was under his stare on the way to the bed, wanting nothing more than to throw the cup at him. The cup, a fist, his blade.

"What's wrong with you, Bailin? You're far too quiet. You've been scheming."

Bane said nothing and kept his head down as he held the cup towards his grandfather.

With shaky hands, he tried to raise it to his lips but didn't seem to have the strength.

"Well, help me, boy."

Was he ill? Was this the reason why he hadn't seen him about the castle? Why Felina was overseeing all the important decisions?

He placed his palms beneath the old man's hands and helped raise the cup to his puckered lips.

You killed my mother.

Water ran down his chin and splashed onto his bed robes, yet the Baron's sunken eyes never left Bane's.

"Where's your sister? If she's been meddling with that hedge knight again, I'll have him sent south; you see if I don't."

The cup tumbled as the old man began to cough, his entire body contorting as he struggled to breathe.

Bane glanced at the door, expecting somebody to rush in after hearing the noise, yet nobody came.

The fit subsided and the Baron eased himself back into the pillows, the pain dissolving from his face.

"So, you've finally come to kill your father. It's long past time, Bailin. I thought you'd have done it at Winter's feast."

The man cackled, which turned into another violent fit of coughing.

"Probably for the best that you waited until the castle thought you away in the south. Not that anyone would blame you."

Bane stared at his grandfather. A part of him wondered how he could be of the same blood, and another part wished that he'd never stumbled across him. And a smaller part hoped that he would choke and die.

"Get it done then, Bailin. Take my pillow and place it over my face. In truth, you'd be doing me a favour. My mind isn't my own. My thoughts are so scattered that I sometimes struggle to remember who I am. Go on, take it."

The Baron moved unexpectedly quickly, grasping Bane's wrist and shoving a pillow into his hand.

"End it. Please."

The pillow was soft, duck down, the finest cotton, embroidered with the Shankil coat of arms. Could it really be used as a means to kill?

His grandfather took a wheezing breath, fought a cough back down and then sunk into his bed, lids slowly closing, yet Bane got the impression he was still being watched between the grey lashes.

The old man began to snore. An ugly throaty clacking caught in his throat.

Bane gripped the pillow in both hands.

You killed my mother.

There were worse ways to die, and the Baron was reaching the end of his life anyway. Perhaps helping him through the final door was a mercy.

He leaned across the bed, kneeling upon the sheets as he stretched over his grandfather. Adjusted his weight so he could get a better position above him.

Bane took a breath, held it and then tucked the pillow under the Baron's head, propping him so his airways were clearer.

When he eased himself back, he became aware of a presence behind him.

Simultaneously, he spun, grasping the hilt of his sword as he set his feet apart.

The tall figure in the shadows of the corner of the room remained still.

"How long were you there?" Bane asked, easing his fingers from his sword.

"Long enough to know that I can now trust you with my father's life," Glance replied as he stepped out of the shadows. "I'm sorry, Bane. This was a test."

"You mean I was supposed to find this room and not the Watch Tower?"

Glance nodded and then put his fingers to his lips and gestured for Bane to follow him.

The balcony door creaked as Glance pushed it open, went outside and then closed it again behind them.

The night was fresh, the stars were out, and frost was creating a white sheet out of the bailey and practice grounds below.

"So far, you've been the perfect student. A keen learner, brave, honourable to a fault, yet I still needed to be sure how far your loyalties went."

There was no torch on the balcony and they were both hidden within darkness, yet Bane got the impression that Glance was smiling.

"I followed you through the tunnels but came out through a different door and was in place to watch you enter my father's chamber. It wasn't hard for him to believe you were Bailin. The likeness is remarkable. Yet I almost intervened when he gave you the pillow."

"What is wrong with him?"

Glance stepped to the balustrade, rested his elbows on the stonework and leaned out.

"Old age. His mind hasn't been his own for some time. There are days when he doesn't even know who I am. Others when he remembers the smallest of details from when he was a boy. He might be right – to kill him may have been a mercy. And at one point I thought you would have."

Bane swallowed - he didn't know how close he was to doing it.

He joined his uncle on the balustrade and leaned out, staring down as two guards were patrolling the grounds and seeking out a natural path that would keep him within the shadows of them.

"Do you forgive me?" Glance asked. "It was a mean thing to do."

Bane shrugged. He felt anger, a little hurt at being betrayed, but shook the thought away.

"You had your reasons."

"I did, and now you've proven yourself to be loyal. I can leave you here knowing that a Garik is present in the castle."

Bane turned to face Glance.

"You're leaving?"

His uncle nodded.

"Tomorrow. My father is ill and I don't think this cold northern winter is doing his health any good. I will be escorting him south to spend the harsh seasons in a warmer climate. It might help him unburden his mind. And you'll be busy with learning sword skills and letters. I hear Cuthbur has invited you out on a hunt with him."

Bane smiled.

"It was Lady Felina's idea. She wants us to get used to each other's company outside the practice yard."

"Very wise. My sister would make the perfect Baron if ever women were allowed to rule. But before I go, let me give you a final task that must be done before I return."

Glanced produced a purse from inside his tunic and dropped it into Bane's palm.

"This is for Nan Hilga. You're to leave it on her table. Without her knowing how it got there. You're to be indivisible at all times."

"Nan Hilga? What's it for?" Bane asked, hefting the purse and guessing there were more than a few marks inside.

"Recompense for the tome you're going to steal from her. The same book with which I delivered on the first night we met. You know the one."

"Yes. It was thick with a black binding," Bane said, not wanting to say more."

"Indeed, Master Bane. But don't be coy. You know what was in the book. Come, there are to be no secrets between us."

Without thinking, Bane touched his foramen with the Fug mark, the thorns hidden beneath his dark shirt.

He felt that he was betraying Gelwin when he pulled the sleeve of his jerkin up to the elbow and exposed his arm to the moonlight. She had said to never show anyone, although Glance didn't seem surprised.

"Remarkable," he said as he gently took Bane's arm and inspected it.

He rubbed the tip of a thorn with his thumb and winced.

A bead of blood ran down the pad of his thumb.

"I had my suspicions when Nan Hilga asked me to acquire the book," Glance said, putting it in his mouth. "Have you done anything with it?"

I killed a man. His name was Raif.

"No. I'm not sure what I would do with it. It's a mark, a tattoo."

Glance shook his head as he let go of Bane's arm.

"Then I have a second task for you. When you've acquired the tome, read it."

****

Bane awoke early the next day, opening only one eye as he washed in the basin and dressed into britches, a light shirt and a tunic. He slipped on the vambrace as it was hot, sweaty work in the practice yard, and he would need to roll his sleeves up. He only opened his other eye when the sun had risen enough to chase the shadows into the corners of the walls. He helped himself to a wedge of cheese and yesterday's bread as he silently stalked through the corridors, avoiding everyone and out in the yard.

He arrived at the practice yard before the other fledglings and was shocked to find that steel swords were in the selection barrel instead of the usual wooden ones.

"Time to up the game," Jarl said as he dropped the shields beside the swords. "Nothing helps fledglings learn how to use a shield quicker than when they're up against steel."

Bullif dropped the rest of the shields beside the others and gave a stern nod of approval.

"Don't think about using your own sword in place of one of these," Bullif continued, tapping the practice swords. "You'll blunt it against the inferior steel."

"Or worse, you might cut down one of the other fledglings," Jarl added.

Bullif snorted.

"Worse for sword to get blunt than lose a fledgling," he grunted and then tried to grin, yet it didn't seem to fit his face.

The rest of the fledglings arrived and stared at the steel swords. Except Hemmel, who sauntered to the barrel and picked one out before swinging it around.

"This is going to hurt. Well, it's going to hurt some of you, anyway," he chuckled.

Cuthbur rolled his eyes at the statement while he plucked a sword from the barrel and came to stand beside Bane.

"Are you looking forward to the hunt tomorrow? Jarl reckons there are a few boars on the forest fringes. One of them is particularly nasty. He's been said to attack the guards when they're on patrol."

Bane nodded.

"Sounds like fun. What are we hunting with?"

Cuthbur shrugged.

"We'll be spectating mostly. But my mother will have a bow, and I'm sure Jarl will have one too. She's quite the shot, my mother."

Bane couldn't imagine Lady Felina using a bow, but then, what did he know about Lords and Ladies?

"Quiet," Bullif hissed, and the group of fledglings ceased talking immediately. They knew that if they didn't, it would be ten circuits of the practice yard carrying a sword above their heads. Which was a struggle with the wooden ones. The steel was a lot heavier.

"Go through your forms," Jarl ordered, watching intently as the boys began to work through sets of forms, all of them now able to perform well enough for them to be effective, if not to Bullif's liking.

Bane lost himself in the dance of steel, his world shrinking to just himself, each motion flowing seamlessly into the next.

He became vaguely aware of Bullif watching from his periphery and felt satisfaction as the warrior gave a subtle nod before moving onto Bon, his harsh tones stinging as the stableboy put his feet too close together and toppled over.

After, they were told to pair off and face each other.

"Who's going to bout against me," Hemmel said as he swaggered amongst the fledglings, making a show of brandishing his steel sword.

"Garik, knock this whelp down a peg or two," Jarl said as he walked between them.

Hemmel glanced up at him and Bane smiled back.

Over the weeks the group had gotten closer together, each of the boys having their own strong points and weaknesses. Hemmel's strong point was his ability with the blade. His weakness was his boasting and overconfidence. Bane thought that it was part of his personality and couldn't be changed.

"Sir," Bane said as he snapped to attention and wandered over to Hemmel, winking at the taller lad.

Hemmel swallowed something in his throat; the cockiness dampened somewhat.

They faced off, as did the rest of the fledglings. And waited for Jarl's command.

"Fight."

Hemmel came straight in with a lunge. His blade darted out before Jarl had finished the word.

Instinct took over Bane's body as he brought his shield about while stepping back, easily catching the blow, yet it was strong enough to rattle the handle and armrest. He deflected it away while coming back with a thrust of his own.

Hemmel dodged, slipping into Dancing Thistle and butted the rim of his shield against Bane's, hard enough to loosen the arm bracket, yet it still held.

Bane grinned. It was a good attack, and he barely parried the sweeping cut from the blade, the morning sun glinting from the steel, the clash of the two metals as it met his.

"Stop smiling at each other like maids dancing around the Maypole. Put your opponent down," Bullif growled as he watched, shaking his head.

Hemmel gritted his teeth, leaned away from Bane's arcing cut and caught him a glancing blow to the shoulder.

"You've been practising," Bane said as he rolled his shoulder and pushed through the pain.

"I have," Hemmel admitted, switching forms and coming in high, using his height to full advantage. "I need to keep on top of you."

Bane caught a flurry of jabs to the shield, each rattling the arm bracket. He could feel the nails working loose.

Dancing from Rising Wind to Stalking Crane, Bane sidestepped around a vicious thrust, Hemmel's blade sliding beneath his arm, hooked a foot around an ankle and drove his elbow into Hemmel's sternum.

He heard his opponent gasp, but the tall youth twisted away and came back quicker, using several forms to get through Bane's defence.

"Good," Jarl said as he came to watch, as did some of the fledglings who had finished their bouts.

Steel clashed against steel, Bane wondering if Hemmel would win this.

"Nice," Jarl said as Hemmel leaned away from an ill-judged slice and came back with an overhead lunge, narrowly missing Bane's head.

The rest of the fledglings had finished and now formed a rough circle around them, Bullif nodding approvingly while Cuthbur winced as Bane caught another blow to the same shoulder.

"This one will be mine," Hemmel roared as he suddenly broke away from a form, taking Bane by surprise, swinging out with his shield, the rim clattering against Bane's and dislodging the arm bracket completely.

He managed to catch another body shuddering blow and the shield broke apart.

Bane ducked the next attack and rolled behind Hemmel.

Now shield-less, he grasped his sword with both hands and deflected the next cut and thrust.

Seeing that his opponent was almost bested, Hemmel came on stronger, using both shield and sword to batter him.

With a final swing of his shield, he knocked Bane's sword wide, leaving the other side of his body exposed.

On impulse, Bane brought his shield about to catch the oncoming sword, yet it wasn't there; it was on the ground in pieces.

He'd lost the bout. Hemmel would strike his naked arm and then follow up with a jab to the chest.

Unable to stop the momentum, Bane braced himself for the pain which would erupt as the blunt steel struck.

Time slowed as Hemmel leaned it, jaw clenched as his blade cut into Bane's forearm.

White heat exploded from Bane's elbow to his wrist, the vambrace shredding before his gaze and the thorn tattoo came alive.

His arm was a thriving tangle of needle-sharp points, catching the oncoming steel and repelling it with such force that the sword flung high, propelling Hemmel away.

Impulses overriding his shock, Bane dropped the thorn-bristling arm, dipped his shoulder and drove forward into the startled youth, knocking him to the ground.

Flapping his arm to cover the tattoo with the torn fabric that remained, Bane put his boot on Hemmel's chest and his sword to his heart.

It was a win, and a good bout like that would normally be met with approving claps and nods, yet there was only silence.

They'd seen it. Bane could read their faces as they stared at him and at the arm of the tunic, which was torn open as if ravaged by a wolf.

Cuthbur had his mouth open as if to say something but then closed it, bafflement creasing his brow. Bon's jaw was hanging slack as if attached to his skull by a broken hinge.

Jarl picked up the shredded vambrace and stared at it before tossing the useless strips of leather to the ground.

"Looks like you'll need a new one," he said, breaking the silence. "Right, you lot, pick someone else and let's carry on."

When nobody moved he clapped his hands together to get them going.

The fledglings slowly partnered up with each other, some glancing back before they began clashing steel against steel again.

"How?" was all Hemmel said as he propped himself up onto his elbows, sweat and dirt smeared across his forehead.

"It doesn't matter how. It was a good bout. You're vastly improving and will do your father proud," Jarl said as he grasped the boy's hand and pulled him to his feet.

"But he had no shield," he continued, staring from the blade in his hand to Bane's arm.

"The vambrace had steel rods, that's all. But your blow managed to smash them to pieces. That would have been a win for you. Now pair up with Bon."

Jarl waited until Hemmel had gone. He stared at Bane before leaving, looking as confused as the rest of them.

When they were alone, Jarl steered Bane around the corner of the rock, away from view.

"Now, are you going to tell me how in the fugging ring did you do that?"

He felt a little shame at revealing his secret to Glance the previous night but also, if he was being honest with himself, relief.

Checking that there were no prying eyes, Bane pulled the torn material aside and held his arm out to the old knight.

Jarl leaned closer, inspecting the tattoo with curious fascination. He was about to press a finger to it when Bane pulled back.

"I wouldn't. It seems that anyone who touches it gets cut."

Jarl pulled his hand away and glanced around before leaning against the rock.

"I've seen nothing like it. And to repel steel like that. Is it witchcraft?"

Bane shrugged as he covered the tattoo back up.

"I wish I knew. I was left out for the Fug when I was a day old. The first tide took me away from Crookfell, but returned me later with this. It's been hidden beneath a vambrace for most of my life. Very few people know about it."

"What else can it do," Jarl asked, wearily glancing back at the arm.

Bane shook his head.

"I don't know. I didn't know it could do what it did."

He remained where he was for a time, watching Jarl as he chewed on his lip, deep in thought.

He was expecting to be told that he could no longer be a fledgling. That freaks like him don't belong in the castle.

"What are you thinking," he asked, unable to prolong the inevitable and wishing that he had chosen a different shield. One that wouldn't have broken apart, then none of this would have happened. But then, he respected Jarl enough not to have secrets.

"I'm thinking we need to get you a new vambrace, and if you're sworn to protect young Cuthbur, you'll need to tell him. And I can't keep this from Lady Felina."

Relief flooded Bane, but then he wondered what Cuthbur and his mother would think.

"You're coming on the hunt tomorrow. It might be best that we tell them then. Now, I suggest you pick up another shield and join your friends. And keep that thing covered."

****

It was another star-filled night; the few shreds of cloud streaked across the full moon. If he was out in the open, he still wouldn't be easy to see, but as he slowly prowled through the trees to Nan Hilga's house, he was invisible.

Midnight had long passed, and no lights were on in the hovel, yet the fine tendrils of a dying fire floated up from the chimney, letting him know that Hilga had not long gone to bed.

Silence was his companion as he crept along the side of the stone building and peered into the window.

The room within was shrouded in darkness; only the smouldering embers that glowed lazily from the hearth lit the chamber enough to reveal that Hilga was in the other room.

Holding his breath, Bane pressed lightly on the window and slid a thin strip of copper into the crack, a loop already twisted into one end.

Glance had taught him how to unlock this particular window. His uncle told him that he'd needed to enter on a number of occasions this way.

He rolled the wire between finger and thumb, the wire swivelling until the loop hooked over the small bolt, and then, ever so slowly, slid it free.

Once he pulled the wire back through and stowed it in one of his many pockets, he carefully swung the window open and delicately climbed inside.

He was like a prowling cat, unseen, the master of shadow. The King of the dark.

With a well-practised drop, he landed on the floor, bending his knees to absorb the noise and straightened up, a smile on his face at the accomplishment.

He did it.

His first attempt at entering a home was a success, although he felt the guilt of it being the home of Nan Hilga.

The tome he needed was on a shelf and he confidently took a step towards it, placing the pouch of coins on the table and whispering an apology to Hilga.

It was then that his cloak snagged against a candle stick and pulled it from its stand.

Helpless, he turned to see it clatter against the floor, the ironwork making enough noise to make up for all the silences he had acquired through the night and more.

He flinched, heart hammering inside his chest as he sought an escape, gaze darting to the door, but Hilga's voice came from the opposite side.

"Not very good at stealing, are you," Nan Hilga said as she struck a strike box and lit a lamp.

She was sitting in her chair, stick held in a knobbly grasp while wearing a knowing smirk.

She picked up the bag of coins, hefted it in her palms and then placed it inside her pocket.

Bane looked to the door, but what was the point? He had been caught.

Shame filled him as he dropped onto the stool, sighing deeply as he thought of an excuse but couldn't come up with anything. And he loathed to lie to her after all she had done.

"I came for the tome, Nan Hilga. I'm sorry," he said, wondering what she would do. She could have him tried for robbery. She could have the castle lock him up. And what would his uncle say? Or worse, would Lady Felina have him stripped of his rights and banished from the castle.

For the second time that day, Bane wished he could start it over again. Twice now he was in peril of losing everything.

The stern wrinkles around Nan Hilga's eyes stretched as she began to cackle.

"Young Glance said you might be visiting," she chuckled. "He'd already asked for the tome and told me how you might try using the quiet ways."

"You knew?"

Nan Hilga nodded.

"Go on then, take it," she said, pointing her stick at the shelf.

Bane lifted it down, the skin of the book feeling brittle.

"Careful with it, mind. It's old. I'd say a few hundred years older than me."

"Thank you," Bane said, shame still burning his cheeks.

Nan Hilga smiled warmly.

"You've filled out a bit and standing taller. Castle life must be treating you well."

Bane returned the smile.

"It has. I'm now personal bodyguard to Master Cuthbur, once I've been trained."

"Gelwin would be proud of you. Young Nel, too."

Bane felt a sudden pang of loss. He missed Gelwin terribly. And also the mother he never had.

He nodded thanks and crossed the room to the open window.

"Use the door. And don't worry, none. Glance has never been able to sneak up on me, either."

Bane closed the door behind him, realising that Nan Hilga had been the only constant in his life. Well, apart from Dodd, no doubt he would be in the tavern or sleeping off a hangover.

He passed through the trees and untied his mare from where he'd left her.

She greeted him by trying to bite his elbow as he climbed into the saddle. But he was used to that now.

He tapped her flank with his heels and set off back to the castle, mixed feelings clouding his mind.

He only hoped the tome would give him some answers. But first, he needed to learn how to read it.

18

The Hunt

The mare snorted as Bane clucked his tongue, edging her into line beside Cuthbur and the rest of the hunting party.

Snow coated the ground, seeming to wash the countryside clean.

"Easy, boy," Cuthbur soothed his stallion, who had begun to stomp impatiently on the frozen ground. "I think your mare is in season. Dart doesn't usually get this skittish. Unless it's the other horses. He's not used to riding in such a large party."

Bane couldn't give an opinion. He'd only ever ridden with Glance or by himself.

"Do you think we really need twenty to hunt down a few boars?" Cuthbur asked.

Bane stroked his mount's neck as he stared at the group of men and horses, all eager to set out into the forest. There were ten on horseback with bows and another ten on foot carrying pikes.

"I guess we'll need to span out to cover the ground. In the forest it wouldn't be hard to run away from a small number. But twenty will cast a large enough net," Bane replied.

He caught Jarl's gaze as the knight was in conversation with Lady Felina and wondered if he had revealed his secret yet. He didn't think so as she hadn't looked his way.

"Are you not getting your bow ready?" Bane asked, seeing that Cuthbur's bow was over his shoulder, the string pressing into thick furs.

"There's no point. Mother warned me to stay on the periphery. The boars have been known to attack horses."

Bane watched as Lady Felina readied her bow, nocking an arrow to the string but only partially putting pressure on it.

Jarl put a horn to his lips and gave a single blast, and they were off.

Bane gripped tightly to the reins as the mare suddenly broke into a trot and needed to pull her back level with the rest.

The party moved as one, the pikeman leading the way, fanning out as they entered the tree line, boots crunching through the frost, breaths visible in the still air.

The naked limbs bristled with ice as he pushed his mount between two oaks, ducking so the hilt of his sword didn't catch on the low-hanging burghs.

The forest was quiet, the animals aware of the approaching men and remained hidden.

They followed a deer track that took them closer to the foothills, the mountain looming high through the canopy, the silver ring of fog on its ascent.

Seeing the Fug reminded Bane that there was something he needed to say to Cuthbur.

The track skirted a shallow stream and Jarl and Felina rode through the water to the opposite bank, taking most of the riders and pikeman with them.

Bane knew the forest well from his life as a forager and realised that the track would take them to the fringes of the foothills in the opposite direction from Crookfell.

The stream would fork after the bend with the branch on their side leading to a gully before rejoining further down.

"Glad we had a break from sword practice this morning," Cuthbur said, rubbing at his chest where he had taken a jab from another fledgling yesterday. "Sometimes I think Bullif likes to see us beaten."

Bane grinned.

"I expect he does," Bane said, remembering the extra lessons he was receiving from the warrior with his own sword. The forms were the same, but because they didn't use shields, he took the brunt of the attacks on his arms and legs. Yet he got a sense that there was mutual respect between Master and student.

They came to the fork in the stream and the main party disappeared one way while Bane and Cuthbur went the other.

The trees grew thicker along the bank, so they needed to head inwards a couple of spans, keeping the stream in sight as they followed a natural curve that swept along the gully.

A short blast of Jarl's horn echoed from somewhere to their right, startling the horses, followed by the shouting of men.

"Fug it," the rider who had accompanied them said, staring out through the trees. "Seems I should have gone with your mother. They'll have the first kill."

Sir Hoskin, a knight from a town Bane had never heard of - way down in the south in a part of the country he had never heard of. Bane thought him arrogant and rude. What the Crookfell folk would have called a Goldy Pig - rich, entitled and with a self-righteous arrogance.

Sir Hoskin kicked his horse into moving closer to the gully, attempting to ride up the side to get a better view as the shouts of men across the stream rose and the barking screeches of an animal filled the air.

He reached the top of the gully and stood on his stirrups, leaning across the saddle horn.

"They have it," he yelled down to Cuthbur, not addressing Bane. It seemed he wasn't good enough to be included in the exchange.

Cuthbur nudged his stallion towards the knight intending on joining him on the rise, eager to see his mother in action, but there was a sudden explosion of motion from the bottom of the gully.

Cuthbur reined his horse in as a huge boar rushed up the rise, squealing angrily as it drove its tusks into Sir Hoskin's horse.

Bane had never seen a boar up close but had heard stories of the beasts. And this one was right out of a bard's tale.

The collision was so violent that it knocked the defenceless horse over, taking the knight down with it in a tangle of screams and squeals.

Cuthbur's stallion reared up, hooves kicking the air, wild eyes seeking a way to escape while its rider clung to its neck.

Bane kicked his mare's flanks to get to Cuthbur while the two pikemen ran at the boar, weapons levelled before them as they thrust their pikes into the beast.

The squealing intensified as the boar thrashed its head from side to side as it backed away from the dead horse.

It turned on the pikemen, blood glistening from the sharp horns on either side of its snarling mouth, the hunched muscles on its back that were of a height with the men, bunched as it came on.

Cuthbur's stallion reared again, this time with such force that he couldn't hold on and was flung from the saddle.

He landed on his back, head bouncing from the ground as the stallion ran off through the trees, stirrups flapping from the riderless saddle.

Bane was off his mare in an instant and ran to Cuthbur's side, aware that his own mount hadn't stayed around and had shot off in the opposite direction.

Cuthbur struggled into a sitting position, his face slack and dazed. Then he glanced to the boar on the rise and his eyes went wide.

The beast tipped its head back and screeched in rage, biting down on the shaft of a pike, its teeth easily crunching through the thick wood and breaking it in two.

The men backed away, skin going as white as the undisturbed frost - not the patches covered in steaming blood, while Sir Hoskin moaned from beneath the mess of his dead horse.

"By the All-Mother," one of the men murmured as the boar lowered its head, snorting steam as it scraped the ground with its feet, readying to charge.

Bane turned Cuthbur's face up to his own and placed a finger to his lips, then pointed towards the closest tree with branches low enough for them to grasp.

Cuthbur nodded that he understood and slowly stood. A yelp escaped him as he put weight on a foot and would have collapsed if Bane hadn't caught him.

The sound caught the boar's attention, its large head swivelling on a thick neck as it screeched again.

The men used the momentary distraction to run, sprinting down the rise into the gully and began to flounder across the stream.

They were going for help, but Bane realised that before the rest of the party would get to them, the boar would have charged.

The beast began to scrape the ground again, this time its head lowered in their direction, large haunches bunching up as it readied to charge.

The tree that was climbable was the same distance away as the boar was to them.

They wouldn't make it in time - not both.

Cuthbert realised the facts at the same instance and let go of Bane's arm.

"Run. You'll make it," he said as he pulled the bow from around his shoulder and, with shaking fingers, nocked an arrow.

"I'm the one that's supposed to be protecting you, remember?" Bane said as he drew his sword, eyes fixed on the ginormous boar.

"Then we're both going to die," Cuthbur said, swallowing hard as he brought his bow up and stretched the string until his fingers touched his ear.

"Most likely," Bane agreed, setting his feet and wondering if there was any point. The monster would be a mass of charging meat, a solid wall weighing heavier than two horses.

"My first hunt and my last."

As Cuthbur finished the sentence, the boar charged.

It was a broiling mass of unstoppable carnage, a pike still left embedded in its flank bouncing with the movement, but the beast didn't notice, its hate-filled eyes locked solely on them.

Cuthbur let loose the arrow and it shot past the boar, skittering into the trees and missing completely.

Not that it would have done anything more than annoy it should it have hit.

Bane lowered his legs as the monster came on, baring down on them, leading with lethal tusks.

At the final moment, he dived to the side and shoved Cuthbur as hard as he could.

They both hit the frozen ground, the beast snagging Bane's cloak and tearing it from his neck.

Cuthbur yelped again, the wind driven from him as he rolled onto his back.

Bane was already on his feet, taking long strides and putting distance between himself and the boy he was to protect.

The boar squealed in frustration as he circled around a tree, never losing its momentum as it came on again, a tusk scraping along the ground as it shook its head and gouging a furrow from the hard earth.

Bane rolled out of the way, feeling the hot breath of the beast and was up on his feet, ready for the next charge, but the boar chose an easier target, seeing Cuthbert scrambling away, using his hands to drag his injured leg.

There was no escape for him.

"Here, pig," Bane yelled, attempting to draw the boar's attention yet it was clear the beast wouldn't be swayed.

Its screeches became wilder as it narrowed the distance to the prey.

Cuthbur kicked his legs as he struggled, a scream rising from him as he knew his attempts were useless, arms rising as the monster rushed closer.

Bane forgot himself as he bounded towards Cuthbur and slid between beast and friend.

His sword was held before him, tip poised and aimed at the central mass of the raging boar, so close now that he saw the individual bristles of the wiry fur and the sweat beneath.

He became aware of horses riding hard from the stream and several arrows thudded into the flank of the beast, yet they had no effect.

Instinct took control of Bane as he braced for the impact. It was as if his body was not his own as he drove the blade into the hard forest floor and brought his tattooed arm up.

Intense pain engulfed his forearm as an explosion of shredded cloth filled his vision, the boar vanishing behind a black screen of thorns that thrived in a circular motion until they formed a round shield.

The monster collided with the thriving thorns, propelling Bane backwards into Cuthbur. Yet his sword, scraping deeper into the earth, anchored him.

When he slid to a stop it took a moment for his mind to catch up with what he was seeing.

On its back, legs kicking the air, was the boar. Its screeches bouncing around the forest in rage.

Without hesitation, Bane sprinted towards the floundering beast, the thorns in his arms shrinking back into the tattoo as he leapt upon the exposed belly and drove his sword through the soft flesh.

Blood fountained up from the open wound, the screech becoming a siren's scream, its head thrashing desperately as Bane twisted the blade.

And then it went still.

A last shuddering breath escaped the boar, steam floating out from the slack jaw.

Bewildered, Bane looked down at his arm. Shreds of cloth dangled from his sleeve, the tattoo showing beneath.

One word kept repeating in his head.

How?

Hooves splashed through the stream as the party of hunters crossed, water broiling up onto the banks as they galloped towards them.

"Cuthbur?" Lady Felina yelled as she brought her mare to a halt next to her son and dismounted. "Are you hurt?"

Cuthbur sat up and slowly shook his head, his gaze never leaving Bane's.

"I think I twisted my ankle, but other than that, no. I, I thought I was going to die," Cuthbur admitted.

Bane felt every stare. Cuthbur's, his mother's, Jarl's and the knights on horseback. They scrutinised him as if he were a witch. As if he were the master of dark magic.

Jarl nudged his mount closer, the skittish horse whinnying in complaint at being close to the huge boar, even though it was dead.

"Your tattoo, I take it?" he whispered so only Bane would hear.

Bane didn't need to answer. His tunic was shredded from wrist to elbow - and Jarl was at the front of the party as they came across the stream and would have been close enough to see what happened.

The retired knight turned in his saddle to address the rest of the group.

"I watched it stumble. Probably a lucky arrow in the right place. Still, if it hadn't been for Master Garik taking advantage, I dare say things would have ended differently. Well done, lad."

A cheer rose up from the rest of the party, knights and pikemen alike, bringing a warmth to Bane's face that he wished he could control.

"And look at the size of the beast," said another as he came closer. He was a younger knight whom Bane had seen around the castle but had never spoken to. "Its head will look fine displayed in the trophy room, wouldn't you say, Lady Felina? This is truly a tale for the bards."

"Indeed, Sir Darinpor. And we should have a feast. A feast to celebrate not only the hunt but Master Garik himself, who has now twice saved my son."

His cheeks now burning, Bane was relieved to hear a muffled cry.

"Help me," Sir Hoskin pleaded from beneath his dead horse.

As others rushed to the aid of the fallen knight and attention diverted away, Bane pulled his sword free from the boar, creating a sucking squelch, gore dripping from the blade.

He clambered down from its belly and caught the rag Jarl had tossed him and wiped the sword clean before slipping it back into its scabbard.

Amidst a great deal of grunting and a little chuckling, the knights and the pikemen pulled Sir Hoskin from beneath his horse.

Pale-faced and flustered, it seemed the man's only injury was his pride.

He stared open-mouthed at the corpse of the boar, his eyes growing wider as Sir Darinpor explained who had felled it.

Two more pikemen appeared at the other side of the clearing, bringing Cuthbur's and Bane's horses.

Bane's mare stomped the ground and refused to come any closer, no matter how hard the pikeman pulled on her reins.

Bane went to her, soothing her with a gentle stroke to the neck before leading her towards the group.

They helped Cuthbur into the saddle, and then the party headed back, Sir Hoskin having to share a saddle with another knight.

The pikemen remained to bring back the two boars which were killed that day.

Bane rode beside Cuthbur as they followed a deer track out of the forest. Neither of them spoke, although Cuthbur kept glancing Bane's way, the frown never leaving his brow.

It wasn't until they were clear of the forest and the bulk of the party was ahead of them that Cuthbur slowed.

"How?"

His eyes fell on Bane's arm, the one with the shredded sleeve.

They were now at the back of the group and out of earshot from others.

Bane slowly rolled the torn fabric of his tunic up to reveal the tattoo. The thorns seemed longer somehow, more deadly as if seeing them come alive before had added weight to the ink.

"I'm Fug marked," Bane said, twisting his arm so that Cuthbur caught it all. When he reached out as others had done before, Bane pulled it away.

"It'll cut you if you touch it," he explained, wishing that he had more answers. Yet the vents of the day had only brought more questions.

"Fug marked?"

Bane nodded and then explained how he had come by the tattoo.

To his credit, Cuthbur listened without interruption, his frown deepening at times, mouth open as if to ask a question and then closed again.

Afterwards, there came an awkward silence where the two of them rode without speaking. Occasionally there was a snatch of conversation from the party ahead as a word caught in the wind.

As the castle came into view, Cuthbur leaned closer and slowed.

"So, what happened in the practice yard yesterday with Hemmel - that was also the tattoo?"

"Yes," Bane admitted, feeling encouragement at the question. "By right, Hemmel did win the bout, as my shield fell apart, leaving me exposed."

"But your tattoo saved your arm. As it saved both our lives today."

Cuthbur smiled.

"Forgive my quietness. I'm a slow thinker sometimes. And this was something that needed a lot of thought."

Bane returned the smile.

"I'm only glad you didn't have me tried as a witch."

Cuthber laughed.

"What, and miss out on having a god-marked bodyguard at my side? No, I believe fates have brought us together, Bane. And I am glad of it. Does anyone else know of this secret?"

Bane shrugged as he counted them off in his head – those that were alive anyway. Nan Hilga, Dodd, Glance and Jarl.

"There's five, including you," he said, not knowing if the raiders recognised what it was. Raif certainly knew.

"Is there any point in covering it up," Cuthbur asked as they rode through the gates. "If it's going to shred whatever you're wearing anyway."

He put a finger to his lips in thought.

"Maybe the leather smith could put something together. Something that would split in two when called upon. A special vambrace or something."

Bane laughed as he tried to imagine a leather contraption on his arm that opened and closed, yet couldn't quite put it together in his mind.

"I doubt it would work. I still don't fully know what it does other than act as a shield," and a way to slit open arteries in the neck, he might have added but didn't.

"I do have an old tome that speaks of it, although I need to learn to read."

"I'll read the tome. If you will allow it."

Bane scratched at his arm, feeling the thorns bristling along the surface.

"That does make sense. If you don't mind."

Cuthbur grinned.

"I could do with something other than Military Tactics and The Art of Diplomacy to read. Besides, I dare say I'll be off my feet for a few days."

The horses followed those in front until they reached the stables. Jarl dismounted and came to Cuthbur, taking the reins from him.

"Come now, Master Cuthbur, let's have the healers look at you. I doubt you'll be well enough for the practice yard come tomorrow."

Bane watched them leave before handing his mount over to Bon, who came out from the stables, face beaming with pride.

"Is it true?" he asked, playfully thumping Bane on the shoulder. "Did you slay a boar with only your sword?"

"Not only a boar," Sir Darinpor said as he handed the reins to another stableboy. "It was a monster. The biggest beast on this side of the Fug. And he faced it off as though it were a badger."

The knight bowed, tipping his hat as he mimicked a sword thrust in the air.

"A single blow and the monster was slain. I won't lie, Garik, I heard the rumours about what you did at Crookfell with those raiders and thought they were more likely embellished, but from what I witnessed today, I believe every word."

The knight bowed again as he backed away and then went to join the other knights as they began to discuss the coming feast.

Bon was now staring at him with his mouth open, his teeth clashing together as he snapped it shut.

"I wish I was there," he said, absently stroking the horse which had become impatient with waiting outside and wanted to join the others in the stables.

"It wasn't that courageous. I got lucky, is all. The boar stumbled and I managed to stick it before it got back to its feet."

"Still, wish I was there."

There came a shout from within, and the Stable Master's booming voice echoed out.

"Bon?"

Bon cringed as he gave Bane an apologetic smile before disappearing inside.

Alone once again, Bane made his way across the castle grounds to the servant's entrance, stalking in his silent ways and unconsciously manoeuvring out of the line of sight of people.

He crept through the door, his boots making the lightest of touches along the stone as he meandered through the many corridors and steps, avoiding being seen by anyone.

Once in his chamber he closed the door and removed the torn tunic. Hopefully a tailor could mend it. It would be a shame to waste the material.

From his wardrobe he snatched an old shirt and slipped it on. Then taking a lamp, made his way through the secret door and worked his way through the tunnels to the study.

It was eerily quiet in the large circular room. Even more so now that Glance was away. He retrieved the tome he had not quite stolen from Nan Hilga and sat by the window.

Carefully he turned the pages until he found the image that matched his tattoo.

The ink had faded to grey on the brittle paper, but the size and shape were perfectly drawn, as was the pattern of the twine beneath. Whoever drew the picture was a skilled artist.

He brought the book closer to his face as he tried to decipher the writing.

The words were small. A tangled swirling text of several lines.

Bane had learned a few of the letters and some short words since beginning his reading lessons and only recognised some here. One of them was a short word of only three letters.

He traced the letters with his finger, skin scraping along the paper.

TYR

He pronounced the sound it made, stumbling with the word until it fit.

Then it came to him.

Weeks ago, Glance had instructed him to look at all the covers of the books in the study. To become familiar with them so if he needed anything, he knew where to search.

He thought it was a waste of his time as he couldn't read any, yet he persisted and was glad he did. He knew where one of the books was that had a similar word on its spine to the one in the tome.

TYR.

It took him a moment to locate the book and then brought it back to the chair.

He blew dust from the cover, revealing that there was an illustration. It was so faded that he could make out a head and a partial torso and arm. The rest was lost.

This tome was even older than the one he already had.

The spine creaked as he delicately opened it, the pages giving off a musty smell and what writing remained had become so faded it was all but lost to the brown specks that were eating the paper.

Yet determined to find some clues to the tattoo, he slowly turned each page. Some began to tear while others were stuck together, but eventually, he came to the middle.

Gently, he lifted the book closer to the window and, as he tilted it, caught the outline of an illustration.

It was a battle. Immense dog like creatures and serpents fighting against men. At the centre of the battle were two giants fighting each other. One had a snake-like head and fought with a curved blade and spear, while the other was human-shaped and wielded a sword and what appeared to be a black circular shield.

The snake-headed giant had thrust the blade of his spear into the torso of the other, yet from the picture, Bane saw that the giant was mid-swing to severing his attacker's head.

Bane softly blew air over the page and cleared some of the dust, revealing the shield wasn't as smooth as it first appeared. The artist drew the thorns so intricately that he recognised the pattern.

He had seen it earlier that day when he deflected the boar. And the same pattern swirled beneath his sleeve now.

What did it mean?

He studied the illustration more, seeing how realistic the battle seemed. It was as if the artist had been there. Yet that couldn't be true. The giants were not real. And neither were dog people who fought on two legs.

Then, as he looked at the backdrop, he almost dropped the book.

He recognised the area. The Fug wasn't there, but the mountain was identical. And from the angle of the view, the battle was taking place where the castle was standing.

He turned through the rest of the pages. There were a couple more images, yet time had faded them to nothing.

When he closed the book, he traced a finger over the word again.

Tyr.

He said it out load before he closed the tome and set it down next to the other.

Perhaps there were more books in the study with that word on it. He decided to commit the rest of the day to searching.

19

Through The Mist

He'd found nothing more in the study of Tyr. He didn't know if the word was the giant's name or was translated as thorns in the old tongue. He hoped Cuthbur might find more among the decaying pages of the tome he left earlier on his way to the practice yard. It had been snowing then, and an icy chill descended from the mountain, yet he'd soon worked up a sweat - as did the rest of the fledglings.

When they were finished, they pestered him with questions about the boar and how he had brought it down. Even Bullif was interested.

He was glad when he finally left and made his way back, hoping that Cuthbur might have found something.

He was almost through the servant's door when Belle came marching out, fists by her side as she stumbled into him.

"Beg your pardon, Sir...Bane?"

Bane smiled at her, yet Belle didn't smile back.

Her eyes were red and swollen as if she had been crying, and she began to fuss with the hem of her dress as she glanced away.

"Belle, what is it?"

Before she had the chance to answer, Randel was pacing down the corridor towards them, his face pinched and stern. On his side was another maid, older than Belle, smirking.

"Forgive me, Master Garik," Randel said, glaring at Belle, who had stepped away and put a little distance between them. Her head was downcast, but Bane got the feeling she was crying again.

"Belle, come with me," Randel insisted as he gestured with his finger for her to follow. "It's bad enough that I receive complaints about you from other staff, and you've been told about being over-familiar with people above your station. And now I catch you attempting to talk with a man of title."

"It's because she's a turnip plucker, Mr Randel. they can't help it," the maid said and then glanced away as Randel frowned.

Belle sniffed as she raised her face, red eyes catching Bane's briefly before returning to the floor.

He guessed she was on the edge of quitting the castle. And from the smugness on the other girl's face, Bane thought that was exactly what they wanted.

With her lips pressed tightly together, Belle raised her head again, a resolve coming over her as if coming to a decision, but before she spoke, Bane stepped closer.

"It was I that bumped into her, Randel. And that was only to ask if she would be my guest to the feast this evening."

Randel opened his mouth, his frown softening as he addressed him.

"The feast in your name, Sir. Might I congratulate you on your hunt."

Bane nodded, hiding the irritation he was feeling. "However, Master Garik, inviting a maid as your guest is out of the question. Young Belle will be required to serve at the feast. And stations should never mix."

The smugness returned to the older maid, her gaze locking with Belle's as her smirk widened.

Bane had seen the way some knights act around the servants and staff of the castle and cringed at how they spoke with them. He'd promised himself that however life treated him at Garik, he would never speak to the working staff with anything short of respect. But for this one time, he was willing to make an exception.

He stepped closer to Randel, stretching tall so he was peering down his nose.

"I insist, Randel. Belle is to be my guest this evening," he said, putting on a plummy voice to match Sir Hoskin's. "I may choose who I please. If you have any issues with that, please take it up with the Baron."

"But Sir, the Baron isn't resident at the moment," Randel replied, flustered. "It would be quite inappropriate for you to be seen with a maid…"

Bane didn't know what the next words were going to be as he stepped closer, forcing the Head of Staff to take a step back.

"A maid? Like my mother was?" he said, then turned his attention to the other girl who had stopped staring at Belle, her mouth falling open. "A turnip plucker, like myself?"

Bane grinned the way he had seen Bullif do before he jabbed an exposed part of your body that wasn't protected in the practice yard. He felt satisfaction as the girl stepped behind Randel.

"By inviting my friend, Belle, I am staying with my own kind."

Bane leaned closer.

"And if anyone treats her differently because she is Crookfell born then they will learn to regret it."

He caught the maid's eyes as he spoke, hoping that his reputation would stop the bullying.

After a moment, Randel cleared his throat and regained his composure.

"Very well, Sir. I will see to the arrangements."

The Head of Staff gave a curt nod and marched off down the corridor, the maid at his heels seeming a lot less smug.

"And she will need the rest of the afternoon off to prepare," Bane called after them.

Randel paused long enough to confirm he had heard with another nod before carrying on.

"Bane? What have you done?" Belle asked, reaching out to grasp his hand. "You'll ruin it for yourself."

"I'm not worried about me. My bloodline - bastard born or not - gives me some privileges."

"Thank you," she said and leaned up to kiss him on his cheek. "That was the kindest thing anyone has ever done."

"I'm only returning the kindness you and Dew gave me in the village," Bane said, feeling the heat from the kiss as he stepped away. It lingered, along with Belle's intense gaze.

"How is Dew?" he asked, trying to change the subject.

Belle shook her head.

"I don't know. I've not been home in weeks and only catch fleeting words with my mother as she delivers the kindling."

Bane worried as Belle's face suddenly turned white.

"I have nothing to wear to the feast," she blurted out. "I have only my uniform."

"Then I'll take you home. You've suddenly got a free afternoon," he chuckled. "Have you ever ridden on a horse before?

It wasn't long before they were both laughing as Bane steered the mare down the valley towards Crookfell, Belle clinging to his waist.

She was wearing his winter cloak over her shoulder, and every time he glanced around, she beamed back at him, never looking happier.

As the valley bottom gave way to the open land, Bane tapped his heel to the mare's flank, and she began to trot.

Belle shrieked and clung tighter.

"I'm going to fall off," she laughed.

"No, you won't," Bane said, allowing the mare to break into a canter, her main billowing in the freezing air.

He slowed as they entered the village, steering the horse past the homes he had once avoided, the folk coming out to see who was riding past.

It wasn't long before doors were opening, and people were standing outside, gawping.

When they passed the swine pens, Mr Gobbin stared open-mouthed, about to tip his hat to them, when recognition twisted his features.

Bane ignored him, clucking his tongue to encourage the horse on while Belle childishly blew him a kiss.

When they skirted the forge, Girant came and waved, his young son coming out with him, dressed in a small leather apron like his father.

It was one of the only places Bane missed when he left for the castle. But he was glad he did. It wouldn't have been long before young Tomm would be working the bellows.

As they rode up the narrow lane to the lumber yard, they noticed that Belle's mother was already out on the front porch, stacking kindling into bundles to be tied.

When she saw them coming she dropped the kindling she'd been holding, hands going to her mouth.

"Belle?" she said anxiously as she met them, catching Bane's eye before she looked down and attempted to curtsy.

"There's no need for that, Mrs Camwell," Bane said as he climbed from the horse and offered Belle his hand, yet she had already slid off and came rushing into her mother's embrace.

"You've not been told to leave, have you?"

Belle shook her head.

"No. But let me tell you while you help me get ready for the feast."

Mrs Camwell shook her head.

"Feast?"

"Yes. Bane has invited me to be his guest at the castle this evening."

"You mean Master Garik?"

"Just, Bane," Bane said. I'm still the same boy who used to split your wood, Mrs Camwell."

"Nonsense, Master Garik, Bane. You bring my Belle from the castle, riding through the village on a horse - this will be the talk of Crookfell for some time," she laughed. "My Belle on a horse. But let us not stand out here talking. Come inside, and let's have a proper natter. Tell me more of this feast."

Bane heard the familiar thwack of an axe meeting wood from around the back of the property.

"I think I'll take a stroll if that's fine with you ladies," he said, leaving them to catch up.

He found Dew behind a stack of freshly split logs. The tall youth set a log down on the stump and hit it with the axe, the blade catching the edge and sending it spinning back into the pile.

"Fug it," Dew hissed.

He hastily bent down to pick up another, pausing as Bane's shadow fell over him.

"Need a stacker?" Bane asked, grinning at his friend.

Dew glanced up, brows coming together for a moment before a smile lit his face.

"No, I'll stack. You were much better at splitting."

Bane removed his cloak and rolled up his sleeves before taking the axe from his friend.

Dew placed a log on the stump and Bane split it down the centre, the two halves falling away and making a satisfying thud.

They worked in silence for a time, Bane enjoying the familiarity, the smoothness of the worn axe handle, and the motion to his shoulders.

"You've filled out," Dew said after a time. "You must be fed well at the castle."

"I eat like a pig, if truth be told," Bane laughed. "And work just as hard.

They caught up while they worked, the afternoon passing quickly until the last log was split. Afterwards, they sat beneath the oak and watched the Fug roll down the mountain. It was like old times as if he had never gone to the castle at all.

The afternoon rolled by, and it wasn't long before they returned to the cottage. Dew's mother was smiling by the door as Belle came out.

Bane watched her step through the doorway, dressed in a red lacy frock with a velvet cloak. Her hair was now out of the string-tied ponytail and hung to her shoulders in dark, shiny ringlets, the setting sun lighting a shy smile.

Her cheeks reddened as she caught him staring.

"Doesn't she look a picture," Mrs Camwell said, beaming.

Bane swallowed the catching lump in his throat.

"Err, yes," he heard himself say, unable to think of anything else, his mind suddenly thinking how his fingers would feel running through her ringlets.

"I'm ready to go to the feast," Belle said, holding her head high as she glided towards the horse.

Bane helped her into the saddle and held the reins.

"Are you not climbing on with me?"

Bane looked at the dress, something that her mother had been saving, and shook his head. He didn't want to ruffle it up, and besides, he was suddenly aware of how sweaty he was. Funny how it had never bothered him before.

"I'll walk you," he said, wondering why he felt self-cautious.

They said goodbye to Dew and Mrs Camwell and made their way back to the village, taking the outer path so as not to ride through the mud near the swine pens.

The snow was pristine along the empty barrier between the village and the foothills, the Fug breaking the tree line as it neared the trial stone.

Bane had never noticed how beautiful it was before. He had thought of taking Belle along the track to his mother and auntie's grave. He didn't know why. His mind seemed muddled, and he couldn't help but keep glancing back at her and feeling that she was watching him too.

As they neared the stone ruins of the barn, Girant appeared with his wife and son, the three of them having come out to enjoy the calm weather, young Tomm running through the snow, giggling joyously as he made strange patterns.

Bane waved out and was greeted with a smile from both doting parents, feeling proud of the fact that the Smith and his wife were taking in every detail of Belle.

For a moment, his head was back in the hovel he grew up in. The long hard day labouring for Dodd and was grateful for the way things had worked out.

"Tomm, not so close," he heard Girant's wife call out as the young boy ran closer to the border land. But it seemed that Tomm was having too much fun to listen.

The Fug came on, flowing over the snow in its silent possession of the land it was swallowing.

"Tomm," Girant boomed louder, an urgency to his voice.

The boy had no room for thought other than continuing the outwards arc of his run, laughing as he ran towards the danger.

"Tomm!" Girant repeated as he lumbered after his son, the huge man a great deal slower.

"Bane," Belle said, feeling the anguish they were all experiencing, her hand going to her mouth.

Bane knew that Girant would never reach his son, and that Tomm was oblivious to the danger.

He tossed the reins to Belle and sprinted across the open snow, hoping that he would reach Tomm before the silver mist.

"Tomm," he bellowed as he ran, bounding through the thick white powder, his cloak billowing behind him. "Tomm."

The boy passed the trial stone, giggling as he stumbled and then caught himself before running on, his gaze on the ground.

"Tomm," Bane heard his mother scream from where she was with Belle, the two of them watching on in terror.

The Fug swept down, the silver wall looming high as it welcomed the boy, engulfing him in a heartbeat.

One moment he was there, full of life and then next, gone.

Bane felt the scream from his mother, the cry from his father, and heard Belle scream his name before he sprinted on and dived into the Fug, leaving all sounds behind him.

The mist was all consuming. It's freezing embrace clung to him as if crushing all warmth from his body.

"Da?" cried the boy through the blind whiteness.

Bane could see nothing. He placed one foot in front of the other and pushed towards the boy.

A wild growl pierced the vapour, an animalistic hunger as if sensing food. It was followed by more of its kind. A pack, scrambling to reach the prey first.

Desperate and blind to the white, Bane flung out his arms and immediately grasped something solid.

He heard a shriek and felt a thrashing of small feet kick into him.

"Tomm, it's alright. It's me," Bane said as he knelt and grasped the boy's shoulders.

Through the mire, he could make out Tomm's frightened face, tears welling in his eyes.

When he recognised Bane, he flung his arms around him.

That's when he heard the deep snarl over his back.

Taking a deep breath, Bane gently pushed Tomm to arm's length and then drew his sword.

"Stay close to me," he said as he slowly turned, not wanting to make any hasty moves should it entice the hidden beast.

A small hand grasped the leg of his britches as he brought his blade overhead, adopting a defensive stance.

Low growls, high pitch snarls and guttural laughter circled them, sounding like they were in the eye of a storm of malevolent monsters. A maelstrom of teeth and claws that were waiting to lash out, to cut, to tear, to gut and devour them.

Swift moving shadows darted across his vision, large shapes bounding across – Bane turned with it all, circling, switching his blade from high to low as he moved, keeping Tomm at his heel.

He would have moved towards the edge of the Fug if he could, but there were no points of reference and nowhere to head to. They were as likely to move deeper into the Fug than move away from it.

Which made him realise the Fug was ascending the mountain. If they were standing still then it should have passed over them, yet the God's Breath had taken them with it.

Then the laughter got louder, drowning out the guttural bestial noises and as the Fug began to push away, leaving them in a dome of darkness, Bane recognised the shapes to be human.

"You enter the Fug, you become the Fug – you become one of us," came a deep voice, old and raspy.

"You become Draugr."

Bane slipped positions as the words came from different places, as if each shape were speaking at the same time.

Then something came rushing out, a flash of steel and Bane brought his sword about and caught the blade of another.

Laughter from a hundred souls.

A fleeting shadow, Bane ducked and felt the air shift above, spun and deflected a spear.

He became aware of a steady rhythm, as if drums were beating, the sound growing as the attacks came on.

Steel rang against steel, laughter intensified, the drum beat quickened.

"Not the boy," Bane pleaded as he fought the invisible enemy, parrying an ancient broadsword and thrusting out, catching flesh.

"Sacrifice," The mist answered. "Blood for the Draugr."

A hideous face peeled forward, flesh torn and eaten, a rictus grin below empty sockets.

Bane twisted, cut down and sliced through gristle and bone and the head came away from the rotting body - a horned helmet rolling off.

"Sacrifice. Then take me," Bane bellowed, jabbing out, reversing his grip, slashing back, dipping and driving a shoulder into another haggard body.

"Leave the boy, be."

The whistling of air and Bane leaned away from the spiked ball of a morning star, swinging close enough to notice the specks of rust in the aged iron.

"So be it," the bodiless said in unison.

Something large loomed out of the fog and snatched Tomm. It happened so quickly that Bane only registered what happened after it was too late.

"No," he yelled, swinging wildly.

"Fear not, brave warrior. The boy has been returned to the land of the living. You, however, will be Draugr."

The drums grew louder as the fighters came on, each taking a turn, slicing, thrusting and cutting. Some more accurate than others, yet none broke Bane's defences.

He was getting tired, and they fought without fatigue, a relentless onslaught of rotting flesh and sharpened iron.

"He's Draugr," he heard a voice say. "Fights like he's the blood of Thor in him," agreed another. "Will make a grand Draugr when he falls," they laughed.

A blade cut through the mist, scraped over his chest, a hammer about to take his head.

Spinning Thistle became Ascending Dawn as he dodged the hammer and then took a sword down his thigh.

The pain inflamed immediately as he fell to one knee, raising his sword and catching a descending mace.

He didn't have time to react to the spear point as it came from nowhere and ran up his inner arm, slicing through cloth and leather.

There was a change in the beat of the drums and several shapes loomed out of the mist together, hideous shapes that were once men, now wasting away, decayed and baring the wounds from a life long gone.

Bane knew that this was the moment his life would end. By some strange twist, choosing to take it when he had just begun to experience happiness.

He watched the old swords, the ancient axes, maces, hammers, and thought only of Belle.

Rising, he went to meet his doom. He cut up with his blade, severed the arm of the first, turned his shoulder to block an arcing axe and felt the familiar fire of heat along his arm.

The thorns burst through his sleeve, thriving in a swirling mass that instantly formed a shield.

He caught the blade of a weapon - an axe and propelled it through the mist, the wielder still clinging to the shaft and knocking others down as they went.

He spun to meet the next attack, but it didn't come.

As he slowly turned, he found that he was surrounded by a wall of the disfigured dead. All of them staring.

Knuckles creaked, bones clicked, joints clacked as they watched him, the mist receding and revealing more rows of them, withdrawing until the many became an endless sea of creatures that were once men.

"Blood of Tyr," said the closer one, standing a little taller than his brethren, some portion of flesh left to his face. "The time draws close. You have been marked by the Wycum, and she calls."

His gaze lingered on Bane's thorns.

Bane struggled to remain on his feet, the strength of the endless fighting finally catching up, the injuries now throbbing.

"Blood Of Tyr," Bane repeated, glancing down at the shield of thorns as it shrank back into his tattoo. "A giant?"

The Draugr laughed, the tendons along his cheeks stretching and tearing.

"Tyr is no giant. He is a god," he said. "You must speak with the Wycum. Go now. Seek her out. The time has come for war."

Others then stepped closer, some being jostled and pushed from the mass of felled warriors behind.

"We Draugr grow restless. The fight is coming," they said as one.

Bane stepped back but was met with the Draugr behind, all of them pressing in on him.

"The fight is coming," they repeated, closing tighter, crushing him.

Through the press, the Fug returned, and all became white.

****

Alruna heard the Fug pass above, the howling shrieks and animal snarls battering at the bunker door, the old wood rattling in her hands.

The first tide was always the more violent, but it would soon pass.

She glanced at her father sitting on the bench, his coughing becoming worse in the damp air. Geri snuggled into him, rubbing her huge head against his leg.

When he caught Alruna watching he shook his head.

"It's nothing."

Alruna nodded.

"Aye, Da. Like it was nothing last night when you were coughing up blood."

"I said it's nothing," he growled, coughing into his sleeve and turning away from her.

He'd been hard with her over the few days since she'd put Ferric through the final door.

She'd also felt a coldness from the rest of the village, but she had expected that. Everyone avoided her, especially the men. Yesterday, Ganlin had stumbled over a barrel in his haste to get away from her.

Her hand shook as she gripped the handle, a final growl from above, yet the runes held.

When the wood finally settled, she slid the bolt and flung the door open, desperate to get out of the confined bunker.

Freki followed her out, bounding up the ladder in a fluid motion of black fur.

The ground had been covered in snow before the winter chill set in, but after the Fug had passed there was a layer of ice glistening over the surface.

Alruna paused at the top to offer her father a hand. As she helped pull him free of the hole, she noticed a spotting of blood on his sleeve.

"Maybe you ought to have a talk with Old Ma Bunt," she said, nodding towards the other side of the mountain where Clan Lothrid was perched in the low crags.

"I'll not be talking with any witch, girl. It'll pass, always has before."

Alruna watched him clamber up the rise to the hut, the fire inside still smouldering, the cauldron of stew bubbling above.

He had one hand on the doorframe when he stopped; head turned towards a lump on the ground by the empty fire pit.

Alruna got a sickening feeling in her gut.

The lump was in the shape of a man, the snow starting to settle over dark clothes.

"He wasn't there before we went down," Boran said, reaching for his sword as he stepped closer.

Alruna already had her axe in hand, Freki at her side.

"No, he wasn't," Alruna agreed, which meant that the Fug had left him there, curled up on his side, back towards them.

"He's not one of ours," her father said as he placed his boot against the stranger's shoulder and shoved him onto his back.

He rolled, a cloak covering his face but not the deep gash in his thigh or cuts in his shoulder and arms.

"Why didn't the Fug claim him?" Boran muttered. "He should be Draugr."

A gust swept down the mountainside, carrying a flurry of snow. As it passed the body, it tussled the cloak and blew it flat, revealing a young face.

It was a face that Alruna had been waking to each morning, one she couldn't go to sleep without being in her thoughts. It was seared into her soul the night its owner slit Raif's throat.

Bane.

The Bane of the Crookfell, the bane of her life.

She'd dreamt of killing him. Had his image front and centre as she fought against the men in the village, hacked at him as she split wood, driving with such rage that she might kill him with her feelings alone.

Another icy gust cut across them, as cold as Alruna's blood.

As it touched the boy he stirred, a shallow breath, a rise of the chest, a fluttering of his lids.

Alruna pounced, axe raised high and coming down hard.

Her father easily snatched the axe from her grasp and flung an arm around her waist.

"No, girl," he said, pulling her away, having to strain as she struggled in his grasp, and although old, was still a good deal stronger than her.

"I want to kill him," she screamed, thrashing her legs and arms, kicking wildly and then dropping her weight so she fell through his hold.

"Alruna," he shouted, but she had already rolled out of his reach – was up, had somehow taken her father's sword and was now taking long strides towards the Crookfell boy.

She had no idea why the Fug had chosen to spit him out here, but she wasn't going to waste this opportunity.

Bane's grey eyes were now staring at her, confusion written in them, perhaps pain.

Well things were about to get a lot more painful.

The rage was rising within her, the sword trembling in her hands as she brought it down, cleaving through the skull of her brother's killer.

Her oath was fulfilled.

The blade was less than a finger width from embedding into Bane's head when an immense mass struck her midriff, and she was knocked backwards.

Her vision filled with the white ground and blue sky before she hit the ground, the wind driven from her.

When she raised up onto her elbows, Freki was protectively squatting in front of the boy, a low growl coming from the leopard, teeth bared.

"Traitor," Alruna said, rolling onto her knees and rising to her feet.

Mercifully, she still held her father's sword.

"Out of my way, cat, or I'll cut you down with him," she warned, circling the pair, the boy still watching, confused, while Freki padded at his side, putting herself between Raif's killer and her owner.

"Alruna, listen," Boran pleaded as he tried to rest a calming hand on her shoulder.

She shrugged it off.

"Why is he still breathing?"

"Listen, girl. Do you think the gods would have brought him here for you to simply kill? Or do you think he has a purpose?"

"His purpose is to die. And I made an oath."

Her father made to grab for his sword, yet she easily dodged him, but couldn't get past the shadow leopard who was protecting the boy as if he was her own cub.

"And the Wycum mark on his arm? I've never seen anything so strong. It means something."

"Means something? It means he's a freak. He isn't even Norse. He's no Viking. He's never even been this side of the Fug. And he's got Raif's sword."

"I'm telling you, Alruna. No, I'm ordering you as Clan Chief, as your father – leave him be."

"I will, after I've gutted him," she said, making to leap but before her feet left the ground, Freki pounced on her, pinning her into the snow, and then Geri sat on her legs, the huge cat lying heavy.

Boran paced past her. She childishly made a grab for his boots, but he was already at the boy, leaning over him and pressing a cloth to the blood leaking from a gash in his thigh.

A scream of frustration left Alruna's chest, and she went still.

"Fine. Alright, I won't kill him. Now get off me, stupid cat," she snapped at Geri.

The shadow leopard looked to Boran, who gave a single nod.

"Leave the blade there," he said.

She dropped the sword and slowly came towards them as her father knelt and lifted the boy's head, pressing the back of his hand to his brow.

"You're safe now, lad. Stay in the land of the living – we'll fetch a healer," he said and then glanced up at Alruna.

"Go fetch Old Ma Bunt. Tell her to hurry."

Alruna narrowed her eyes, the smouldering heat of anger glowing fiercely beneath the surface.

She knelt closer to Bane, cocked her arm back and punched him full in the face.

20

The Wycum

Bane couldn't feel his arms - he lost all sensation in his hands, in his feet, body – all he could feel was the fire pulsing through his thigh. It's what dragged him out of the darkness he was engulfed in.

There was something in his mouth. His tongue felt swollen as he probed his teeth and inner cheek.

It all throbbed with each pulse. Then he remembered the last thing he saw.

Alruna's fist.

His lids took an age to open, as if stuck with dried treacle, his head pounding as if something was crushing it.

"He's coming round," he heard Nan Hilga say, although she sounded different.

When the haze began to shrink from his vision, he found that he was in a dark, damp room lit by a single lamp. The voice he thought belonged to Nan Hilga was, in fact, a different elderly lady, as old, as wiry and hunched over him, prodding the wound in his leg while sucking on her gums.

"His wounds won't kill him," she said, placing a hand not too gently on his brow.

"Food, drink, and a little rest. That's all he needs."

The chamber was cramped. The only furniture was the single bench he was lying on. There were no windows and only a ladder leading to a hatch that was the way out.

A raider he recognised, the older one with the beard that was there on the night he killed Raif, was standing behind her, a large shadow leopard at his feet. And standing in the corner, leaning against the wall, was Alruna, glowering with rage.

He caught the tendons on her hand stretch as she gripped the shaft of a nasty-looking bearded axe. He guessed that it was the presence of the others that was keeping her from using that axe on him.

"Can you hear me, lad?" the old lady that was not Nan Hilga asked.

"Aye," Bane said as he worked spit around his mouth. "Where am I?"

"In a tight spot," the man answered. "You're in my village and only just this side of the living. And I wouldn't be surprised to find that by this evening, you'll be on the other."

Bane felt a presence at his leg; another shadow leopard, smaller and younger than the other, curled up and rubbed her head against his good leg. It was the same cat that he'd found in the forest some time ago.

"Why did the Fug drop you in my village?"

Through the pounding in his head, Bane remembered the fight with the Draugr in the mist, the struggle that should have been the end of him.

He hoped Tomm manged to find his parents again. And what of Belle?

"Answer my father, boy," Alruna hissed, moving away from the wall, the axe slipping from the loop in her belt to her hand.

Bane was glad to see that the man who he took to be her father held out an arm to stop her from passing him, although he didn't know how long that protection would last.

"The Draugr. They told me to seek out the Wycum?" Bane replied, the last name sounding strange as if it was some sacred word he had no right to use.

"The Wycum," the old lady said, leaning away from him. "What business is this you've brought me to, Boran? I want no part of it."

"I could end this business now," Alruna said, making to get passed Boran.

She backed away with a glare from her father and a growl from the shadow cat at Bane's feet.

"Why must you seek out the Wycum?" Boran asked, ignoring both women.

Bane struggled into a sitting position, his thigh screaming at him to stop, the crudely stitched twine that weaved the wound closed, stretching tight.

He shook his head as he rolled back the shreds of cloth which was once his sleeve.

"I entered the Fug for reasons other than my own, and I fought the Draugr. They would have finished me if not for this," he said, holding out his arm. "They say there is a war coming, and I must seek out the Wycum."

The hatch door suddenly began to rattle violently, the wild snarls and growls of beasts attacking from the other side, claws and teeth scraping at the wood.

Instinctively, Bane went for his sword, sure that the monsters would break through - they didn't, and he realised that he no longer had his sword. It was now strapped to Alruna's back. It fit her well as she climbed the ladder to hold tight to the hatch handle.

He couldn't blame her. She had more right to it than he did.

The others didn't seem to react to the noise battering at the door.

"Is the Wycum here?" he asked.

The old lady glanced to Boran, who shook his head.

"The Wycum dwells at the peak of the mountain. Only a very few have found her."

The noise passed with a final trembling on the wood, and then Alruna slid a bolt back and pushed herself out as if she couldn't bear to share the same place as the murderer of her brother.

Boran watched her go and Bane felt the cat at his feet stir, yet both remained.

"I killed her brother," Bane admitted, unable to meet Boran's intense gaze.

He didn't know why he was admitting this, especially as he guessed that the person he was admitting it to must be the father of both. And why did he feel a need to defend the girl who had punched him in the face?

"Aye, lad. And the only reason you're still alive is that I know you didn't intend to kill my son."

Boran held his hand up, finger and thumb almost touching.

"But you're this close to me finishing you. And Alruna doesn't need that."

Boran helped the elder from the bunker and then came for him, offering a shoulder as he helped him out of the hole in the ground.

"So, this is how you survive living on the mountain with the Fug," Bane said as he pulled himself free of the hatch, wincing as his thigh reminded him he had an injury.

He noticed the runes carved into the wood around the door and tried to commit them to memory. If Glance was here, he would have wanted to know.

"My hut is here," Boran said, pointing to a small shack not unlike the one he had grown up in. "You have sanctuary until the morning tide. After that, I won't hold my daughter back."

Bane nodded, catching Alruna stalk off into the woods, a final glance narrowed at him.

"If it's the Wycum you seek, you need to run into the Fug as it flows up the mountain.

"Run?" Bane said as he took a lumbering step towards the hut, his skin pulling tight over the stitches, a searing pain up his leg.

He took another step and heard the healer grunt something before she ambled away, her staff digging into the earth.

"If what Raif said is true. You'll need to speak with your clan chief, Old Ma Bunt. Rhondu, needs to learn of what may be coming."

"I'll speak not a word," Old Ma Bunt said as she made her way down the mountain, not looking back.

Bane couldn't bear the pain any longer and needed to sit down. The shadow leopard was by his side as he hobbled through the doorway and fell onto one of the three cots, flinching as he expected an axe through the back of his head.

Boran followed him in, looking at where he was, opened his mouth as if to say something and stopped.

"I can move", Bane offered, realising that he must have fallen into Raif's empty bed.

Boran shook his head.

"Stay where you are. It matters none, now."

Mountain stew was bubbling in the cauldron, reminding Bane that he hadn't eaten since the morning he entered the Fug.

Boran took a clay bowl down from a shelf, filled it with the stew and passed it to him.

As Bane greedily ate, a large man appeared in the doorway.

Bane recognised him as the giant of a raider who had been there on the same night he killed Raif.

He had a hammer in his hands and looked ready to use it.

He pointed the head towards Bane.

"Alruna told me he was here," he said, his booming voice filling the small hut.

"Aye, Hadlo," Boran said. "Did she send you to kill him?"

The giant set the shaft of his hammer on the floor.

"Aye."

Boran nodded as he relaxed back in the chair. "Thought she might have."

Both men stared at him as he ate, gazes falling to his arm and the tattoo beneath the shredded sleeve.

Bane swallowed the meat in his mouth. It was chewy and made more so with the scrutiny from the men.

"Alruna said you fought the Draugr," Hadlo said. "Did you fight a man a little older than yourself? Tall, slim?"

Bane put the bowl down. It was clear his answer meant something to the giant.

"I don't believe so, no. The ones that I could see were old, a long time dead."

Hadlo nodded thoughtfully.

"Well, if you're going back into the Fug tomorrow, and if you see him. Tell him…Tell him his Da was proud of what he did."

Bane nodded.

"I will."

Boran offered him more of the stew, but Bane shook his head. He felt too awkward with the pair watching.

"We'll leave you to it, lad. I'll come back in the morning to let you into the bunker. Once the Fug passes, you'll no longer have my protection. Do you understand?"

Bane inclined his head.

"And I wouldn't go leaving this hut. My daughter is out there and will no doubt take your head."

Boran stared at him for a moment longer, then left. He paused at the doorway, his glower boring into him before he closed the door.

Alone, except for the cat, Bane helped himself to more stew and then sat back on the bunk, taking in the rest of the hut.

It was as simple as the home he grew up in. It had a fire, cots and a chair. The bare essentials to living.

From what he'd seen, the raiders were much like the Crookfell folk; only the Norsemen needed a place to shelter from the Fug twice a day.

It was a wonder why they never left the mountain.

He finished his bowl and lay back. Sleep was what his body demanded now, and it was the last chance he would get before he would run back into the Fug.

He checked the stitches in his leg.

The healer, Old Ma Bunt, had sewed the cut well, if not a little ugly. But how was he to run tomorrow? Surely the stitches would tear, and then he would be no use to anyone. But he guessed nobody this side of the Fug cared.

Feeling fatigued, Bane laid his head back and closed his eyes.

He couldn't leave. He guessed the hut was being watched. And there was no way back to Crookfell without passing through the Fug.

"Looks like it's just the two of us," he said to the shadow leopard.

She had grown some since he first set her free months ago. If she wasn't full-sized, she wasn't far off. Not quite as large as the other cat which trailed Boran like a second shadow, but she was nearly there.

"Just going to rest my eyes," he told her, stroking the back of her large ears.

She purred as she leaned into him, a deep vibration that travelled through her huge chest into his leg.

He only meant to lightly nap, but it wasn't long before the darkness pulled him down into the land of sleep.

Alruna crept out of the bunker where she and her father had been sleeping. His light snores were the only sound as Geri slept beside him.

She'd had her eyes shut a long time before his, taking on the slow rhythmic breathing, even faking the odd intake of breath, the gentle moan of somebody having a dream.

At one point she thought he would remain awake all night, sitting vigil should she try to leave, yet mercifully, he began to drift, as did Geri.

She waited a while more, counted another hundred snores and then gently crept up the ladder and out in the open.

A freezing fog clung to the side of the mountain, hiding her from view as she made the short distance to the hut, slipping her axe free from the loop in her belt.

She held it with a reverse grip, the blade cold against her bare forearm.

The door was shut, but she wasn't going in that way. She placed hands against the sill of the window and peered inside.

The boy was asleep in Raif's cot. The cat curled up on the floor beside him.

Using the axe, she pried the window open and slipped inside, landing deftly onto the packed mud floor.

She waited to see if anyone would wake, but the boy and Freki remained still.

Placing her feet down carefully, she tiptoed the short distance to the cot and raised her axe, gripping it with both hands.

As easy as splitting a turnip.

Bane was facing the ceiling, eyes closed and mouth partially open.

She lowered the blade so it was hovering above his scalp, checked that Freki hadn't stirred and then raised the axe.

A simple fall of her arm, no effort needed to end him. And her father wasn't here to stop her.

Bane stirred, mumbled something intelligible and then went still.

Alruna let go of the breath she'd been holding and gripped tightly to the shaft.

She leaned closer, seeing his face upside down, their noses almost touching.

Do it now. End him. Keep your oath.

Like splitting a turnip.

His breathing stopped, lids fluttering open as his gaze locked with hers.

He had the greyest eyes. No fear in them as if he knew this time was coming.

"You killed Raif," she said, wanting to put as much venom behind the words as she could, but instead, they spilt out as a whimper. "You killed my brother."

Bane went crossed-eyed as he looked at the blade and then stared through it at her.

"I did. I wish I hadn't," he said, so close that his breath brushed her damp cheeks.

"Wishing won't bring him back."

A lone tear ran down her jaw, rolled to the end of her chin and fell, striking Bane on the side of his mouth.

Time slowed, the pair of them locked over Raif's bed. The axe trembling within her weakening grip.

Kill him.

"I hate you."

Bane slowly nodded.

"And you will die in the Fug tomorrow."

Bane swallowed, the lump in his throat bobbing.

"I expect so."

Alruna sniffed the tears back and pulled away. Then, putting her back to him, he stalked out of the hut through the door.

****

Bane didn't sleep the rest of the night. The lingering threat of death loomed heavy in the air. He was sure that Alruna was going to finish him.

He wiped away her tear that was drying on the side of his face.

If it wasn't for his leg, he might have tried to escape. Yet he knew that the Fug was already on its ascent, and he needed to be inside one of the bunkers before it swept through the village.

The cat, Freki, stirred by his side as someone filled the doorway, a bell tolling not too far away.

"It's time, lad. Come with me."

Pain stabbed through his leg as he clambered to his feet and throbbed with each step as he followed the clan chief to the hatch in the ground.

He climbed down the ladder and settled on the bench. Alruna was standing in the corner, the hilt of her brother's sword poking over her shoulder, hand resting on her axe.

She could still end him here.

Another bell tolled, this one closer, and Boran descended the ladder, closing the door behind him and sliding a thick bolt across.

"Have you no other weapon, lad?" he asked, frowning down at him.

"I have a knife," he admitted. "And, well, this," he said, rolling the shreds of his sleeve up to reveal the tattoo.

Boran glanced at his daughter, who shook her head.

"He's not having Raif's sword."

Her glare said there was no arguing with that.

Bane couldn't blame her. What would be the point in giving a sword to somebody who was about to die?

Another bell tolled, and the door began to rattle; the animalistic shrieks and howls soon followed.

"Once it passes, you need to be up and out running after it," Boran said, struggling to hold the hatch, which violently shook.

Bane nodded, feeling that he wouldn't be able to run fast into anything.

He cast a glance to Alruna, who was still glowering.

"You might need to hold your cat back. I don't want her following and getting herself killed."

Alruna clicked her fingers and the leopard padded over to her.

The rattling became more vicious and then it ebbed.

As soon as another bell rang further up the hill, Boran pulled the bolt on the door and flung it open.

Bane breathed deeply and glanced at Alruna.

"I'm sorry," he said and then scrambled up the ladder. The clan chief was at the top, a hand held out towards him, Bane took it and was yanked through the hatch.

Once out he saw that the Fug was flowing up the mountain, the silver mist sweeping through the village.

"Run!" Boran commanded.

Bane pushed on, pumping his arms to compensate for the injury in his leg.

It pulsed with agony, screaming at him to stop, but he struggled through it.

He stumbled over a tree root, flailed his arms wildly to keep on his feet and drove on, head up, focusing on the Fug; he was almost there, the vapour within touching distance.

He reached out, fingers passing through the silver tendrils, feeling the icy touch, forcing his legs on, the burning becoming excruciating.

With the next step his boot clipped another root and he stumbled, hands flying wild, ready to catch himself, but there was nothing to grasp.

Another bounding step and he went down.

Then a firm hand took him under the elbow, guided him up and pushed him up.

"Fugging run, boy," Alruna grunted as she guided him on, gripping tightly to his arm, pulling him with her.

They both ran through the mist.

The Fug engulfed the pair of them in a world of silver.

Bane lost all sense of where he was. The only thing he could feel was the warmth of Alruna's arm alongside his, her hand gripping tightly.

21

Demons OF The Sand

Bailin crawled to the edge of the ridge which overlooked Fort Palsin, a squat square building surrounded by four high walls. Any sign of the King or his men was lost to the bodies which lay scattered amongst the inner walls. From this distance, he couldn't tell which side they were on or even if they were human.

Nothing stirred.

It had been a hard two-week ride, pushing the mounts and the men through each day and night, stopping only to catch the briefest snatches of sleep or to swap horses.

The messenger slithered up next to him, his face hidden within the gloom.

"The King will be in the central building," he said, pointing to the wood and stone block sitting alone at the centre of the fort. "There were enough provisions inside for them to hold up until help arrived."

"It's been nearly a month since you left. How can you be sure he's still in there?" Bailin asked, staring through the darkness but only making out strange shadows and stranger shapes. The windows of the building were boarded shut, but if there was someone inside, then surely torch light would come out.

"I can't believe my King is dead, Sir. If I must go in alone, I will," the messenger said.

Jin was his name, and Bailin had come to like the man over the time travelling south with him.

"Jin, I don't believe the King has passed through the final door. And my men and I will break through the fort and rescue anyone still alive in the building."

Jin nodded, a fleeting smile crossing his lips.

"Thank you, Sir. I want to come with you," Jin said, pulling a short sword from his belt.

"I have some skill with a blade, and you'll need the numbers. We're only twenty, and there must be a hundred down there."

Bailin grinned, admiring the courage of the messenger.

"My men and I fight a certain way – we've fought together in many battles. I'm sure we can handle what's down there," Bailing said, squeezing Jin's shoulder. "And we will need someone to watch the horses. If the King is down there, we'll need a swift exit and a swifter ride out. And I wouldn't trust anyone else, my friend."

"You honour me, Sir," Jin said as he nodded gratefully, crawling back to allow room for Sir Godlin.

"It doesn't look good," the knight said, rubbing his beard as he glanced down at the fort before them. "And whatever those creatures down there are, I don't think they're men."

"I'd have to agree with you. But man or beast, we must cut through them to reach the King. Are the men ready?"

Godlin nodded.

"They all know what must be done. And they're eager to spill blood."

Bailin nodded. He knew the men were as scared as himself. It wasn't natural not to be. But they also knew that to admit as such was to admit defeat.

"Good. Then let's not keep our King waiting. And bring the tar."

He scurried back, collected his helmet from his pack and stood in front of the small band of Garik men, proud of every single one of them.

"Let's keep this short, sharp and brutal. You know what I'm asking. If you want to back out, now is the time. There will be no shame in it."

Nobody stepped forward and he didn't expect them to. Before every battle he always gave the men a chance to leave, especially when there was a real chance of them dying.

"Men of Garik, you know what to do, what's expected of you. We live as men…"

"But fight like gods," the men roared back, the Division's motto said before each battle.

Bailin walked up and down the line, clashing blades with each.

Godlin followed, daubing tar on every shield in a certain way.

"Might I ask what the tar is for, Sir?" Jin said as he watched the routine.

"Preparing for the worst," Bailin answered as he clashed swords against the final knight in line.

They were ready.

"Stay with the horses, my friend. Should things not go our way, ride to the capital. Ride hard and don't stop until you get there."

Jin nodded that he understood and went to stand by his horse.

"Good luck, Sir," he said.

Bailin grinned as he slipped on his helmet and went to stand with his men.

He began the approach, leading from the front as he always did, Godlin by his side, broadsword cocked onto his shoulder.

The gates loomed in front of them, open and unprotected, dark shapes moving within the walls, the glint of sharpened steel catching the moon, and what seemed like teeth and claws.

Bailin picked up the pace, armoured boots slamming into the mud, shield held tight to his side, the tar running down the polished surface.

"We live as men," he growled, teeth clenched as he began to run.

"But fight as gods," his blade brothers replied.

He entered through the gate, slamming a shield out wide and catching a shape that loomed from the darkness.

It was solid, larger than a man, claws scraping against the edge.

A painful howl filled the air as the knight behind thrust out a sword, and hot liquid spattered across Bailin's face.

He drove on, hearing the thuds of steel finding marks, screams of pain, the scraping of steel on shields. The building wasn't far, a wall of beasts surrounding it.

They were in the shape of men. Tall, lythe and hunched, with long teeth and snarls.

Jackels of the dessert. Sand demons.

"We live as men," he shouted, sword raised as he bounded into the first, cutting down, finding flesh, sweeping back, slicing through a neck – the head tumbling away; a painful snarl locked in the jackal's expression.

"But fight like gods."

Godlin's broad sword swept through a beast's torso and stuck into the devil beyond; another jackal hacked at him with a jagged length of iron, which could barely be called a sword.

Bailin caught it, turned his blade and arced it up.

Dark blood squirted from the stump of an arm, its owner howling, but its mouth was soon filled by the broad sword as it came back.

Bailin was briefly aware of teeth spinning past his vision as he slammed his shield into one of two demons directly in front of him, his sword driving out and skewing the other in the chest.

They fell away to reveal the door to the building.

Without saying a word, he spun and put his back to the door, defending Godlin as the large knight rammed the old wood with a heavy shoulder.

The door gave after the second hit, and the knight was inside, shouting that he was a man of Garik.

Bailin left him as he joined his men, making a crescent shape as they protected the door, waiting for the King to come out.

The hordes of demons in front fanned out to surround them, eager snarls, evil intent glowing from yellow eyes, yet none came close enough to kill.

Bailin quickly counted his men as they faced the foe. Mercifully, they were all there, shields locked and blades ready to use.

A clatter came from over his shoulder as Godlin returned alone.

"It's empty," he said, shaking his head. "The building is deserted. There's been nobody here for weeks."

"Empty? Was the King here at all?" Bailin asked.

"No," came the answer, although not from Godlin. The voice came from the gate at the other side of the fort where a lone figure stood, the demons parting for him as he stepped forward.

"The King was never in danger. He wasn't here when we attacked," he said, coming close enough for Bailin to recognise.

"Jin?"

The messenger laughed as the jackals began to kneel, bowing their heads low as he passed them.

"Yes, Blood of Tyr, although not Jin the messenger. I am Jin, a ghast of these jackals."

Bailin watched him approach, grin widening so it didn't fit the human form, teeth growing longer and his nose elongating to match that of his brethren.

The knights about Bailin jostled as they locked their shields tighter, blades poised above, ready to strike out.

Jin laughed, the kneeling demons rising and then following the trickster, their teeth displaying through malicious grins, claws tightening around the crude, jagged lengths of iron.

"Hold," Bailin ordered his men, feeling the tension rise.

Jin paused at the edge of the crescent, opening his arms to encompass the band of men before him, now fully in the Jackal form, although he was wider and darker in colour.

"Know this, Blood of Tyr. You will not live to see another dawn. None of you will," he said, sweeping his claws in front of the men.

"What is this madness?" Sir Godlin said, cocking his broadsword onto his shoulder. "Were we so easily tricked?"

Bailin shrugged, wondering if he could reach this ghost with his blade - he didn't think so.

Jin stepped a little closer, leaning in, yellow eyes soaking up Bailin hungrily.

"Why the need for all this?" Bailin asked, slowly sliding his foot closer, buying some time and putting himself within range.

"There is a war coming. In fact, it's already here, within these lands. A war that's been fought for thousands of years. Ever since the mighty Gharl and Tyr fought in the North."

Jin barked out a laugh as he glanced down at Bailin's boot and stepped back, large teeth catching the moonlight.

"My god, Gharl, sits on his throne in the far south, awaiting the head of Tyr. Only then will the war be won, and my kind will rule the world. The time of men is coming to an end."

"What about the Emperor?" Bailin asked. "Although we've been fighting him for years, he still hosts the largest army in the world. His fleets, his land forces."

"Emperor Saliman is a tool. A puppet. Gharl is behind his every move. He whispers in his ear, pushing him, using him, forcing him to do his bidding. Why else has he been attacking your shores?"

Bailin had often wondered why the Emperor persisted in attacking his homeland. Had he been a puppet all this time?

"Tyr fell in a long-ago battle. His body is hidden within Garik Mountain, the pathetic Fug a means of protection, as weak as it is," Jin barked out another hideous laugh. "And you believe that Garik castle was built to keep things from coming down from the mountain, beasts from the Fug, or the Norsemen from your door. No. the castle was originally built to keep jackals out."

The rest of the jackals began to laugh, all of them coming closer, sniffing the air, thick tongues running over long teeth. Their number was so large that it filled the space between them and the fort's gate.

"But why go to all the trouble of tricking me? It seems a little specific. I'm only the son of a baron," Bailin asked.

"Because, Blood of Tyr, an army of my brethren are heading north as we speak. They're large enough to break through the castle, to steal what lies at its belly and then march through the Fug."

"What lies at the belly of Garik castle?" Bailin asked. "I've lived there all my life. There are only ancient foundations."

Jin shook his head.

"There is a way to break through the Fug, a means for a small number of jackals to break clear of the mist and what lies within. Yet it matters not. Our number is great enough to crush the Draugr, should we not take the castle."

"You still haven't answered my question, demon. Why bring me here?" Bailin asked, becoming impatient with the gloating ghast.

"Because the mighty god Gharl knows things, can read patterns hidden within the threads of life. Can see that a threat still lies within the North. A long distant relative of Tyr. You."

Jin tipped his head back and howled, the jackals around joining in until the howling filled the night, a sound that made the hairs on the back of his neck rise.

"Steady," Sir Godlin warned the knights.

When the howling subsided, Jin returned his attention to Bailin.

"And with you months away from home, trapped and about to die, there is no threat."

Bailin watched as the large doors on the fort walls began to close, the wood slamming with an eery finality.

Jin stepped closer, his legs bent backwards in the way that canine's legs did, long claws clicking along the ground.

"I will eat what is left of you, Blood of Tyr. Your flesh will bring me strength. The rest of your worthless band shall be torn apart to feed my brethren."

He stepped closer still, saliva dripping from large fangs, the rest of the jackals closing in.

"You are mine."

Bailin glanced at Godlin and his men, all of them holding strong, twenty against a hundred or more demons of the sand.

"There is no escape, Blood of Tyr. You are trapped in here with us," Jin said, then frowned as Bailin grinned back.

"No, ghast of the dessert," Bailin said as he nodded to Godlin, who stroked a strike box along his shield, the daubed tar immediately taking flame, the fire soon spreading along all the locked shields and brightening the fort.

"You are trapped in here with me," Bailin laughed.

The closer jackals raised arms to protect themselves from the sudden light and from the special runes that had been painted with the black sticky substance, now aflame.

Bailin twisted the hand that held the shield, gripped tightly to his sword, and then sliced through Jin's head.

He watched it tumble through the air, a spray of blood circling out, and before it landed, he had already killed another.

"We live as men," he bellowed.

"But fight like gods," the knights cried, the sound of steel meeting flesh mixing with the howls and shrieks of pain that filled the night.

22

Mountain Peak

The Fug choked them in its freezing, silver embrace, clutching them tight as it pulled them along its whirling currents.

Dark shapes loomed from the mist, some animal, some manlike, but all staring with hate, with hunger.

Bane felt Alruna's grip tighten as they turned, his leg screaming at him to stop.

Then the snarls and growls came, coming closer the further they travelled, followed by the deep rumble of laughter.

"Stay back," Alruna screamed at them and Bane felt her grip go as she drew her axe and spun to face each demon, but none attacked. "We seek the Wycum."

The only answer was more laughter and guttural grunts of hunger.

A draugr suddenly lurched through the vapour, sword held high, expression set in grim determination, its eyes white and sunken.

Alruna ducked the cut, rose and came back at him, her axe slicing through its ribs, the blade scraping across bones, yet the draugr turned as if not feeling a thing.

Bane went for his sword and realised it wasn't on his back but on Alruna's.

"Look out," he warned as the draugr brought his sword about, twisted sinew stretching, dried skin puckering around an old wound across its back.

Alruna moved swiftly, stepping out of reach to avoid the swing and hacked down into the draugr's hip.

It grunted, tried to take another step, began to topple, its gaping mouth widening as Alruna drew her brother's sword and sliced through its neck.

There was no blood, only a dark gaping hole that widened as the dead creature fell over, the injury yawning like a second mouth.

More shapes circled them, the beat of a faraway drum growing louder and faster.

Bane and Alruna put their backs to each other, staring out at the threat which could come at any time and from any direction.

"Give me your sword," Bane said over his shoulder.

"Odin will need to pry Raif's sword from my dying fingers before I give it to you," Alruna spat back.

"Your axe, then."

Something came out of the mist on Alruna's side, a clattering of steel against steel, a grunt cut short and then a grey hand landing on the ground – still gripping a sword.

"No."

Bane pulled a knife from his belt; the small blade wouldn't do anything against a proper weapon but it was the only thing to defend himself with.

"Why did you come with me? You could have stayed," he said, staring into the silver vapour but seeing nothing.

"I don't know," Alruna said. "I already regret my decision."

Something else came out of the gloom on her side, a large Viking with what looked like a rope mark around its neck. It held a large, vicious, double-bladed axe, the blades as jagged as the creature itself.

Alruna moved quickly, dropping into a roll, coming up behind it and slicing her sword across its knee, severing the tendons.

It dropped, large teeth grimacing through the tufts of a grey beard.

Bane slipped around and jabbed his knife through the draugr's head, the small blade punching through the skull.

The draugr yelled and his fist connected with Bane's bad leg.

Pain erupted up his thigh as if been struck by a hammer blow.

He went down, saw the shadow of the double-bladed axe follow, and tried to roll away but was blocked by another punch.

He screamed as he twisted and thrust the knife into the torso of the draugr, stabbing again and again into the chest.

The draugr roared but the injuries didn't affect him other than make him angrier.

With one meaty hand, he raised the axe, ready to finish Bane off, yet Alruna slipped through and cut the arm through at the elbow, followed by slamming her own axe into the back of its fractured skull.

Bane scrambled away on hands and knees as the beast fell, its body bouncing once before becoming still.

"Get up," Alruna yelled at him, reaching her arm under his and yanking him to his feet.

Again, they placed their backs to each other, only this time Alruna reluctantly gave him the axe.

"I want it back afterwards."

Bane took the axe and hefted it in his hands.

"I'm better with a sword," he said.

Alruna glared at him over her shoulder, eyes narrowing to hateful slits.

"The axe is fine," he said and then faced out, altering his feet to match the shapes which moved beyond the veil, silhouettes shifting, ready to strike.

"We seek the Wycum," he yelled, raising his arm to show them the tattoo. "I am Blood of Tyr."

He didn't know if there was any truth to that statement but knew that it meant something to the draugr.

"Only one may seek out the Wycum. Blood of Tyr. And that must be you," came the voices from the gloom, speaking in unison.

"No. Alruna is with me."

"She will become one of us. She will be draugr."

There was a shuffling beyond the mist and a taller shape stepped out of the mist. He was younger, his skin pale but not the grey of the other creatures.

"Jhora?" Alruna said, taking a step towards him but pausing as the newcomer held out a hand to hold her back.

"I am no longer Jhora, Alruna. I am draugr."

He was solemn, but Bane could tell that he had once enjoyed life. He now had many scars and injuries. A nasty gash opened down the length of his chest, revealing the white bone beneath.

"You must leave the Fug, Alruna. You must do so now. Come with me and I will take you out of the mist, although you will be some way from the peak. Only the Blood of Tyr may remain to reach the Wycum."

Alruna glanced back to Bane.

"The Fug will take him to the Wycum?"

The draugr that was Jhora nodded.

"But you must leave now. Come," he beckoned, stepping back through the mist.

"No," Bane said, stepping with Alruna. "We go together. We can both climb to the peak. Both find this Wycum."

Alruna shrugged as she plucked the axe back from his grasp.

"I still might kill you," she said.

Bane believed her yet also knew that he couldn't leave her alone on the mountaintop. Not so far up away from her village. He felt he owed her father that.

She snaked an arm under him and took the weight from his injured leg as they followed the tall draugr through the mist.

Other shapes moved to come at them, steel and iron glinting as if ready to cut them down, yet none made a move.

"They hold back because only one draugr may fight at a time. This fight is mine."

"Your father is proud of you, Jhora, of what you did," Bane said, realising that this must be the draugr that the giant Viking back at the village spoke of. This was his son.

"Wrong, Blood of Tyr. I have no father."

The mist flowed differently then, the tendrils of vapour thinning out, and Bane caught snatches of greens and blues.

"Jhora, why do they call me Blood of Tyr?"

The draugr paused, his pallid skin stretching into a frown, eyes cloudy yet still holding some colour to his irises.

Because you hold the blood of the mighty god of war, the same god that sleeps in the mountain. Tyr is restless and awaits the time when he can take the head of Gharl, the demon god of the south."

"I have the blood of Tyr?"

"The Wycum will explain all. There is a war coming."

Bane wanted to ask more, but he stumbled over something hidden below the vapour and, as he fell, took Alruna with him.

They both tumbled, rolling several times, flashes of grey, blue and white until they came to a stop in a tangle of limbs in the snow.

When his vision caught up, he found that they were on the side of the mountain, in a deep drift clinging to the side of a grey cliff face, the world looming a long way below. The castle was so small it was only a dull smudge, a speck sitting on the edge of a forest that was so far away he couldn't make out anything other than the green canopy.

"Get off me," Alruna said, pulling her arm out from under him and yanking a leg free, which was trapped beneath his back.

She stood, looked up to the top of the cliff face, the wind dusting the snow from the top, and then back down below.

"Fugging...Fug," she screamed, veins pulsing in her temple, the skin around her jaw becoming red as she went to strike her axe into the rock but stopped at the last moment.

She turned to him, took a step, raised the axe, and Bane knew that this was the time, yet she took a deep breath, and the axe fell into the snow.

"Fug it."

She sat down heavily, staring up at the Fug as it disappeared up the mountain, reaching the summit and sweeping back down.

It flowed over them, blocking the sky momentarily before disappearing below, dropping from sight.

"Why didn't I stay in the fugging, bunker?"

Bane sat up, fingers already going numb from the air which was stealing the breath from him.

"You can go back. Only I need to seek the Wycum."

Alruna didn't look at him, her jaw clenching as she stared up the mountain to the peak.

"Shut up."

Bane gasped as he put weight on his leg and struggled up onto his feet, gripping the spindly trunk of the only tree on the slope.

He studied the route he would need to take to the peak and realised that he would need to climb a sheer vertical wall.

It would be near impossible on a good day, but in winter and carrying an injury, he had no hope.

Alruna stared at him and then up at the summit and came to the same conclusion.

"You're going to die," she said and rose, picked her axe out of the snow and slipped the shaft into the loop on her belt.

Her boots crunched through the snow as she descended the slope, her legs disappearing to the knees as she floundered, her vest and shirt inadequate to the biting winds and thick ice.

"Where are you going?" he shouted to her back, but she ignored him.

The slope gave way to an overhang which dropped to a steep ridge, a rock jutted out with icicles dangling beneath.

Bane watched until she disappeared and thought that she could possibly be the last person he saw. The last he spoke with. It was a shame the words were so harsh, yet he couldn't blame her.

A gust cut across the slope, carrying ice and stinging his face.

He pulled his cloak in tight about him as he limped to the granite wall, fingers numb as he pressed them to the rough surface.

There was no way he would be going up it without wings.

Stepping sideways, he crept along the bottom of the wall, working his way to the edge.

The drop down would take an age, most likely ending with him being impaled on the ferns some many spans below.

He gripped a small crevice, wedging as far into the crag as he could and leaned out.

The surface on this side seemed a better climb. There were more places to set his feet and grip, but if he fell, it would be to certain death.

The top of the crags seemed even less inviting. Long icicles dangled drown from an overhang, each as long as a sword, sharpened by the harsh winds which battered this unprotected side of the mountain.

The afternoon sun was already on its descent; daylight would soon be running out, and he didn't want to be resting on the slope overnight.

Ignoring the drop, Bane leaned out as far as he could, pressing the toe of his boot into a wide crack. It was his bad leg, and he knew the stretch was going to hurt.

Steeling himself, he held his breath and then pushed upwards and grasped the small jut of rock.

The tips of his fingers scraped over harsh granite, slipping to the edge but mercifully found purchase.

Putting his weight onto his hand, he kicked the snow free from another crag and placed his foot inside and then reached up to the next.

Now he was fully away from the slope, one false move and it would be a messy end for him.

His mind wandered to Belle as he climbed, hoping that she somehow found her way back to the castle. None of this was her fault. It wasn't anyone's fault, and he got the feeling that the Fug had somehow enticed Tomm into its misty embrace, hoping to entice Bane and trap him.

Maybe he was always fated to seek out the Wycum. He only wished it had been an easier journey.

He heaved himself up, repeating the same movements, kicking out the snow from the crevasses, gripping to the best handholds and pulling himself bit by bit up the wall.

The wind tore at him, any feeling in his fingers long lost. He needed to watch each movement he made until he was sure his hands responded how he wanted them to.

If he died here, would Glance worry where he was? Would Cuthbur? Jarl?

With each reach, he tried to push his friends from his mind, yet they kept coming back.

"Focus," he berated himself.

By the fourth reach, his fingers were bleeding, and his legs and arms were trembling with fatigue.

He risked a glance down and judged he was about halfway. If he was going to change his mind and try to go back down and wait for the morning, now was the time.

Feeling a sudden dizziness come over him, he closed his eyes and clung to the wall - willing himself to climb. It was as if his body wasn't his own.

He knew he couldn't remain where he was much longer. The stew from the previous evening was all he had to take him up. If he didn't move now, he wouldn't make it. He doubted he would make it anyway.

"Move," he willed himself and reached up to the next hold, pulled, kicked the snow with his boot, and drove a foot into the crack. Reach, grasp and pull.

He blotted out the pain and tried to breathe how Glance had taught him. Be self-aware yet alone from the bodily senses.

Before he knew it, he was at the icicles, staring up and wondering how he was going to get around.

There was no way to avoid them – he needed to go through and over.

Clenching his teeth, he stretched out and grasped the first. Testing it with a tug before committing the weight of his body to it.

It held.

He swung out into oblivion, grasped the next along and let go of the crags with his feet.

Suspended above the world, his cloak billowing in the wind, Bane worked his way along to the edge of the overhang, blood mixing with the ice and snow, making each hold more slippery than the last.

He tried to take his mind away from everything but the long spikes of ice, having to force his hands to work until he was at the edge.

There was only one handhold he could see, a small jut of rock which was out of reach.

Then it started to snow. Thick white chunks filled the air mixed with hail as it swirled about him, blinding his vision while scouring exposed skin.

Ignoring the drop below, Bane worked his legs back and forth until he had enough momentum to swing up.

He let go of the icicles and momentarily had no contact with the mountain at all.

He wasn't going to reach it.

It was a foolish judgment, and then his fingers brushed the tip of the rock and he gripped as tightly as he could.

Hanging from only the finger of one hand, he slowly reached higher, his entire body shaking with fatigue, his legs kicking at nothing.

Desperately he reached up for the next place but found none, the movement breaking the hold on the only place he had.

A scream released from his chest as he lunged upwards, a last attempt at grasping onto anything.

He slipped out into nothing.

Terror consumed him. This was the end. There was no coming back from such a fall.

He only hoped he would find Gelwin and his mother in the afterlife.

Then, as his mind turned to Belle, his head jerked, and he slammed into the icicles, his jaw bouncing from a large spire and dislodging it.

"Fuggin climb, boy."

His scalp on fire, Bane frantically reached up and gripped the ledge as someone yanked up on his hair.

Making a silent prayer to the All-Mother, Bane found purchase through the snow and heaved himself over, the effort made easy as he was being pulled from above.

When he was finally on flat ground, he rolled onto his back and stared up into Alruna's angry face.

"Fugging village folk can't climb, can't fight, can't do anything but fugging bleat like goats," she said, leaving him there as she paced away from the edge crouching into the rock where it naturally concaved, blowing air into her fingers.

Bane gathered his breath and clambered to his feet, pulling his hood up against the wind and hail, the pellets of ice stinging anything that still had enough blood in it to feel.

He glanced at her prints in the snow and realised that she had climbed the vertical wall, which he didn't even attempt.

"Thank you," he said, his teeth beginning to chatter.

She said nothing, only turned her head.

Yesterday she had wanted to kill him, and now she saved his life.

Bane squatted beside her, pulling his weak leg out straight. Cramp locked his thigh muscle, and he could tell from the blood seeping through his britches that the stitches in his wound had most likely broken.

The rock they were sheltering against had a ledge which wound crookedly upwards, disappearing into dark clouds thick with swirling hail.

The summit was still some way beyond the grey veil.

"We can't be that far from it now," Bane said, struggling up and using the rock to pull himself to his feet. "The Wycum must be through the cloud."

He took a lumbering step until his leg gave way, and he crashed to the floor.

"Stupid," Alruna said, gripping him by the jerkin and hauling him closer.

"We must wait until the morning. We can't climb blind," she said, lifting him into a sitting position and not too gently shoving him against the rock.

Bane had never felt so tired or so cold before.

"Th..th..thank you," he mumbled, his entire body now shivering - he thought he might cause an avalanche.

Alruna said nothing, her body shaking as much as his, yet she didn't complain.

"Why did you come back?"

She ignored him, only stared at her feet and then pulled her knees into her chest as the snow drove against the rock, the starting of a drift building about them.

Bane shifted closer to Alruna, thinking they would survive the night better, sharing body heat, yet the closer he shuffled to her, the further she pulled away.

"Please, take my cloak," Bane offered, untying it from around his neck and giving it to her.

She balled it in her hands and tossed it back.

If Bane had the capacity to shrug, he would have, yet the cold battering his body stole that ability away.

Hail bounced from the rock behind them, dropping down, rolling into his collar and stinging his skin.

Bane fought with the wind to put his cloak back on and pulled the hood up tight. If Alruna would rather freeze to death than accept anything from him, then that was her decision, as foolish as it was.

Darkness descended, the sky becoming indistinguishable from the mountain or the drop over the snow which Bane felt building about his feet.

He wouldn't be surprised to find themselves buried by the morning when they woke – if they woke.

The cloak stretched to cover his legs when he drew them in, pulling each side over him into a cocoon.

It was enough to keep the wind out, yet the unforgiving cold was still biting through every damp layer he was wearing.

Later in the night, he heard scraping as Alruna shifted and then felt his cloak being pulled open and her cold body sliding in close to his.

He said nothing as he slipped an arm over her shoulder and drew the cloak over both of them.

It wasn't long before he felt Alruna's head fall gently against his shoulder.

He woke first, his body racked with cramps, from his throbbing legs to the fingers, which were either still numb or raw with scrapes and scratches.

Alruna slept on, her head wedged into the crook of his neck, arm laying across his chest as she gently snored, yet she was surprisingly warm.

He kept still, even though he'd lost all feeling down that side.

The shared body heat was what had saved them during the night. It wasn't an unpleasant feeling. The girl lying against him.

****

Alruna opened her eyes.

At first, she thought she had fallen into the bunker, but the light was wrong. As her mind caught up with where she was, her heart began to thump, the memories of the previous day coming back.

She'd never experienced a cold like what attacked them last night. Death would have claimed her if she hadn't found shelter within Bane's cloak or used the heat from his body. His arm was protectively over her, and hers draped across his chest.

She hated him, a cruel, savage hatred, but she didn't want to move away from the warmth. She'd not had this closeness to another in a long time, and she couldn't deny that it felt good.

She often wondered what it would be like to press up against a boy in the village as she had seen some of the women do. Yet there were none she liked and only a few her own age.

The sun penetrated the top of the drift, lighting up Bane's face.

That wasn't too unpleasant, either. A little rough from the climb, a healing scab, a bruise across his jaw where she'd thumped him, yet not too shabby for it.

Then the guilt hit.

Raif came to the forefront of her mind and she sat up, flinging Bane's arm from her shoulder and instantly regretted it.

The drift that had covered them in the night fell away, dislodging the snow that had collected above the rock they had sheltered beneath. It dropped down on them in a large white curtain.

In her haste to be away from his touch, Alruna stepped backwards, her feet slipping through the powder and the next thing she knew, she was on her back, sliding from the rock with the falling snow.

Her head collided with the granite, and then she fell away, tumbling out into nothing.

"Alruna?" came Bane's panicked voice from above and her fall came to a jolting halt, her leg wrenched tight as her boot snagged against something.

No, Bane had her foot, straining as he sat down heavily and then scrambled away, dragging her up with him.

The sword on her back clattered against rock as she briefly glanced down and wished she hadn't.

The ground was a long way, the trees so small at the bottom that she would be smashed to an unrecognisable pulp if she fell.

Fear hit her. An all-consuming terror which shook through her entire core.

As soon as her hand grasped solid ground, she heaved herself up and held tight to Bane, his solidness suddenly becoming the only thing with which she felt safe.

The confusion on his face softened as he held her tight, pulling her further into the rock, and they both collapsed to the floor, feet wedged so they wouldn't move.

"We're closer than you think," Bane said, his soft tones whispering close to her ear.

She felt the heat from his breath and thought he might touch her with those soft lips.

"We shall never be close," she hissed, the guilt from before returning, although she had no desire to pull away from his hold.

"No. I didn't mean us; I meant the peak. Look."

Feeling foolish, Alruna raised her head and found that they were on the edge of a summit, a small saddle in the rocks with a natural ledge leading to the top, only a few spans away.

"Then let's not sit here getting cosy. I want off this mountain and away from you as soon as possible," she said, yet there was no hostility in her tone, and she was in no hurry to release him.

She felt a loss as he let go and brushed himself off. He limped several steps, hand pressed to his injured thigh, which he was partly dragging along. Yet he moved with a determination of one that had come so far.

She couldn't deny that he had and couldn't help but admire him for all he'd gone through.

"You killed Raif," she said, the words coming out as a sob as she followed, lifting his arm over her shoulder and bearing the weight of his weaker side.

"I did," he replied, face stern as he stared ahead. "And that night has haunted me ever since. Every time I oil and sharpen his sword, every time I draw it."

Freezing gusts swept across them as they slowly made progress along the ridge, threatening to sweep them off completely.

"I can't forgive you. And you're not having the sword back," she said, not knowing why she felt the need to talk.

"I know. And if I could go back and change things, I would."

He winced as he moved, but she didn't know if that was from the pain in his leg or from the conversation. Perhaps both.

The thin ledge became thinner as it skirted the saddle, yet there seemed to be ancient steps carved into the rock, leading through a tall crevice at the summit.

This must have been the way Raif had come. He had trodden on these very rocks when he sought out the Wycum for himself.

The blue sky gave way to dark clouds again, and the snow began to come down, yet mercifully, they made it to the crevice, wide enough for them to pass through.

Bane no longer needed her help as he gripped the side of the rock, taking a step at a time.

She followed him inside the crevice which was some kind of cave shaped from the rocks itself. The steps led up and through a dark mouth.

He hesitated on the threshold, stared into the gloom and then stepped through.

Alruna followed, feeling a warmer air coming out of the cave.

Worn steps led them down, twisting and winding until they came out into a small cavern, more of a grotto if such a thing could exist on a mountain.

Tendrils of smoke spiralled up through cracks in the floor, and a smell of rotten eggs filled the air, yet it was warm, almost stuffy.

A shadow in the corner of the grotto suddenly shifted, and Bane gasped, instinctively going for the sword on his back that wasn't there.

It was a creature, hunched over with its face hidden beneath a shroud.

Alruna pulled the sword from her back and passed the axe to Bane.

"You'll not need those here," the shadow said as it shuffled closer, raising crooked fingers towards the weapons. The voice was as old as the mountain, full of gravel or rocks, yet there was strength there. Alruna got the impression that it was female, although the shroud that covered it didn't offer much in the way of the shape beneath.

"We seek the Wycum," Bane said, lowering the axe.

The creature slowly nodded as it gestured for them to follow.

"The Wycum is impatient, come, come."

They followed the creature, Alruna once again taking Bane's arm and pulling it over her shoulder.

They stepped through a hidden arch that was naturally disguised with rocks, more steps taking them further into the bowels of the mountain. Then they emerged into a larger cavern, a bubbling stream of steaming water snaking through the centre and disappearing through a fissure in the wall.

"Who is it that seeks the Wycum?" the creature asked, turning to them.

Alruna caught the lower part of a jaw, the flesh grey and cracked.

"I do. Bane. Bane Garik, son of Bailin."

Alruna glanced at him.

"You're who now?" she asked, realising that they could have easily snatched him the night that Raif died, and her brother may still have lived.

"You're Bailin Shankil's son?" she asked.

"I'm his bastard," Bane said, shrugging.

The creature lifted her veil, revealing that she was indeed as old as the mountain.

Her cheeks and brow had deeper wrinkles than the rocks themselves, her eyes sunken and were more draugr like than human.

"Bastard or not, it matters none. You're still Blood of Tyr," she said, coming close enough to grasp his arm.

"Are you the Wycum?" he asked.

"Wycum, yes. I remember marking you, boy. A day old, left out for the Fug."

Alruna watched Bane. He flinched as the ancient one rubbed her thumb over the mark, the thorns reacting to her touch.

She didn't know about him being left out to die as a baby. He had a harder start than most, yet in the short time she'd known him, he'd never complained.

"This mark has tasted blood already. The thorns have grown strong, yes?"

Bane nodded, his gaze catching Alruna's briefly.

"Good. That is good. Now, you must refresh yourself. Take a moment to bathe your wounds," the Wycum said, pointing at the bubbling stream. "I must speak with this child in private, for she has something to ask, no?"

Alruna stepped back, the intense stare locking with hers.

"Come, come," the Wycum said, taking her hand and leading her to the back of the cavern and down more steps.

Alruna glanced at Bane before she descended, wondering if she would see him again and why she cared.

"I don't have anything to ask you," Alruna said as the steps came out into another grotto-like chamber, a shallow pool of dark liquid flowing out of the wall before dropping down and running along a channel which passed through the wall on the other side.

"Then why are you here? You have doubts that need amending, yes. The same question that brought your brother to the mountain."

"Raif came to be marked like my father was," Alruna snapped. "My father, Boran Lothrun."

"No, child - you're too afraid to ask the question because you already know the answer."

Alruna was about to deny it, the words forming on her lips, yet the doubt was real, the question too.

"Was my father ever marked by you? Did he seek you out?"

The ancient one smiled, the crags and fissures in her face twisting, yellow teeth worn down like old tombstones, clashing together as she cackled.

"You already know the answer, girl."

She and Raif had found a jar of ink years ago. Hidden high up on the mountain where the goats sometimes went when being stubborn. It was hidden within the hollow of an old tree. There were needles in the jar.

They left the find and told their father, who denied its existence. When they returned, the jar was gone.

She never knew Raif had the same doubts growing up.

"If it makes you feel any better, child, I've only ever marked three people."

"The clan tradition has always been a lie?"

She didn't know if that made it better or not. Her father had lied to her, had lied to the entire village.

"You already know, child. Now come here so I might mark a fourth."

Alruna frowned down at her. She was a head shorter yet seemed to possess a power.

"What do you mean?"

The Wycum grasped her hand and pulled her close to the channel of dark liquid.

"I mean to mark you, child. There is a war coming, and you've proven yourself. Now give me your arm."

Alruna didn't think she could pull her arm free even if she wanted to. The ancient had a vice-like grip as she produced a long needle. She dipped the tip into the dark flow and then tapped it into the soft underside of the wrist.

Alruna winced as the Wycum worked, the needle making small rapid jabs, her own blood coming to the surface in small beads.

"The Blood of Tyr will work well with you; I can tell it's already going to be strong."

23

Jackels At the Gate

Daylight broke over the crest of the ridge which overlooked Fort Palsin, yet it wasn't as bright as the flames which engulfed the old structure and walls, the bodies of the many dead piled up inside, adding fuel to the raging fire.

Bailin was standing with his men as they watched the thick smoke rise into the dawn, the stench of burning flesh filling the air.

"Do you believe what he said, that ghast?" Sir Godlin asked, his face crusted with dried blood and soot, beard blackened with dirt and sweat.

Bailin slowly nodded.

"I wish I didn't, but I believe every word. It all makes sense now, the endless warring with the Empire, the loss of his armies as he threw them into impossible battles he would never win. This god of the desert, Gharl and his hold over the south. Jin had no reason to lie. We were lucky to come out with only scrapes."

Godlin leaned back and spat onto the ground, nodding towards the rest of the men who were sat on the rise, hands on knees, heads tipped back, still heaving from the hard fight and then the building of pyres for the dead.

"So, we ride hard back to Garik castle and defend its walls from the army of jackals heading its way?"

Bailin rested his hand on the pommel of his sword, knuckles scabbed and thick with dried blood - luckily not his own.

It had been a harsh fight. The jackals fought tooth and claw or with anything else they could get their paws on. Yet they were no match for Bailin's knights. They fought as one. A highly disciplined unit of men fighting with honour, skill and brutal prowess. They had the better steel, the sharper weapons and the ability to use it all. Not to mention the runes daubed on the shields with tar. Runes of Tyr, a protection against demons.

They'd used the tar in the past, but it became more of a tradition with the Garik division. One that had turned last night's trap into a slaughter.

Bailin glanced at his men. They were dog-tired, yet he needed to push them a little more.

"No. The Jackals will be there within a day or two, and we're what, a couple of months away? We must pray that they are spotted before they attack and that the walls hold against them until help arrives."

He wiped his hand across his jaw, the stubble scraping the dirt from his palm.

"Choose a trusted knight to ride directly to the Capital, Nork. We need to send a message to the King and warn him of what's happening. Then, send another two knights to ride hard up the King's Road to meet up with Shull and the rest of the division. Tell them to head directly for Nork. If Jin is right and the war is about to break across our shores, then they'll be needed there."

Godlin raised his brows, looking worried all of a sudden.

"And the rest of us?"

"We push south to the coast and see what's happening for ourselves. If you were the Emperor with a fleet the size of his and wanted to land it in one go, where would you choose?"

Godlin scratched his beard.

"Lymport. It's got the largest harbour, and the mouth of river Dwent flows from there right up country, passing Nork. And it's deep enough to float war galleys."

"My thoughts exactly. Now, get the men ready. We move out as soon as the fort becomes ash."

****

Bane sank lower into the hot water, the steam rising and touching his bare skin. The many cuts and grazes stung like hundreds of individual flames, yet the soothing feeling of the bubbles caressing his body pushed the pain away. He left his clothes discarded on a rock, a rare smile finding his lips as the water swept over his shoulders.

Holding his breath, he submerged totally beneath the surface, the past harsh days dissolving away.

The flames on his skin softened to a gentle buzz and even the injury in his thigh was little more than an itch.

He was floating as the Wycum came shuffling back into the cavern, and as he saw Alruna behind her, he suddenly became aware that he was naked.

He floundered deeper as he caught her smirking, trying to cover himself the best he could.

"Sink into the waters, girl. The Fug will be reaching us soon, and you must travel back down the mountain with it."

Alruna began to undress, her belt falling to the ground before she grasped her vest, pausing to glance at Bane while raising an eyebrow.

His face flushing with heat, Bane put his back to her, hearing the rustle of discarded clothes followed by a splash.

He turned to find that she had dropped into the water and had gone under. She remained beneath the surface for a time before coming up. Her warrior's braid flicked over as she threw her head back, droplets splashing him as she came closer.

"The cuts on your face have gone," she said, the reflection of water sparkling across her cheeks and lighting up her blue eyes.

Bane hadn't really noticed how beautiful she was until then.

Then became aware once again of how naked he was, and how close she was coming, and then how naked she was too.

"You're going red."

Bane turned away.

"No, I'm not," he argued, then a thought came to him.

He tenderly felt for the injury along his thigh and was shocked to find that it wasn't there.

"My leg's healed," he said, his smile returning.

The Wycum stepped closer to the water and perched herself on a rock which wasn't there before.

"The waters are warmed by Tyr's blood. It'll cleanse most wounds," she said, "But won't bring back the dead. Which is what will happen to the pair of you if you don't prepare the castle for an invasion."

"Invasion?" Alruna asked, slipping closer. It was then that Bane noticed that she had a tattoo on her wrist. It was a band like his own when he was younger. But they were not thorns. They looked like a ring of forest ivy.

"Yes, Gharl thinks he is the only one who can see patterns in the sky, whispers from the trees and death upon the winds. A war has been raging since the time of the small gods. A war that most thought was over."

The Wycum shuffled closer, her craggy hands gripping a stalagmite which was poking from the water's edge.

"As we speak, there is a wave of jackals marching on Garik. They'll be there by tomorrow's moon. The demons must not break the walls. They must not be allowed to enter the castle."

"Demons? What about Crookfell?"

The Wycum smashed a gnarled fist into her palm.

"They'll be crushed. Food to feed the desert dogs, as will anyone caught outside the walls."

Bane looked to Alruna, who was shaking her head.

"What about the Fug? Will my clan, our villages be safe behind the silver veil?"

"Only if the castle holds. But ask yourself, Alruna Lothrun. Why do you think they need to break into the castle? There is something hidden within that will allow them to pass through the Fug. Then ask yourself another question. Why have the Norse been here all these centuries."

Alruna stared at the Wycum, a subtle shake to her head.

"As the last true battle came to an end, Tyr and Gharl gave each other mortal wounds. They were both carried away by their own. Gharl to the deserts of the south, and Tyr was brought here. The war will end when the head is removed from either god. The Vikings volunteered their best fighters, battle-hardened Drengrs, to remain to protect the mountain and the body of Tyr. Those are your ancestors, girl. And with Tyr's last breath, he created the Fug. His breath that contains the dead that have fallen in battle."

"And if Gharl wins, it will be bad?" Bane asked.

The Wycum stared solemnly at him.

"If the desert god wins, then the jackals will inherit the world and the day of man will come to an end."

Alruna shared a look with him then, the redness in her cheeks paling.

"How big is this wave of jackals that are coming?" she asked.

"I don't know, but it will be big enough to do the task. A lethal strike force of demons that were bred to fight. If they attacked without warning, the castle would fall. That is why I brought you here. Your task, both of you, is to prepare, to fight, to die if needs be. Survive the wave, and the North may stand a chance, regroup and fight back. You will only achieve this by standing together."

"Stand together?" Alruna said, the grimace she'd worn back at the village finding its way onto her face once again.

She pulled away from him, her jaw clenching.

"It's what I told your brother, girl. This is bigger than any petty feud."

"He killed my brother."

The Wycum moved so quickly that her arm became a blur of grey as she grasped Alruna around the wrist with the tattoo and yanked her closer.

"Raif was already dying, girl. He'd been mortally wounded by the draugr. He would have been one of them now if you hadn't burnt his body on a pyre. It was only his strength and courage that kept him going as long as he did. Otherwise, he'd be wearing this mark and not you."

Bane heard the words, yet it took a moment for their importance to sink in.

"Raif was already dying? I didn't kill him?"

Alruna elbowed him in the ribs, a snarl parting her lips.

"You killed him, boy. I was there, remember?"

The Wycum hissed and gripped tighter to Alruna's wrist, forcing a gasp from her.

"I suspect the boy was defending himself, and if the mark took the life, then your brother lives on in Bane."

Alruna yanked her arm free and glared at the pair of them, yet it seemed some of the hate had dropped, along with the snarl.

She swam to her clothes and climbed out, forgetting that she was naked or not caring. Bane turned away, feeling his cheeks grow warm again.

"This wave of jackals will hit hard and destroy everything if they succeed. You must not let that happen. The castle must stand strong if it is to remain in the war. Do you understand, child?"

Bane was taken aback by the severity of the Wycum, the white eyes becoming darker, a red glint to the cloudy irises.

"I found a book in the castle. It was old, yet the pictures within seemed real as if the person drawing them was there."

"Yes, child." The ancient said, sitting back, her voice becoming soft again. "I was there, in a younger form, but I fought by Tyr's side. It was I who recorded the last battle. I that hid the secret in the castle, and it is I alone who has remained in the mountain, awaiting this day. Now come, the Fug approaches."

Bane was reluctant to climb out of the warm water and back into the freezing air.

He glanced to make sure that Alruna wasn't looking and then hopped out and quickly put his clothes on, feeling rejuvenated for being in the healing waters.

"Go now. Leave the way you came. The Fug won't wait for you, and neither will it harm you," the Wycum said, pointing towards the archway they came through.

Alruna said nothing as she marched past him, her shoulder brushing his, not too gently.

Shaking his head, he glanced once more at the ancient, yet she had already shuffled to the side of the cavern and leaned against the wall, her features taking on the crags and fissures in the rock itself.

It was as if she wasn't there at all.

Putting his back to her, he followed Alruna out into the brightness of the day, the Fug already ascending towards them.

They paced in silence towards the silver vapour. Her jaw set hard as she acted as though he wasn't there.

"Will you bring your fighters to the castle?" he asked. "Will you help us defend against these demons?"

When she didn't answer, he made to grab her shoulder, but she flinched away.

"I heard you, boy," she snapped, turning on him so viciously that he thought she might push him off the saddle and out into oblivion. "And the choice isn't up to me. My father is Clan Chief, and he can only speak for our clan."

"No," Bane said, taking her hand and holding her wrist up to reveal the tattoo. "You're Wycum marked. Doesn't that mean that you are clan leader?"

She snatched it away and nearly fell, only Bane grabbing her hand again preventing it.

"It's not that simple," she said, looking away to the advancing wall of fog.

It billowed towards them, devouring them completely, and the only thing that Bane felt was the warmth from her hand as she gripped it tighter.

As before, the shapes in the gloom moved around them, snarls and grunts echoing through the mist. They turned, Alruna reaching for her axe, yet they were not attacked.

"I will warn the castle and get it ready for these jackals," Bane said, turning Alruna so he faced her. "The Wycum is right. We must swallow this feud. This war is bigger than any of us. "Will you come?"

Alruna said nothing, her scowl deepening, yet she didn't look away and didn't let go.

"I'll never forgive you, Bane."

It was the first time she had used his name, and it felt good hearing it from her mouth.

"I don't expect you to."

"And I still hate you."

Bane nodded.

"I know."

She took a deep breath and swallowed a choking sob.

"I will come. And I will try to bring others, but I cannot command them to fight for the castle."

The mist swirled about them, tussling his cloak and almost drawing him off his feet.

"That is all I ask," he managed to say.

Alruna turned her head, her gaze cast down as she chewed the inside of her cheek.

"You'll need this."

She unbuckled the scabbard from her back and handed him Raif's sword.

"After the fight, I'll want it back."

Bane took the harness and strapped it on, feeling the familiar weight against his back.

"Thank you."

She stared at him, lips drawn tight, yet the hate had gone from her eyes.

"Shut up."

The Fug swirled more aggressively, and Bane felt himself falling, Alruna stumbling the other way, and then she was lost. He fought his way towards her, but the shapes came for him, large hands shoving him the other way.

He might have gone for his sword, but the vapour suddenly evaporated, and he found himself on the edge of Crookfell.

The disorientating feeling of being dropped forced him to his knees, catching himself in the snow.

Over his shoulder, he watched the Fug depart, the silver mist flowing away from him and hoped that Alruna was dropped safely in her village.

"Bane?" he heard a cry from across the other side of the open ground. He glanced up to see that Dew and Belle were running towards him.

"Bane?" Belle cried again as she slammed into him, almost knocking him from his feet.

"I thought you went through the final door," she said, reaching around and squeezing tight.

"What happened?" Dew asked, giving him a playful punch on the shoulder. "Belle told me you disappeared into the Fug and then made me sit here until you came out.

"How did you know I would come out?"

Belle pulled away as she beamed.

"Of course you would. You're the only one who has ever gone into the Fug and come back out. And if you can do it as a babe, then why not a man."

"Did little Tomm come out?"

Belle nodded. "Right after you went in. He said there were monsters and that you protected him. So, what happened?"

"I'll tell you later, but listen, we don't have a lot of time. The castle is about to be attacked. I need you to help me get all the folk in Crookfell to the castle."

"Attacked? By whom?" Dew asked, looking worried.

"I'll explain later. Just get them to the castle. Do you think you can do that?"

Dew and Belle glanced at each other before nodding.

"Good. Now, I don't suppose you kept hold of my horse?"

Dew grinned.

"It's at home. Ma's being doting over it as if it were a newborn," Belle said.

Before midday, Bane was riding the mare hard across the valley, not slowing as he galloped through the gate of the castle, hooves slamming over stone.

He rode past the stables and across the bailey, barely avoiding two guards on patrol. They leapt out of the way, shouting at his back, but Bane spurred the horse on, climbing the stairs and trotting down the narrow lanes until he reached the main entrance to the castle.

Two sentries came forward as he leapt down and threw the reins to one of them.

"Send word to the gatehouse that the people of Crookfell are coming and to not deny them entry," he said to the other.

They stared on, not reacting.

"We're under attack or will be soon. Now go," he said, spurring the men into action.

He put his back to them as he ran through the tall arch, collided with a serving girl, stopped long enough to pick her up, apologised and then pressed on.

His boots slammed up the stairs, which he took two at a time, reached the top and ran along the corridor towards Lady Felina's chambers.

Before he reached the door, it swung open, and he ran into Jarl.

"Steady, lad," he said, huge hands grasping his shoulders. "We missed you at the feast last night. Lady Felina toasted…What's wrong."

"We haven't long. Is she here?"

Jarl nodded as he gestured through the door, a worried frown creasing his brow.

"Master Bane," Lady Felina said as he rushed in, her easy smile dropping.

She was perched in her chair, skirts flowing out and touching the floor, a book in her lap.

"My Lady, I've just returned from the mountain," he said, catching his breath. "I've been warned that the castle is about to be attacked."

"I don't understand. The mountain? And attacked by who?" Felina asked, rising from her chair.

"Lad, you're not making any sense," Jarl put in, closing the door behind him.

"Please, believe me, my Lady. I went through the Fug yesterday. It carried me up the mountain to the Wycum."

He explained all that he could, leaving out the parts that were not essential.

When he was finished, Felina glanced at Jarl, her expression unreadable.

"What will you have me do, my Lady?" the retired knight asked.

"I think it's quite clear what we must do, Jarl. We prepare for war."

****

Alruna found her father in the bunker with both cats. Once the Fug had passed, he threw open the hatch and almost fell back down the ladder when his eyes locked on her.

"Alruna?" he said, eyes blotchy and red. "I saw the Fug claim you. Watched you disappear and I thought I'd never see you again," voice catching on the last word.

She took his hand and pulled him up and out, his arms flinging around her and not letting go.

"Da, we have to talk," she said, twisting away from his grip, and then was almost bowled over my Freki.

The leopard raised up on hind legs, her front paws pressing down on her shoulders as she licked her face.

Boran then gasped.

"You have got the mark of the Wycum," he said, taking her hand and rubbing his thumb over her tattoo.

He winced as he drew it back, a bead of blood dropping from the pad.

"Aye, and this one's real," she said, looking at the fading band around his arm.

At least he had the shame to look to the floor.

"I was going to tell you, Alruna. When the time was right, when you were ready to lead the clan."

"The jar of ink Raif and I found?"

Boran nodded as they wandered to the hut, the cats following.

"Aye. The thing is, that's the way it was always done. The secret passed from chief to chief. Not that it's needed any more," he said, staring at her wrist again.

Alruna turned it over, admiring the tattoo of the interwoven ivy that seemed so real. She rubbed her own finger across the drawn vine and marvelled at the way it moved, the leaves rising and falling, the edges feeling as though she could pluck one.

"Da, we've got a fight coming. We need to gather all the men in the village and send word to the other clans. What Raif warned us is true. The Wycum told me herself. There's a war coming, and we'll need to fight."

"And the boy?"

"Bane. He was with me. He's now at the castle, preparing for a battle. They're about to be attacked by demons. The castle must not fall."

She took her father's hand.

"Will you help me raise the clans? We must cross the Fug and aid the castle."

Boran sat down in his chair, leaned back and shook his head.

"That is now no longer my job, Alruna," he said, eyes falling once again to the mark on her wrist. "You are now clan chief."

24

Moon Of The Desert Dogs

The day had been harsh. The entire castle was busy preparing for the coming battle; even the people of Crookfell had pitched in, digging more defences around the walls, felling trees and sharpening large stakes from the trunks. Pits had been dug with spikes at the bottom, and barrels of oil dotted about, ready to light so the demons couldn't approach unseen in the dark.

Anyone of fighting age and willing were gathered by the knights. They were to wait in the bailey and used as reserves if needed. Archers were posted along the walls and buckets of rocks were scattered along the battlements, ready to be dropped on the attackers.

Bane was standing on the battlements with Lady Felina, who was dressed in britches, tunic and polished armour. Cuthbur was at her side while Jarl was at the other, leaning out and staring down at the progress below.

"I wish my brothers were here," Felina said. "Bailin could probably hold the jackals back alone, and Glance knows the castle inside and out – knows all the secret ways. Surely, he had knowledge of this hidden key they are after."

"At least your father is safe," Jarl said, and I'm sure help will come once the messengers reach him."

Felina inclined her head as she went to join the knight, staring down at the grounds.

"Is there any sign of the Vikings?" she asked, lines deepening along her smooth forehead.

"No, my lady. But they will come," Bane replied, hoping that Alruna could persuade her people to fight.

The day was setting and the first of the riders that had been sent out to spot the approaching wave had returned with news of a dust cloud approaching across the open ground.

That dust cloud was now visible.

It loomed high in the darkening sky, an omen of things to come.

Another rider then came thundering along the King's Road, pushing his mount to a lather as he came through the gate.

"This doesn't look good," Jarl said. A moment later, the trumpets sounded along the walls.

Then the rider was rushing up the stairs to join them on the wall, falling to a knee before Lady Felina.

"I saw them, my Lady. The wave of demons, they'll be here by dusk."

"How many?" Jarl asked.

"No fewer than ten thousand, Sir. It was hard to judge. They didn't move like men. They ran on all fours, a sea of them. But they could easily be double that number, maybe more."

Lady Felina nodded solemnly as she dismissed the rider. She then summoned the captain of the guard.

"Ensure everyone is within the walls and close the gates," she ordered. "And light the barrels."

They were silent for a time as they watched the dust cloud approach, a dust cloud formed from the many thousands of paws thundering towards them.

"Will the raiders come?" Cuthbur asked, seeming small inside the armour which matched his mother's.

"They'll come," Bane reassured him, then watched the blood drain from Cuthbur's face.

"What's that noise? That rumble?"

Jarl's worried expression turned to Felina as they all heard the sound of thunder.

"They'll be here a lot sooner than dusk," he said and then leaned out over the battlements again.

"Is everyone inside?" he bellowed down. "Then close the gates."

The rumble grew louder, a tremor passing through the stone beneath them, the looming doom above growing darker.

"There," an archer shouted, pointing out beyond the valley.

Bane couldn't see it at first, then on the ridge of the valley wall appeared a lone dog with wide haunches and a short muzzle. It reared up on its hind legs, head raised to the sky and howled.

The cry cut through Bane, a malicious tone filled with hate. It was soon joined by others, many others, growing louder along with the thunder. And then a swarm of dogs crested the valley wall, flowing over it and racing down the other side. The numbers were so vast, and their bodies so tightly packed that the snow beneath was lost to sight. It appeared as though a blanket was being pulled over the countryside. A wicked, raging cover full of teeth and claws.

"By the All-Mother," the closest archer said as he began to nock an arrow, fingers trembling as he drew the string back.

"Easy," Jarl warned, "Make every arrow count."

Up and down the wall, men were getting ready, either with bow or barrel. Some appeared shocked, others scared – faces going white. Most of them had rarely left the castle, and only a few had ever been in a battle before.

The jackals kept coming, a raging river of dark bodies, ebbing and flowing with their own current, a torrent of evil heading directly for the castle.

"Hold," A captain ordered, steadying the archers along the wall.

The people in the bailey remained quiet, the younger ones cowering away from the doors. Even the horses whinnied and stamped the ground, sensing something coming.

"Hold."

An over-eager soldier let his arrow loose early, staring after the shaft of wood as if he couldn't believe it went.

It struck the ground midway between the attacking dogs and the castle.

The snarls and barks were building now, mixing with the howls and something else, a deeper rumble from within the endless pack.

Bane leaned closer and saw a huge jackal, twice the size of the rest. It ran at the centre of a diamond formation, flowing faster than the swarm.

"Hold!"

"It's a ghast," Cuthbur said, eyes making large circles as he raised a finger towards the huge beast. "They were mentioned in the tome Bane gave me. It's the commander of the wave. Larger, smarter and some have the ability to morph into men."

"Then that's the one to bring down first," Jarl said, signalling for the guard commander and passing on the information. He went up the line, instructing the captains.

"Loose!"

Bows thrummed as the volley of arrows raised up high, arcing gracefully before falling like metal tipped rain.

They fell into the leading edge of the jackals, puncturing skulls and embedding into shoulders, backs, and legs. One went through the throat of a baying dog, cutting the howl short.

The dead fell and were stampeded by those behind, becoming lost in the flood that came on.

None of the arrows reached the Ghast.

"Loose," screamed the captains again in unison.

Another volley went up, filling the evening with long shafts, cutting silently through the air before thumping into flesh.

More jackals went down, trampled flat by their brethren as they came on. The fallen lost beneath so many thundering claws.

Bane watched each volley go up and come down onto the mass of animals and knew if they had ten times as many archers with ten times as many arrows, it still wouldn't be enough.

"Brace the gate," a captain bellowed over the battlements.

Lady Felina gripped the pommel of her sword as the front of the charging dogs struck the gate, the ancient wood shaking violently.

Many jackals fell into the pits, some being driven by their own kind onto the sharpened stakes, high-pitch screeching as they died.

The howls rose in pitch, a vicious attack of claws scraping against stone.

The people in the bailey began to back away, nervous glances coming up to the wall to where Jarl ordered them to prepare.

"The gate won't hold them long," Jarl said as he leaned over the edge.

Archers were raining arrows down, shooting one arrow after another while the guards threw the heavy rocks down.

Bane could see that Jarl was right. The beasts would be coming in soon. And the larger dog, the ghast, seemed to know it.

It slowed its advance and now stood on its hind legs, pulling a large, jagged sword from a strap on its back.

It grinned up at Lady Felina as he pointed the blade at her, an evil glint in his eyes.

"Break the gates and climb the wall, my brothers, for tonight we dine on men," he growled, the jackals about him howling as they pushed for the door. Others scrambled for the wall.

There was an almighty thump and the sound of splintering wood erupted below.

One of the guards throwing the rocks pointed down, shock written on his face.

"They're climbing up. There's too many of them," he said and then found the strength to lift the barrel from the wall and tipped its contents over, followed by the barrel.

He then leapt back and drew his sword, but before it was out of the sheath, a jackal had breached the wall and leapt at him, fangs biting down into his neck and sending twin jets of blood spraying from either side of its jaws.

It was bigger and faster than Bane thought possible. Tearing a chuck of flesh away before kicking the dying guard over.

It was a head taller than Jarl, howling before it pounced on an archer who was concentrating over the battlements.

He screamed as claws raked down his back, flailing with his arms, the bow discarded.

It all happened in a heartbeat.

A knight beside the pair drove his sword through the beast's chest and kicked him back over the wall. But he was soon replaced by three more.

"They're coming in," yelled one of the guards below, the men in the bailey backing away.

"My Lady, I think you ought to find refuge in the castle," Jarl said, flinching as another mighty thump struck the gate.

"My place is with my people. And I'll not hide behind doors waiting for them to come in," she snapped, drawing her sword.

Bane was expecting Jarl to argue, but instead, he grinned.

"That's what I expected," he replied, drawing his own sword and picking up his shield.

He then turned to Bane.

"Take Cuthbur and join the other fledglings, lad. We'll hold them back as long as we can."

Bane slipped his blade from his back.

"I'd rather fight with you," he said, hearing more splintering wood followed by gasps below.

He looked back to the wall to find more jackals had scaled it and were now coming over.

Lady Felina gave her son a kiss on the brow before turning on Bane.

"No. You swore an oath to protect Cuthbur, and you'll damn well keep it. Now do as Jarl says and join the fledglings," she said, then leaned closer and kissed Bane's cheek.

"Go."

"Yes, my Lady," Bane said and then, nodding to Cuthbur, they both ran down the stairs, leaving the sounds of desperate fighting behind them as they pushed through the crowds to the other fledglings.

The open ground was a mass of movement: guards lining up in front of the disintegrating gates, archers in front in two rows, the first kneeling.

Behind them were more knights and soldiers who hadn't gone south with Bailin's division. Bullif was commanding them, shouting for them to draw their blades as the gate rattled again, loose masonry falling from the huge iron-cast hinges.

Amidst the chaos, Bane spotted the fledglings huddled around the volunteers from the village. Hemmel was trying to bring order to the gathered men, but the Crookfell folk were having none of it.

He shook his head as Bane arrived.

"They're a thick-headed bunch, these turnip pluckers," he said.

Bane scanned over them as he drew closer, seeing Dew and his father, Mr Gobbin and his son Kulby, Girant and a few other men, but not many. He thought he caught the top of Dodd's head towards the back, but wasn't sure.

"Aye, well, us turnip pluckers don't have it as easy as you castle folk," Bane said, slapping Hemmel on the shoulder.

The tall youth laughed.

"Forgot you were one of them, Garik. Can you get them to at least form a line?"

The fledglings had been put in charge of the villagers who had no experience with weapons, save for Kulby. But it was clear that the Crookfell folk were not about to take orders from who they considered to be still boys.

The gate banged again, and this time, something cracked, and the oak planking began to fall apart.

"Listen up," Bane said, stepping in front of Hemmel, sword still in his hand. He used it to point to the beasts that were beginning to squeeze through, teeth gnawing at the wood, claws tearing chunks away. And then he gestured to the jackals that had breached the wall and were now fighting with the guards and knights above.

"We are the last line of defence if those desert dogs get through them. And the last line needs to be a fugging line."

There were murmurs from the men, jostling as they tried to step alongside each other.

"And if we fail, then those animals will make for the castle and the people within. Your wives, your children."

He saw Dew's father nodding along with Girant.

Bane held up his arm. He thought there was no point in covering the tattoo and so now wore a leather vest over a shirt; the sleeves rolled back.

"I am one of you. I am of Crookfell stock. You forced me once to be tried by the Fug. I passed. I've defended the village against raiders, I've brought you here today within these walls to offer protection."

"You offer us death," Dodd said, stepping between Mr Gobbin and the smithy. "We would have been better where we were."

"You'd have been food for those beasts," Cuthbur snapped. "And you will address my friend as Sir, as is his title."

Dodd spat on the ground, words forming from his grimace when Girant turned on him, grasping his collar and heaving from the floor with one arm.

The smithy's other arm was cocked back, large hand curling into a fist.

"Your lad has saved my livelihood, has saved my boy Tomm and has helped damn near everyone from Crookfell, and you go against him?"

"Fugging boy's spawn of Death," Dodd said, "He's…"

Whatever Dodd was going to say next was lost beneath Girant's fist as he smashed into his face, a lone tooth spinning out across the ground and getting lost in the snow.

The smithy then dropped Dodd's unconscious body to the ground, where he landed in a heap.

"That was well done, Girant," Dew's father said.

The Gobbins dragged the body to the wall and then came back to line up with the rest, the men seeming more cooperative.

"Good, now listen to Hemmel," Bane said as he walked amongst them. "He's the son of a knight and knows his way around a sword and shield better than all of you put together."

Hemmel puffed his chest out at that.

The men nodded and began to form into a better line, shields held how Hammel demonstrated, sword slack by their sides.

"The gate's breached," shouted one of the guards as the archers began to loose arrows at the jackals coming in through the broken barrier.

Large jaws snapped at the men, claws raking down torsos and backs, teeth clamping onto arms, legs and necks.

The noise was deafening.

Screams of pain, wails from the injured, cries from those being savaged drowning out the moans of the dying. And above them all was the clashing of steel on iron, the guttural snarls and barks of the attacking jackals.

Amidst the chaotic violence, Bane caught sight of Bullif, his blade a silver blur as he cut down dog after dog, his movements calm and precise. It wasn't long before there were several dead beasts around him, dark liquid spilling from open wounds.

"Hold yourselves steady, men," Hemmel warned, fingers nervously twitching on his hilt, a film of sweat plastering his hair to his head.

Bane had to admire his resilience, keeping his head before an oncoming wave of demons and standing his ground.

He was a natural leader.

The first jackal clambered past the soldiers, paws slamming into the snow as it bounded towards them. "Steady," Cuthbur yelled, swinging his shield before him, teeth gritted as he shifted his feet.

The beasts leapt at them, and Cuthbur and Hemmel stepped in to meet the attack, shields raised to deflect claws and teeth, and as they turned, their swords struck from either side, both slipping between ribs.

The dog was dead before it hit the ground, blood spattering over the trampled slush.

"See?" Hemmel said, turning to the villagers. "They die just like the rest of us."

Cuthbur grinned up at Bane, a foot upon the leaking carcass.

That's when a pair of jackals sprang over Bullif and the soldiers, one stumbling but gaining its feet as they launched at Cuthbur and Hemmel, who were standing out front of the line.

Bane was already moving as the demons came on, one of them pulling a long strip of jagged iron from its back and brandishing it like a sword.

His training took over, his feet moving with practised impulse, his torso twisting as he slashed down with his blade before the unarmed jackal had time to respond.

Then brought his shield arm about to block the arcing strip of iron, the thorns in his arm swirling out to create the shield.

He felt the impact; the force deflected outwards, a charge-filled crack that repelled the demon, sending the limb that held the jagged blade high.

Bane spun away, keeping his momentum going, adopting Spinning Thistle, his sword slicing through the neck, feeling the bone part and then watching the head tumble away, the body collapsing with the other.

There were gasps from the villagers and the fledgelings, but Bane put that behind him as he faced more jackals that were breaking through.

"Protect the entrance," he shouted over his shoulder as the fledglings formed up, Cuthbur on his left while Hemmel stepped to his right.

"We can win this, right?" Hemmel asked, staring up at the fighting on the battlements, the knights struggling with the demons on the walls, the soldiers at the gate.

"We live as men, but fight as gods," Cuthbur answered.

"What?" Hemmel asked, staring past Bane.

"It's what my uncle Bailin cries when going into battle. At least that's what Glance tells me."

"Bailin, the Shadow of the North," Hemmel said, grinning.

"Then let's use it. We live as men," he shouted, thrusting his sword in the air. "But fight as gods."

He was already charging at the rushing demons, shield held before him.

"He's far too overconfident," Cuthbur said as they ran after him.

"Aye," Bane said as he thrust his own sword into the air, "But most of the time, that's how he wins. We live as men…"

"But fight as gods," Cuthbur finished.

Bane felt a sense of pride mixing with fear as he heard the words ring out behind as the rest of the fledglings ran with them, Bon almost tripping over his scabbard straps and was caught by Girant, the huge smithy lumbering into a sprint, hammer in one fist, a sword in the other.

They slammed into the jackals, claws and strips of sharpened iron scraping over steel, the dogs desperately trying to find purchase and break through the line, yet the fledglings worked together, cutting, chopping and hacking into the beasts.

Bane danced through the forms, his blade an extension of his arm, the shield of thorns propelling the vicious attacks.

A demon slipped beneath a thrust, snarling up at him, long teeth dripping with saliva.

He drove the circle of thorns down, the rim of sharp needles driving into flesh and tearing into its exposed back.

Its howl was cut short when Kulby's sword smashed its skull open.

Bane nodded a thanks and then went on to the next jackal, the demons seeming to come from everywhere.

Someone grunted over his shoulder, a blur of motion as Girant's hammer smashed into a furry chest – a soldier screaming as he shoved the head of a demon away from his neck, the jaws clamping instead on a shoulder – Bullif slicing through flesh – Cuthbur driving through an exposed throat; carnage greater than any of them had experienced before.

"Alruna, where are you?" Bane hissed as he dropped into a roll to avoid teeth clashing onto his thigh.

He came up, slicing through a stomach and then cut through a hamstring on the backswing - Hemmel stepping in and taking the jackal's head, blood splashing across his face.

There was an almighty roar from the fighting soldiers, and a huge jackal bounded through them, long claws ripping through exposed flesh.

"It's the ghost," Cuthbur yelled, pointing his sword at the ginormous demon.

Bullif stepped over the dead, laying about his feet and letting his steel sing, danced about the ghost, sword arcing round to chop into its ribs, but at the final moment, the ghost shifted.

Its body morphed from beast to human, the paw becoming a hand before it caught Bullif's wrist, twisting as he slashed claws down the sergeant's chest.

Bullif yelled as he threw a punch, but the demon laughed as he lifted and threw him into the advancing soldiers, the blow hard enough to knock them all down.

"Break into the castle, find the key," the ghost bellowed, his human voice becoming a howl as he became the giant jackal again and bounded towards the fledglings, the last line of defence.

"We live as men," Hemmel shouted as he rushed towards the ghost, blade held out, jaw clenched in determination.

"But fight as gods," the rest of them called out as they followed the tallest youth who seemed afraid of nothing.

The ghast had Bullif's blade, which looked small in his claws. He swiped it at Hemmel, who parried it easily and stepped inside the ghost's range, bringing his blade up to drive it through its heart.

There was a shimmer and the ghost twisted sideways, Hemmel's momentum carrying him through and onto Bullif's sword.

"No," Bane yelled as he ducked the claws from another, catching Hemmel as he fell, the sword now wrenched out, leaving a deep cut through the breastplate, blood bubbling out.

Hemmel shook with a final shuddering breath and went still, head lolling back and eyes staring up into nothing.

"Bane." Cuthbur shrieked, and Bane managed to wedge his shield of thorns between himself and the ghost before claws gouged him open.

He felt the now familiar force driving the demon back, a sharp intake of breath from the beast, followed by laughter.

"Blood of Tyr?" the ghost said, morphing into human form as he leaned away from Bane's thrust, coming back with a burst of jabs, his arm a blur of motion.

Bane stepped away, taking them all on the shield, setting his feet to begin the forms, yet the huge jackal pushed on, slashing and cutting, his free hand becoming a claw as he swiped the air above Bane, its head elongating, fangs extending.

Misjudging a blow, Bane caught the hilt as it slammed into his chest, knocking him onto his back, the wind driven from him.

Trying to suck in air, he rolled away, a canine foot thudding into the earth where his head had just been.

"You don't move like a man," the ghast said, lashing out with a claw and then blade, pushing Bane back towards the servant's entrance.

"That's because I only live as one," Bane growled, catching the body of Hemmel in the churned mud, head lying in Cuthbur's lap.

He parried the ghast's blade, spun into Swooping Crane and slid the rim of his shield across the beast's side, tearing through flesh and fur.

"But I fight as a god."

He brought his blade around, slipped it beneath a claw and rammed the tip down through the shin bone.

The blur this time was more rapid, the shimmer between beast and human happening so fast Bane's vision only registered the change after it happened, by which time he'd been struck in the chest again, a foot knocking him clear into the air before he slammed onto the ground.

The back of his head hit the boot of a fallen soldier and brought white fizzing dots to the corner of his sight.

"And you'll die like one, too."

The ghost leapt into the air, reversing the grip on his sword as he came down, the tip of the blade poised above Bane's heart.

Girant's hammer struck the ghost in its side, sending him crashing into the mud, the blade grazing down Bane's cheek.

It stung as he rolled away from the jaws as they opened up and snapped at him, yet it was struck by the hammer again and followed by the heavy overswing from Kulby's sword.

The ghost gathered itself and backhanded Girant before he struck again. The huge smith stumbled backwards and fell unconscious in a heap.

The jackal then turned on Kulby, about to run him through, but Mr Gobbin came charging out of nowhere, Bon at his side, and the pair thrust their swords at the beast.

The demon screamed in frustration, backed up and swiped its arm, knocking both fledgling and swine herder over as if they were made of straw.

"Get inside the castle," the demon yelled again, shoving one of its brothers towards the locked doors.

Now the line had become a tangled mess, the jackals dodging through the gaps and bounding up the stairs, shoulders smashing through the wood and falling through.

Screams erupted from within as more desert dogs ran inside.

Bane could do nothing but stare after them.

He'd failed.

He pushed the thoughts away as he brought the thorns about on impulse and caught a thrust, yet was too slow to avoid the claw.

Pain burst along the gashes up his chest as he watched the paw carry on its upward arc, drops of his own blood following.

His mind was full of pain, fire, fear, anguish and loss; Bane watched the steel cut through the air, silver light reflecting from its keen edge.

Jarl was fighting alongside Lady Felina, back-to-back, as they tried desperately to hold the demons at bay, the knights fighting as best they could, outnumbered and with many fallen bodies torn and mutilated.

Bane caught the sword with the thorns and heaved up, but the ghost came back, grinning like a wolf in a bard's tale.

Bane moved his head away from a cut, the blade biting into the earth and flicking dirt into his face.

He caught Hemmel's unmoving body, Cuthbur watching on in horror.

They'd lost.

Screams followed the smashing of glass from inside the castle as more jackals ran inside.

Girant was down, Bon and a dozen others. The rest of the fledglings, the villagers, Dew and his father, were busy fighting with the demons that hadn't gone inside the building.

He stared up at the ghost as he loomed closer, now holding the sword - Bullif's sword - above him so that Bane had to stare along the blade from tip to hilt.

Death was coming. It's what he deserved for failing. Yet, above the failure, he felt hurt that Alruna didn't come.

Wherever she was, he hoped she was regretting her decision.

25

Dark Forest Ivy

Alruna was already regretting her decision as she clung to the rope. The grappling hook that was scraping precariously close to the edge of the sill above was the only thing preventing her from falling to the frozen ground below.

"Should have fugging come earlier," she grunted to herself as she swung a leg up onto the window ledge and heaved herself up.

If she had, they might have been able to come through the gate instead of having to climb through the back, using the same route of entry that her father and Raif had done months before on the night of her brother's death.

She'd wasted an entire day explaining the situation to her clan and the surrounding villages. The other clan leaders were less than cooperative when she asked them to supply men.

When the negotiations broke down, and the arguing had no effect, she was left with threats, which partly worked - the mark on her arm added some weight to them.

Apparently, her deeds at the challenge had reached even the furthest of clans on the other side of the mountain. Her name whispered as she swore by Odin himself that if they didn't commit men to the cause, then she would be using her axe on them.

In the end, her father stepped in and came up with a solution, as very few of the gathered men believed there was an approaching wave of demons.

They agreed to form a band of a hundred men, warriors from each of the clans, and wait on a hill overlooking the castle. If these so-called desert dogs turned up, they would cross the Fug and give aid. If the demons didn't show up, then they could go home.

Alruna had bitten her nails to the quick as she waited, fearing more for being named a liar than having to fight the jackals if they did attack the castle.

When the dust cloud became visible, and the rumble of uncountable beasts came from the south, she felt relief – which swiftly became fear again as she witnessed them crash against the walls.

Now, standing on a window ledge trying to break into the castle to give aid, she felt more annoyed than scared.

"If you slide your knife into the edge of the lead, you'll be able to prise a pane out enough to squeeze your arm through and unlock it," her father said from below, teeth gritted as he climbed the rope.

"Prise it open?" Alruna called down as she raised her boot off the sill and drove her heel through the glass, shattering an entire side.

Her father shook his head as he struggled onto the sill, Alruna gripped the back of his jerkin and hauled him up.

"We're not here to help preserve the castle," she said as she kicked the broken shards from the frame and climbed inside.

The chamber was large, and at its centre was the biggest bed Alruna had ever seen. Thick cotton sheets and pillows that would swallow your head.

"This belongs to the Baron's grandson?" she asked, taking in the polished wood, the paintings on the wall, and the wardrobes, which were no doubt full of good quality clothes. "This is why the castle people are so soft."

Other men climbed through the window. Wide-shouldered, thick furs and bristling with steel. Muddy boots smeared the rugs, greasy hands gripping the drapes.

Hadlo clambered through, and as the giant of a man turned, the shield on his back knocked a shelf down, the things on top smashing as they struck the floor.

Boran shook his head, and Alruna dropped the grin that she was wearing.

"Are they tied fast?" Hadlo bellowed out of the broken window.

He leaned out, grasped the rope, and began to pull it in, others around him taking the slack as they heaved, the coils rubbing against the frame.

Then, large paws grasped the sill, and Geri sprang through, followed by Freki. The two of them seemed less than impressed with the way they were tied together and hauled up the wall.

When they were untied, they padded across to Alruna and her father.

It's getting a bit cosy in here," her father said, watching the rest of the men still climbing through.

Before things got too cramped, Alruna shoved open the door and made her way down the corridor, axe held slack by her side, Freki prowling beside her.

The inside of the building was like a maze. Staircases leading up and down, doors at every turn, and the rich furnishings and carpet made her feel like she was in a totally different world.

Would they ever find a way out?

She kept catching herself glancing at the Wycum mark and wondering what it did. Would it become a shield like Bane's or something else?

It was prodded and poked back at her village, the men inspecting it to make sure it was real, every one of them managing to cut themselves on the dark ivy leaves. Alruna felt the blood soaking into the tattoo, the vine growing thicker, the leaves wider as the ink became alive. It was as though the nourishment forced the growth, for when she awoke in the early hours, the tattoo was no longer a single ring around her wrist. It had now spread to her elbow, coiling around her flesh in an intricate pattern.

A door suddenly burst open, and a short man in a neat uniform stepped out, squealing as he saw her.

Alruna shoved him up against the wall, the blade of her axe pressing into his neck.

"Please don't kill me," he pleaded in a piping voice. "I'm but a servant, not a fighter."

There was a dark stain spreading around the groin of his britches, drips splattering the floor.

"No, really?" Alruna asked, unable to keep the sarcasm from her voice as she raised a brow.

She withdrew the blade and let him go.

"How do we get down to the wall?" she asked, but the blubbering man sagged to the floor, hands covering his face.

She turned to her father, shaking her head.

"Soft."

She caught movement from the other side of the door and stepped through.

It was a large hall full of women, children and the elderly. A sorry sight of tears, faces becoming ashen with horror as they watched her enter, followed by her father and some of the men.

Alruna said nothing as she crossed the room and stared out of the window at the battle below.

It was carnage outside. The walls, grounds and outbuildings were a broiling mass of fighting. Jackals outnumbered the men, the bodies of the fallen strewn about like discarded dolls - man and dogs alike.

She turned to the women, realised that she was still brandishing her axe and lowered it to her side.

"We're here to give aid to the castle. Now, will one of you show me how to get out?"

Freki and Geri stalked amongst the men, whiskers twitching as they sniffed the air.

A nervous muttering came from one group of women who were sitting apart from the rest. They were dressed in rough spun wool and had harder lines on their faces. One of which was of an age with Old Ma Bunt. She approached, staff clicking on the floor as her gaze fell on Alruna's arm.

"Fug marked like the boy," she muttered, sucking on her tooth. "Of the clans are you, lass?"

"Aye."

The old lady nodded, taking in the rest of the men and the cats.

"Then you better get out there and start helping, lass. No point dawdling in here."

Alruna threw her hands in the air in frustration, one of which was still holding the axe, which of course, was no help.

"That's what I'm trying to do. Will somebody show us the fugging way out before the dogs kill all your men folk and come inside for you?"

Amidst the cries of terror and whimpering, a lone girl stood out as she came forward.

"I'll show you, come with me," she said, her voice shy and timid.

A pretty little thing in a maid's uniform, Alruna thought – delicate and tidy like the castle folk, yet she wore a warn expression like the women in the other group.

"Well done," the old one said, sneering across the room. "It takes a turnip plucker to show bravery when the castle folk should be leading."

Some of the other maids turned away, some even cowering behind the tall pillars as if hiding would make the situation go.

"Now be careful, lass," she continued, grasping the maid's hand.

"I will, Nan Hilga."

Then another woman rose and rushed to the girl, throwing her arms around her.

"And mind you come straight back, Belle," she said, dabbing at her eyes.

Fighting impatience, Alruna strode through the men to the door and out into the corridor.

Thankfully, the girl followed, head down as she passed her.

"This way."

Alruna followed the girl, who she judged to be around her own age, maybe a little younger, walking with an elegance Alruna knew she would never possess.

"Bane has a mark like yours," the girl said, glancing over her narrow shoulders.

A pang of jealousy flamed through Alruna at the mention of the boy's name coming from this Belle's lips.

"You know him?" she asked, almost demanded.

Belle must have picked up on it too, because she looked away, the lines of a scowl briefly flashing across her brow before it vanished.

"We grew up together," she said, leading them down another corridor which was much the same as the one they were on.

Alruna caught the fast fingers of some of the men as they passed silver candle sticks or other things which could be spirited into pockets.

"He's a friend. A good friend."

Alruna didn't like the way the girl said that, as if the word implied something more. Then she berated herself for caring. It was nothing to her if Bane wanted to spend time with this girl who was the opposite of herself. Smelling of lavender and soap, hair neatly held back with a fancy bow, clothes neatly pressed and clinging to her.

They passed a mirror and Alruna caught her reflection – leather britches, mottled fur vest, bare arms dirt smeared and blotchy from the cold.

"Is that the cat that Bane rescued?" Belle asked, leaning down and showing no fear as she stroked Freki, the leopard arching its back with pleasure.

"What?"

"Yes. She was trapped – he freed her. We wanted him to keep her, but Sir Garik said that because she tasted his blood, they might be bonded. That's why he took her away."

"She tasted his blood?" Alruna snapped, feeling a need to slap the girl. She took a breath and calmed her anger.

Now it all made sense. Freki's loyalty to Bane.

She stared down at the shadow leopard, feeling betrayed.

The corridor gave way to stairs that led down into a large hall. A rug ran the full length, a plinth at its centre with a large bowl sitting on the top. It was white with fancy blue pictures around its body.

"They call it a vase," her father explained when he caught her inspecting it.

"Vase," Alruna repeated. "What's it for?"

Boran shrugged.

"How should I know?"

Through the window, she could see the fighting carrying on, a raised sword, the clattering of shields, and the wild slashing actions of the dogs.

The girl paused partway and pointed to a large door at the other side.

"That'll take you out into the grounds," she said and then flinched as a loud crash clattered against the door from the other side. It was soon followed by another, and then it burst inwards, splintered wood skittering along the floor as a huge jackal burst inside.

It landed on all fours but slowly rose on its hind legs as it grinned at them, teeth needle-sharp, as long as her little finger, claws longer still.

There was a moment of stillness as the beast took them in, hunger in its eyes. And then it sprang.

Her father was the first to move, shield held before him as he ran at the dog, Geri by his side. Others followed, a wild cry of Odin ringing in the air amongst the barks and snarls as the men got over the initial shock at seeing the demon and charged.

Claws struck wood as her father collided with it, teeth biting down on the rim and tearing a chunk from the top.

He crouched, ready to leap, but Hadlo's hammer whistled through the air and crunched into its skull, flattening it to the ground.

The victory was short-lived as more dogs poured through the ruined entrance, clambering over each other in their haste to get to them.

Alruna was vaguely aware of Belle backing away into a corner.

"Run back upstairs," Alruna screamed as she swallowed her fear and ran to meet the demons, axe already in motion.

The men must see her fighting. A clan leader should lead by example, her father had once told her.

Freki leapt upon the back of another jackal, her claws digging into flesh as she sank her teeth into the back of its cranium. It collapsed, a final breath releasing from its chest.

The hall became a battleground of its own, the men – her men – bravely cutting into the dogs which came through the doors, an unrelenting wave of beasts.

Her father brought a jackal down with a blow to its ribs, Geri tore the throat from another. Even Ganlin was thrusting a blade into a belly, blood gushing up his arm and splattering his face.

All about her the carnage grew thicker, more vicious, her arm tiring from swinging the axe, chopping and hacking.

She made to cut into an approaching demon, but as her arm descended it sprang up, catching her wrist, its teeth about to sink into her neck.

Desperately, she flung her free arm in the way, expecting the jaws to clamp down, yet the tattoo sprang to life.

Long cords of ivy shot outwards, wrapping around the jackal's nose and mouth, forcing it closed.

Alruna clenched her fist, and the cords snapped together, the leaves twisting, the vines digging through flesh.

The demon tried to scream; the sound muffled as Alruna yanked hard to the side and snapped its neck.

As it fell, the vines unwrapped themselves and shrunk back into the tattoo.

She might have marvelled at what she had done if another beast hadn't chosen that moment to charge at her father.

Boran fell back, shield high, yet the jackal clawed into it, found purchase and then wrenched it away.

Without thinking, Alruna stepped towards them, although they were on the other side of the hall and reached out with her open hand.

Tendrils of ivy shot from the tattoo, the vines weaving over her hand and through her fingers, arrow-fast as they latched around the demon's ankles.

Yanking back, she pulled the beast off his feet, the tendrils winding backwards and dragging the creature with them.

It tried to scrabble away, digging into the stone floor, but the strength of the ivy was far greater than the dog's, and as it reached her, she dropped the axe down on its head.

The ivy retracted into the tattoo once again, becoming still, as if hadn't just come alive and helped kill two demons.

She caught her father watching her, along with Hadlo and most of the men. There were still more jackals, but they were beaten down, the rest of them broken, dead or dismembered.

When the last was killed, Ganlin having driven his sword through its open jaw, it flopped against the plinth at the centre of the hall and then went still. Unlike the plinth, which tipped to the point of toppling over before settling back, the vase rolled to one edge, about to roll off – the girl, Belle, wincing - yet it impossibly rocked back, swaying until becoming still.

Alruna stepped over the tangle of demons, seeing the smashed windows, the broken panes, and the torn rug and felt that the vase was somehow mocking her.

Childishly, she shoved it from the plinth and grinned at the satisfying sound it made as it smashed into a thousand pieces.

She glanced up, expecting Belle to be scowling, yet the girl was staring out of the broken door and the approaching demons which were rushing their way.

"Don't let them enter," Alruna shouted, and Hadlo stepped into the doorway, his hammer impacting into the first to come through, slamming through a chest and doubling it over.

The men ran through the gap, forcing the desert dogs back.

"Shield wall," she screamed, her throat now becoming saw.

Wood slammed against wood as the Vikings locked shields, muscles straining, boots sliding in the slushy mud, yet they held.

Alruna followed them out, torches and burning braziers lighting the violence, flames reflecting from the glassy eyes of the fallen, the menacing leers of the jackals and the wide eyes of the men locked in battle.

Then Belle was running, hands to her mouth.

"Bane?" she yelled, terror paling her skin.

Through the chaos, Alruna saw Bane on his back, the largest Jackel in the castle standing above him, the long blade of a sword pressed to his throat.

A panic rose inside her as she realised he was about to die.

****

Saliva dripped from the ghast's fangs, falling onto the blade, the bead it formed glowing red with the reflections from the flames.

Bane wasn't afraid to die, but he was ashamed of failing. He tried to move his tattooed arm, but the beast had his full weight on it, its foot pressing the shield of thorns into the mud. Its other pinning down the hand which held the sword.

Defenceless and about to be killed, Bane stared up at his killer, filling his chest with his final breath as he strained one last time.

It was over.

Then the face of the ghast briefly shimmered, taking on a human form long enough for Bane to recognise startled surprise.

A large black shape filled his vision a moment before crashing into the ghast.

The pressure released from his arms, Bane rolled onto his front and clambered to his feet, spinning to defend himself from the ghast, but it was fighting with a shadow leopard.

"Freki?"

The pair were thrashing at each other. Teeth, claws, tearing into flesh, into fur and then the demon brought his sword arm back, about to thrust it into the cat.

Bane darted forward, ready to parry the blow, but instead, long green shoots unfurled from over his shoulder in a green blur and wrapped around the ghost's wrist.

It was ivy. Twisting and curling as it bit into flesh until there was a snap.

The demon roared and the blade fell.

Without hesitation, Bane brought his sword about, ready to slice through the exposed neck, but the beast saw him coming and struck him with a backhanded blow.

It ripped free of the ivy and lunged for him, jaw opening wide, fangs biting down.

An axe thudded into its shoulder, grubby hands gripping the shaft, a tattoo along a forearm.

"Thought you weren't coming," Bane said, feeling hope fill him again.

"Needed to check you were using my brother's sword correctly," she replied, wrenching her axe free.

The ghost roared a second time, sunken eyes blazing with fury as it lashed out, catching Alruna on the side of the head, knocking her down, and then went for Bane.

Dropping to a knee, Bane felt the air above him shift as claws raked through his hair.

He tried to cut up with his blade, found empty space, slammed an elbow into its sternum and then drove the rim of his thorny shield up, feeling flesh tear beneath it.

The creature howled, a scream filled with hate, with pain - yellow eyes focusing on him.

Tendrils of ivy suddenly weaved towards the ghost and found its neck, curled around, blood leaking through the leaves which were digging through the throat, tightening.

Bane spun, adopting Rising Star and sliced the shield across its chest, continuing the turn while reversing the grip on his blade and drove it through its heart.

As he pulled it free, the ivy vines writhed around the neck, shrinking tighter, choking until it cut right through.

The head fell from the shoulders and thudded into the mud, the body collapsing on top of it.

Bane slowly turned back to the castle and saw the shield wall defending the entrance, then glanced up at the wall, feeling relief at seeing Jarl and Lady Felina still fighting, the knights getting the better of the remaining jackals.

More of the beasts began to close in on Bane and Alruna, circling them, fury and hunger edging their snarls.

Alruna put her back to his as they faced them off. He felt her breathing, a growl resonating through her chest, axe hanging loose and dripping with blood.

"At least if we both die, you won't need to kill me." Bane said over his shoulder.

Alruna made a swing for a jackal that came close but missed.

"Who said I still won't?"

The circle around them drew tighter, teeth snapping, claws slashing, and Bane knew they were about to strike, most likely all coming at once.

He wished he had final words to say, maybe a last moment with Belle, yet where he was somehow felt right, as if Alruna was destined to die by his side.

As the demons closed in, Bane felt a subtle change, a shift of the battle as the knights upon the wall were coming down the steps, rushing to aid those in the bailey.

It seemed the desert dogs around them sensed it too, for they suddenly backed away, searching for an escape.

"Fugging finish them," Alruna screamed as she gave chase, axe swinging, ivy shooting from her arm and catching a jackal around the legs and bringing it down.

A simple drop of her weapon and the head was cleaved in two.

The Viking shield wall collapsed as they charged at the beasts, war cries erupting from lungs, steel flying, shadow leopards tearing and biting.

Fledglings, village folk, soldiers and knights – they all swiftly dispatched the remaining jackals until there were none left standing.

****

Flames flickered from the torches and the braziers about the grounds, smoke drifting over corpses, man and beast alike. Bullif limped to the broken body of the ghast and retrieved his sword, caught Bane watching and gave a sullen nod before moving off to join the soldiers as they tended to the wounded and the dying.

Bane walked around in a daze, grief from seeing Hemmel laid out with the others that had fallen, relief when he caught sight of Dew and his father, shared a worn smile with Cuthbur, who was back with his mother on the castle steps.

He didn't know when it happened, but he found himself on the ground, back pressed up to Alruna's, a strange comfort in each other's silent company.

They didn't speak. They didn't need to.

Boran and the giant were debating with the other Vikings, none of whom seemed to have fallen during the battle.

Then Belle found him and rushed to his side, grasping his hands and pulling him to his feet.

"I was so worried," she said, stepping close and crushing him in a hug. "I couldn't bear the thought of losing you."

She stepped back long enough to kiss his lips before embracing him again.

Alruna sniffed, glanced up and shook her head. She was about to leave when Lady Felina came over, Jarl and some of the high-ranking knights with her.

Her armour now scratched, dented and missing a greave, Lady Felina still possessed dignity.

A smile curled her lips as Bane bowed his head and knelt, feeling every graze, cut and bruise over his battered body. When he rose, he found that all attention was on Alruna, who was glaring at Felina. She folded her arms and raised a brow.

"Kneel before the Baron's daughter," Sir Hoskin demanded, and Bane noted that his armour seemed too clean to have been in a fight.

Alruna found enough scorn for both of them.

She stepped closer to Hoskin, a hand resting on the shaft of her axe.

"I kneel before no one," she said, hawking up phlegm and spitting on the knight's polished breastplate.

Another step and she was close enough to bite his nose – Bane thought she might, but Hoskin backed away, trying to form words, yet all that came out was a stammered squeak.

"There's no need to kneel. You've done us a great service," Felina said, unfazed, her smile widening as Boran came to join them. "I'm not afraid to admit that if not for your intervention, the castle would have fallen. We are grateful for your kindness."

"How grateful?" Alruna asked, ignoring her father, trying to step between them, rubbing a hand over a weary face.

"What my daughter means, My Lady is that we would like to open links for trade between the castle and the clans."

"Trade?" Alruna snapped. "We came across the Fug, fought beasts from the south, risked our own men. How about payment? How about gold, silver, steel?"

Bane watched the exchange and noticed the Vikings rising and slowly edging closer, twitchy fingers hovering dangerously close to weapons. Jarl and the knights began to fan out, tightening bucklers and loosening blades from scabbards.

Deep growls rumbled from the shadow leopards, archers unslung bows. The giant Viking cocked a hammer onto his shoulder, Girant stretched his neck one way and then the other as he squared off with him.

Tension hung heavy around them, like oiled tinder beneath dry wood, awaiting a single spark.

Lady Felina smiled at Alruna, yet her gaze was calculating.

"Of course, my young friend. I'll negotiate a payment with your father."

"Why? I'm Clan Chief. You'll negotiate with me. Five gold coins for each of my men. Twenty score swine, steel and a smith to work it. Oh, and access to the King's Road."

"What? That's ridiculous," Sir Hoskin said from behind the knights.

Lady Felina quieted him by raising a hand, narrow eyes never leaving Alruna's.

"You've been thinking about this for some time," she said.

Alruna grinned.

"Chiefs need to be thinkers, isn't that right, Da?"

Boran only watched the exchange, his expression caught between frustration and surprise.

"Seems a fair price for coming to our aid, if not a little late," Lady Felina said, gesturing for Sir Hoskin to come forward. "I'll have my clerk draft the treaty for you to sign."

"Treaty?" Alruna said and then spat on her palm and thrust it toward Felina. "You're dealing with the clans. Paper means fug all."

Felina glanced down at the hand and smiled.

"As you wish." She turned to Hoskin and then glanced back at the offered hand.

Grimacing, Hoskin took the hand, wincing as Alruna gripped harder than needed.

Bane let out the breath he'd been holding as the Vikings eased back and the knights relaxed.

"We'll return in the morning for the coin and the swine," Alruna said, swaggering over to the Vikings. She glanced once at Bane, a sadness becoming aloof as she slapped the big Viking on the shoulder.

She turned once more to Lady Felina.

"There's a bit of a mess inside the castle. Those desert dogs wanted to smash things," she said and then strutted out of the grounds, heading for the destroyed gate.

Her men followed, Boran smiling apologetically as he gave a curt nod and went with the rest.

Freki padded after them, head turning towards Bane as if struggling to come to a decision. She stared for a moment, tail drooping, and then padded away.

Bane thought that if he gave the command, the cat would have stayed. But knew that she needed to be with her own kind in the mountains.

Then Lady Felina approached, hands reaching out and cupping his face.

She placed a kiss on his brow.

"And you, nephew, are the reason why the castle still stands. We all owe you a huge debt. You will forever have our gratitude. If not for your warning and your valiant courage, we would all be dead."

Bane suddenly became aware of all the people staring at him. The knights, Bullif, soldiers, guards, the folk of Crookfell and everyone else.

"And my brother would have been proud."

Bane watched her leave, Cuthbur by her side, along with the knights.

Jarl remained, dimples forming in his beard as he grinned.

"You fight like your father," he said, nodding to himself. "And there's no teaching that kind of skill."

He put an arm around his shoulder as he led him away, steering him back towards the castle.

"Lady Felina's right. Wherever he is now, Bailin would be proud of you."

26

Fight Like Gods

Bailin stared down at the docks filled with Imperial war gallies and along the beaches on either side, shallow draft ships filling the sea from one end to the other, hulls resting on the sand, smaller boats ferrying soldiers to the shore.

Torches lit the night, running as far as the eye could see in both directions.

"You were right," he said, turning to Godlin, who was crouching beside him, jaw set firm, worried eyes scanning the vast armies below.

He was glad he sent the youngest knight back along the King's Road, riding hard to the capital to warn the King of their findings.

They were hidden within the veil of a willow, his knights catching a rest from the hard ride.

"I've never seen numbers this great before. And there are jackals amongst them. Ghasts too," Godlin said, shaking his head in disbelief.

Bailin brushed the branches aside as he stepped out into the moonlight, the smell of smoke and the grease of meat filling the air.

"It's the start of the end," he said, catching the shouts of slave masters harshly abusing the poor wretches that were dragging siege engines ashore. The cracks of whips cutting through the screams, the dismantled bodies of catapults, scorpions and long-bladed scythes piled along with a stockpile of spears and swords.

Countless square formations of a hundred score soldiers covered the sand in an endless chequered pattern - waves crashing relentlessly behind them, salt spraying yet they remained still, disciplined.

The knights followed him out into the open, lining up either side.

"You've got that look in your eye," Godlin said, nodding to himself before watching the mass of enemies before them. "What will you have us do?"

Bailin adjusted the straps of his scabbard and picked up his shield, the tar already daubed in the shape of runes.

He turned to his second and grasped his arm in a warrior's grip.

"Ride to the capital," Bailin said, placing his helmet over his head.

"And you, my Lord?"

Bailin dropped the visor down, seeing through the slits in the front.

He knew that Lamport had fallen, and enemy scouts would already be en route to the next town or village upriver. He wished there was a way to slow the advancing army and buy his countrymen some time.

"I'm thinking tonight might be the night I'll embrace Nel again," he said.

I will embrace you as I always do.

Godlin nodded as he drew his long sword and reached for his helmet, the other knights hefting shields onto arms, steel finding hands.

"I'll not ask you to come," Bailin said to his men.

Godlin grinned.

"You don't need to. Besides, it will be interesting to test these southern dogs," he said, taking a strike box and putting a spark to the tar.

Bailin's shield lit up, the flames running along the runes, catching alight the next shield until they were all aflame.

Shouts erupted from the beach as they were noticed, rank upon rank of imperial soldiers turned as one. A sea of sharpened steel.

Ghosts howled, jackals closed in, teeth and claws itching to tear them to shreds.

Bailin drew his sword and stalked towards the Empire, his pace picking up into a run, his men fanning out either side – a lone tear falling against a storm.

His thoughts going to the North, to Garik and to his son that he would be leaving behind – hoping that he would find a place in the new world.

"We live as men," he screamed at the enemy he was racing to meet.

Godlin and his blade brothers raised their swords, shouting as one.

"But fight as gods!"

THE END

Acknowledgments

Firstly, I would like to thank my wife for being one of the driving forces behind my books. Without her reading my work and critiquing where needed, the stories wouldn't be what they are.

Secondly, I would like to thank Karen Fuller who has read Gallows Born, chapter by chapter as the words spilled onto the keyboard. A loyal arc reader who has been there from the very start of my writing career.

Thirdly, I would like to thank Stephen Logan, Gill and Derek Horne – my small arc team, who have also read Gallows Born and given their honest opinions.

And lastly, I would like to thank you, the reader for giving my book the chance – and hopefully enjoying it.

Printed in Dunstable, United Kingdom